PRAISE FOR
ACCIDENTALLY CATTY

"This light, comedic paranormal romance delivers simple, unencumbered entertainment. A lively pace, the bonds of friendship, and bright humor aided by vampiric sarcasm make for a breezy read with charming characters and no shortage of drama. Cassidy's fans are sure to enjoy this, while newcomers will be reminded of MaryJanice Davidson's or Kimberly Frost's work."
— *Monsters and Critics*

"I have been a fan of Dakota's since *The Accidental Werewolf*, book one of this series. I loved all of the books in the series, but I think this book is my favorite . . . *Accidentally Catty* is very funny, cute, and sexy."
— *Night Owl Reviews*

"A fun read with some meat to it that will have people looking at you wondering why you're laughing if you're out in public." — *Fresh Fiction*

ACCIDENTALLY DEMONIC

"The Accidental series by Ms. Cassidy gets better and better with each book. The snark, the HAWT, the characters, it's all a winning combination."
— *Bitten by Books*

"An outstanding paranormal romance . . . Dakota Cassidy delivers snappy dialogue, hot sex scenes, and secondary characters that are just too funny . . . *Accidentally Demonic* is a hold-your-sides, laugh-out-loud book. With vampires, werewolves, and demons running around, paranormal romance will never be the same."
— *The Romance Readers Connection*

"Dakota Cassidy's books make me laugh and laugh. They are such great fun that I always look forward to the next one with gusto . . . I totally loved this book with a capital 'L.'"
— *Fresh Fiction*

THE ACCIDENTAL HUMAN

"I highly enjoyed every moment of Dakota Cassidy's *The Accidental Human* . . . A paranormal romance with a strong dose of humor."
—*Errant Dreams*

"A delightful, at times droll, contemporary tale starring a decidedly human heroine . . . Dakota Cassidy provides a fitting twisted ending to this amusingly warm urban romantic fantasy." —*Genre Go Round Reviews*

"The final member of Cassidy's trio of decidedly offbeat friends faces her toughest challenge, but that doesn't mean there isn't humor to spare! With emotion, laughter, and some pathos, Cassidy serves up another winner!" —*RT Book Reviews*

ACCIDENTALLY DEAD

"A laugh-out-loud follow-up to *The Accidental Werewolf*, and it's a winner . . . Ms. Cassidy is an up-and-comer in the world of paranormal romance." —*Fresh Fiction*

"An enjoyable, humorous satire that takes a bite out of the vampire romance subgenre . . . Fans will appreciate the nonstop hilarity."
—*Genre Go Round Reviews*

THE ACCIDENTAL WEREWOLF

"Cassidy, a prolific author of erotica, has ventured into MaryJanice Davidson territory with a humorous, sexy tale." —*Booklist*

"If Bridget Jones became a lycanthrope, she might be Marty. Fun and flirty humor is cleverly interspersed with dramatic mystery and action. It's hard to know which character to love best, though—Keegan or Muffin, the toy poodle that steals more than one scene." —*The Eternal Night*

"A riot! Marty's internal dialogue will have you howling, and her antics will keep the laughs coming. If you love paranormal with a comedic twist, you'll love this book." —*Romance Junkies*

"A lighthearted romp . . . [An] entertaining tale with an alpha twist."
—*Midwest Book Review*

THE
ACCIDENTAL GENIE

DAKOTA CASSIDY

BERKLEY SENSATION, NEW YORK

THE BERKLEY PUBLISHING GROUP
Published by the Penguin Group
Penguin Group (USA) Inc.
375 Hudson Street, New York, New York 10014, USA
Penguin Group (Canada), 90 Eglinton Avenue East, Suite 700, Toronto, Ontario M4P 2Y3, Canada
(a division of Pearson Penguin Canada Inc.) • Penguin Books Ltd., 80 Strand, London WC2R 0RL,
England • Penguin Group Ireland, 25 St. Stephen's Green, Dublin 2, Ireland (a division of Penguin
Books Ltd.) • Penguin Group (Australia), 250 Camberwell Road, Camberwell, Victoria 3124, Australia
(a division of Pearson Australia Group Pty. Ltd.) • Penguin Books India Pvt. Ltd., 11 Community
Centre, Panchsheel Park, New Delhi—110 017, India • Penguin Group (NZ), 67 Apollo Drive,
Rosedale, Auckland 0632, New Zealand (a division of Pearson New Zealand Ltd.) • Penguin Books
(South Africa) (Pty.) Ltd., 24 Sturdee Avenue, Rosebank, Johannesburg 2196, South Africa

Penguin Books Ltd., Registered Offices: 80 Strand, London WC2R 0RL, England

This book is an original publication of The Berkley Publishing Group.

PUBLISHING HISTORY
Berkley Sensation trade paperback edition / December 2012

Library of Congress Cataloging-in-Publication Data

Cassidy, Dakota.
The accidental genie / Dakota Cassidy.—Berkley Sensation trade paperback ed.
p. cm.
ISBN 978-0-425-25324-3
1. Jinn—Fiction.   2. Werewolves—Fiction.   3. Vampires—Fiction.
4. Paranormal fiction.   5. Humorous fiction.   I. Title
PS3603.A8685A63 2012
813'.6—dc23   2012032338

PRINTED IN THE UNITED STATES OF AMERICA

10 9 8 7 6 5 4 3 2 1

ACKNOWLEDGMENTS

A million thanks to—

Betzi Cable—who won a contest of mine and was willing to let me immortalize her on paper. I hope I do her fun, friendly personality and Facebook posts justice.

Charlene Gibbons (I love to *Psych* enable her!)—who, at a charity auction, outbid everyone else for a shot at being a character in this book. You warmed my heart with your gracious response to winning, and for that, I hope in return, I properly depict the goodness of your kind soul. ☺

AP—Dude, the title *The Accidental Caribou* and moose-bits will always have a special place in my heart. *Always.*

Autumn—because she's an awesome fan and she sent me an email with an idea that turned out to be pure gold—you rulez, darlin'!

The many reruns I watched of *I Dream of Jeannie* and the incomparable Barbara Eden. When I was six, I wanted to be just like her, and she was who inspired my infamous pretend blonde ponytail made out of a white baby blanket. Thanks for so many happy, happy memories and for giving my wild imagination a visual.

My Facebook/Twitter fans—you guys are hardcore! I love that you'll offer me suggestions about my current works in progress, and I love it even more when I end up using them as I did with Erica and Dan's! Love you all so hard!

My brother, Chris, and my SIL, Cathy—because they had an idea made of genius that helped me plot this book!

Most of all, this is for the late L. A. Banks. In all my author travels, conventions, and online interactions, she always stood out as a prime example of warmth and graciousness. From the moment I first met her in Pittsburgh, I adored the ease with which she laughed. I adored her all-inclusive nature, and never to be forgotten, I adored her Randy Jackson impression at a panel we did together. L.A. was everything I want to be when I grow up. She was all things good and kind, and I'll always count myself blessed to have shared time with her. Wherever you are, my friend, it's a much brighter place with plenty of big L.A. hugs to go around.

Dakota Cassidy ☺

AUTHOR'S NOTE

I've totally run in a million different directions with djinn folklore. Some of it came from my love of the Disney movie *Aladdin* and the sitcom *I Dream of Jeannie*, and some of it was all just part of my imagination. A lot of it was pop culture's take on genies. I've made my own rules (which shouldn't surprise you) and created my own idea of what a genie's world would be like. My intent is never to insult or offend anyone who celebrates a particular belief in any culture. My apologies in advance if I have. If I've gotten something wrong, any and all mistakes are mine.

CHAPTER 1

"Thank you for calling OOPS. We're here to serve all your paranormal crisis needs. This is Wanda . . . er, Sloan Flaherty—werewolf at large. How can I help you?" His voice was bored and robotic as he read the greeting he'd been told to repeat if he had to answer the phones. To amuse himself, Sloan leaned back in his chair and threw his feet up on Nina's desk with a sly grin.

Nina Blackman-Statleon, one of his sister-in-law Marty's best friends, would gnaw his foot clear off if she caught him—which only made him smile wider. He loved to razz Nina, badass vampire and all round easily irritated female.

He waited for the person on the other end of the line to speak while he took great pleasure in peeling Nina's sticky pads apart and making the shape of a Christmas tree on her desktop out of the assorted pink, green, and blue squares.

A female voice, rich with hesitance and a thread of what Sloan clearly pinpointed with his razor-sharp wolfie skills as fear, said, "Um, hello?"

Sloan fought a yawn. How he'd been talked into answering the

OOPS phones while Marty and her friends went off shopping left him scratching his head. Those women could talk a man out of his penile implant given an hour and a couple of Nina's imposing threats.

"Yeah. Hi. This is Sloan." He cleared his throat, Marty's warning still ringing in his ears. *If someone calls and they sound alone and afraid, remember to make a withdrawal from your sensitivity account, Sloan Flaherty,* she'd threatened followed by Nina, who'd said, *You fuck this up, and I'll eat your arm clear off.*

He straightened in his chair, injecting warmth into his voice. "How can I help you?" he purred, then cringed. Okay. That sounded just a little too 1-900-Sex-MeUp.

But the caller didn't notice. The return answer was tinny and filled with static. "Is this for real?"

"Is what for real?" He popped a Cheetos in his mouth, lifting the phone away from his lips to block out the abrasive crunch.

"This Out in the Open Paranormal Support?"

"Oh, it's for real." Sloan fought a snort. Maybe a little crazy but totally real. His brother, Keegan, hadn't loved the idea of his wife, Marty, and her friends starting up a help line for those in need of support after a paranormal accident.

Each woman at OOPS, a vampire, werewolf, werevamp, and demon respectively, was the product of an accidental paranormal incident. That was how Keegan met Marty in the first place. While in werewolf form, he'd accidentally bitten her when she was walking her poodle, Muffin, fell in love, and eventually married her.

Then a cluster of coincidences happened, leaving Marty's friends bitten and turned into shapeshifters, too. This had led the four women to believe there had to be others like them. Others who'd been turned, not necessarily with malicious intent but rather in a bizarre turn of events. Keegan didn't think the stats on that were very high, and frankly, he'd agreed with his big brother at the time.

Nor had his brother believed any paranormal accident victim

would actually call to ask for help from the operation the women had so carefully set up. But not even his brother, alpha male of their pack with a bossy streak a mile wide, could push Marty around when she set her mind to something.

So the four women, women Sloan was exposed to on an ongoing basis because his brother was married to one of them, had set up a cheap basement office on the off chance there'd be walk-ins. They also had a 1-800 number and website for global support.

Marty was a force when she wanted something, and she never did anything halfway, Keegan had explained with as much manly as he could muster for being so whipped.

What Keegan avoided copping to was the fact that he was totally besotted with his accidentally turned wife, and he couldn't say no to her blue eyes and the pretty pout of her lips. There was no force to it at all, just mad love on both their parts. Mad love that made them both behave like complete idiots.

Sloan wasn't a fan of complete idiot—or a commitment like marriage or anything that tied him to anyone for longer than the time it took to scope out a mutually satisfying, yet completely no-strings-attached arrangement. At least, that used to be the case. For the past year, he'd been rethinking his life plan.

The crackling static on the other end of the line grew louder, recapturing his attention. "Can you explain what exactly it is that you do? I mean, I googled the words *paranormal* and *help*, which was just a wildly random lucky guess in terms of my predicament, and a total shot in the dark in my panic. You guys were second only to the show *Paranormal State*. Did I miss something somewhere? OOPS came up as a help line for people who've had paranormal *accidents*. I can't seem to make the connection between being haunted and the word *accident*. How does something like that happen by accident? Either a ghost wants to haunt you or it doesn't. There's so much room for interpretation here."

Leave it to Marty, part owner of Bobbie-Sue Cosmetics and their marketing guru, to have OOPS all up in Google's business, with ads for their service and mega tags galore. It was to be expected that when the average human heard the word *paranormal*, their television-saturated minds went instantly to ghosts and Melinda Gordon. "Uh, well, I'm told they specialize in what's called a paranormal crisis."

"They?"

"Us. Sorry. *Us.*" Marty would kill him if he scared off a potential client. He wouldn't worry so much about it if not for the fact that Marty could nag a dead man to death. Add Nina, Casey, and Wanda to the mix, stir, and being nagged to death was no longer just an expression of speech—it was a real possibility.

"I can't get to the OOPS site for more information. My phone just won't download it. I was lucky to nab the phone number before it crashed. So I'm sort of going in blind."

That was probably because Marty had more shiny on that site than Tiffany's. Only Lover of All Things Decorated Marty would have a site designed with pictures of sparkly vampires enclosed in a red circle with a big X over it. Nina the vampire said it was to reassure those who thought they might have been turned into vamps that they wouldn't sparkle in the sunlight—a fear that was common these days, according to her.

"Are you still there?"

Yeah. Sloan looked at his watch. Unfortunately, he was still here. "Sorry. Yes. I'm still here."

"So can you define a paranormal crisis for me? Does it mean you have ghosts in your house or dead people making your walls bleed? You know, the disembodied voice that tells you to *Get out!* Is OOPS like *Ghostbusters*? Because I'm not sure that's what I'm in the market for."

How did you define the kind of crazy that was paranormal? "First, before we go any further and waste not just my time, but yours, I have to ask you some questions."

"About?"

"About whether you're really in crisis or not." Because according to Nina, crisis was a matter of fucking opinion and just because you liked a raw T-bone, it didn't necessarily qualify you for an induction into Werewolf U.

She breathed into the phone, long and shaky. "Oh. Of course. Fine. Ask away. It's not like I'm going anywhere. Maybe ever from the looks of things."

Sloan smoothed out the crumpled paper questionnaire the women had so carefully designed to determine if they were really talking to someone who'd been accidentally turned or a crackpot fuckwit, as Nina called them, who was just messing with them because they thought it was LOL funny to ask Marty if she would eat their algebra teachers. "First, do you have any bite marks on your neck or any-where on your person, for that matter?" Experience with Nina's sister Phoebe had taught him neck bites weren't the only way to create a vampire.

There was a stirring on the other end of the line and then she replied, "Hang on. I'm digging out my compact because the mirror in here is cracked. Oh, it's so disgusting and dirty here. Thank God I had my purse with me when this happened."

Silence prevailed, broken only by the sound of what he thought might be beer cans crashing together. He was very familiar with that melodic tone. Very. "Okay. I'm looking and no. No bite marks on my neck or anywhere."

Sloan checked off *no* in the "Signs You Might Be a Vampire" sec-tion. "How about sudden and excessive hair growth?"

"I'm not sure how to answer that because it's pretty personal in nature, don't you think?"

Sloan dragged a hand through his hair, gritting his teeth. "Look. I'm just doing my job, and what I mean by excessive and sudden hair growth is like the hair on your legs."

"No. No sudden and excessive anything, for which you'd hear me express my undying gratitude, but I'm not sure if what I'm experiencing is the lesser of two evils. Whatever that evil happens to be."

Sloan flicked the pen top in impatience, hoping to get this over with quickly. Where the hell did those women go to shop? Sri Lanka? "Moving right along. Horns?"

"Like the kind on a bike? You know—toot-toot? Or the kind in a symphony orchestra?"

"No. No bikes. No orchestras. No toot-toot. I mean the kind on your head. Like the devil. You know, evil-evil?"

This time, whoever she was, she let out a small gasp of unmistakable horror. "No! No horns. What the heck kinds of questions are these, anyway?"

"The paranormal kind. Next up, any burning in the tips of your fingers or the urge to eat rodents?"

She choked out a cough, her next words angry and clipped. "Clearly, I've made a mistake. I thought you helped people in paranormal crisis? Is this some kind of joke? Because if I'm wasting my cell battery on some joke, I have to warn you, I have a bit of a temper, and I have a black belt in karate. If we ever meet in person, you'll regret being so cruel when I'm in so much trouble!"

She'd begun to sound a little frantic, for which he realized he was responsible. Sloan tried to add a nurturing tone to his voice. The tone Wanda said was very important to the newly turned. "Again, I'm just doing my job. Please remain calm. If I don't determine whether you're pranking me or not, my sister-in-law will see my head roll. I'm in enough trouble with my pack already. I don't need her adding to it. If you knew what Marty, that's my sister-in-law, was like, a steamroller disguised in designer shoes I can't pronounce the makers of, you'd understand where I'm coming from. So how about we determine what exactly the issue is with you so I can go back to my Cheetos and you can extend the life of your cell battery?"

"Your pack? Did you say *pack*?" Disbelief littered her words.

"You bet'cha. I meant my werewolf pack. I'm part of a pack." Not that this woman would believe what he said. The girls had warned him proof might be necessary. Which blew if he was going to have to shift. He didn't have a spare set of clothes.

"I think you're one smoke short of a pack, mister. Listen, is there someone else I can speak with?"

"For the moment, I'm all you've got, lady."

"Damn."

"Ditto."

She sighed in crystal-clear irritation. "Fine. Ask away."

Sloan's lips thinned, his nurturing tone all but drying up. "So no burning in your fingertips?"

"Not unless you count the itch to kill the man who did this to me. No. No burning."

"No desire to eat small animals or their larger counterparts—like maybe a moose?"

A long rasp of a sigh came before she answered, "No. I don't want to eat big game."

Sloan squinted at the questionnaire. Well. That was that. She didn't fit any of the profiles the girls had laid out. Their time here was done. "All right, then, seems you're not anything we've ever heard of. You don't fit any of the profiles I have listed on my form. Looks like you're cleared for takeoff. No crisis. Have a great, non-paranormal day." Good luck. Later. He prepared to hang up, but her desperate cry stopped him cold.

"Wait!" she screeched into his ear.

Fuck. "For?"

"Even though I don't have any of the issues you listed, I do so have a crisis!" she cried in exasperation.

Sloan pictured a woman stomping her feet in a childish rage and fought a devilish grin. "Well, you don't have any of the issues we have experience with. That means you're not a vampire, werewolf, demon, or a cougar, or any derivative thereof. Seriously, lady. If you're not any of those things, what else is there?"

"You can *really* turn into one of those . . . those things?" she squeaked.

"Or a combination of them. We're called shapeshifters, among other things." Many other things.

"Shut the front door," she muttered. "Do you mean you shift like those creatures on that show *Supernatural*? That's disgusting! They're all so horrible and——and gooey!"

Sloan sighed. Yes, those creatures on TV were disgusting, and they'd given all paranormals a bad name. *Thank you, Sam and Dean Winchester.* "What you've seen on TV isn't exactly an accurate or fair depiction of who we are. In fact, it's a little overblown. We're not all bloodthirsty human hunters. As a matter of fact, you didn't even know we existed until I told you we did because we keep a low profile and live peacefully amongst you. No gooey. No disgusting."

She was sarcastically contrite when she replied, "Oh. Of course. I'm sorry. It was incredibly insensitive of me to think you'd be remotely like those vicious savages on a TV show. Where are my paranormal manners?"

Sloan clenched his teeth, fighting to keep his professional hat on. The one Casey said he'd better not let slip because Nina had done enough of that to last them all their eternal lifetimes combined. "Anyway, that still brings us back to square one. You don't have any of the outlined symptoms we specialize in. So I don't think OOPS can help." And the Cowboys and the Giants were playing. There was a six-pack and some beef jerky to buy. Gotta go.

Her gasp was of outrage mingled with the static that kept coming and going over the connection. "You're just going to blow me off? Well, I'm sorry I'm not hairy enough to meet your stringent criteria for a paranormal emergency. What kind of outfit are you running here? I thought this was supposed to be a help line for people in crisis?"

Sloan reached for his coat from the back of the chair. "It is. Apparently, you have the wrong crisis for this help line."

"You're not really telling me being stuck in a bottle doesn't qualify as a paranormal crisis, are you?" she shouted.

"Have you been drinking?" Sloan winced, peering over his shoulder. If the girls heard him say something like that to a possible client, there'd be no end to their torment about his insensitivity.

"No, you nominee for most unhelpful customer service rep ever, I haven't been drinking!"

"Well, *you* mentioned the bottle. Not me, lady," he offered dryly, convinced she'd been slamming a few back.

"I said I was stuck *in* a bottle. *In-in-in!* I'm not *on* the bottle! I swear on my dead Uncle Orvis's grave! Just listen to me. *Please.* I'm a caterer. I was catering this swank over-the-top party when I opened what looked like a very old bottle of gin. At least I think it was old. I've never heard of old gin, but it was really dusty, and it said *gin* on it. So what do I know? I don't drink—though that could change at any given time. Anyway, I was just replenishing the gin for the bar. And I did . . . Er, replenish. Oh, boy, I did. I opened the bottle and . . . Anyway, the next thing I know, this guy, dressed a lot like someone from my assistant's niece's favorite movie, *Aladdin*, like poofy pants and all and a T-shirt that said, 'Sorry About What Happens Later,' pops out of the bottle in a puff of some nasty, green smoke, smelling like a week-old *CSI* crime scene and starts dancing around like he'd just won a harem of women."

"An Aladdin guy . . ."

"Yes!" she shouted. "So, I scream. He screams back. We both scream together, he mutters some gibberish in a Joe Pesci kind of way, does this crazy fun house laugh, and the next thing I know, I'm in this bottle. *A gin bottle.* I know it's the same gin bottle because I can read the letters G-I-N on it. Only it's backward because, you know, I'm on the inside looking out—*of a bottle!* A bottle. A. Bottle. Aaaa bottle!"

"Got it. A bottle." Sloan yawned, covering his mouth with his knuckles.

"And, God, it reeks in here. And it's a filthy mess. There are beer cans all over the place, cigarette butts stacked in artful pyramids, sweat socks that look like someone mud wrestled in them, and if you can believe it, a velvet wall hanging of Elvis from his jumpsuit days. Which to me says somebody had way too much time on their hands. Is that good enough for you, Sloan the Werewolf? Is that enough crisis?" She hissed the words. "And lastly, put that in your not-a-paranormal-crisis-that-fits-your-stupid-profile pipe and smoke it!"

Sloan blinked when her increasingly hysterical rant ended. If she was a crank call, she was a damn good actress. To be safe, and keep him from the wrath of Nina, he decided to trust she wasn't bullshitting him. He gave the form he had in front of him another swift glance.

Nope.

Not a single mention about being trapped in a bottle. Time warp? Yes. Bottle? No. So what did that accidentally make her? Wait. Bottle plus Aladdin-like guy plus poufy pants equaled . . . A genie? Shit and piss. He knew as much about the djinn as he did feminine protection. Though, somewhere he remembered hearing they could be nasty little bastards when provoked. But then, there was a lot of false information floating around on the Internet about werewolves, too.

Goddamn it. Why couldn't she just be something simple like a werewolf? Or a hedgehog? He knew jack shit about anything other than being a werewolf.

When he got his hands on Marty, he was going to kill her for leaving him here alone under the guise of "Oh, Sloan, stop being such a baby. Hardly anyone ever calls on a Sunday afternoon." He grabbed his phone and texted Marty a 911 and waited.

Nothing. That was just fucking terrific.

"Hey, werewolf? Are you still there? Or did you hang up because this is just too outlandish to believe, you being a *werewolf* and all," she said with a scoff. "Did you hear a word I said? I'm trapped in a bottle! Oh, my God, a bottle!"

Sloan winced, his eyes moving as quickly as they could over the counselor trainee pamphlet Marty had left him with. There it was. *At all costs, keep the client calm.* "I heard you. But it says here I have to try to keep you calm while we figure this out." He couldn't tell her what he suspected or she'd lose it all together—then he'd never find her. And, yes, he'd go looking for her, because he liked his living environment to be ball buster–free.

"Calm? *Calm?*" she screeched. "I'm trapped in a bottle! You be the calm. I, on the other hand, am going to be the whirlwind of flipped completely out!"

And then the tears started. Huge gulping, snot-riddled sobs that, according to the *How to Comfort Your New Client When in Paranormal Crisis* pamphlet, was expected and supposed to be handled with the utmost compassion.

And tissues.

Not one of his stronger suits. Though, he hated to see a woman cry—or in this case, hear it. It turned him to so much mush, and he'd promise almost anything to stop it. Christ, he hated a woman's tears. "Shhhh—shh-shh. I'll help you, I promise. Now do you know where you are? Are you still at the party you catered?"

There was a long, shuddering breath and then, "No. Not exactly."

"Meaning?"

"It's absolutely humiliating. I don't know if I can tell you."

He was growing impatient with her again. Though, if he was honest, he kinda wanted to see a chick in a bottle. For curiosity purposes only. "Lady, do you want me to come get you or not? Because if not, I have a game I wanna catch."

"You'll come get me? Really?" She sniffled the words.

He looked at his cell phone again. No text from Marty. Shit. "I'll come get you," he soothed with a solemn tone. If he didn't, Keegan would give him hell for days for upsetting Marty. Not on his list of favorite things.

"I'm in the garbage can at the end of my client's driveway."

Placing the back of his hand over his mouth, Sloan muffled his hyena-like laughter and wiped the tears forming at the corner of his eyes on his forearm.

"You're laughing!" she accused with an outraged tone.

Sloan rocked back and forth, covering his snorts before sitting back up and taking a deep, long breath. "I'm sorry. Sorrysorrysorry. Just give me a second, okay?" he managed to wheeze out, covering the earpiece of the phone and bending at the waist again to still his fits of inappropriate laughter.

Four more deep breaths later, and he was back. He cleared his throat, and rolled his head on his neck. "Okay, do you have an address for the garbage can?"

Garbage can. Hah.

As she ran off her location, Sloan typed it into his phone's GPS and pulled up directions to a pretty ritzy suburb in Long Island. "It's gonna take about thirty minutes to get to you with traffic—hang tight, okay? Oh, and what's your name?" In all this, he'd forgotten to ask her name.

There was a pause and then, "You'll laugh again, and I'm a little shaky right now. Usually, I can take a joke. But at this stage, your high-pitched, girl-at-a-slumber-party giggle might break me . . ."

He straightened, shrugging his jacket on as he made his way to the door. "Swear I won't. I'm all laughed out."

"It's Jeannie. Jeannie Carlyle."

Sloan's eyebrow rose. "As in *I Dream of?*"

Her answer was reluctant. "Yessss."

Priceless.

Okay, so he wasn't all laughed out.

SLOAN came to a screeching halt precisely in front of the garbage can Jeannie was supposed to be in and jumped out of his car, scoping the dark street to see if anyone was looking. He tucked his chin into the front of his jacket, pulling his knit cap over his head to brace himself against the harsh winter wind.

A quick glance at the mini-mansion with its rounded shrubs and cascading fountains made him wonder if there weren't security cameras somewhere beyond those wrought iron gates. He tugged his knit cap low over his brow and hunkered into his jacket.

He managed to find the garbage can without trouble, yet he paused and sniffed his surroundings. Well, this was definitely the place. So if this Jeannie was punking him, she'd gone to great lengths to do it. His spidey senses, though, told him she was legit.

With a flip of his wrist, Sloan wasted no time popping open the garbage can's top and using his flashlight to locate the bottle Jeannie said she was in. Her cell phone's battery had died ten minutes into the trip over from OOPS, making him worry about that fragile state she claimed. If she freaked out and word got back to the girls, he was in for some sensitivity boot camp.

He located the bottle easily enough under some newspapers.

Lifting it out, he held it up to the streetlamp. It looked just like any other liquor bottle. He couldn't see a damned thing but some murky remnants of amber liquid. It sloshed when he shook it.

Tucking it into his jacket, Sloan got back in his car and took off down the winding road, following it until he left the small suburb and found a 7-Eleven. Whipping his car into the parking lot, he threw it into park and pulled the bottle out to hold it up again.

Sloan squinted. Shit. Maybe he'd gotten the wrong bottle? Putting his eye to the open mouth of it, he peered inside. The sting of something sharp to his eyeball made his head snap back.

He put the bottle to his lips, swiping at his watery eye with his thumb. "Jeannie? What the hell was that?" he yelped now putting it to his ear to see if she responded.

"A beer can—which, if you could see this pigsty, would put ninety-nine bottles of beer on the wall to shame, and, yes! Yes, it's me! Oh, thank God you came!" she yelped back, her relief evident.

The bottle gave off a slight humming vibration beneath his hand. Holy. Shit. "I'd hold off on thanking the man upstairs," he said into the glass rim. "I'm not sure where we go from here because all of the paranormal experts are out designer discount shopping and can't come to the damn phone right now." He clenched his jaw. Damn that gaggle of women. "Suggestions?"

"You know what, when this is all over, if these invisible OOPS people give me one of those customer feedback forms to fill out, you're screwed. You're the expert here! How should I know what's next?"

Right, right, right. The expert. Shit. Think, Sloan. Without warning her, he tipped the bottle upside down and gave it a hard shake, watching the opening to see if she did the obvious and fell out.

Nothing but some leftover drops of liquid. "You still in there?"

"Don't you mean am I concussed and battered?" she yelled at him, her anger echoing in his ear.

Damn. "Look. I'm doing my best here, okay? I'm still new to this. Just give me a minute to think."

And then it hit him. *I Dream of Jeannie.* He put the bottle back to his lips and talked into it. "Did you ever watch *I Dream of Jeannie?* You know the show with Larry Hagman and the hot blonde in those fluffy pants?"

There was that rasp of a sigh again. "I know this is an admission I'll regret, but, yeah. I arranged my pillows on my bed to look like the inside of Jeannie's bottle, and if you only knew at this very moment how familiar I am with fluffy pants. So, what of it, expert?"

He didn't remember a whole lot about the show other than the cute blonde with the ponytail, but he remembered a little something . . . It was a feeble suggestion at this point, but it was all he had until he could locate those women. "Do you remember how Major Nelson got Jeannie out of the bottle?"

"I can't remember. I only know that if you don't get me out of here soon, I'm going to asphyxiate from the stench, and it won't matter if I get out of here."

Sloan slid down in the front seat of his car when he noticed customers of the convenience store were staring at him while he talked into a bottle like some nut out on a day pass from the crazy house. "He rubbed the bottle."

He heard her scoff. "Weak, Sloan Flaherty. Weak."

Rolling his tongue along the inside of his cheek, he pressed the bottle to his lips. "Got a better plan?"

She sighed a sigh that whispered in his ear, sending a chill along his spine. "No. So go ahead. Rub away."

Heh.

"Hang on to something, then. Things might get bumpy." Without waiting for an answer, Sloan put the bottle between his two hands and gave it a brisk rub, then set it on the passenger seat.

And waited.

His nostrils flared. Was that the scent of beer and stale cigarettes filling the interior of his car? His head swung around just as his car began to rock like they'd hit an eight point five on the Richter.

Sloan grabbed for the steering wheel, leaning forward and clinging to it with one hand while protecting the bottle on the seat with the other. The violent shaking lifted the front end of the car right off its wheels. It humped the paved parking lot like a lover, lifting up and slamming back down, over and over.

And then she was there. In the passenger seat beside him.

A disheveled, raven-haired pixie with cigarette butts stuck to her chin-length hair and a crushed beer can in the purse she clung to.

Wearing sapphire blue harem pants and a matching wisp of satin bra.

Multicolored smoke surrounded her, then drifted away and disappeared, leaving glittery rainbow trails.

Her mouth, red and plump, fell open as her light blue eyes met his, glazed and shiny.

Sloan's mouth fell open for a moment, too. He wasn't sure what he'd expected her to look like, but it wasn't the cute little package she'd turned out to be. Though, definitely not his type, he liked 'em leggy and blonde. Yes. That was what he liked. Or had liked.

Sloan was the first to react. He put a hand on her shoulder, giving it a light squeeze, noticing her skin warm and supple beneath his fingertips. "Jeannie? Are you okay?"

Her wide eyes fixed on him, and she visibly cringed at the touch of his hand, but recovered quickly. "*You're* the werewolf?"

Sloan gave her a cocky grin. "You wanna see the proof?"

Jeannie shook her head hard. The glint of the store's display light through the windshield caught the chocolate and red highlights in her wavy hair and highlighted her cute nose. "Where the hell are my clothes and what is *this*?" she asked, plucking at the filmy pants covering her shapely thighs, then lifting her feet to reveal jewel-encrusted slippers, pointy toed and tipped with tassels. "I look like MC Hammer!" she virtually shouted, spitting the veiled material of her fez from her mouth.

"Whoomp, there it is."

"No. That's 'Can't Touch This,' wolf man."

He reared his head back and laughed for the third time that night. "That's *were*wolf."

"Not laughing here." She threw her arms over her chest with a shiver.

"Maybe it was a parting gift from your friend?" Sloan guessed, pulling off his jacket and draping it along the back of her seat for her to use. "I don't know. Like I said—this"—he waved his hand along her length—her very sexy, rounded length—"isn't our specialty. Anyway, you're out of the bottle, and that's all that matters. Are you okay? I mean, physically?"

Jeannie's return expression was bland when she burrowed into his coat, pulling it tight to her chest. "Is anyone ever really the same after being pushed through an opening the size of a donut hole only to end up wearing a fez?" She flicked the hat on her head with two fingers.

Sloan chuckled. "You make a valid point. So, I guess that's it, right? You're out of the bottle. Mission accomplished. Go team." He held his fist forward for her to knock. This ought to shut Marty up.

Jeannie's eyes were still glassy, but she managed to knock fists with him with a weak stab and a slight shudder of her shoulders.

"You want a ride back to your car?" He reached for the gearshift to put it into reverse.

She nodded her head affirmatively. "Yes, master," was her throaty, sinfully enticing reply.

Sloan kept his foot on the brake and cocked his head in surprised confusion. "I said, do you want a ride back to your car?"

"Yes, *maaaaster*," came out of her mouth once more, only this time in a warbled almost cry while her lips twisted in distaste.

Sloan paused with a frown. "Did you just call me master? *Master?*"
Very. Kinky.

It was clear she was struggling to keep her lips from moving, but
it was as though some invisible entity were forcing the phrase from
her lips. "Yes, master," she all but spat.

Now her eyes weren't just glazed. They were glazed and wide
with shock and maybe even some horror, if he was reading the drop
of her jaw right. Jeannie clapped a hand over her mouth with such
force, it echoed in the car.

Okay, this had gone from a little weird—because let's face it, he
knew weird—to full-on whacked. Wherever this was going, he
wasn't going with. She was alive. She didn't have any discernible
injuries, and excluding the strange way she'd come by her cute outfit, no paranormal abilities. It was time to call this rodeo. No way
was he revealing what he'd thought earlier.

Jeannie blinked, then frowned, clearly choosing her words with
caution. "I'd like to go home now," she whimpered around her fist.
"Please."

"Home. I'm on it." Lifting his foot off the brake, Sloan backed
out of the parking lot and made a beeline back toward the house
where he'd found her. They rode in relative silence, Jeannie tucking
her purse and his jacket to her once barely covered breasts and Sloan
trying to keep his eyes off them.

Woman in crisis, ass. No breast watching for you.

They slid to a halt right back where they started. Simultaneously,
they reached for their respective door handles, Jeannie's hand shaky,
Sloan's impatient to get out and get her safely to her car before anything else happened.

He made his way around to her side of the car, placing his hand
at her elbow and catching a whiff of the fruity scent she wore. Sloan
plucked a lingering cigarette butt from her hair with gentle fingers.
"Where's your car, Jeannie? Give me the keys. I'll go get it for you."

She tipped her purse up to the streetlamp and pulled out her keys, handing them to him, hesitance in her eyes. "It's just outside of the back gate." She breathed a sigh of evident relief that her statement didn't include the word *master*.

"Why don't you wait in the car where it's warm?" he suggested from over his shoulder. If he hurried, he could still catch the last half of the game.

Footsteps sounded behind him. He paused and turned to find Jeannie to the rear of him, her heels visibly digging into the pavement, her body at an awkward slant. "Did you hear me? You can wait in the car."

She wobbled, putting her hands out to steady herself. "Oh, I heard you just fine. Apparently, my feet don't have their listening ears on."

He shoved his hands into the pockets of his jeans, rocking back on his heels. "Your feet?" Now what? Had they sprouted wings? At least that would have some paranormal qualities to it.

"You heard me. My feet aren't cooperating. Each time you take a step, my feet literally mirror your footsteps, and there's nothing I can do to stop it."

"That's crazy," he replied, sarcasm seeping into his words before he could prevent it.

She crossed her arms over her chest, the arms of his jacket hanging over her hands. "You'd know crazy, now wouldn't you, *expert*?"

Sloan threw his hands up in defeat and turned to stomp off to find her car. The faster he got her into it, the faster he could go home.

But the echo of her slippers stalked his ears. Sloan pivoted on his heel to find her but a couple hundred feet from him.

Jeannie's eyes narrowed, glittering in the glow of the lamplight with an I-told-you-so glint to them.

Rolling his tongue along his cheek, he took a step backward to test her theory.

As though someone were pushing her from behind, she teetered forward, fighting the unwanted movement of her feet. When she began to stumble, Sloan rushed forward, catching her so she wouldn't crash to the hard pavement.

Jeannie slumped in his arms with a growl of frustration, bracing her hands on his forearms. Their bodies pressed closer, making Sloan inhale sharply. He set her from him with a hard glance. "I think we have a problem."

"Ya think, *master*?" The fatal word flew from her mouth like a bullet, crashing through her clenched teeth. She screamed then, her face turning a shade of red Sloan couldn't remember seeing before.

That was just before she disappeared in a cloud of perfumed, lavender-colored smoke.

Sloan waved away the smoke, and when it cleared, he was still alone.

This paranormal incident was brought to you by the words *yes* and *master*.

CHAPTER
2

"Is this outfit some kind of pathetic ploy for attention, Jeannie Carlyle?" Betzi, her menu planner and chef for Cee-Gee Catering, drawled the question from her position on Jeannie's moss green couch.

The surface was covered in boxes of sales receipts and client orders Jeannie could never find the time to organize. Betzi swung her legs over the arm of the sofa with a yawn, casually flipping through the current issue of *Cosmo*.

When Jeannie, who was still marveling at the technique with which she'd arrived on her doorstep, Sloan strangely in tow, didn't answer, Betzi peered over the top of her magazine, a smirk on her face, her light brown eyes dancing with amusement. "Well? Don't give me the eyeball. Answer the question. Do you need some love or something? Because I have to tell you, boss, I'm kind of tired tonight—it was that damned yoga instructor that did it to me. Well, that and all his downward-facing dog. He has so much energy. Sexy as hell, but phew—much work. Oh, and the twins are in your bedroom—snarling and, I'm sure, taking great pleasure in eating those fluffy stripper thongs you got at the flea market."

Jeannie shot Betzi the most infuriated glare her eyeballs would allow without falling out of her head. Tonight was not the night to hear about another of Betzi's sexual escapades—most especially if it involved downward-facing dog and a sweaty yoga instructor.

When she'd managed to poof herself back to her brownstone's front door amidst this new smoke-and-mirrors technique she'd acquired, she'd burst through the door to her friend's astonished gazes, introduced Sloan, acquiring more astonished gazes, and proceeded to explain her arrival and the preceding nightmare of her bottle captivity.

So it was an explanation that was just this shy of outlandish? Surely they knew her well enough to know she'd never make something like this up . . .

Jeannie spread her arms wide, indicating her flimsy ensemble and being extra careful to keep her back to Sloan. "Of course this is a ploy for attention, Betzi Cable. First, there's my festive fez—what about that doesn't scream I want attention? Then there's my harem pants. Because I'm all about absolutely anything that will show off all the cellulite on my ass and how so not firm my abs are."

She pushed Sloan's jacket out of the way and pinched at the small roll of flesh exposed just under her ribs, making a face. "And who doesn't want to flaunt their miniscule, thirty-four B fun bags in this armor they call a push-up bra? Fun bags that closely resemble a can of freshly popped dinner rolls all oozing out the sides?"

"Ohhh, but it's such pretty material—all that gauze . . . So delicate, and look at the intricacy of the waistband of your MC Hammer pants. I mean, you just don't run into that kind of embroidery anymore these days," Charlene, Jeannie's assistant muttered in her best divert-the-crazy-in-this-situation tone.

Usually her lyrical Australian accent soothed Jeannie. Tonight, it just made her want to throw her mate on the barbie. Clearly, they weren't getting the picture here. She had a 911 on her hands.

Charlene tweaked the leg of Jeannie's harem pants and forced a bright grin. "And those shoes, mate?" She nodded her thumbs-up. "To. Die. For. So authentic."

Jeannie let out a puff of pent-up air and planted her hands on her hips in a frustrated gesture. "Right, because in my desperate ploy for attention, I definitely want my attention-grabbing outfit to have only the most intricate embroidery."

Charlene gnawed on her lip—one of her many nervous reactions when she didn't know what to say. "You know, I could've stayed home. I had plenty of work to do for that beast of a bride, Willow Sanders. I didn't have to come over to make sure Betzi didn't suffocate the twins with a pillow or give them too much canned dog food. You do remember what happens then, don't you? It leads to oose-lay oopy-pay." She whispered the words, her eyes flitting to the floor in shame. "It took us three cleanings with that carpet cleaner and four gallons of solution to get the mess all up the last time she fed them her leftovers from The Dawg House. I was just trying to help," she huffed, clearly offended by Jeannie's harsh tone.

"You know how you can help, Charlene?" Jeannie asked, her voice tight, her temper flaring.

Charlene's face instantly brightened, her wringing hands stilled. Sweet and genuine, she answered, "Name it. I'm in. Whatever you need, and I do mean whatever."

Jeannie narrowed her eyes in the vicinity of the alleged werewolf Sloan Flaherty, gorgeously quiet while he watched the women interact. Waving a hand in his general direction, she snorted. "Tell me what to do with *him*."

Betzi dropped the magazine on the couch and smiled in Sloan's direction with a coquettish slant to her lips. She smoothed her pixie-cut dark hair behind her ears and slipped to the edge of the cushion

with a wink. "I'll tell you what I'd like to *do* with him, but it's probably not fit for polite company. Oh, and Ms. Charlene Gibbons, who
blushes if you use the word *vagina*. Now, usually, that wouldn't stop
me, but seeing as you ran rampant with this fascinating, though
maybe a little outdated, maneuver in order to nab a man—I'm sticking to the employer/employee code and keeping my all-out lust for
hot stuff on the inside." She made a circle with her finger around her
lower torso. "But a warning for all future endeavors. The next time
you go on a long overdue man spree, leaving me and my lady parts
behind to babysit Benito and Boris, and you don't bring me home
any leftover doggie bags of the male persuasion, I'm breaking up
with you and going to work for that pig Aleksi."

Jeannie's eyes rolled upward. She gritted her teeth and fought
for composure. Not an easy task in harem pants. "I cannot believe
you'd threaten me with that cheesy Russian rip-off of Sandra Lee.
He makes those crescent rolls from scratch like Pillsbury is suddenly
making Big Macs. And I did *not* go on a man spree. I told you what
happened," she insisted, peevish in tone.

That Betzi and Charlene were having trouble believing her explanation for showing up here in this getup with a man she couldn't get
more than a few hundred feet from without being forced directly
back toward his vicinity by some invisible force came as no surprise.

She was having trouble believing it, too. But still . . .

Betzi rose, waving a dismissive hand at Jeannie before sauntering
toward Sloan, who was still looking rather confused, and was now
sitting on the ottoman that matched her burgundy chair, covered in
her almost identical dogs Boris's and Benito's hair. "Yeah, yeah. There
was a bottle of booze, and a bald Aladdin guy with a single braid
down his back, and he wore parachute pants, and a phone call and
some sort of paranormal something or other and then *him*. The, uh,
werewolf," she enunciated in slow syllables. "Look, friend, here's the
thing. If this isn't a ploy for attention, or some whacky way of acting

out slash losing your marbles because of all work and no play or a date in all the time I've worked for you makes for a dull, maybe even mental Jeannie Carlyle—then just say it. Never mind. I'll say it. Your hormones finally caught up with you. No shame in that, boss."

Jeannie began to protest, but Betzi held up her hand and snapped her fingers together while Charlene's eyes darted between her boss and her coworker with nervousness. She backed away, stumbling over a throw rug before righting herself and biting her lip.

"Look, you don't need a reason to admit you have needs, *mi amiga*. I always say if your hormones are calling—answer the damn phone. But you definitely didn't have to make up this elaborate story about being trapped inside a gin bottle because you want to sleep with a guy who likes to role-play and has a fetish for Barbara Eden. There's nothing wrong with a little kinkity-kink. I'm just going to be thankful you didn't hook up with a man-child who likes to wear diapers. There's also nothing wrong with a one-night stand. Don't be ashamed of your needs, Jeannie. Own those bitches." Betzi punched the air with a slow, unenthusiastic fist for emphasis.

"Okay, ladies. That's enough," Sloan said, jumping up, a disgusted scowl on his beautifully chiseled face. "I can assure you I do not wear diapers, and have never, not even once, considered them as an accoutrement to anything sexual."

Charlene clasped her hands together at her breast and sighed with a dreamy rasp. "Ohhh, he knows what the word *accoutrement* means. He's a smart one-night stand. Way to pick 'em, Jeannie." She, too, punctuated her statement with a much more enthusiastic fist pump than Betzi's and gave Jeannie an encouraging smile.

"For the last time, he is not a one-night stand!" Jeannie yelped with a stomp of her bejeweled foot, making the tassels on her shoes quiver. "What I told you about how this all happened is true, Betzi Cable! I didn't pick him up at the party I catered, and I definitely don't want to have a one-night stand with him!"

Sloan beat the place on his chest where his heart was with a fist. "Ow. That cuts so deep." He gave her a somber glance, but his eyes, a light blue and hooded by dark lashes, gleamed.

Crossing her arms over her chest, Jeannie stood in front of him, just barely reaching the top of his broad shoulder. "My heartfelt apologies."

Sloan put a hand on her shoulder, using a light grip, one that while she was sure wasn't meant to, nonetheless made her shiver. "No, no. No need to apologize. You're on edge. I'd be on edge if I were wearing gauze, too. No amount of intricate embroidery can make up for that."

Jeannie's chin lifted as she shrugged his hand away. His big, unfamiliar, warm, sexy hand. Stranger danger. "This isn't funny, Sloan."

"I'll say."

Jeannie backed up with slow steps, careful not to hit the corner of her messy desk. Since they'd both arrived at her brownstone in a puff of lavender smoke smack-dab on her doorstep, she'd had no choice but to invite him in because she couldn't get very far without him. He'd had the very same look she knew mirrored hers. Utter confusion.

And what had that *master* thing been about? The word had slipped off her tongue like she'd always addressed strange men in that manner—though, she'd discovered, if she bit her tongue hard enough, she could now choke back the word. The use of that particular title troubled her far more than some whacky genie costume. Jeannie Carlyle was nobody's bitch. So, yeah. "Why can't I get away from you?" she asked with a frown of discontent.

"Because I'm irresistible?"

Jeannie wrinkled her nose and shook her head. "No, I'm pretty sure that's not it."

His lean jaw clenched. "Look, I don't know what's going on. It's like I said, I have no information on genies or whatever it is you are.

I'm a werewolf. Genies and werewolves don't play in the same sandbox. But Marty, Nina, and Wanda will be here soon to help figure this out. Nina just texted me to say they're on their way."

Yeah. She vaguely recalled him explaining the three magical women that were going to tip her paranormal world right side up again by helping her get through her paranormal crisis. "And then what happens? Shorty, Tina, and LaShonda wave their magic wands and make everything okay?"

"It's *Marty, Nina*, and *Wanda*," he emphasized, his eyes somber. "I'd get that right, if I were you, specifically Nina's name. She's probably the meanest woman alive. No, I take that back. There's no probably about it. She *is* the meanest woman alive. I can't make any promises for your safety if you get her name wrong. Just a heads-up. As to what happens next?" Sloan shrugged his wide shoulders. "Can't say for sure. I've never been involved in their little support group or any of the adventures they seem to manage to get tangled up in. I was just answering the phones for them because Marty made me. She's my sister-in-law, another werewolf, and when she wants something, you give it to her or she badgers you until you do."

It might be crazy to even consider such myths existed, but after tonight, who was the crazy one if she didn't at least give this paranormal explanation some serious credibility. There was no denying she'd been trapped in a gin bottle. There was no denying a man had popped out of the gin bottle just before she'd been sucked into it.

OMG. Mulder had been right. The truth really was out there.

Located in a gin bottle full of stale cigarette butts and piles of beer cans.

The slight throb of her temple increased. She rubbed it with an errant finger and gathered more of her thoughts. "So this kind of thing has happened before? They've helped other people who've had accidents like me?"

Sloan's forehead wrinkled in thought. He jammed his hands into

the pockets of his jacket. "Twice, I think. So far anyway. I dunno. I
don't keep track. Like I said, I was just at OOPS helping out while
they shopped—or something. They don't get many serious calls.
Most of them are pranks."

"So how did you get here again? To my house?" When her lavender smoke had cleared, and she'd realized where she was, Sloan had
been right behind her like they had some invisible leash binding them
together.

Sloan planted his hands on his hips, making his leather jacket
crinkle. "It was the craziest damn thing. One minute you were there,
right in the middle of the road at that guy's mansion—the next you
were gone and I was right behind you. Poof. You know the rest.
Puffs of girlie-smelling smoke—me outside your house, et cetera."

Betzi circled the two of them, her heart-shaped face full of mischief. "Okay. I think it's time for Charlene and me to hit the bricks.
You guys go back to your one thousand and one Arabian nights fantasy, and I'll call you in the morning for the juicy details after I plan
that menu for the Morgans, yes?"

"No!" Jeannie shouted, clutching Betzi's hand, panic racing
through her veins. "No way are you leaving me here alone when I
have more creatures coming!"

Sloan clucked his tongue in clear admonishment again. "Another
tip from me to you. Ixnay on the word *eatures-cray*. If I wasn't sure
Nina'd be mad as hell that you called her Tina, I'm positive she'd eat
your lungs for lunch for calling her a creature. I don't want to scare
you, but I think it's only fair to tell you Nina can be very touchy and
confrontational. Not to mention, she has absolutely no filter from
brain to mouth. We're called paranormals. I'm a werewolf just like
Marty. Nina's a vampire, and Wanda's half werewolf, half vampire.
Period."

Charlene's eyes, pretty and blue, went wide behind her stylish
glasses. "I think this"—she flapped her hands between Jeannie and

Sloan from behind Betzi—"whatever it is, has just become much too weird for me. This is role-playing gone extreme. You're both in way too deep for my comfort level. Beware the Dungeons and Dragons syndrome, mate," Charlene warned with a slight hitch to her worried words and a fearful expression.

A loud knock at her front door had Sloan moving through the women at a rapid pace and Jeannie hot on his heels, unable to keep herself from following him. She shot Charlene and Betzi a see-what-I-mean glare when she scurried past them with shuffling feet and yelped in panic, "Would you guys keep an eye on the twins in the bedroom? You know what they're like with strangers."

Betzi herded Charlene toward Jeannie's bedroom with a nod and one very clear skeptical eyebrow raised.

"Thank Christ. That's probably the girls," he said over his shoulder as though their appearance was going to make everything all better.

Right. Shorty, Dina, and Tawanda.

Jeannie stopped short only to fall into his wide back, and for a brief moment, she reveled at how hard and secure it felt. She pressed her hands to his lean waist to catch herself, only to yank them away as though she'd been burned.

A naturally gorgeous brunette leered back at Jeannie from the other side of her chain lock. Her pale face, peeking out from a black hoodie, eerie and beautiful, didn't look too pleased. Ah. This must be the infamous Lena.

She wormed her fingers under the chain and flipped the pair her middle finger. "Open the fucking door, fleabag. See this?" She pried her lips apart with her free hand and opened her mouth wide with a rough grunt, encouraging them to look. "See my fucking fang? It's broken, goddamn it. This is the kind of shit that happens when you send blondie into a full-on freak with your 911 texts, Sloan. She hit the fire hydrant outside with that big SUV Keegan bought her so she'd have room for all her bullshit designer shopping hauls. I clipped my friggin' fang on the dashboard, numbnuts. For that shit? You gotta pay."

As Sloan let the chain slip, he popped the door open and backed away, and on cue, Jeannie went with him. Her eyes went wide while she gazed in openmouthed horror at the woman's teeth.

She really did have fangs. Like really. The unbroken one, long and so white it glowed, hung over her lower lip when she closed her mouth, jagged and sharp.

The brunette circled Sloan and Jeannie, her almond-shaped, coal black eyes narrowed, her long, lean body throwing off a cagey sort of energy. She waved a slim finger in Jeannie's direction. "So, this is her?"

Jeannie nodded numbly, unable to tear her eyes from this beautiful creature's mouth. Still stunned, she created a million reasons in her mind, beyond the obvious, as to why someone would possess incisors the size of tusks. "This is her," she acknowledged.

The woman gave Sloan a hard shove to his shoulder with a flat palm, using such force, Jeannie saw him plant his feet more firmly on her tiled entryway to prevent himself from bucking backward. "Is she fucking on fire, Sloan?"

Sloan smiled at her, his eyes clearly taunting. "Look, Jeannie. It's the OOPS organization's friendly community vampire. Bet she wants to be your neighbor."

"Did you hear me?" the alleged vampire rasped around her fang. "I said, 'Is she fucking on fire?'"

"Why ever do you ask, vampire?" Sloan cooed at her.

"Because Jesus Christ and a flippin' calico kitten, you got Marty so worked up with all your 'hurry the hell up, I wanna get away from this chick's texts, she rushed over here assholes and elbows and took out a fire hydrant in the process. Now I have a broken fang. Do you have any idea how painful that shit is? I'll be goddamned. I'm not supposed to feel any pain unless you stake the shit outta me, but bustin' a freakin' tooth is like hella painful? Jesus, this vampire shit," she muttered, her tone disgusted, her angry eyes pinning Sloan to the wall.

Seeing the tension mount between the two, Jeannie thought to intervene. She spoke the words before she was able to stop herself. Regret was for sissies anyway. "You're Katrina, right?"

"Nina," she hissed at Jeannie, her eyes flashing. "And you're Ali Baba's main squeeze, right? Did you hook up with a Groupon or some shit for belly-dancing classes or what?"

Jeannie eyed the gorgeous albeit pale woman while repeating her name over and over again in her head. She so sucked at names. They took time to remember. Time and repetition. "No. I'm Ah-ladd-in's squeeze. Ali lost his Baba a long time ago. Now he's just boring and old. But wow. That Aladdin." She gave a low whistle.

Nina smirked, her tooth somehow smaller now. "Good, you've still got your chuckles. You'll need it wearing that. Way to rock the flimsy, lady."

"So you're the one who's supposed to help me? My friendly and supportive paranormal crisis counselor?" Because this Dina—she mentally corrected herself, *damn, Nina*—appeared neither helpful nor friendly.

Sloan snorted.

Nina planted her hands inside the pockets of her hoodie. "Oh, sure, I'll help you. I won't like a single second of it, but I'll help, because my two bleeding heart BFFs make me do it. But it damn well won't be 'cus I like it."

"Can anyone make you do anything? I didn't get the impression someone of your caliber could be made to do what she didn't want to." Jeannie didn't mean it as a slur at all. She really meant it. At well over five inches taller than Jeannie, Nina-Tina-Dina had Amazonian properties. No way was she going to poke the caged beast.

Sloan was immediately in Nina's path. He shot Jeannie a pointed look. His handsome face held a warning. "Stopping now. Remember the warning I gave you?"

Jeannie nodded obediently. Right, right. "Yes, massster . . ." She bit her tongue and winced. If she focused, she'd found she could control her words. "I mean, right—she's the meanest woman alive. Don't rile her."

Nina cracked her knuckles and glared at Sloan before her eyes fell back on Jeannie. "He said that about me?"

Totally ready to do whatever she had to in order to ingratiate her-self to this beast with big teeth, because honestly, this Bettina—er, *Nina*—was her manna from heaven, she planned Operation Suck-up. If giving up the Reluctant to Help Her Sloan was what would appease Nina, too bad. It was a dog-eat-dog world.

So Jeannie nodded furiously. "He did. He said not to call you a creature or forget your name because you're confrontational. He also said you have no filter from your brain to your mouth. Totally said you were the meanest woman alive."

Nina's face went from dark to light in seconds, a smile wreathing her beautiful face. "At least he got something right."

"Then I shall forever call you Meanest Woman Alive. How's Mean for short?" Jeannie asked.

Sloan mouthed the words *suck-up* at her, his gorgeous lips trans-fixing her gaze.

Nina's head fell back on her slender shoulders when she cackled. "I guess if you had to fuck up, playah, you fucked up with a chick who's got some swingin' tenders. Booyah, Romeo." She clapped him on the shoulder.

Sloan shook his dark head. "Oh, no, I did not, as you so callously put it, *fuck up*. I was answering *your* phones when this went down. I did exactly what you said to do when I answered, too. I was sensi-tive. Kind. Warm even. And I rescued the damsel in bottle distress, but I definitely didn't create her or her predicament because, had I? She would have been blonde and about six inches taller."

Jeannie glared at Sloan. "I find that so surprising, Sloan the Werewolf. Would she have been empty of head, too?"

Sloan clucked his tongue and redirected his gaze at Nina. "My work here is done. Over. Now. So where's my car? I think I can still catch the highlights of the game on ESPN. Did you pick it up on your way over here?"

Jeannie gave him a mocking disappointed pout and poked at his chest. "That's it? You're just going to leave without any concern for the outcome of my not-blonde-enough well-being?"

He eyeballed Jeannie without an ounce of sympathy. "Um, yep."

Nina smacked her lips, her face full of amusement. "You'll probably have to wait on that, chicken shit."

Now Sloan's eyes narrowed. "Why do I have to wait, vampire?"

In that moment, a petite blonde rushed in, her pretty face flushed, her trendy purple heels clacking on the floor. She threw her arms around Sloan's neck, the length of her long ponytail bobbing against her stylish, deep purple coat. "I'm sorry! I'll pay for it. Swear on my Louboutins!"

Sloan put his hands on her waist and set her from him. The look he gave her was hesitant, yet Jeannie also noted a hint of fondness in it. "Pay for *what*, Marty?"

"Hoo, boy," another voice, soft and sweet exclaimed. The woman that belonged to the voice stopped in front of Jeannie. She was tall, slender, and dressed like some modern-day Audrey Hepburn. Though, Audrey probably would have had her forehead and left cheek waxed. The tufts of hair poking from those spots on the woman's face definitely deserved investigation, but that wouldn't come from Jeannie Carlyle, PI.

She didn't want to know . . .

"First, my apologies for this." She touched the hair on her cheek.

"In times of great stress, I still have a little trouble controlling my shift. It'll be gone in a matter of moments."

Jeannie scanned the woman before her. Her chestnut brown hair was pulled into a loose bun at the back of her head, her makeup, while artfully applied, was meant only to enhance rather than wow.

"Sloan? Maybe we should wait to talk about this until after we've talked to Jeannie? She is our first priority, after all." Tugging off her leather gloves, she dropped them into a matching large taupe hand-bag dangling from the crook of her elbow. "So clearly, by the look of your outfit, you're a genie. Er, *Jeannie*. I'm so sorry we weren't here sooner. We took a personal day that went a little long."

Nina sidled up to her and bumped Jeannie's shoulder with hers. "Know why we were fucking long? Because blondie over there"—she pointed a finger at the woman in purple standing next to Sloan—"just couldn't fucking decide which dress would best enhance her fat ass and hairy legs."

"And we're off," Sloan muttered on a cackle, stretching his bulky arms in front of him before crossing them in front of his chest.

The elegant woman's sigh was long and maybe even a little tor-tured to Jeannie's ears. She ignored the Amazon Nina and instead addressed Sloan. "So Jeannie's aware of the nature of our origins?"

Sloan nodded, his eyebrow cocked. "Oh, she's very aware. And if she wasn't before, she is now, due to Fangalina here." He thumbed a finger at Nina.

With a matter-of-fact nod back at Sloan, the pretty woman gazed at Jeannie, her eyes warm. "So, introductions, then? I'm Wanda Schwartz-Jefferson. Werevamp—which explains the hair on my face. Two paranormals in one." She smiled and held out her hand. A hand Jeannie blatantly hesitated taking.

Wanda gave her another encouraging smile and inched her hand closer to Jeannie's. "Promise you won't get cooties if you shake my hand. Swear it on Nina's cursed life."

Jeannie sobered and stuck out her hand, letting Wanda take hers. "I'm sorry. That was rude. It's this bra—it pinches the brain cells that control my manners."

Wanda chuckled, shrugging out of her bone-hued jacket and placing it carefully on the hook by the front door. "A sense of humor is always helpful in a situation like this."

"Marty Flaherty, straight up werewolf," the perky blonde with more shiny bracelets on her wrist than you could buy in bulk at Claire's said.

Jeannie blinked at the woman with the long mane of shiny hair. "Flaherty? As in related to Sloan the Werewolf Flaherty?"

Her mouth pinched at the corners when she made a sour, but playful expression. "Damn. I've been had. There's just no hiding him, is there?"

"To be fair, he did answer my call of distress," Jeannie defended, even if Sloan wanted to get away as fast as he could now.

Nina's snort was loud and abrasive. "I'd be all kinds of distressed, too, if I was wearing the shit you got slapped on your lady lumps like you just hit the Victoria's Secret for Genies in Istanbul. It's like twelve degrees outside, Jasmine. You shoulda brought your magic carpet to keep you warm." She paused for a moment, clearly pondering her cleverness, then threw her head back and laughed.

Sloan circled the women, his footsteps impatient. "Before you girls go any further with your paranormal spiel, where's my car parked? I have to go—game to catch and all." He tacked on a smile to his unfeeling words.

Wanda's hand went immediately to Sloan's shoulder. Her words were clearly measured. "Sloan, about your car . . ."

Sloan's jaw hitched upward as did one raven eyebrow. "You did grab my car, didn't you? Marty has the spare key. She gave it to you, right, Wanda?"

Marty took two steps backward and hid behind Wanda, placing

her hands on her friend's shoulder and using her as though she were a human shield. She closed her eyes and gulped. "Oh, God, I'm sorry. I'm soooo sorry. Swear on the pack I'll fix it."

Sloan cleared his throat; a tic in his jaw that fascinated Jeannie began to pulse. "What is there to fix, Marty?"

"So it was like this," she began from behind Wanda's back. "It's sort of *your* fault. *You* had me in a full-on freak with all your texts to hurry it up. I was rushing to get here to *you*, to help, so you wouldn't have to suffer anymore, and because you're not exactly Mr. Sensitive. You did make it sound like the world was coming to an end—you'd think you were stuck with the Unabomber, not a cute little brunette like Jeannie."

"Marty . . ." Sloan's tone held a warning. The muscles in his forearms flexed and his thighs visibly tensed beneath his tight jeans.

Marty flapped her hands, her bracelets jangling. She poked her head over Wanda's shoulder. "Anyway, I was rushing and I'm still not used to the SUV. It's big. Really big. And Wanda and I were busy chatting about the most fabulous knockoff Badgley Mischka I found today and then—"

"Boom, baby!" Nina shouted, slamming her palms together to make a loud crack and following up with devilish laughter. "She nailed that restored piece of fucking metal like you nail chicks, hard and fast, werewolf. Made me slam my fang right into the dashboard of your precious can on wheels."

Marty pursed her lips. "Shut up, Nina! Let me finish explaining."

Sloan's hand immediately went upward, his lips becoming a thin line. "Wait. You hit my car? My rebuilt-from-the-ground-up '66 Mustang? The one I spent two years working on? You *hit it*?" His voice raised a couple of notches.

Jeannie noted his struggle to keep his anger in check. It was just a car . . . but it was one Sloan clearly loved. Her feet shifted to move away due to the fact that he looked like he was going to blow, but the invisible force that kept her tethered to him rooted her to the spot.

"Oh, she did more than hit it," Nina said with antagonistic properties. "She rammed that fucker so hard it folded like a junkie in a meth lab."

"Damn it, Marty!" he roared in a whoosh of air; his sharp cheekbones wisped red with anger. "I told Keegan you shouldn't be allowed to drive something so big. You were dangerous enough in that stupid convertible you had. Giving you a car the size of *The Partridge Family* tour bus was just more indulgence on the part of my brother, who doesn't understand the word *no*." He shot Nina an angry glare. "I thought you said she hit a fire hydrant, Nina?"

Nina shrugged with indifference, clearly unconcerned about Sloan's precious piece of metal. She slapped him on the back with an amicable grin. "Oh, she did, dude. That was *after* she slammed into your tuna can on wheels, knocked it out of the way, and drove up over the fucking curb. It's how I broke my fang. Because I was driving your hunk of junk, dude. So, I guess, somebody's gonna need to make nice with the Geico gecko in the very near future."

Sloan's eyes bulged for a mere moment before they narrowed in Marty's direction. Menace lurked in them. He took an imposing step forward, parting Wanda from Marty without touching either of them. "I should have known better," he seethed. "What the hell was I thinking leaving something as simple as picking up my car to the three of you? It's like leaving Larry, Curly, and Moe to organize world peace!"

Wanda finally spoke, her voice tight but composed. "Now, Sloan, there's no need to be so rude. It can be fixed. Stop overreacting."

"Fixed?" he yelled, his fists in a tight clench. "Fixed, Wanda? It took two years for me to rebuild that car. You know what this is like, Wanda? It's akin to me running over your stupid, and according to you, priceless Hummel collection. You know, the one you spent half of your life scouring eBay to complete?"

Wanda's eyes went wide when she gasped. Her finger shot up under Sloan's flaring nostrils. "Don't you call them stupid, mister! Don't you dare make fun of my Hummels!"

"Dude!" Nina yelped, taking a protective stance in front of Wanda. "It's just a fucking car. Knock it the fuck off and let's get to the biz at hand. I'm sick of these yapping women. I need quiet, and I need it soon. Now you've gone and added another broad to this shit wreck of babble." She thumbed over her shoulder at Jeannie. "So shut the hell up and lay off."

Jeannie blanched at the tension between the three women and Sloan, her stomach knotting. She hated yelling and she especially hated discord.

Sloan whipped around and began to pace, the crinkle of his jacket ringing in Jeannie's ears. "Just a *fucking car*, Nina? Excuse my foul language, Jeannie, but is your garden gnome collection in that creepy Harry Potter maze of trees in your backyard just a *fucking garden gnome* collection, Nina? Or is it important to you? Because I remember tripping over one of those ugly things at Greg's five millionth birthday party last year and you nearly losing your wee mind because I chipped its freaky garden gnome hat."

Okay. Things were getting ugly. Cars and Hummels and garden gnomes aside, she needed help. Real help. Screw uptight Sloan and his classic, rebuilt car. Sloan could catch a cab.

Jeannie tapped him on the shoulder and cleared her throat. "Look, I don't want to interrupt the battle of the Most Important Possessions, but I've had a really long night, and the sooner you can—"

"You leave my goddamn garden gnomes out of it, ass sniffer!" Nina spat, cornering Sloan until Jeannie was almost pressed up against the wall. Her movements were freakishly swift, making Jeannie's heart pump with fear.

But Sloan obviously didn't fear Nina in quite the way he'd preached she should. "Back off, vampire."

"The hell," Nina taunted, snapping her teeth together. It was clear she thoroughly enjoyed razzing Sloan. Whatever the friction between them was about, there was an underlying amusement in it for both of them Jeannie didn't quite understand.

She peeked around his back to see Sloan glowering down at Nina, his eyes dark and dangerous. "You know, Nina, I'm sick and damned tired of your thug tactics." He jammed a hand into his thick, dark hair in clear frustration. "Swear to Christ, there are times when I wish I was a woman, because if I were, oh, lady—I could finally get away with—"

Sloan didn't get to finish his sentence.

But, Jeannie reflected, he might be in the market to borrow her painfully tight push-up bra and some liquid eyeliner.

Oh, dear.

CHAPTER 3

No one moved.

Not even Nina, who'd been coiled like a tightly wound spring just seconds ago.

Ohhh. Jeannie's mouth fell open in horror when she stepped from behind Sloan after more of that crazy lavender smoke had cleared. She shoved her fist into it to keep from squealing while a rush of tingly heat spread from her toes to the top of her head.

Wanda's elegant face had gone slack—her tastefully made-up eyes wide.

Marty pressed her hands to her cheeks and frowned.

Not surprisingly, Nina was the first to recover. She took a swaggered step away from them and scanned Sloan from head to toe.

Then she smiled. Wide. Devilish even. "Niiiice hooters." Her whistle was clear and sharp, cutting through the still silent room. "Would ya look at those, Marty? Perky, right? And look at his ass. It's like the one you have when you wear that fucking Booty Pop."

Marty's nod was as slow as her words. "Yeah . . . perky . . . No Booty Pop required . . ." she mumbled with a tone in the key of awe.

Sloan stared at them all, his eyes, now complete with a beautiful fringe of lashes, were wide, too. He looked down at his newly acquired lady lumps, plucking his T-shirt outward at an awkward angle with a gasp. "Oh, my God!" he squealed, much, Jeannie supposed, like any woman who had breasts as fine as his would.

But then he snapped his ruby red lips shut when he obviously heard the words that shot out of his mouth had a very feminine, almost Valley Girl hitch to their tone. With a stomp of his foot, he planted a hand on his curvy hip and glared at Jeannie.

Jeannie winced as she took a few steps backward to assess the full damage. Sloan's dark hair hung in beautiful long tresses around his face, the almost blue highlights glossy under her living room lamp.

His very made-up-with-more-makeup-than-a-MAC-display-rack face was cakey with foundation, and the blush on his cheekbones made him look like a clown. He was, quite frankly, a parody of a woman. It looked like he'd been playing with his mother's makeup and had failed dismally.

She bit her lip when she took in the sag of his once tight-fitting jeans. They bunched at his waist and thighs, yet were much too tight in the area of his derriere. Once a luscious thing to behold, it was now a backend to rival the likes of even J.Lo. Though still totally luscious.

Had she done this? Had she turned Sloan into this nightmare version of a woman?

Jesus. He was coyote ugly. So ugly, he was a candidate for the Chew Your Arm Off in Order to Get Away from Your Drunk Hookup on the Morning After club.

It had to have been her. There'd been that strange lavender smoke—smoke that, even now, still dissipated in flirtatious tendrils all around Sloan.

But how?

Nina crossed her arms over her chest. "God, you're an ass face of a woman. So I guess sometimes you get what you wish for, eh, flea bait?"

"The wish!" Wanda gasped, her purse rocking on the crook of her arm when she whipped around to face Jeannie. "Sloan wished to be a woman . . . Oh, sweet mother. Jeannie can grant wishes."

Oh. Jeannie blanched.

How wishtastic.

"I swear, Marty," Sloan complained with a hint of whine, brushing his luxurious locks from his face with a swipe of his hand. "I don't know how you women do it. This is—well," he drawled, "it's just awful. Yes. Awful." He shook his head, fighting a rush of tears. "I mean, I feel so overwhelmed right now. One minute I want to lie down on the floor and cry like a two-year-old, and the next, I want to challenge Nina to a hair-pulling contest because she has more fabulous hair than me. It's in-san-ity!" He pouted, then frowned because his lower lip had jutted forward of its own free will.

Fuck. Had he just said that all girlified while his hand flew around in the air? In delicate fashion, to boot? The rush of uncontrollable emotions raging through him assaulted each nerve in his body in unmerciful womanly waves.

He couldn't stop his disturbingly over-the-top responses. The moment he thought better of them was the moment they flew from his lips.

He felt raw and out of control, on the verge of tears, and—of all unmanly things—touchy and ultrasensitive. Thank God the girls had talked Jeannie into coming back to the OOPS offices where they had their paranormal index cardholder with all their connections.

He just wouldn't have been able to stand Jeannie's friends silently laughing at him, too. It was enough that Marty, Nina, and Wanda had cackled like hens the entire ride over. They'd texted him more than one LOL along with helpful makeup tips and the URL for the Spanx website while Jeannie, still glued to his side, sputtered snorts of laughter.

Thankfully, Betzi and Charlene had agreed to let Jeannie call them when she was done handling her *escapade*, as Betzi had titled it.

"Know what all that whine is about, Sloan?" Nina asked.

"Wha . . . aa . . . t?" He was sniveling. Christ and a prostitute, he was sniveling, much in the way he'd heard Marty do when she watched those Lifetime movies—or when she wanted her way with his brother Keegan.

"That's called PMS, girlie," Nina taunted, holding up a hand mirror she'd dug out of the OOPS bathroom so Sloan could see what he looked like. "Know what makes that boo-boo all better? Oreo cookies and some Midol. You want I should hit the twenty-four-hour drugstore on Seventh?"

Sloan swiped the air again in Nina's direction with a furious hand and pink-glazed nails. "You leave me alone, you mean beast! I'd rather eat hot coals than have you do anything for me!" he cried out.

Cried.

Oh, fuck all. Sloan lifted his foot, his now silver high-heeled foot, to begin to stomp around some more, only to fight back the urge with the clench of his teeth.

He pressed his fingers to his eyes to keep from sobbing and took a sniffling gulp of air. "Oh. My. God. Make this stop! I just can't bear it a second longer! Not a second!" Sloan whipped a warning finger up in front of Marty, who'd crossed the room with sympathy written all over her face. He didn't want pity. He wanted balls.

That thought made him blanch. Did he still have balls? He couldn't look.

This was all Marty's fault. If she hadn't made him feel so guilty for not supporting her venture with OOPS, he'd have never answered the phones so she could have some alone time with the girls, and he wouldn't now be shedding tears, talking with his hands, cramping, and craving a bag of chips double dipped in chocolate ice cream and hot fudge sauce.

Jeannie placed her palm on his arm, giving it a squeeze. Despite his womanly appearance, her hand made him think straight, manly things—technically, at this stage of the game, making him a lesbian. "I'm sorry, Sloan. I don't even know how it happened. It just did. You know, in that puff-of-smoke thing. But if it makes you feel any better, you know, if we can't fix this, what you're experiencing, er, displaying is a really exaggerated version of how it feels to be a woman. Well, maybe not the Midol and Oreos, but the rest . . . Like you're hormonal times a billion." She patted his arm again, her eyes reflecting her share of bewilderment.

Her tender, nurturing tone wrought more tears from eyes he would have sworn were all cried out. But taking into account he was utterly sick with jealousy that Jeannie had such perfectly symmetrical, almond-shaped eyes—it made sense.

After looking in that hand mirror the beast kept waving in front of him, Sloan found he sorely lacked in the feminine department. Sorely.

"Don't," he heard himself squeak, putting a hand between them. Jesus. What was it with the hand thing? "I can't bear your pity. I'm a mess." Again, even as the words escaped his lips, he couldn't believe they were coming from his mouth.

Marty patted his shoulder and pulled a tissue from the sleeve of her fabulous, long-sleeved maxi dress. Sloan bit the inside of his lip when he summed up Marty with three words that were as foreign to him as how to use a mascara wand. *Maxi dress* and *fabulous*. All in one sentence. Oh, God.

She tilted his chin up and swiped at his tears. "Stop. You'll ruin your makeup."

"Loook at me," he moaned. "I'm hideous. Simply hideous!"

"And fucking whiny," Nina added, just so there'd be extra tears.

His finger was immediately up in the air again and then, he was waving it in accusatory fashion at Nina. "If I wasn't sure before, Nina, I am now. You're not a woman. You couldn't be, you unfeeling, angry little viper. You're insensitive and crude and you dress like you just left some Goth party where people cut themselves while they play Halo."

Nina winked, adjusting her hoodie around her face. "Well, I've been telling you for years I'm more man than you'll ever be. Guess I was fucking right. Now quit adding to the already overweight load of broads on my back and shut up. We have a problem—one we know diddly about. Jeannie can obviously grant wishes. Yours at least, for sure. So the first thing would be to nix the word *wish* totally from your vocabulary. Everybody clear on that shit? No wishing for fucking anything. Though Marty might want to wish her Booty Pop was real so she doesn't have to wear those two slabs of poufy material over her bag of bulldogs anymore."

"Nina." Wanda let out a low warning growl, sending her friend a scowl filled with discontent. "We're absolutely not going to begin this way again. No more yelling and threatening and in general taking far too much pleasure in someone else's pain. Now, you will sit. You will sit without uttering another word unless it's supportive and warm, and you will smile like you just ate someone's limb clear off while you do it. I will not have you offend another client."

Jeannie clacked her jeweled slippers together when she glanced at Nina and Wanda. "I'm not offended. I thought it was pretty funny."

Nina grinned. "I like her. She can stay. At least until some crazy shit's about to go down and we have to save her life. Then she has to hit the bricks."

Marty crossed the room and splayed her fingers over Nina's mouth, placing her other hand on her shoulder as leverage. She cocked Nina's head back and peered into her friend's coal black eyes. "I'm going to remind you of your husband's words after the last disaster you created. If you don't learn to keep your mouth in check, he'll hand you over to clan rule himself. Remember those words, Nina? Remember *why* he said those words. You remember Phoebe, don't you, bulldozer? The sister you turned into a vampire in one angry shove?"

Nina's chin lifted and her eyes narrowed to black slits in her head, but when Marty slid her fingers down to her chin, her lips pressed tightly together in compressed silence.

Marty rocked Nina's head up and down, making the long, dark cascade of her hair fall out of her hoodie and tumble over her shoulder. "Why, yes, Marty," she mimicked her friend. "Yes, I remember every word my adorably fed up husband Greg said, and I'm going to do whatever it takes to heed those words, because I do not want my head chopped off at dawn in front of my entire clan of vampires. No chopped heads. None. It's messy, and neither Wanda nor myself can fit your beheading into our tight schedules. Not to mention, I find myself faltering on what to wear to a beheading."

Nina ripped Marty's hand from her chin with a snide smile. "Maybe you should ask Mistress Sloan?"

Marty slapped her hand back over Nina's mouth.

Jeannie was instantly on her bejeweled feet, the chair the girls had so graciously sat her in tipping over and clattering to the floor. The look of panic on her face made Sloan want to reach out and squeeze her hand in comfort.

Oh, ick. Comfort her? If it weren't for her, he'd be home right now, watching the game. This girl thing—this sympathizing with a woman he hardly knew—was work, not to mention everything he hated.

Jeannie's stiff frame straightened. "Okay. You had me at the head-chopping thing. I don't know what that means, and while I'm sure you'd all be good enough to explain it, because you've been nothing but gracious to me. Well, except for on the drive over when I thought Gina, Trina, Farina was going to attempt warp speed, and she so awesomely offered to do something I can't even repeat to my intestines if I didn't stop backseat driving. But that was just a simple misunderstanding. I mean, I'd threaten to eat someone's intestines like they were a spaghetti dinner if they interfered with my audition for NASCAR, too. It's only natural. So no explanation needed. I'll just go. You know. Home. To my house . . . I think I can figure this out on my own."

"It's fucking *Nina*."

Jeannie nodded absently. "Right. Sorry. Fucking Nina. The vampire who turned her sister into a vampire, too."

Wanda, Sloan noted, sensed Jeannie's rising panic and went instantly to her side. She wrapped an arm around Jeannie's shoulder and patted, steering her back to the chair. "It's all right, Jeannie. I can see you're panicked. But I promise you, if you go home, you'll only be right back here again in need of our help. Don't be frightened. We would never hurt you." She eyed Nina with a familiar warning look Sloan often saw pass between the women.

He watched Jeannie's shoulders go rigid through eyes that were sticky with mascara. Until she looked deep into Wanda's compassionate eyes, and then he saw her face transform from frightened deer in the headlights to one of tentative trust.

He'd give Wanda that. She had a way of creating calm in the midst of complete chaos. She was always who soothed Nina when she went off on a tirade, and she was the peacemaker between her friends. Jeannie was in good hands with Wanda.

Sloan crossed the room, his ankles buckling at awkward angles in his heels, in order to place his hand on Jeannie's shoulder and give it a squeeze. "It's all good, girlfriend. Wanda will take care of you," he reassured her, then realized he'd called her *girlfriend*.

Jesus and fuck.

Sloan eyed Jeannie as she took a deep breath. "Okay, so let me get this straight because everything's very crooked right now. What we have so far is this: I can grant wishes, and I'm responsible for Sloan's cramping and the ugliest high heels I've ever seen in my life."

Nina snorted, but her lips remained compressed. Good thing, too, Sloan noted, or now he'd officially be able to take a bitch out and get away with it. Being a woman and all.

Wanda's eyes went warm when they focused in on Jeannie. "I think you did, honey, and until we know what's going on, I think we'll all have to be very careful about the things we say out loud. On our way over, I googled genies and the djinn. While I'll admit to watching a lot of *I Dream of Jeannie* as a child, I guess I just always thought Hollywood had Westernized it—maybe romanticized genies and their powers. Anyway, I went to Wiki and all sorts of places, and they all back up the TV show's theory. So if the myths really are true, Sloan gets three wishes courtesy of you."

Sloan paused for a moment and decided he'd better take matters into his own hands before menopause set in—or he got pregnant. Wait. Did he have the equipment to get pregnant? Shit. He didn't want to know. "I wish I was a man again!" he yelled into the room without hesitation, making Jeannie and the girls jump.

Out of thin air, the mysterious lavender smoke appeared once more, swirling around Jeannie and creating a thick cloud of jasmine-scented haze.

The very spiky heat he'd felt the second he'd wished he was a woman overcame him again, whooshing upward toward his skull, then racing back down to his toes. It was like being on some crazy hormonal rollercoaster with a slow rise and a sharp fall.

As suddenly as it began was how suddenly it ended.

Sloan rocked forward on his feet, catching himself just before he fell on top of Jeannie.

And then there was more of that crazy silence.

His gaze went immediately to his chest. He sighed in relief.

There was indeed someone in the universe looking out for him.

Wanda smiled up at him, her eyes twinkling. "Well, that's one problem solved. However, folks, we have another problem, and I imagine it could be prohibitive to you, Sloan. Maybe more so you than even Jeannie."

"Now what?" he asked gruffly while he ran his hands over his arms and checked to be sure his feet were out of those damn heels.

Wanda clucked her tongue. "If the legend of genies in fact holds true, and I guess after that little bit of magic gone horribly wrong, it has some merit." She poked a finger in his chest. "You, Sloan Flaherty, have just inherited a genie to call your very own."

"What the hell does that mean?"

"It means Jeannie, God help her and forgive me for using the word, is in essence, your slave."

YES. This was crazier than crazy. It was cray-cray to the tenth power.

Yes. She wanted to fly the cuckoo's nest right now and never look back.

Yes. The more she heard these women chatter around her in the basement office of OOPS with its pressboard matching desks, stacks of multicolored sticky notes in decorative Christmas tree shapes, and a lone JUST SAY NO TO DRUGS poster, the more she was convinced they were, in fact, truly the definition of crazy.

Yes. The pamphlet they'd handed her filled with their paranormal testimonials was absolutely crazy. But it was, Nina insisted, necessary to speed up the process of rambling disbelief and overall too much carrying-on and sometimes even rocking and drooling by the bewildered client.

They'd paid good money to have them made up, she'd said, so they could cut through the bullshit explanations and get to the business at hand. It was a quieter process to read the trio's traumas rather than *see* them, Nina assured her. There were fewer horrified tears and more silent contemplation, which was just how Nina liked it.

Plus, Nina added, she was "sick to fucking death of proving to people they were real in freak-show fashion." If those afflicted chose not to believe, they could kiss her pale, vampire ass.

The brochure, beautifully made-up with pictures of each of the women in their before and after paranormal forms, well, except Nina, whose square was empty because she didn't photograph, read like some script from a movie with three or four sequels. There were paragraphs filled with their personal encounters involving poodles and a werewolf, hygienists, fangs, hell, cougars, mixed breeds of paranormals, and all sorts of mad-assery Jeannie couldn't quite process.

How could any of this be really real?

Yet, she'd been well and truly stuck in a gin bottle. That had been real. She'd turned Sloan into a woman. That had also been real. Nina did have fangs that miraculously healed in just an hour after meeting her with a broken one. Wanda's tufts of stray hair from her "shift" had magically disappeared, too.

So who was she to be so judgy?

There was no one else to trust. Trust wasn't something that came easy to her. In fact, she was probably a front-runner for finding people who were about as untrustworthy as a crooked politician. Her track record spoke for itself. She'd been scammed once before, and it had ruined her entire life.

But she really had been stuck in a bottle. She had.

So if these people said she was Sloan's slave, then slave it was. She'd just suck it up until she could find a way out of these crazy harem pants.

Even if the very idea of catering to a man's every whim made her gag a little. Okay. A lot.

Looking down at the sapphire blue fabric covering her legs, Jeannie decided if she was going to pay for that trust later by way of her death, it was just as well. She'd rather die than wear this skimpy piece of flimsy material another second anyway. "So is that why I can't get more than a couple hundred feet from him before I feel like he's got a leash on me?"

Wanda held up a finger, her expression one of uncertainty. "Now, that I'm still pretty unclear on. I didn't find any information about that at all. Yes, in some antiquated way, Sloan, for lack of a better word, owns you. But I can't find anything that has to do with being attached to him in this manner."

"So this is really like all those reruns I used to watch of *I Dream of Jeannie*? Really?" Jeannie squawked. Man, had she been shafted. Jeannie's bottle was cute and had lots of pretty pillows. It was nothing like the piece of shit she'd been stuck in.

Wanda nodded her head, her expression grim. "I think so. I think what happened was you replaced the genie trapped in the bottle. When he managed to get out, someone had to go back in—that someone was you."

"Speaking of the bottle," Sloan interrupted. "Who was this guy you were catering the party for anyway, Jeannie? Maybe he has something to do with this?"

Jeannie shrugged her shoulders. "He was just a regular client like any other client. He hired me to cater, I catered. There was nothing unusual about him at all."

Wanda massaged her temples, and said, "I've got feelers out on the man that hired Jeannie. If anyone in our circle knows about him, we'll know soon enough."

Sloan sighed, his beautifully handsome face tight with tension, a face that, even in her anxiety, Jeannie couldn't help but take a moment to admire. "So, back to the business at hand. This means we can't go anywhere without each other? That's why I ended up back at her place in all the smelly smoke—because I'm her *master*?"

"Well, if the folklore holds true, you did let her out of the bottle, Sloan. Don't you remember *I Dream of Jeannie*, brother-in-law?" Marty asked. "You must have at least watched it just to see Jeannie in her hot costume. Major Nelson was the one who set her free, and that meant she became his genie." She crossed her arms in front of her and blinked her eyes in the same way Barbara Eden had, her blonde ponytail bobbing behind her. "Remember that?"

"Wow. You're really good at that," Jeannie said, an almost smile crossing her lips. "You wanna wear this?" She plucked at the veil under her chin.

Marty chuckled but shook her head in vehement fashion. "Not if it means I'm attached to him. No chance in hell."

Nina slapped her feet up on her desk and tucked her fingertips under her armpits. "Know what this means, don't you, ass sniffer? This means no more free-range cootchie-la-la till you figure this shit out."

Wanda threw a sticky pad at Nina, clocking her on the top of her head. "Remember the wrath of the clan? Zip it."

Clan. Right. She'd read that word in the pamphlet, too. Being a vampire meant you had a clan. She took a deep breath while she processed more of the information she'd read. Bits of it were still very fuzzy, but she was determined to eventually wrap her brain around all of it. "So where do I go from here? How do I make this go away?"

Wanda crossed her legs at her ankles, her eyes hesitant. "Do you want honesty?"

"Always." Maybe. No. Yes. *Suck it up, Carlyle.*

Wanda blew out a puff of air, her rosy cheeks expanding. "We've never experienced anyone who was able to change back. We've had several cases now, and none of them resulted in a return to their former lifestyles."

Jeannie gulped, twisting her fingers into the filmy fabric on her legs. "So I'll always be attached to Sloan? I'll always have to call him master?"

Wanda popped her lips and gave a slight shrug. "I'm only giving you our stats thus far, Jeannie, meaning OOPS and our experiences. We've never dealt with someone who's been turned into a genie. I'm just telling you where we are at this point."

"And we're still really new to this, Jeannie," Marty comforted, her blue eyes warm. "We've only been doing this for a couple of years, and we've dealt with several paranormal events. They just didn't include genies. Who knows what could happen? Maybe when we learn more about what happened to you, we'll find out the solution is a simple one and you can go back to your life as you knew it."

One she'd fought long and hard for. She bit the inside of her mouth hard before speaking in order to keep a scream of frustration from seeping out into the room. "So until then I'm stuck with *him*?"

"Hey! I have feelings here. And I can think of worse people to be stuck with," Sloan protested.

"Name them," Jeannie dared, fighting the urge to roll her head on her neck in challenge.

Sloan's mouth slammed shut to the tune of Nina's snort.

"Okay, so let's do this," Wanda offered in her compassionate way. "It's late. We're all tired, and we don't have a lot of information right now anyway. I can't seem to locate Darnell, who's our go-to guy because he's been around for an eternity—"

"Darnell?" There were more of these paranormal people? Wait. Of course there were. How could she have forgotten all that she'd read?

"The demon," Sloan chimed in, wiggling his eyebrows when she expressed her shock.

"Yes. Darnell's a demon, as is my sister Casey," Wanda noted. "Her testimonial's in the pamphlet if you think you can possibly absorb anything else tonight. Anyway, Darnell's very knowledgeable about the paranormal in general, and if he doesn't know about it, he can usually find something out. So why don't we wait until he contacts us? For now, go home and get some rest. We'll follow you and stay with you in case you need us."

Jeannie still couldn't believe she was so definitively linked to this man. "With *him*?"

Wanda patted her thigh. "It appears you don't have a choice."

"Choices are overrated, right?" Jeannie said with a nervous wince, her heart crashing against her ribs.

Wanda gave her another hesitant yet probing glance. "You're taking this awfully well, Jeannie, and while I admire that, I hope you'll read our pamphlet on delayed reactions to your accident and the seven stages of grief. All of which you'll eventually experience while you go through your adjustment period."

Being tethered to a man as gorgeous as Sloan would certainly take adjusting to. "The only stage I'm experiencing right now is the one called mourning, wherein I mourn the fact that I'm not attached to Clive Owen or Daniel Craig."

The three women looked at each other with some sort of secret glance she couldn't quite interpret.

"Fuck," Nina grumbled. "Get your Barbie pink marabou mules and that made-from-the-eye-of-newt, five-thousand-dollar nighttime moisturizing cream, Marty. We're gonna be braiding each other's hair and playing dress up tonight. Shit. Shit. Shit."

Jeannie let her confusion show. She looked to Wanda, who had become her beacon in a long, dark night.

Wanda sighed and shook her head at Nina, her eyes admonishing. "What Nina's unfiltered response means is that you'll need us with you for the inevitable crash to reality. We want you to feel safe and well cared for."

"So Nina's going to come to my place and nurture me?" Jeannie joked, trying to keep her breathing steady.

"Yeah. That would be me. I nurture your organs until I'm ready to eat them for my midnight snack."

Ironically, Jeannie believed Nina really would dine on her organs. No hesitation.

Marty began to move around the colorless basement office of OOPS, gathering items to jam in her large tote bag. She held up what Jeannie thought was a first-aid kit until she read the small print. It was a paranormal kit. "Just in case you have powers that are dormant and we need to deal with them."

Nina lobbed a bright green bottle of sunscreen in the bag Marty had. "Don't forget the fucking tissues with lotion, blondie. This is gonna be a wet one."

Jeannie was a little freaked out, but she wasn't going to crash. That was ridiculous. She wasn't a crasher. She was a fighter.

Yes, indeed.

So she was crashing.

Hard and fast in nasty snot-dripping gulps, and it had happened almost the moment she'd entered her bedroom and saw that Betzi and Charlene had changed her sheets and made her bed. Clean sheets comforted her. Her friends knew it. They just didn't know why.

Most likely they'd done it after Wanda had called and explained Jeannie was going to be fragile for a time, and they should expect sudden outbursts of emotion. The gesture was a reminder of her post-genie life—and it touched a raw nerve.

Now she could just wish her bed made itself, right? No, wait.

Her new owner Sloan could do it. Owner. Slave. Master. The words kept rolling around in her brain until she wanted to scream from the absurdity of them.

Jeannie sat at the edge of her bed, rocking back and forth while Boris and Benito cocked their heads and whined at the gulping sobs erupting from her throat. "Oh, my God. I'm—I'm a—a genieeee!"

Nina stuffed a crumpled tissue into her palm with one hand and scratched Benito's head with the other. "Wipe," she ordered gruffly. "Your nose is snotty. It's disgusting."

Jeannie's head fell forward, her chin touching her chest while tears streamed down her face. "And I'm attached to hi—hi—hi . . ."

Marty nodded, her arm around Jeannie's shoulders as she rocked her in a soothing sway. "Him. Yes. You're attached to Sloan, but he's really not so bad, Jeannie. He just hasn't grown entirely up. He has good attributes, too. He loves children and animals and . . . and . . ."

"Brewskies and blondes," Nina finished for her. "He's like a trillion years old, Marty. If it ain't happened yet, it prolly ain't ever gonna fuckin' happen. Being attached to Jeannie might be a good thing for him. Maybe it'll keep his wandering noodle in his drawers so he doesn't bring the pack a good case of the clap."

"Oh, Godddd!" she wailed, thoughtless to the fact that Sloan was just outside the door and would likely hear every horrible thing she said about him.

This wasn't as much about Sloan, despite his insensitive attitude toward her plight. It was the being-attached-to-any-man gig that she despised. She'd worked long and hard for her independence and a semi-healthy mental state. She'd broken free twelve years ago when she was twenty-three—and she wanted to stay that way.

Free.

From any man. Maybe forever. How uncanny the very thing she'd vowed never to let happen again had happened again—a man owned her, even if it was by circumstance rather than her poor decision making. And in a push-up bra and fez, no less.

Nina offered comfort in what she'd come to silently title The Nina Way. She placed an awkward hand on Jeannie's thigh and patted it before putting her hand back in the pocket of her hoodie as though touching Jeannie burned. "It's okay, Jeannie. I'd cry, too, if I was stuck with that womanizing mutt."

"Womanizing mutt with super ears who can hear you because he has no choice but to be right outside the door, Nina!" Sloan called out, thumping against the wood.

"Vampire who doesn't give a shit right behind that door, Sloan!" Nina hollered back.

Wanda nudged Nina and clucked her tongue, smoothing her hand over her prim flannel nightgown. "Quiet, Elvira. Let Jeannie mourn in peace. Don't make me remind you of the horrors that await you should you screw this up."

Pressing her fist to her forehead, Jeannie wailed, "I can't be stuck to a maaaan . . . I have a demanding business to run and employees to pay. How will it look if I'm calling him master and following him around like some love-starved teenager?"

"Hot?" Sloan called.

"Shut up, Sloan!" the three women yelled in unison.

Marty wiggled her pink mules. "First, let's look at the bright side. At least you're not stuck in that genie outfit, right? I mean, it was cute and all, but now we know you still have fashion choices." She plucked at Jeannie's worn bathrobe and wrinkled her nose. "Second, we'll figure it out, I promise. Sloan knows how to use a knife—he can cut tomato peels into decorative rose petals or something. Peel potatoes. We'll make sure he's useful to your catering business."

"I'm not peeling potatoes."

"Sloan?" Nina hollered, startling Boris and Benito. "Shut the fuck up, or I'm gonna come out there and punch you in the head. Stop making shit worse so Jeannie can get all this crap out of her system, and I can get some goddamn sleep."

God, how inconsiderate of her. While the women had changed into their nightwear and settled in, Jeannie had succumbed to the suggestion that she take a hot bath and read more of the OOPS pamphlet. Among the many hair-raising passages, she'd read about all the things Nina had either given up or needed in order to keep her eternity in tip-top shape. One of them was vampire sleep.

Blowing her nose into the tissue, Jeannie fought to control her tears and forced herself to be a gracious hostess to the people who had been kind enough to offer to watch over her. "I'm so sorry, Meanest Woman Alive. You need your vampire sleep, right?"

Nina pulled the sleeves of her pajama hoodie over her hands and rolled her eyes. "Just fucking finish, okay? We haven't had a crier in a long time. It's takin' the shit right outta me."

She took a shuddering inhale of air. Okay. No more feeling sorry for herself. Life had changed, even if it was only for the moment. She'd dealt with plenty of change in her lifetime, and she'd done it without being given the opportunity to look back.

And while that change hadn't exactly involved granting wishes and skimpy harem pants, she'd have taken this kind of change over the one she'd experienced what seemed a lifetime ago.

Two deep breaths later and she was on her feet, ready to regain any small measure of control she could manage. "I'm done." She brushed her hands together in a gesture of finality.

Nina shook her head, her coal black eyes skeptical. "That's what all the noobs say. Until round two."

Jeannie shook her finger, ignoring the throb of her red eyes. "No-no. I'm really done. Any more gut-wrenching sobs will occur privately. Promise. So let's figure out sleeping arrangements. I have a spare bedroom and a pullout couch. Oh, and a few weeks off to figure out this madness before I have a big wedding to cater. Until then, Betzi and Charlene can handle things."

"I call the bed," Marty hollered playfully, making Boris and Benito sit up and bark when she hopped off the edge of Jeannie's bed and bolted for the door.

"Fuck you, Marty!" Nina yelled, racing after her in a blur of limbs and feet.

Wanda slid gracefully off the bed to the tune of Nina and Marty's bickering banter. She smiled in what appeared to be an apology. "I'll go check to be sure they don't have a pillow fight."

"Motherfucking motherfucker!" Nina bellowed from the guest bedroom. The tone to her expletives, filled with palpable anxiety, sent a chill up Jeannie's spine.

Jeannie and Wanda looked at one another—their gazes mirrored the same question. *Now what?*

Jeannie didn't have a choice but to scramble down her short hallway filled with boxes of silver serving platters she hadn't had the chance to bring to storage as Sloan literally dragged her by their invisible tether.

Wanda rushed in behind them, pushing past Sloan and Jeannie to cock her head at her friend. "Nina?"

Jeannie tightened her flannel bathrobe around her neck while she watched wisps of lavender smoke feather around Nina's head. Her stomach lurched. *No.* She hadn't felt a thing. Not a single tingle. No wave of heat. Nothing. She gulped. "Where's Marty?"

"Fucking hell," Nina muttered, throwing the pillow she held back on the bed with such force it burst open, revealing the cushiony foam.

Wanda grabbed her arm, her face frantic. "Nina? What happened?"

"We were fucking fighting over the stupid bed. You know, the way we fight over everything. Next thing I know, she's gone. Just like that."

Realization spread over Wanda's freshly washed face. "You didn't make a wish, did you? Mary, mother of God, Nina . . . you didn't!"

Nina, usually so growly and fierce, scrunched her nose up. She almost looked contrite. That alone brought Jeannie to silent panic. Nina didn't seem like the type who let remorse anywhere near her.

Nina's eyes fell to the floor, away from Wanda's scowling gaze. "Not fucking out loud . . . Swear, it was subconscious, Wanda. I think shit like that all the time about her—about everyone. I didn't say it out loud because we have the wishmaker over here to worry about."

Jeannie gasped, stepping in front of Sloan, her chest tight with fear. "But I didn't feel a thing. When I turned Sloan into a woman, I felt it. I knew I'd done it!"

"What exactly did you wish for, Nina?" Wanda hissed the words, so obviously fighting for composure a vein popped out in her forehead.

She jammed her hands into the pocket of her hoodie with a sullen pout. "You're not gonna like it."

"Like we'd expect less, Nina?" Sloan quipped, but his tone was heavy.

Nina didn't even make an attempt to lob a snarling retort at Sloan.

Oh, hell. It must have been a horrible wish. Jeannie's stomach took a nosedive. She clenched her hands together and held her breath.

"Nina?" Wanda shook her arm hard, her voice tight.

Nina pressed her fingertips to the bridge of her nose. When she answered, her tone was stoic. "Fine. I fucking wished she'd fall off the face of the planet."

If this legend or myth or whatever were true, that made wish number three. The last wish she was capable of granting . . .

Oh, Jesus Christ and a pair of MC Hammer pants.

CHAPTER
4

Sloan ran his hand over his hair and let out a ragged sigh. "That's just perfect. The *planet*, Nina? Could you have been any more descriptive? Maybe a little less all-encompassing?"

But Nina still didn't rise to the bait, making it clear to Jeannie that despite her bickering with Marty and all the name-calling, she cared a great deal about her. "I swear, I only *thought* the words. I didn't say them out loud. Jesus Christ and a Shetland pony."

Fear for Marty's safety, and the possibility she was now granting random, unspoken wishes, made Jeannie shiver. She spoke the words that pulsed in her brain without thinking. "Hang on a second. I thought I could only grant *Sloan* wishes and he's used two now. Nina's makes three. How did I mind-meld Nina's wish? And if Sloan owns me"—she fought a gag reflex at the word—"isn't he in charge of who gets a wish?"

Wanda was pacing now, treading a path back and forth on the hardwood floor with her white ballet slippers, her hand in her hair. "I don't know. None of this makes sense. Not that much ever does in most cases. I must have uttered those words a thousand times since we started OOPS. Very déjà vu. We've got to find Marty—that's all I know."

Jeannie grabbed Sloan's arm, letting her fingers sink into the leather of the jacket she'd returned when she'd changed into her pajamas. "Wish her back! Go ahead. Just say it." She closed her eyes, praying when Sloan spoke the words, some lavender smoke would appear.

Sloan's pause made her eyes pop open. "Let's do this! What are you waiting for?"

He put a hand on her shoulder, leaving a warm imprint that left her uncomfortable for a brief moment until she took a cleansing breath, letting her panic subside, only to find what Sloan's hand really did was leave her quivering all over. "Hold on. I've been reading a little about genies online while you women shredded my very person in that bedroom, and wording this wish is crucial to having the proper results. I read a story, whether it's true or not is anyone's guess, but this guy wished his headache away. You'd think aspirin or something would be involved, right? No. In fact, quite the opposite. He lost his head. *Literally.*"

Jeannie's stomach heaved, making her wrap her arms around her waist. "But the other wishes you made turned out okay. Well, as okay as a wish for a man to be a woman can turn out," Jeannie protested. Sloan's reluctance was wasting precious time. What if Marty was all alone somewhere—in the dark?

Jeannie shuddered inwardly at the thought, stuffing her unwanted memories back into the metaphoric Pandora's box in her mind.

Nina clenched her fists into tight balls, the thin blue veins under her skin visibly tense. "None of this makes any fucking sense, Wanda. If Sloan only gets three wishes like all that *Aladdin* Disney bullshit, then how did I get one of them? How did Jeannie read my goddamn mind and virtually hear what I was thinking? Can she read minds, too? And what if that really was the last wish she had to give?"

Wanda held up a finger to her lips, her eyes flashing. "Quiet!" she snapped. "Let me think. Nina, go check my phone and see if Darnell's gotten back to me yet. Sloan, take Jeannie and think about what we're going to tell Keegan when he calls looking for his wife."

Sloan's expression was instantly full of concern. Looking to Jeannie, he held out his hand to her. "C'mon, wishmaker, we have some serious thinking to do."

She wanted to take his hand, feel the warm, lean length of his fingers. She wanted to let him lead her out of the guest bedroom and have it mean nothing more than just that. But her fears, her pathetic, ongoing issues just wouldn't allow it.

Instead, Jeannie brushed past Sloan and the scent of his woodsy cologne without so much as touching him. She made her way to her living room, flipping on the lights as she went. She felt Sloan's presence behind her and heard him flop down on her puffy recliner.

Sitting on the edge of her matching couch, Jeannie asked, "Keegan? That's Marty's husband, right? The man responsible for turning her into a werewolf?"

Sloan sighed, dragging his hand through his hair. "That's him. He's also going to be the werewolf who turns anything he can get his hands on inside out until we find her."

Jeannie's heart clenched at that kind of love. Oh, God, what had she done? "He really loves her . . ."

"He really can't see straight where she's concerned."

Perfect. An angry werewolf who would look to her as the responsible Marty-napping party. "How long have they been married?"

Sloan's face softened before he cleared his throat. "Four years. They have a little girl, Hollis, my niece."

A child. She'd taken a mother from her child. "And a dog, if I remember reading that pamphlet correctly, right? Cake or Brownie or something?"

Sloan chuckled a warm and deep sound that slithered along her nerve endings. "You really blow at names. It's Muffin. Yes. And they have the perfect all-American werewolf dream together."

Jeannie's ears picked up on tension in Sloan's voice—tension and something else. "Do I hear bitter in your tone?"

"No. You hear the that's-their-dream-not-mine tone."

"I did notice everyone has a lot to say about your very active love life." They'd all made it clear Sloan liked blonde women, booze, and football, and women, and more women.

At least he was honest.

His raven eyebrow swung upward, but his lips thinned. "I'm confident I won't lose my womanizer title any time soon."

God, she was bad at small talk, but she felt they should at least know a little about each other. They were sort of rocking the Siamese twin thing . . . "So you don't want children and a family?"

"I don't want to be pressured to have them is what I don't want."

Jeannie tucked her fist under her chin. "Why would anyone pressure you?"

"Because when you belong to a pack, the pack wants you to keep their seed strong and reproduce more little pack members."

"A pack . . . Oh, right. I remember reading about that in the OOPS brochure. You belong to a pack and Nina belongs to a clan, and you all coexist peacefully with humans, though most of us aren't even aware you exist."

His nod was curt, his lips thinned. "Right. The pack."

Jeannie pulled the one pillow from the couch Boris and Benito hadn't slobbered all over to her lap and wrapped her arms around it. "Now I definitely hear bitter."

"I guess maybe you do." His answer was reluctant if not honest, the hard line of his stubbled jaw tense.

Definitely a touchy subject. She was pretty good at gauging people's lines in the sand, and she was even better at not crossing them. Jeannie took a mental step back so as not to smudge that line. "So this pack-reproduction thing, it sounds pretty antiquated. Not unlike our new slave-master relationship."

Now his face expressed true distaste. "How about we don't use that word anymore. I don't want a slave."

"Right. No slaves. Though, I'd bet if I were blonde and five-ten, you wouldn't be so quick to dismiss my new title." She grinned.

Sloan didn't.

In fact, he looked almost angry. The shadows the lamplight played over his face made his jaw harder and more angular. "I like women and I make no bones about it. I like women who go away when the good times are gone—which usually isn't longer than twenty-four hours. But I'm never disrespectful to them by not sharing my honest intentions when liking them. I don't lie to them, and I would never dub any woman my slave—especially not you. And you're not blonde or even close to five-ten. Point officially moot."

Hot button. Though, Jeannie still couldn't quite grasp why. So he liked one-night stands? At least he was free enough about his needs to pursue them. That was something to be admired. One-night stands implied he never gave too much of himself. Never allowed himself to be lost in a sticky entanglement. "So the pack and its antiquation . . ."

His lips turned up on either side for a brief, shining moment. One she filed away in her brain to recall when he wasn't smiling. Which was often. "It's not as antiquated as it was. Since Marty and her quote-unquote 'accident,' the pack's loosened up a little. She's helped them to see that love conquers all or some such crap."

"You don't believe in love?" *OMG. Shut up, Jeannie. Why would you care?*

"Do you?"

"I asked first," she said with a small, teasing grin, avoiding any focus on her.

"I asked second."

Jeannie looked down at the floor, her eyes counting the slats of her wood flooring. "I can't say for sure. I haven't experienced it."

"You've never been in love?" Sloan sounded surprised.

She was, after all, thirty-five. Most would naturally assume she'd been in love at least once. At one point in time, she'd thought she was, but she'd learned. Oh, she'd learned. "And you have?"

His smile was fond and it stirred something inside Jeannie similar to a green-eyed monster. "Yeah. I have."

"I feel faint." She hid her ridiculous notion of envy by joking.

"Want me to wish you up some smelling salts?"

Jeannie smiled, then immediately frowned when she thought about Sloan's brother and how angry he'd be if they didn't find Marty. "I want you to wish me up a way to keep your brother Keegan from killing me for shipping his wife off to parts unknown."

Sloan sat up and placed his elbows on his knees; his eyes were intense when she caught his gaze. "I won't let him kill you."

"Chivalrous."

He shrugged his shoulders, the leather of his jacket crinkling. "Probably not so much. I'm really just looking out for my best interests. Who knows what could happen to me if something happens to you. We're sort of connected." He used a finger to indicate the space between them.

"What was I thinking?"

"You were thinking like a woman—wishfully. Something I hope never to do again."

She let her chin fall to her chest with a snort. "Too much estrogen, not enough logic?"

"Undoubtedly."

Jeannie shook her finger at him. "We ain't the sissy gender, and don't you forget it."

"How do you stand all those highs and lows? It was brutal. And those heels? Jesus . . ." he muttered, though he was smiling again and that somehow made everything shiny.

"I think you just got a huge dose of it all at once. It's not always like that."

"I'll take your word for it."

"So wishing for Marty to come back—what should we do?" The knot in her stomach returned, tightening into a painful coil of nerves.

Sloan's hands gripped the arms of the chair he sat in. "We should word the wish *very* carefully. The trouble is we have no way of knowing if Nina used up my last wish, or if you're Wishes-Unlimited—or if you'll never be able to grant another wish again. We need to find out more about your origins before we take chances. If you were a werewolf, this would be easy. We'd have a steak. You'd learn to shift, find the best the market has to offer in razors, and you'd find some nice guy in our pack and discover the true joys of falling in love with some lucky pack male."

She mocked a huge sigh. "Bummer that. Every girl who's turned into a werewolf wants love and steak—oh, and a good razor."

Sloan didn't laugh, his expression somber. "We can't afford to waste or mince words with Marty at stake."

Jeannie shuddered. "I'm afraid . . . for Marty. Where do you think she is?" Again, the feeling that she could be somewhere dark and dank made Jeannie's heart race. She hated the dark—and dirty sheets. Not necessarily in that order. Thus, she imagined everyone else did, too, and it was all she could do not to crawl out of her skin with the memory of it or the fear that Marty was somewhere unmerciful, feeling that way, too.

Sloan's look was thoughtful, but then he grinned. "I think, wherever she is, she's making someone crazy with her color wheels and makeup advice. But Marty's pretty tough. I promise she can take care of herself."

Her head cocked to the tone in his voice. "Is that admiration I hear?"

"She's my sister-in-law."

"Doesn't mean you have to like her. I know plenty of people who hate their in-laws."

"Fair enough," he conceded with a nod. "For all her clothes, makeup, hair, and damn well annoying perkiness, she's been good for our family and the pack. She lightened them up with her jokes and why-does-everything-have-to-be-so-doom-and-gloom-all-the-time attitude. Since she joined the pack, a lot has changed, including the strict no werewolf-human relationships. I also admire that she can get my brother, a diehard tight-ass, to do almost anything if she just bats her eyelashes and smiles. He was pretty uptight before Marty, but he's a whole helluva lot easier to be around now. And she gave him Hollis—who also wraps Keegan around her toddler finger. If I'm honest, she does the same to me. Hollis, that is." Sloan followed the admission with a doting smile.

Jeannie bit back a disturbing sting of disappointment. She'd never experienced that kind of romantic hold on a man. *Because you've only experienced one man, Jeannie, and that didn't work out so well, now did it?* "God, I feel shitty now."

"This isn't your fault, Jeannie."

The sympathetic tone in his voice made her flush with an uncomfortable heat. She slapped her hands on the pillow in her lap. "You know what? I absolutely know that. I didn't ask to be thrown in a bottle. I also didn't know taking me out of that bottle would cause so much harm. If there's one thing I've learned in thera—" She shook her head. "If there's one thing I've learned in life, it's to place blame where it deserves to be placed. I place it squarely on MC Hammer pants. What I mean when I say I feel shitty is simply this—Marty's obviously a good person. She came over here the moment you called her, and she was only trying to help me—a virtual stranger. That says something about a person's heart and the good contained therein. The last thing she deserved was to vanish into thin air."

Sloan snorted, crossing his ankles. "Yeah. Maybe you could have just made her mouth disappear?"

Jeannie chuckled, but the lighthearted moment didn't last for long before reality settled back in by way of a cold lump of trepidation in her stomach. She squeezed the pillow tight, digging her fingers into it. "What are we going to do?"

"We're going to not panic, but we are going to think rationally."

"The bottle."

His head shook emphatically while his eyes chastised her. "Nuh-uh-uh. No booze, young lady. We need your brain to be fully functioning on the off chance someone slips and makes a wish from, say, the far-off regions of the Netherlands."

She sighed, wrinkling her nose. "I don't mean booze. I mean the bottle I was stuck in. Maybe there's a clue in it? Maybe I can get back into it somehow and look around? Please say it's still in your car."

"What's left of my car," he mumbled bitterly.

Jeannie made a face of admonishment. "We have a missing were-wolf. Bad time to grudge."

Sloan was up on his feet and heading for her front door before she could stop him, his long legs taking big strides. "Good idea. Lemme go check. Sit tight."

Jeannie slid off the couch in a rumpled heap before she could catch herself, cracking her head on the coffee table on the way down. "Wait!" she yelped as she was dragged across the floor like a dust mop, swishing into some tossed-aside shoes.

Sloan stopped short and whipped around; his face held dismay when she crashed into the wall and bounced back. "Shit! You're bleeding."

Her hand went to her forehead and her fingers felt a small gash. Sloan knelt down beside her. "I forgot we're—you know . . . Damn.

I'm sorry." He bracketed her face with his hands, only to have her tense up and reach for his wrists. "Let me see," he ordered, gripping the sides of her head and letting his thumbs run over her temple.

Panic, as unwarranted as it was, swelled deep in her chest, rising up and threatening to choke her. "Don't! I'm fine," she said, pushing his hands away with a frantic shove.

Confusion glittered in his blue eyes. "Just let me look to be sure you don't need stitches." Sloan's grip, by no means harsh, tightened ever so slightly, and again Jeannie attempted to scurry away, thrashing her head from side to side, making it pound.

"Please stop!" she cried with rising panic, but catching the concern on his face made her force herself to tamp down her fear. She softened her voice, struggling to paste a smile on her face, though her eyes couldn't quite meet his. "I'm fine. Promise."

Sloan let her go, holding his hands up like white flags. His eyes weren't filled with the anger she expected, but something else. She just couldn't figure out what. "I would never hurt you, Jeannie. If we're going to be stuck together like this for an unforeseen amount of time, I need you to know that."

She scooted backward on her haunches, finding the couch and using it to shimmy her way upward. "I know that. Of course, I know that. It just hurt a little when you touched it, that's all."

Jeannie heard herself try to convince Sloan, but it was weak and pathetic and ridiculously overacted. *Of course you know, Jeannie. You know that rationally. So how about you give that mostly dormant monster inside you a final resting place? Don't let down your guard, but seriously— ease up.*

Smiling, she looked Sloan directly in the eye with determination— purposely—so that all her dark secrets would remain just that. Dark and secretive. "Now let's go find that bottle."

He swept his arm toward the door, but the tentative ease between them had turned tense and uncomfortable. "After you."

* * *

SLOAN shook the bottle much the way he had when he first found Jeannie, keeping a good distance between the two of them on the couch. While he tried to focus on the possibility there was something that could help them inside the bottle, he was having trouble keeping that focus for the flat-out fear he'd seen in Jeannie's eyes when he'd tried to help her.

Prying wasn't his thing. He never asked questions of the women he'd once dated because he really didn't want to know how they felt or even if they felt. They knew that going in. It was an unspoken rule of the one-night, at most, weeklong stand.

Yet, this was different. He was officially different, and that was the only explanation he could find to explain this irrational, exceptionally unfamiliar feeling he had for Jeannie.

She'd touched something in him—something primal and protective—without saying a word about her feelings. Now he found himself wanting to know what or who had done something so heinous to her that she'd display such raw fear toward him.

And he wanted to *hear* how she felt about it.

He tried to chalk it up to the residual girl-factor that might still linger inside him after his bout as a woman, but watching her do whatever it took to avoid any kind of physical contact with him was tearing up little pieces of his gut.

Jeannie interrupted his train of thought with a question. She poked him in the arm, making him look up at her cute, heart-shaped face and really see it. See how blue her eyes were. Note how full her lips were.

She waved a hand in front of his face and pointed to the gin bottle. "Hello in there? How do you suppose I get back in there? If I can get back in, maybe I'll find out who was in the bottle before me under a pile of dirty socks or something. You know, like a pay stub or a bill . . ."

"Do genies pay bills? Collect genie unemployment?" Sloan teased just to see if he could make her smile again.

Instead, she wrinkled her cute nose. "I don't know about the former resident of that bottle, but this noob genie does and she really wants to be able to keep doing so without you stuck to her. No offense. So abracadabra me back in. You're in charge." She waved her fingers at the bottle, indicating he should somehow know how to get her back in.

Sloan cocked his head. "How do you propose I do that?"

"Well, what did you do to get me out?"

"I rubbed it."

"Right. So rub again already." She waved her delicate hands at the bottle in a circular motion.

No. He didn't like this. What if they couldn't get her back out? What if she was stuck in there forever, alone and afraid? *What if you're turning into a pussy, Sloan?*

No. That wasn't it at all. Concern for her safety wasn't pussy. "This is too fluky for me. How do we know if there's any consistency to this, Jeannie? What if you get back in and can't get back out? It's not like we've had any rhyme or reason to any of this. You granted Nina a wish you didn't even hear, for Christ's sake." He warred with his words, trying to keep them even, but some of his worry seeped out in his tone anyway.

She closed her pretty eyes and tucked a piece of her dark hair behind her ear like she was dealing with a toddler who required more patience than she had to offer. When she opened them, her words were laced with a definite hint of desperation.

"*Please*, Sloan. We have to help find Marty. I'll never be able to live with myself if I don't at least try. There has to be something in there that tells us who was in that bottle. Aside from the fact that the prior tenant was a complete slob, and last I checked, Hoarders Anonymous didn't have a list of its members we might peruse, I don't recall many clues as to who this mystical dude was. But I also wasn't looking for clues because I was panicked. I just wanted to get the hell out. I can only vaguely remember what he looked like. It did happen fast. So without much of a physical description to put on Genie Land's milk cartons, we need something to go on. If he was stuck in that bottle for even just a short period of time, he must have left behind some clues to his identity other than an ass-load of laundry."

"Seriously. Do genies have forms of ID? Driver's license—social security card?" he asked, his sarcasm intentionally biting to hide his earlier wussylike response.

"Well, it would seem werewolves and vampires do . . ." she countered.

Touché. His gut tightened again, uncomfortably so, whether she had a point or not. "I don't feel good about this."

"Then think about big be-hootered blondes and beer while you rub. I hear that always makes you feel good." Her words were sarcastic, but the twinkle in her bright eyes was amused, and it relaxed the tension in his shoulders a little.

Yet, her urgency to take one for the team puzzled him. But maybe she was right, and finding Marty before Keegan knew she was missing was probably the healthiest course of action for all concerned.

Keegan was fiercely protective of his wife. Sloan wasn't so sure he'd remember Jeannie was a woman when he found out her mishap had created Marty's disappearance. "Okay, look, any small sign of trouble and you're out. Take your phone and call me if you feel even a little apprehensive."

She patted the pocket of her bathrobe, showing him the lump her cell made beneath the flannel stripes. "The only thing I feel apprehensive about is digging through his pile of filthy socks. I mean, I'm messy and disorganized, but he's an epic sock hoarder. Or he has an adverse fear of Clorox."

Sloan chuckled. Whatever haunted her, she did her best to keep it at bay with her sense of humor. He held up the bottle. Its simple lines glowed amber in the living room light. "Okay, here we go." He placed it between his palms and gave it a brisk rub, almost hoping nothing would happen.

Their gazes met, Jeannie's filled with disappointment. She rolled her eyes at him. "Oh, c'mon, Flaherty. Weak. Very weak. You can do better than that. Rub harder," she demanded, planting her hands on her luscious round hips.

He gave it another go, forcing himself to focus on the bottle rather than how petite Jeannie was all swallowed up in a bathrobe that was three sizes too big for her while she demanded he rub.

The floor beneath his feet gave a slight rumble and the lights blinked on and off as though they were winking conspiratorially.

Jeannie's small gasp rang in his ears, and then she was gone in her trademark puff of lavender-colored smoke.

Sloan didn't have time to worry she'd landed somewhere unsafe. His phone vibrated in his jacket pocket two seconds later. "Jeannie?"

"We did it!"

Her joyful response made his chest tight. He scratched at it as though it would relieve the stupidly foreign feeling. "We did."

"Okay, here we go." There was a pause and a couple of grunts before she was back on the line. "God. I should have brought a shovel with me. There are piles everywhere."

He smiled. "Men," Sloan muttered his solidarity with her into the phone.

She snorted, filling his ear with a crackle. "Filthy animals, the lot of you."

"Okay, so aside from the obvious male-pattern piles, tell me what you're seeing." Sloan held the bottle up to see if he could actually catch a glimpse of her through the amber glass.

"Well, it's just as dreadful as it was when I saw it earlier. I'm seeing a strong indication that some genie AA might be in order. There are a million beer cans in here—and cigarette butts, mounds and mounds of them. It just figures I'd inherit the ghetto bottle." She paused again, and Sloan found he was content to listen to her rhythmic breathing while she rifled through this mysterious genie's personal belongings.

"Oh, my God!"

Sloan slid to the end of the chair, his thighs tight with tension. "What?"

"He has satellite TV and surround sound. Badass," she said after a sharp whistle.

"Jesus, Jeannie," he hissed. "Don't do that."

"Sorry." Then she sighed, ragged and filled with frustration. "I'm not finding anything. Like nothing. I wonder how long he was in here? I mean, don't genies sometimes spend centuries locked up in bottles? Though it would certainly account for the accumulation of all these beer cans, it doesn't account for his lack of anything personal."

There was more silence and then a slight gasp on Jeannie's end of the line, but Sloan didn't panic this time. "Wow," she mumbled, distant and rather vague.

What? Did he have a Maserati in there, too? "Now what? No. Don't tell me. He has a wet bar and a fifty-two-inch flat screen."

"Oh, yeah. He has a flat screen, but there's something else . . ."

"Wait. I know. He has a magic carpet." Sloan snorted at his clever retort.

"God, right answer. You're amazeballs. Ever thought of trying out for *Jeopardy*?"

Sloan made a face, cradling the phone against his ear while he balanced the bottle in his palm. "What?"

"You heard the question."

"Shut up. He has a fifty-two-inch flat screen? Do you think you can hold that long enough for me to rub it back out of there?" He eyed the small opening to the bottle with a skeptical glance.

"Sloan?"

He sighed, still trying to strategize a way to get the flat screen out. "Yes, Jeannie?"

"He has a talking throw rug."

"Magic carpet, dollface!" an unfamiliar voice yelped in protest.

Sloan frowned. "Is now really the time to joke, Jeannie? I'm trying to figure the logistics on squeezing a flat screen out of this tiny opening. Clearly, we have a crisis."

"Sloan."

"Quiet. I'm thinking."

"Sloan!"

"What?"

"No flat screen."

He pouted into the bottle. "That's petty."

"But attention grabbing."

"Indeed. So why can't I have the flat screen again?"

"Did you even hear what I said?"

"Nothing after flat screen." He grimaced with regret. The few women he'd been involved with for longer than a week had often accused him of not listening. He'd considered it nagging him to death and, thus, had dismissed their rambling.

Yet, Jeannie quietly demanded he be at his personal best, and he couldn't quite pinpoint why it made him want to strive to be. She didn't speak words of condemnation, nor did she flash accusing eyes at him. It was just silently a part of her, and it drew him like a fly to one of those bug zappers.

"I said he has a magic carpet—a very angry, opinionated, maybe even just a little bit forward magic carpet."

She didn't just quietly demand he give her his personal best, she was LOL funny, too. "Knock it the hell off, Jeannie. That's too Disney even for me."

"Disney this, buddy," she chirped. "Oh, and do me a favor?"

Her voice sounded muffled and faraway. "I'm always happy to do favors for pretty ladies. Shoot."

"Okay. First, save the pretty stuff. I'm hardly pretty. I'm average at best. Not so horrible you'd want to chew your arm off even when sober, but definitely not the kind of candy a man of your awesome-tastic perfectness likes to unwrap. Second? Get me out of here! Rub the damn lamp, Sloan—hurry!"

His hands fumbled with the bottle at her command, and he winced when he considered he'd probably shaken her up. Steadying the bottle, he rubbed it between his palms like he had before. The low vibration he'd felt in his feet the last time accompanied the action again.

In seconds, Jeannie's silhouette was encased in the familiar lavender smoke along with something he couldn't quite make out. He heard her stumble and hit the floor with a grunt. Rushing to her side, Sloan squinted through the thick cloud until he got a closer glimpse.

Holy shit.

"Look, knight in shining armor, grease up your white steed and ready yourself for battle," Jeannie demanded dryly, plucking at, for all intents and purposes, what appeared to be a worn, faded, blue and green throw rug plastered to her as though it had a suction grip. She blew a puff of air out, making the frayed fringe tickling her nose lift upward. "And be wary, fierce warrior, he's a feisty one."

The rug lifted ever so slightly from Jeannie's lithe frame while dust flew upward in clouds of gray. "Better come wit yer A-game, too, hard body. I'm ready to fight to the death for this dame," it said with a gravelly, determined crunch to its tone.

Damn.

A talking carpet.

He'd have much rather had the flat screen.

CHAPTER 5

Sloan knelt down, placing his palms in front of him, and pressed his cheek to the floor so he was eye level with Jeannie. It was an obvious move on his part to get a handle on what he was seeing.

His jaw fairly unhinged; the full view of his white teeth almost made her laugh. "Unfuckingbelieveable," he muttered, wide-eyed. "Excuse my bad language."

Jeannie gave him *the look* with as much of her left eyeball as she could move. In fact, it was the only thing on her body that was capable of movement, the carpet had her so tightly in its grip. Also to be noted, her housekeeper was clearly a slacker, if the dust balls under her couch were any indication. Good to know.

"I can't believe this," Sloan said again, his beautiful face masked in disbelief.

"You know, I find that statement very unsettling coming from a *werewolf*," she admonished, then coughed from the lingering particles of dust falling around her.

The rug flattened again, then rose up to fold its ends together and stroke Jeannie's cheek. It purred when she tried to move out from under it, pinning her harder to the floor.

Purred.

Jesus Christ.

"You talk . . ." Sloan muttered, his eyes glassy.

"So do you," the carpet shot back with an intentionally sarcastic surprise to its tone.

"Sloan," Jeannie hissed, her fists tight next to her torso. "Help. Me," she mouthed, forcing her body to lay prone so as not to incite suffocation.

Suffocation by throw rug. Irony. She had it.

Sloan ran a hand through his hair, his face still so full of awe it was clearly leaving him immobile. "Who—what . . . *How?*"

The edge of the rug lifted again, its fringe ruffling. The sigh it let loose was long and beleaguered, as though he'd told the how of it a million times before. "Magic carpet, ya know? Blah-blah, blah."

Jeannie wrinkled her nose as more dust fell on her. "Might I make a minor suggestion?"

"You can make anything you want with me, dollface. *Anything.*"

"Consider RugDoctor. STAT."

The carpet chuckled husky and deep with the tone of a thousand cigarettes smoked. "Whatever you say, pretty lady."

She cleared her throat. "I'm Jeannie Carlyle, by the way. Yes, I'm a genie named Jeannie. Ironic, I know."

Jeannie felt rather than saw the carpet's confusion. "I don't get it," he groused.

"Never mind. And you are?"

"You'll laugh."

Hah! "Don't count on it. I'm all laughed out for tonight. Maybe even forever. So hit me."

"Mat."

A giggle bubbled in her throat. "Say again?"

"Mat."

"Like welcome?"

"One and the same."

"So M-A-T?"

"I love a smart broad."

The heavy press of the carpet wasn't enough to keep her chest from heaving upward. The snort rippled from her throat and turned into a fit of loud giggles she had to gasp for breath to contain.

The sound of which must have alerted Wanda and Nina, whose feet thumped down her hall and entered the living room in a skid of slippers.

"Jeannie?" Wanda said on a surprised gasp, almost slipping and falling on top of Sloan. She rebalanced herself and threw a hand to her mouth.

"No fucking way, yo," Nina said with a whisper, kneeling beside Jeannie to examine the carpet, her eyes wide.

Jeannie sighed. "I find it amusing that you three, of all the Are You Kidding Me in Are-you-kidding-me-ville, are so shocked and dismayed by this, yo." Though, it was just a little funny to see a woman who had fangs and could fly in such a state of disbelief.

Nina poked the carpet only to have it growl and snap at her. She backed off immediately and murmured, "Dude, it's not . . . Is that a . . . ?"

Jeannie attempted to nod, lifting her chin when she did to avoid another mouthful of musty fringe. "Dude, it so totally is."

Nina slumped down on the floor, crossing her legs to examine the rug, her flawless face full of wonder. She shook her head. "Shut the fuck up."

Jeannie cocked an eyebrow at her. "Didn't I read in your swanky OOPS pamphlet that you can fly and read minds, Nina? And doesn't Stacy or Tracy or whatever her name is have horns or something—shoot fireballs?"

"Casey," Wanda corrected while she gnawed the tip of her fingernail, her brow furrowed. "Her name is Casey. She's my sister, and, yes, we all have abilities of some kind or another. But this . . ." She gave Jeannie a sheepish glance before falling back into silence.

"Right. So you all have your paranormal gadgets; I guess now I do, too." Even if it was a gadget that smelled like one-hundred-year-old mothballs and an opium den. It rather made her feel as though she fit into this new paranormal world that had been thrust upon her.

"Good point, doll," Mat cooed, then coughed, blowing more dusty air upward.

Sloan finally found his voice and, apparently, his white steed. He leaned over Jeannie, his lips so close to hers she had to close her eyes and exhale a cleansing breath because he smelled so delicious. "Mat?" he growled, low and with a distinct warning.

"Calvin Klein ad?"

Jeannie watched Sloan's teeth clench when he ordered, "Get off the lady."

"Oooor what?"

"Oooor I get the damn Dyson."

Jeannie, finally able to drag a hand out from beneath Mat, held it up under Sloan's nose with a warning of her own in her eyes. Silly as it would appear, she wasn't afraid of something as utterly unbelievable as a talking carpet.

The impossible was . . . well . . . not as impossible as it had been yesterday. "Boys—let's not argue. Though, Mat, I don't mind telling you, I think, with the kung fu grip you have on me, my kidneys have switched places with my spleen. If you could lighten up, it would be appreciated."

Instantly, Mat fell almost limp, the suction he'd created lessening until she was able to slip free of him and scurry backward until she was almost pressed up against Sloan's broad chest. She eyed the carpet with her own disbelief, finally getting a good look at the tattered, unraveling thread and gaping hole of a cigarette burn on his upper-left corner.

Mat slithered up to her feet, staying as close as possible without actually climbing back on top of her. "Sorry, doll. I just wanted ta get the hell outta there. You were my only shot at freedom. Desperate times and all."

Her nod of an answer was solemn. "I know that feeling well." She reached out and patted his matted surface, noting more cigarette burns. "So, speaking of desperation—how'd you get in the bottle to begin with?"

"I was in there with Burt," he replied with gruff ease. As though that was how everyone entered a bottle. With Burt.

Jeannie's eyebrows furrowed together. "Burt."

"Yeah. He was the guy in the bottle before you, doll."

Her stomach fluttered. Finally, a clue and she was going to beat that clue into submission with a good old-fashioned interrogation.

With all the crazy that had occurred tonight, preparing to ask a magic carpet questions about his prior owner should be the icing on her crazy cake. Yet, after all she'd seen—*done*—questioning a throw rug was mere child's play. "The guy in the bottle before me was named Burt? *Burt?*" A genie named Burt was like a boy named Sue.

Mat caressed her thigh. "Yep. Burt."

"And how did you and *Burt* become an item?"

His discontent emanated from his worn threads in the way of a shiver. "Me an' Burt wasn't never no item. I came with the bottle. When Burt was put in the bottle, I became his. He just couldn't use me because he couldn't get out of the bottle. So, there we were, a coupla losers stuck together until you came along. End of story."

"Which means now Jeannie owns you," Sloan said, rolling his tongue in his cheek.

"That's right and all my magical powers, too. So hands off my broad," Mat sneered, rising up until he was eye to carpet with Sloan.

He puffed his top half forward in a Neanderthal gesture before slumping back into a heap on the floor. Then he hacked a phlegm-filled cough, which Jeannie responded to with a pat on his mottled blue and green surface.

Mat rolled against her palm like a contented cat having its back scratched. Jeannie gave him a light poke. "So you've always been in the bottle—before even Burt was? Who did you belong to before Burt?"

Mat scoffed and cleared his throat. "I didn't belong to nobody but the road, sugar. I was cursed and put in the bottle by a bent-outta-shape djinn. Burt, that slimeball slacker, came a long time afterward. It was a lonely go of it."

"So you were alone in the bottle until Burt? How long was Burt in the bottle with you, and why didn't you escape with him when he got out of the bottle?"

"Because you're a whole lot hotter, dollface."

"You didn't answer my question."

"Me and Burt only been together about forty years. But Burt ain't got nuthin' to do with me. I can't ever get outta the bottle unless the palooka that put me there lifts the curse or somebody, like you, gorgeous, takes me with 'em. I was cursed to stay in the bottle. Burt gettin' trapped in there, too, was just what you all call a victim of circumstance."

Everyone paused to digest that for a moment until Sloan asked with a rise to his arrogant eyebrow, "Care to explain the curse part and your involvement?"

"Care to stick it up your ass?" Mat choked out before heaving another cough.

Sloan's brow rose and his blue eyes narrowed. "Care to feel the wrath of a Dyson? I hear they have awesome suction."

Mat shrank back against Jeannie with a shiver, his bravado gone. "Fine. I wasn't always a magic carpet."

Jeannie held up a hand to thwart Sloan and gave Mat an encouraging smile. "Then what were you? A lucky coin, maybe? A rabbit's foot?"

"Yer a funny broad."

"I'm a desperate broad who wants answers. So cough them up, please," she said and batted her eyelashes at him.

"I was a gangster."

But Sloan wasn't going to be deterred. "Magic carpets have gangs?"

"No, ya filthy rat," Mat grumbled with scorn. "Gangsters have gangs. Ya know, speakeasies, tommy guns, prohibition, molls, Capone, the whole kit and caboodle?"

"Hold the fuck on—you were once human?" Nina crowed, now on her feet and pacing the floor in front of Mat.

"Just like you, lady."

Nina sank back to the floor with the second expression of awe Jeannie had seen on her face tonight. "No shit . . ."

Jeannie was instantly sympathetic. She knew what it was to be trapped and helpless. Not once, but now twice in her life. "Who did this to you?"

"I told ya, dollface. A djinn I pissed off."

"Pissed off because?" Wanda cajoled, kneeling beside Mat and the others.

"As I recall," Sloan interjected, "gangsters horned in on legitimate liquor stores and forced the owners to sell their bootleg liquor. Is that what got you into this mess, Mat?"

He blew out a dust-riddled sigh. "Yeah, that's what got me into this mess, bright eyes. I threatened the wrong liquor storeowner, okay? He said I wasn't fit to wipe his shoes on. Next thing I know, I'm a welcome mat stuck in a bottle o' some of the best bootleg gin I had. He told me if I ever got the hell outta the bottle, then everybody'd wipe their feet on me for eternity. He wasn't shittin'.

I thought gettin' the hell out would break the curse. Obviously, no such luck."

Jeannie's heart tightened despite the fact that Mat was, for all intents and purposes and by his own admission, a criminal. "That must have been awful being alone for all these years."

Mat's sigh was long and drawn out. "Just me and my regrets until that filthy scum got thrown in there with me."

Jeannie's glance was sympathetic. "The scum being Burt?"

"Yeah, Burt. Burt and the filthy socks he left lyin' all over me, his disgustin' two-pack-a-day habit, and his crappy music."

Wanda ran a hand over Mat's back, giving it a little scratch. A fond smile flitted across her lips. "So who put Burt in the bottle, Mat?"

"I got no idea, good-lookin'. I just know one minute I was lollin' the day away, dreamin' about my girl, the next that piece of shit was on top of me screamin' somethin' about how he'd get somebody named Nekaar. I think. It was a long time ago. Memory's not so good."

Jeannie's stomach fluttered again. They had a name—one that undoubtedly sounded much more like a genie's name than Burt. "So, you think Nekaar is the name of the genie who put Burt into the bottle?"

Mat flipped over, offering up his underside for scratching. "That was the name Burt used when he said if he ever got ahold of him, he'd drown him in the piss of a thousand camels. The guy who cursed him to the bottle was another one o' those crabby, fancy-talkin' djinns. Not that I can blame the guy. I'd be crabby, too. You seen the pants they gotta wear?"

Jeannie's giggle was soft. "Firsthand. So in order to get into the bottle you have to be cursed?" That didn't make sense. No one had cursed her.

Mat draped himself over her lap. "Only a djinn can curse someone. They're the only ones with the power to do it. The only other way to get in a bottle is to replace someone else. I learned that from Burt and all that yakkin' he did night after night to himself and some guy whose name he never did say. That's how you got in the bottle, dollface. You replaced Burt, and I'm damn sure glad ya did. Not only did you bust me out, but you're much better lookin' 'n him."

Jeannie shook her head. Each time one revelation was made, yet another question arose. "I don't get it. Why wasn't Burt enslaved to me like I am to Sloan?" She threw a finger over her shoulder at her enslaver.

"I prefer the title *recipient by circumstance*, thank you," Sloan teased, shooting her a grin that would melt any sane woman's heart.

"Only thing I can figure is 'cus Burt was a djinn. He cursed you the same way he was cursed, and he did it before you had the chance to figure he was yours for three wishes. If I remember right, didn't he say somethin' when you let him out? I remember a lotta screamin', but it's kinda fuzzy. I was nappin', ya know."

Sloan nodded his head and squeezed her shoulder before removing his hand as quickly as it had landed on her flesh. "I remember you saying he yelled some kind of gibberish," he reminded her.

Jeannie paused in thought, then tugged on her lip. "Oh, my God, I do remember he said something. Well, screamed something, but it didn't make any sense. It all happened so fast . . ."

Mat stirred on her leg. "Yep. It was that damn curse. So I guess he musta cursed you to an eternity in the bottle. Just like me. Which makes us perfect for each other, doll."

She tapped Mat's midsection and clucked her tongue. "Except, if I'm following this curse thing properly, I belong to Sloan because he opened the bottle, but he got lucky because I didn't know the words to this curse that would've trapped him in the bottle."

"Of all the damn luck," Mat muttered.

Jeannie's head spun. "So any thoughts on how I get out of the bottle? Or rather, how I get out of being a genie?"

"There's only one way." Mat's tone held finality to it.

Oh, God. Please don't let it be the kind of way that required a major organ. "What's the way again, Mat?" She held her breath and winced.

"Well, you're a genie now, too. It's like I said before, all ya gotta do is curse someone else to the bottle, but there's no changin' the fact that somebody else's gotta go in if you want out for good."

Anxiety rose in the pit of her stomach, making her hands shake. "That's ridiculous. How could I possibly find someone who's willing to wear MC Hammer pants and a push-up bra so uncomfortable it cuts off your blood supply? Add in the fact that if someone lets you out of that vile, smelly contraption, you're literally indebted to them for life, not to mention a life of servitude. It isn't exactly prime real estate. Who makes these stupid rules up anyway?"

Mat sighed his agreement. "The djinn play hardball, that's no lie."

"And what about Marty?" Jeannie yelped, jumping up from the floor, too worried to sit still anymore. "How do we get her back without screwing it up?"

Mat shimmied upward until he was eye level with Jeannie. "Who the hell's Marty? Is there another guy I gotta plug while he ain't lookin'?"

Jeannie shook her finger at him in fierce admonishment. "There will be absolutely no plugging, Mat. If you're mine, then you have to listen to my orders. No plugging, and that means no one. And Marty isn't a man. Marty's a woman, and somehow, one of these wishes I'm in possession of went haywire and she was wished off the face of the planet."

Mat quivered ever so slightly, his torn threads rippling. "You mean the wet blanket here"—he pointed his fringe in Sloan's direction—"wished a dame gone?"

Nina stomped across the floor and eyeballed the rug. Her face was tight with tension when she jammed it in Mat's vicinity. "Listen up, throw rug. It wasn't Sloan who made the wish. It was fucking me, all right? And I didn't even say that shit out loud. I thought it. So why don't you tell us how we can fix this shit before I gotta get a broom and beat it the hell outta you?"

Mat zipped around Jeannie's back and cowered, his breathing harsh and raspy. "Jesus, she's a scary broad," he whispered against Jeannie's ear. "She made the wish?"

Jeannie nodded, clenching her eyes shut. "She did. In her head, no less."

Mat pressed tighter to her. "Somethin' ain't right. You ain't supposed ta grant wishes to just anybody. Only the guy that got ya outta the bottle can make a wish, and he's only got three shots."

So she was what? Special genie? Her sigh was frustrated and tired. "Well, that's how it happened, and Sloan's already used two wishes, and the third was used without even realizing we were doing it. It seems I'm even able to grant wishes telepathically. Now we're afraid if we don't word another wish with the utmost of care, we'll blow it."

"Good thinkin'. If I heard Burt blow his horn once about how he used ta fool a buncha greedy pushovers with that con before he was cursed to that infernal bottle, I heard it a million times."

Terrific. So Burt was an expert at all things involving bottles and deception. Her stomach clenched into a new knot. "Any thoughts on how to get Marty back without making things worse?"

"I got nuthin', doll."

Sloan pressed his fingers to his temple. "Swell."

Wanda rose now, too, tightening her bathrobe around her slim waist. "I propose this—we wait, and while we wait, you all go get a good night's sleep. We don't have a lot of choice in the matter at this point anyway. Nina's going to pass out if she doesn't get her vampire sleep soon, and Jeannie's had probably the longest day in the history of her days. You can't go to bed without Sloan because, well . . . Anyway, while you all do that, I'll fish around online and see if I can't come up with something on this Nekaar. In the mean-time, pray I hear from Darnell. Maybe there's something obscure I've missed, somewhere I haven't looked—maybe the man whose party you catered had something to do with this. I don't know. So off with all of you." She waved a hand in the direction of Jeannie's bedrooms, distracted and worried.

Nina crossed her arms over her chest in a show of defiance. "No sleep till we find Marty."

Sloan chuckled and draped an arm around Nina's shoulder. "*You?* Lose vampire sleep over *Marty?* Since when are you so selfless?"

Nina flicked his arm so hard it split the leather of his jacket. "I'm a giver like that. Just because she drives me out of my fucking gourd doesn't mean she's not my best friend. But you wouldn't understand that, would you, ass sniffer? Because the only friends you have are the kind you have to dial one–nine hundred to talk to. Now get the fuck off me and go to bed."

Jeannie sensed Sloan clearly hadn't realized just how loyal Nina was to Marty by the concerned expression on his face. He squeezed Nina's arm with genuine reassurance. "I promise we'll find her, Nina, if it's the last thing I do."

"I can't let you both stay up alone. I was a good researcher in high school. Please let me help," Jeannie begged.

Nina shook her head. "Three's a crowd, kiddo. You're gonna need some sleep so we can deal with this shit with clear heads. Not to mention, you got *him* attached to your ass. Go to bed and rest up."

"But vampire sleep . . . Didn't I read that was part of mandatory vampire care?" Jeannie protested.

"I'll be fine. Over time, you build up a tolerance to some things. Fighting off vampire sleep's one of them. Though I goddamn well wish it was a tolerance for Ring Dings."

"You promise to wake me up if you need help, or better yet, if you find something we can do to get Marty back?"

Wanda patted her on the hand and gave her another one of her comforting smiles. "You bet. And I wouldn't worry, Jeannie. Marty can never stay away from a good crisis for long. Not even a crazy wish can keep her nose out of it."

Wanda's attempt at lightening the atmosphere of the room brought only silence. The fear flitting across Nina's face made Jeannie allow Sloan to usher her to her bedroom with only a nod and a quiet "thank you" to the women.

Mat slithered along behind them, the underside of him scraping along her floors in jerky rasps.

Boris and Benito didn't even stir when they entered her room. Her hand reached out to stroke each of their heads before she made her way to the small walk-in closet and searched for some blankets and a pillow. The lump in her throat for the damage she'd erroneously created was thick and hard to swallow around. Biting back tears, she dug around for a clean pillowcase, her fingers tight.

She popped her head around the closet door to find Mat and Sloan together. Sloan sat on the edge of her bed with Mat at his feet.

Jeannie hitched her jaw toward the bed. "Seeing as we're sort of stuck with each other, you take the bed, Sloan. I'll sleep on the floor. All I ask is a little warning if you have to go farther than this room. I don't want to end up concussed because you've got some hot date with your cell phone and Mistress Lavonia."

Mat rippled, his roughed-up threads shivering. "Wait, doll. Are you two stuck together? Like he can't go anywhere without you and vice versa?"

Jeannie let her hands fall to her sides in defeat. "I can't get more than a couple of hundred feet from him without being dragged along like a dog on a leash."

"Aw, hell."

Sloan peered down at Mat. "Aw, hell, what?"

Mat shifted in what looked distinctly like a shrug to Jeannie.

"I can't remember. I just know it ain't no good. I mean, it's real, real bad. Lemme think on it for a little, and I'll let ya know."

Sloan leaned forward, placing his elbows on his thighs as he narrowed his gaze at Mat. "So what is it exactly that you're adding to this equation? I don't see why you can't just sleep in the bottle . . ."

Jeannie rushed to intervene. She felt an odd allegiance to Mat—a bond. One she couldn't explain or quite put into words. Placing a hand on Sloan's shoulder, a hand that trembled when she allowed herself a brief moment to luxuriate in his hard muscles, she gave him a nudge. "Not helping."

"And he is? He smells like a goat and he has a memory like a sieve."

Jeannie captured Sloan's eyes with hers. "Enough. He's my smelly goat for now, and while he's mine, we'll be kind to him. Nothing makes a situation worse than discord." And that was something she'd learned the hard way. Don't poke the caged animals. Stay calm. "So, please, *please* no fighting. Deal?" The desperation in her tone obviously caught Sloan's attention. He leaned back onto the bed and held up his hands in a gesture of submission.

Mat's fringe curled around her toes. "Hate to say it, but he's right, doll. I ain't much help."

She knelt down and gave him an affectionate pat. "Are you kidding? You were a huge help. Without you, we wouldn't have a name to go on. Now I don't know about magic carpets, but genies need sleep, and I think werewolves do, too. So let's try and do what Wanda said and get some rest. Maybe you'll remember what Sloan and I being stuck together means, or Marty will just reappear and we'll only have one problem instead of two."

Mat took her advice and snuggled down into the floor, blowing out a gurgling sigh of contentment. Within seconds, he was snoring.

Sloan patted the space beside him on the bed and she obliged by sitting next to him, leaving at least five inches between them. "A talking carpet. Some kind of crazy, huh?"

"A werewolf and his out-of-control genie. Some kind of crazy, huh?" Jeannie poked him with a teasing finger and a good-natured chuckle.

"You look exhausted, Jeannie. Go on and get into bed. I'm going to do some poking of my own for a little while longer. Just so I can decompress."

"You sure? The floor can get pretty cold."

"Ah, but I have Mat to keep me warm."

"The hell you say," Mat grumbled, rolling away from Sloan's feet before settling under her bedroom window.

Sloan tilted his head toward the top of her wrought iron bed. "Bed."

Jeannie slid up and away from him, regretting the loss of his warm presence almost as much as she feared the very warmth it brought.

Sloan rose and helped her move the few colorful pillows Boris and Benito hadn't torn to shreds. He held the covers up with a smile, indicating she should climb under.

As insignificant as she was sure the act was to Sloan, it made her stomach flutter and her limbs flood with warmth.

When he pulled the covers up over her and tucked them under her chin like she was a child, a small sigh almost escaped her lips. One she had to bite back in order to stifle.

He turned without saying a word, moving toward the lone chair she had in the room, flipping the light off as he went.

"You can leave the light on, if you want. It won't bother me," she croaked, her throat dry and tight from Sloan's kind gesture.

"Werewolf eyes. I can see in the dark," he reminded her, the screen from his phone illuminating the handsome lines of his face.

Right. Werewolf. "Sloan?"

"Uh-huh?" His response was distracted as his fingers moved over the face of his cell.

Boris and Benito dragged their sleep-heavy bodies up to the head of the bed and curled into either side of her, bringing with them the comfort of the familiar. "I'm sorry you got involved in this. I had no idea you'd end up stuck with me just because you opened the bottle, or I never would have asked you to rescue me. I mean, who knew this genie thing would really be just like the shows on TV?"

He looked up then and directly at her, his blue eyes piercing hers. "I can think of worse things to be stuck with, Jeannie."

"Surely you don't mean a clingy blonde?" she teased, her eyes heavy, her heart warm.

"Definitely not on my list of favorites."

She adjusted the pillow under her head, folding her hands behind it. "Promise me something?"

"Does it involve picking out china?" He followed his words with a chuckle that made her smile secretly and her toes tingle.

"China's work. I'm a paper plate kind of girl."

"Just how I like 'em."

"I'm being serious, Sloan."

"As am I."

"Just promise me this—even if it's only an empty promise at best. I need to hear the words out loud, sort of like throwing out some positive energy into the universe."

"Are you one of those health-food fanatics who likes wheat germ and dandelions? Because you picked the wrong guy to end up stuck to. I'm an uncooked beef, starchy carbohydrates, Little Debbie's snack cake kind of guy."

Gak. She hated fake snack cake. "No. I like a steak just as much as the next werewolf. But I do believe in reinforcing the positive. So work with me, okay?"

"Deal."

"Just tell me everything's going to be okay. Tell me that we'll get Marty back, and she'll be as good as new."

"I can promise you whoever has Marty won't want her for long. They'll probably beg us to take her back."

"Sloan. Please?"

There was a slight pause and then Sloan said, "I promise you, Jeannie, whatever it takes, Marty will come back no worse off than when she left, if it's the last thing I do." His tone held a hard edge of determination. The right amount to convince her he meant it.

A tear fought to slip from her eyes and down her cheek, making her hunker farther under the comforter, using the fabric to wipe it away. "Thank you," she whispered into the dark.

He looked at her again, as though he were seeing her for the first time, and it sent a wild rush of a thrill through her. "Good night, Jeannie."

Good night.

CHAPTER
6

Jeannie woke to the quiet of her bedroom. Her heart pounded and her fingers clenched the sheets. Instantly, Marty's image, pretty and perfectly accessorized, raced to penetrate her thick haze of sleep. She sat up too fast, reaching for the nightstand, cluttered in various barrettes and headbands, to steady herself.

It was only eight, but the day outside was as dark as her fear they'd never find Marty. She slipped from the bed and almost tripped over Sloan's large frame now covered up to his square chin by Mat. Boris and Benito had apparently slid off the bed during the night and had positioned themselves around Sloan's head, their contented snoring a sure sign Sloan's and Mat's presence hadn't shook them up in the least.

While she gazed down at this paranormal ball of sleep, it struck her again how truly handsome Sloan was. He wasn't just pretty to look at in dim lighting—he was prettier still in broad daylight.

These werewolves didn't just dabble in the good-looks department, they owned it. As if Marty and all her sunshiny blonde, petite, well-dressed frame hadn't been enough, there was Sloan—dark, sexy, and if she believed what Nina said about him, shallow as a kiddy pool.

Yet, she was okay with that. He clearly wasn't trying to be something he just wasn't, and there was an honesty in that she admired.

A soft knock at the door had her hopping over the pile of them and rushing to grab the handle before they woke.

Wanda peered into the room, her eyes tired, but her appearance otherwise immaculate.

"Please say Marty's back," Jeannie pleaded in a whisper, the rush of fear returning.

Wanda wiggled her finger to indicate Jeannie should come outside the door. Jeannie obliged, pulling the door shut behind her and fighting the invisible tug that let her know she was moving out of the acceptable range of Sloan. "Nothing?"

Wanda shook her head, the deep chestnut of her hair gleaming. "No, but we did find an obscure book about genies online. We called several libraries to locate it before we finally did, and they have it in. It's some big book of genie with curses and spells aplenty. Fictional, I suppose, but then there's you, chock-full of every fictional scenario out there, so we don't want to discount any possible clues. We need you and Sloan to go check it out while we wait here for Darnell and Casey. Casey has a friend who might be able to help. Some old college buddy who's well versed in the djinn."

Jeannie blanched. Darnell's name wrought images of fire and Satan and sins, of which she had many. He'd see right through her ruse and drag her back to hell where she belonged. Her voice trembled when she asked, "Darnell the demon?"

Wanda must've caught the fear in her eyes. She reached out a hand to reassure her by cupping Jeannie's chin. "Yes. Darnell and Casey are demons, but it's not what you think. Neither of them would harm a hair on your head. They aren't the kind of demons who make soul-stealing pacts. Well, Darnell did—sell his soul, that is, but he didn't do it for fame and fortune or a great pair of boobs and a rich husband. His reasons were much more altruistic. As long as he lays low under the radar of hell, minds his business, he's okay. He does bear the burden of eternal life, much like all of us. That alone, losing everyone around you year after year, is a hell all its own. As for Casey, she's just another victim of paranormal circumstance—an accident. Promise you're safe with them." She held up a Boy Scouts' honor gesture.

"And Nina? Did she finally get some sleep?"

"She fucking did not, and I'm a pissier bitch than usual because of it," Nina called from the living room. "So tell Sloan the Slacker in there to get his ass up because the library opens in an hour. If I ain't sleepin', he sure ain't, either."

Jeannie leaned into Wanda and whispered, "She's not going to catch fire is she? Her bio in the pamphlet was pretty graphic, and I definitely remember the words *fry like so much bacon*."

Nina came up behind Wanda and tugged on Jeannie's hair, a white strip of zinc on her nose, sunglasses in place. "No. She's not going to catch fire because she has a barrel's worth of sunscreen on, but she will set you on fire if you don't get to rollin'."

Wanda rolled her eyes at her friend. "Nina's built up a certain amount of tolerance to daylight and avoiding vampire sleep, but as you can see, she's also a foulmouthed beast as a result. Don't fret about Nina. Let's worry about you and finding Marty."

"Marty. That's the most important issue," Jeannie replied, running a hand over her sleep-mussed hair. "I mean, the only issue I have is I'm attached to Sloan. I'm not in any danger. So please, let's just focus on Marty. The rest we'll figure out." She turned to go, but Wanda stopped her while Nina's eyes searched hers, their coal depths swirling.

"You're important, too, Jeannie. Yes, finding Marty is important, but helping you adjust to this life that's been thrust upon you, and finding someone to help you do it, is just as important."

Wanda's words were so intense they made Jeannie stiffen. She didn't know how to respond, so instead she nodded. "I'll go wake up Sleeping Beauty, and we'll get to the library."

She slipped behind the bedroom door and let it close with a hush. Before waking Sloan, she said a silent prayer that this book would have an answer about where Marty was.

Because she just couldn't live with herself if another life was lost due to her.

SLOAN blocked the sharp wind by sheltering Jeannie with his body as they came down the steps of the library and said good-bye to Lollipop. The ever-darkening skies only served to make Lollipop's blonde hair blonder, if that were at all possible.

Jeannie stuck her hand out toward her and smiled. "It was nice meeting you."

Lollipop smiled back with the kind of coquettish, flirty ease Jeannie envied, pulled her into a patchouli-scented hug. "Now you remember what I said about those extensions for your hair and the Booty Pop. It'll change your life. Promise," she said on a wink before wrapping her arms around Sloan's neck and pressing a lingering, wet cherry red kiss to his cheek. "You know where to find me, handsome."

Jeannie knew now, too. Lollipop, named as such because she was, according to her, lickable, could be found at Club Grease Your Pole, where she'd offered to teach Jeannie how to rock Sloan's cradle of love with just three simple moves.

With a wave, Lollipop swished down the steps in four-inch leopard heels, her platinum blonde hair blowing in the wind like a billowy Pantene commercial.

After a quick call to check in on Betzi and Charlene, they'd run into Lollipop as they were leaving the library with no success in finding the book. The librarian said they'd just missed the person who'd checked it out, and she refused to reveal the name of the book borrower—even after Sloan had flirted shamelessly with her.

Jeannie let loose a forlorn sigh as Lollipop's perfect figure disappeared from sight. "So, she was nice."

Sloan looked down at her with a grimace. "Go on and say it."

Jeannie began to walk in the hopes of finding a coffee shop. Coffee had soothing properties. Maybe not the kind that would fix her genie dilemma, but surely it would help reduce the throb in her genie head. "Let's get moving before it starts to snow, and go on and say what?"

Sloan trailed behind her, the scent of his cologne drifting to her nostrils on the cold morning air. "I'm a pig. You won't be an original, but at least it'll all be out in the open."

Jeannie shrugged, dipping her chin into her totally unfashionable, puffy gray jacket. "I don't think you're a pig at all, and I really did think Lollipop was nice. She gave me some very helpful tips on how to find those breast gel things you put in your bra locally. You know, so my breasts will leave men wanting more." It was a tip Jeannie would treasure forever and ever.

His sigh was sharp and followed by a puff of condensation. "Your breasts are fine."

She might have blushed, but for the word *fine* and her breasts linked together in a Sloan sentence. "Well, maybe *fine* isn't the word I want associated with my breasts. Who wants *fine* breasts? Awesome? Sure. Perky? Grand. Voluptuous? Even better. But fine? Boo-hiss," she mocked indignation.

"Okay, they're great."

Jeannie snorted, hanging a left to peer down the sidewalk for signs of coffee. "Not when you put them up against Lollipop's. Hers are stupendous. Men write love songs about taters like that."

"Hers aren't really hers. She bought them, Jeannie. They're fake."

"Oh, contraire, *mon frere*. If she signed the check, that makes them hers."

"Are we really having this conversation?"

Jeannie nodded with a smile, jamming her hands into her jacket. Even in gloves, they were frigid. "We absolutely are. Oh, and I don't think you're a pig at all. You're a little like my hero. I admire your ability to express your sexuality freely while you hop from one bed to another, Sloan. I don't hold it against you at all."

"I don't hop. Men don't hop," he replied, a hint of disgust in his gravelly voice.

"Use whatever verb sounds most manly to your ears. The point is, clearly, if Lollipop is any indication, you're uninhibited about your needs, and you don't allow others to dictate to you what's supposedly socially acceptable. It means you're free. I know you run the risk of all kinds of disease and the potential for your man-bits to fall off in chunks of rotting flesh, but at least you lived while you did it."

He popped his temptingly sinful lips. "Interesting perspective."

She nudged his side as they rounded another corner and came to a desolate dead end that led to a deserted alleyway with no coffee.

Stopping to face him, Jeannie looked up at his amused expression with a serious gaze of her own. "Look, do me a favor. Don't apologize if we run into any more of your many conquests. According to Nina, you've done a lot of chicks all over the tristate. So it's bound to happen simply by law of averages. Instead of sweating it, wear it like your badge of honor. You know, the 'Yeah. That's right. I did her. Isn't she hot?' T-shirt."

Sloan's smile was amused even while his eyebrows bunched together. "I have no words."

Jeannie cocked her eyebrow at him. "Well, I hear it doesn't take you many of those words to get you where you want to be anyway. So why indulge in the unnecessary? Efficiency is premium."

He barked a laugh at her, rocking back on the cracked pavement. "Mind explaining where this attitude comes from? I think you're the only woman on the planet who feels like that."

Her shoulders lifted. This attitude came from hiding. Hiding from life. Hiding from the potential to be hurt. Hiding from her past. But due to the nature of her past, she couldn't explain. Let him think she was just one of those women who was super-evolved rather than simply scarred. "Well, not all the women on the planet know what it is to be inhibited."

Sloan's eyes on her made her look away in discomfort. "I don't want to pry—"

Her shoulders stiffened along with her spine. He was treading into uncomfortable territory for her. Maybe Sloan really didn't care that people knew who he was—but she couldn't afford that luxury. "Then don't," she said between thin lips.

He shook a finger at her, but his smile reappeared in all its yummy goodness. "I call unfair."

"Call whomever you want. If we run into any of my conquests and they offer to show you their pole tricks of the trade, then you can pry."

"Jeannie . . ." His syrupy tone turned brittle with warning.

Her eyes fell to the ground. "Look. I just didn't want you to be uncomfortable about your vast and varied appetite."

"I'm not uncomfortable."

Jeannie waved an admonishing finger at him. "I beg to differ. Just as she approached us, you whispered in my ear, 'Oh, look. It's Lollipop the Librarian.' That you actually expected me to believe Lollipop was a librarian says to me you feel shame that you've seen her on a pole or two in your time. She was gorgeous, Sloan, and while I'm sure there are lots of librarians who're just as hot, she was no librarian."

"I did meet her at the library," he protested, his handsome face reflecting his supposed innocence.

Jeannie rolled her eyes. She pulled her hat farther down on her head when the wind nipped at her ears. "Is there a library near Club Grease Your Pole? Wait. Don't tell me. You met her there while returning Shakespeare's sonnets, right?"

He held his two fingers together and grinned, beautiful and perfect. "So close, but not quite. Dr. Seuss, I think, for Hollis. She loves *Hop on Pop*."

Hollis was Marty's daughter. He read to his niece? Her insides gushed warmth, but she hid it behind her sarcasm. "See my surprise. The point is, don't lie about who you are, Sloan. Own it in all its sordid, live, loud, and proud way. It might not be what everyone labels correct, especially the women in your life, but at least it's honest. So don't insult me by lying. Deal?"

His face held awe and confusion and then more awe. "You are the strangest woman I've ever met."

Jeannie curtsied. "Brunettes are like that. Strange. You've been buried hip-deep in blondes too long to notice, Sloan Flaherty."

"I like you."

Jeannie fought the impulse to scream no! He couldn't possibly like her, and instead she responded with, "Let's see if you're still saying that when you have to pass up sleeping with a leggy hottie named Candy Bar because I can't get far enough away from you to give you your schtuping space."

"I dunno," he drawled and winked, the sweep of his gorgeous

eyelashes falling to his cheek. "Maybe I'm tired of schtuping only blondes, and it's time to branch out."

Jeannie cocked her ear to the howling wind. "Maybe I just heard the four horsemen."

"Then you'd better duck, because it's true," he said on a soft, velvety chuckle.

She wanted to ask why, but that same old demon inside her, the one that had eaten away her ability to have expectations where anyone was concerned, stopped her. She stood silently beside him instead.

But Sloan provided the question for her with a nudge of his shoulder to hers. "You wanna know why?"

"I'm not sure I could handle a revelation so profound, but why not let me guess?" She cleared her throat and raised one eyebrow. "The clap?"

"I don't have to worry about the clap. I'm a werewolf. We don't get or transmit diseases."

How convenient. That made being a womanizer too damn easy. "Oh, I know! Is it that redheads are the new blondes?"

"Nope."

She let her hands drop with a slap beside her in a gesture of helplessness. "Then I'm all out of guesses. I can't possibly see why you'd wean yourself off a steady diet of hot women—especially ones like Lollipop. Oh, my God. They're not fattening, are they?"

Sloan's responding chuckle was muted by a loud crack and a flash of silver Jeannie didn't identify until it was too late.

Sloan keeled over in the blink of an eye, hitting the ground like a tree falling to its fate after being chopped own. Before she had the chance to even consider what had just happened, she heard a familiar sound, one she'd come to despise—it was the press of someone's tongue to their back teeth, one that created a sucking noise.

Jeannie whipped around, a gust of chilled air hitting her square in her eyes, making them water for the sting.

And there she stood. Face-to-face with her past.

MAT grumbled beneath Nina's feet, raising up to nudge her work boot. "Hey, dollface?"

She peered over her laptop at him. "Yeah, Swiffer meat?"

"Somethin' ain't right with Jeannie."

Nina clucked her tongue. "Damn right somethin' ain't right. Dude, she's granting wishes telepathically, and she has a talking carpet that smells like mildew for a sidekick. That's a whole lot wrong in my book, pardner."

"No, no. I mean, I can feel somethin' ain't right. It's like I can tell she's scared. Real scared." He coughed hard.

Nina sat upright, slamming her computer top shut. "Is feeling Jeannie's emotions part of the magic carpet gig?"

"I got no idea. Remember me? The throw rug that ain't never been outta the bottle who was left to rot like some damn corpse?"

Nina sat forward with a jolt. "Jesus. So you don't even know what kind of powers you have?"

Mat trembled. "Got no clue. I just know, Jeannie's in some kinda trouble and she's scared. *Right now.*"

Nina looked to Wanda across the room. Wanda frowned back at her.

"Shit," she muttered, jumping to her feet to stalk toward the door.

Wanda was instantly on her feet, too, grabbing her coat and gloves. She leaned down and stroked Mat's fringe. "Hang tight. We'll find her. Promise."

Mat hacked a phlegm-filled cough in response as the two women flew out the door.

*   *   *

JEANNIE fought to catch her breath, the chilled air coming from her lips in rapid white puffs. Her heart screamed inside her chest when a pair of steel-like arms wrapped around her neck from behind.

He'd found her. Jesus God, he'd found her.

He ran his tongue along the shell of her ear in a sloppy swipe, moaning a low feral sound. "Look who I found. And after all this time. You'd almost make a man think you were hiding from him. That's not what you've been doing, is it? *Hiding?* Because it would break my itty-bitty heart."

Jeannie instantly froze. Her stomach plummeted, her pulse thrashing violently in her ears. The breath drained from her lungs when his voice slithered in a hot puff along her neck. "So how's it goin', petunia? Long time, no play."

Jeannie's throat closed up, keeping her from screaming at Sloan to rouse him. His body lay prone after the whack he'd taken to the head while blood oozed crimson tears from an ugly gash in his forehead.

Panic clawed its way into her throat and stuck there. The wind howled, screeching the coming storm. Carelessly discarded wrappers from the base of a Dumpster rose up in cyclonic cones, swirling above Sloan's head. And still he lay crumpled, his limbs at an odd angle sprawled across the alleyway.

You're on your own, sunshine. But isn't something like this what all that karate and therapy was about, Jeannie? Have you forgotten all the nights you spent reliving that horror, planning this prick's death, only to now turn into a chicken-shit?

Jeannie closed her eyes, but she didn't exhale in order to relieve the pressure in her chest. She wouldn't give him the satisfaction of knowing how terrified she was. "Get off me," she demanded, with little authority and far more weak-kneed terror than she'd have liked.

"But I like being near you," he crooned, jamming his tongue in her ear again. "You always smelled so good. Besides, we have a shit-load of catching up to do. For instance, what made you choose the big city? You were such a country girl."

For all that had been lost because of him, a spike of anger replaced Jeannie's sheer terror. "I didn't get a choice, and you know that, you asshole."

The arm around her neck tightened, restricting her breathing. The same tattoo on his forearm that had once intrigued her now taunted her. Right under her nose, a coiled snake ready to attack writhed beneath his forearm's muscles as if it had come to life.

The stench of an obviously long night in some dark, filthy bar, where collectively an entire set of teeth couldn't be found, rose in her nostrils, suffocating her.

Whiskey. He liked his booze hard.

And still she didn't scream.

Couldn't scream.

Wouldn't scream.

Because screaming meant someone would get hurt. *No, Jeannie, it meant they'd die.* Die.

No, God. Please don't let anyone get hurt. No more hurt.

"So who's the pretty boy?" he growled low and slurred, widening his stance.

Alarm bells sounded in her brain while her skin crawled. Instantly, she went limp, so limp, he had to hold her up. *Relax into it, Jeannie. Show submission.* Jeannie shrugged. "I don't know. You hit an innocent man."

"I've been watching you, sweet lips. You know exactly who he is. You sleepin' with him?"

Don't tell, Jeannie. Pretend you don't know him. Don't tell or he'll die, too. Could werewolves die? She couldn't remember, but she damn well wasn't taking any chances.

Her lips, stiff from the cold, stuck together, but she managed a frigid reply. "I said I don't know who he is. I ran into him while I was looking for coffee. He was giving me directions to a coffee shop."

His hand shot up to the base of her skull, and he wormed his thick fingers into her hair before she knew it had happened. He yanked her head back so that her neck arched painfully, pulling at the tense tendons. "You lie. Who is he, sweet lips?"

"I don't know!" she shouted, forcing herself to compartmentalize her fear. Vermin like him smelled fear. Lived for it. Thrived on it. Fear would weaken her response, dull it. No fear. *Focus, Jeannie. Let go.* "Now get off me." Her ears noted the calm she conveyed, and she gave herself a mental pat on the back. *Focus.*

"Or you'll what, petunia? Beat me up with your fancy karate chops?"

He knew. How long had he known? How long had he been watching her? Terror resurfaced for a moment, and she couldn't think from one karate move to the next. But then she heard her teacher in her head. *Make it count, Jeannie. Make it clean and make it count. Always measure your response for the best result—then strike!*

But more fear rose, swallowing her, swallowing her whole until her fingers were icy, useless sticks and her feet were cement blocks. She fought the shudder in her breath and made herself demand, not request. "I said *let me go.*"

He tightened his hold with a heartless laugh, spreading his fingers across the width of her belly and grinding his chest against her spine. "And I said no. You weren't easy to come by, you know that? I've been looking for you forever. But I still have some of my old contacts, and they finally came through. You thought you could hide from me, didn't you? You've changed. But I'd know my baby anywhere."

Stall, Jeannie. Stall until you win this internal round of chickenshit and can focus long enough to take the bastard out. "That was sort of the point. No one was supposed to find me." Oh, God. How had he found her?

He drew a finger up and down her cheek, digging into her flesh. "You ruined everything, you know. I lost millions of dollars because of you and your stupidity. And my brothers. They're *dead*. Dead, dead, *dead*," he hissed slow and harsh. "I can't forgive that."

Jeannie's eyes narrowed as she found a focal point. "You ruined lives. I can't forgive that."

"Oh, c'mon now," he protested in jest, his laughter a mockery in her burning ears. "I made their lives better. Because of me, their families had food on the table—and good medical care. I helped them, buttercup. *Helped*."

Jeannie's fear took a slight turn at his egotistical view of what he'd done. It bubbled into a tiny seed of rage that, when watered by the insidious visuals in her mind of that day so long ago, began to grow. "You tainted them, Victor," she spat, keeping her body still but throwing all the angry vehemence she could into her statement. *"You ruined them."* You vile, filthy, horrible animal.

Yanking her hair hard, Victor whirled her around to face him, his black eyes glassy and full of rage, his greasy hair in a matted ponytail. "I saved them!" he roared at her, the lean chiseled lines of his face pulsing and rippling with his anger.

Still, Jeannie remained almost limp, but her words, long overdue, silenced for so many years, held the agonizing fury she'd never been able to express. "Is that what you call it, *Victor*? You're a savior now?" she taunted, her eyes connecting with his so he'd see her disgust. "Have you really bought into your God complex? I always thought it was just an act for all of your stoolies, but you really are as stupid as your elementary school education says you are." She worked the muscles of her throat until she drew a glob of phlegm. Pressing her tongue to her lips, she spat at him, launching it directly at his face.

And that was when she knew she'd touched just the right nerve. Victor lifted his free hand high, slicing it through the air and punching her so hard her head might have flung right off her shoulders if she hadn't waited so long for this moment. Prepared for it.

As a result, she didn't flinch.

She welcomed the pain.

For it was an invitation to reciprocate.

In that second, that searing pain-filled second, just as she'd formulated her return plan of attack, Jeannie heard Nina scream her name. It carried to her ears on the wave of the icy, rolling wind.

Victor's look of sheer surprise at the sound of Nina's voice and the stomp of her feet from some faraway place would always stay with Jeannie—suspended—memorialized—burned into her brain.

Chaos erupted when Victor launched her against the Dumpster where Sloan lay, still unconscious; the loud crack of metal meeting her spine brought with it more agonizing, bone-crunching pain. Yet she stumbled to her feet, searching with her rapidly swollen eye for any sign of Victor, panting her anguish at a missed opportunity. One she'd waited what seemed a lifetime for.

She bounced from foot to foot frantically, ready to strike if he caught her from behind again. Rage fueled her, keeping her from seeing that only Nina and Wanda were left.

Nina was the first to get to her. Instantly, she lunged at Jeannie, wrapping her arms around her shoulders and engulfing her much smaller frame. "Jeannie! Stop, for fuck's sake! It's me. He's gone. Stop!" she shouted, finally piercing the red haze of Jeannie's anger with her urgent tone.

Her one good eye scanned the alley, searching for any sign of Victor. Of course he'd run off. It was what all cowards did. When her brain finally absorbed the fact that he was really gone, Jeannie fell limp against Nina's lithe body to signal her surrender. Nina whipped her around. Her eyes, covered in dark glasses, fell on Jeannie's face with a yelp of concern. "What the fuck happened?" Her slim fingers went directly to Jeannie's swollen, throbbing eye. "Jesus, kiddo. Are you okay?"

Jeannie brushed her off, even if doing so left her dizzy. The adrenaline of her fear began to wear off, too, creeping up on her in horrifying realization. But she would not cry. "I'm fine. It's fine." *Fine* was suddenly the word of the day. Her breasts were fine. She was fine. Everything was fine.

Nina's face became a mask of anger not entirely unfamiliar to Jeannie now. "The fuck it's fine, Jeannie. You've got some goddamn shiner there. Now lemme look."

Jeannie fought to stay still in the confines of Nina's palms while the oppressive fear of being held captive, even when her captor meant no harm, threatened to overwhelm her. Nina scrutinized her face, running her fingers over Jeannie's jaw. "Nothing's broken, but we need to get you back to your place and ice this shit before your eyeball pops outta your head."

In the meantime, Wanda had yanked Sloan up and over her shoulder like he was a couple of designer frocks fresh from the half-off rack. Even in the midst of chaos, Jeannie was able to recognize how impossible a feat like that was for almost anyone—anyone human, that is. For the first time, she finally got a real glimpse of this thing called paranormal, and it astounded her. Left her speechless.

Wanda trudged over to them, her elegant face shrouded in worry. She hiked Sloan upward and reached out a gloved hand to Jeannie, trailing it down the side of her face with a wince. "God, he slugged you but good. Jeannie, honey? What happened? We caught just a quick glimpse of the bastard, but I've got his scent committed to memory now. If I ever see him again, if I get my hands on him, I'll kill him!" she spat, her eyes scanning the alleyway, her nostrils flaring.

Nina planted her hands on her hips and waited in her typical demanding fashion. "So what the fuck, kiddo?"

Lie, Jeannie. Lie often. Lie well. But don't put anyone else in danger. At all costs, keep everyone in the dark. The words slipped off her tongue with far more ease than she'd ever be entirely comfortable with. "Mugger. He hit Sloan from behind and knocked him out, then he cornered me in the alleyway. Told me to give him all my money. When he found out I didn't have any, he kind of lost it." She pointed to her swollen eye and gave them a sheepish grin. "I'm okay. Really."

Nina's chin rose, and when she lifted her dark sunglasses to peer intensely at Jeannie, one beautiful eye squinted at her with definite skepticism.

Jeannie felt exposed—naked—but she kept her gaze even with Nina's. All good liars looked you right in the eye.

Nina put an arm around her and led her out of the alleyway just as snow began to fall. "Let's go the fuck home, shawty." She looked over her shoulder at Wanda. "You got a handle on Chicken Little there?"

Jeannie rushed to Sloan's defense, though she kept her eyes on the ground, following the cracks in the pavement. "It's not his fault. This guy came out of nowhere and clobbered him. I guess werewolves aren't immune to being knocked out cold, huh?"

"You go ahead and get Jeannie to the car, Nina—I'm right behind you with her Siamese twin. Don't get too far ahead of us for Jeannie's sake!" Wanda yelled her warning into the bitter cold, putting her head down to stave off the wind.

Nina clamped her arm around Jeannie tight, pulling her close to her strong, lean body. "So before we get in the car, and before I chew you a new one in front of Wanda and everyone else—wanna fucking tell me why you're on a first-name basis with your mugger?"

Jeannie fought the instant urge to stiffen. Keeping the KISS rule in mind, she easily replied, "He told me his name."

"Oh, yeah? How fucking friendly. It's always good to know the name of the dude who caves in your face. Is that some kind of new goddamn mugger etiquette?"

And now turn the question into a question, Jeannie. You're so good at it. It had become like a game to her over the years as she'd practiced her cover story. "How did you *hear* me say his name to begin with? You weren't anywhere in sight just two seconds before he slugged me."

Stopping in front of Marty's SUV, Nina rested the heel of her hand on the doorframe and glared down at her. She used the other to point to her ears. "Vampire. Good hearing. Real good hearing. Fast, too. I've also been known to kick some serious ass. It's good your mugger *Victor* ran the fuck off like the pussy he is. I'd have eaten his man marbles one by one and picked the leftovers out of my teeth with his bones. It's messy."

Shit. If she'd heard Victor's name, what else had Nina heard? Her stomach churned, but she kept her breathing steady. Ignoring the reference to Victor, Jeannie did the next thing on the list of things to do when you were trying to convince someone you weren't a liar. She killed Nina with kindness. "Awww, you'd do that for *me*? You're more awesome than I know what to do with."

But Nina wasn't going to be sugarcoated with Jeannie's charm. "Yeah, I'm awesome and you're full of shit. I don't know why you're lying. I don't know that I care right now. But if it puts a single one of us in danger—I promise to bury that push-up bra with your battered body. That work, cupcake?"

"Aye-aye, Meanest Woman Alive," she agreed jovially, saluting her. "Or how do you feel about MWA? It's easier on the tongue, don't you think? And upon my burial, can we nix the harem pants? They show every ounce of cellulite I have."

Nina pointed to the door of the SUV just as Wanda huffed up the sidewalk, Sloan still unconscious. "In. *Now.*"

Jeannie began to climb into the warmth of the car when just a

few feet away, a man erupted from a small shop, catching her attention. He made such a ruckus, she couldn't help but gape. His sky
blue cap with a red brim that read Burger Mania was in his hand,
and his sparsely hair-covered head was shiny with the freshly falling
snow.

He threw up his middle finger in the direction of the ornately
decorated window, his face the color of Lollipop's lips. Clearly,
he wanted someone to see his ire. "You know what?" he bellowed, clenching his fists and trembling. "Fuck all of you! *Allll of
you!*" he screeched, his pudgy face distorted as he bent at the waist
and stuck his forearm just under his knee. Turning, his backside to
the store's window, he flipped the horrified onlookers his middle
finger again.

A crowd of the employees from the store, wearing identical hats,
had begun to file out, each of them wide-eyed as the man screamed
one last time.

"That's right! You heard me, you bunch of stuck-up, truffle-fry-
loving assholes! I wish you'd all just go to hell! Hell! Hell! Hell!"

The pavement beneath Jeannie's trembled. Just a smidge.

Oh, no. *No. No. No.*

Right before Jeannie's very eyes—every last employee disappeared in a puff of lavender smoke.

Oh, my. When bad wishes happen to good people.

There was a moment of silence before the disgruntled employee
backed away, tripping and stumbling until he broke into a run, his
apron flapping in the breeze, the scent of his fear redolent in Jeannie's nose.

Wanda took one last unaffected glance at the empty sidewalk
before she hurled Sloan in the backseat with a ragged sigh. Like she'd
seen it all before, and this was just one more mundane item to add
to her list of strange.

Nina leaned forward on the doorframe of the SUV. Pressing her cheek against it, she shook her head. "Batgirl?"

Wanda cupped her chin in thoughtful pause, then looked to Nina. "Joker?"

"That was wish number *four*. Get on the fucking bat phone and tell Casey and Darnell we have a 911."

CHAPTER 7

"Hell," Jeannie repeated, then held her breath when she anticipated the sting that would surely follow the cleaning of her wound.

Nina held her head while Sloan dabbed at the side of her eye with antiseptic. "Did *Victor* bust your fucking eardrum, too? I'd be surprised, you know, 'cus he was such a considerate mugger—all wanting to fucking make friends with you and shit. Hey." She nudged Jeannie with a finger. "Maybe you guys could do a secret Santa? You know, seein' as you're all personable."

Nina just wouldn't stop insinuating Jeannie knew Victor. The entire car ride back, Nina had made less-than-subtle references to him.

Sloan's jaw hardened while his fingers ran over her face with gentle strokes. "Damn it, Jeannie. I'm sorry, but I can promise you this: I'll kill that sonofabitch if I ever get my hands on him. Never saw him coming—didn't even single out the puke's thieving smell as anything more than just another human's scent, for Christ's sake."

Jeannie reached out and patted his bulky arm, then put her hand back in her lap. Not because it was unpleasant to touch Sloan. On the contrary. It was divinity times a million.

Rather, it was due to the fact that she was still uncomfortable with gestures of reassurance, which could lead to a reciprocation she wasn't sure she could handle receiving. "It's okay, werewolf. You were too engrossed in hot babes and the defense of your lost love thereof. Worry not. It's just a black eye. They heal, I hear." She knew they did. Firsthand.

Nina's face hardened, giving her cheekbones a sharp definition beneath the low lighting in Jeannie's pink and gray bathroom. "Damn you, Sloan. What the fuck is wrong with you? Jeannie's a live case right now, which means we don't know what kind of assholes could be out there trying to find her. Because there's always an asshole. Always. You know, like every other case we've had where there's some skeery, dangerous dude lookin' to take a bitch out? You have to be aware and not only watch your back, but look the fuck out for the client, too—*always*, plastic boob chaser."

Sloan's breath, minty and fresh, wafted over her face. His eyes shot Nina a disinterested glance. "Forgive me, Gumshoe Nina. I'm new to this. It's kind of my initiation case. It never occurred to me there'd be anything skeery or otherwise looking for Jeannie. So just call me novice. I still don't have my private eye decoder ring yet, remember?"

Jeannie held up a hand between the two of them. Their rising anger, coupled with their antagonistic relationship, made her a little edgy after so much chaos. "First. No arguing on my behalf, okay? I'm fine. It was just a knock in the head. Now, I promise, Meanest Woman Alive, Sloan will be on his toes the next time we venture out. Second, could we get back to the hell thing? Could you explain what that means?"

Nina clucked her tongue. "It means this, I Dream Of: In a fit of rage, that crazy Burger Mania motherfucker wished all those people would go to hell. *You* provided the transportation. Casey and Darnell took care of it, and it's peachy-keen now. Though I hear during the getting-them-out phase, there was a lot of screaming and crying—bucket loads of snot, too. Don't worry. I made sure they didn't remember a thing. They're all back at that deli as if it never happened, and so is the perp who made the wish, and before you ask, yeah, I can toy with your mind. Make you forget—erase shit. But we have a bigger problem than that, kiddo."

Nina's expression made her cringe. They needed another problem like she needed another genie push-up bra. And Nina could mess with your head in more than just the way of intimidation?

Oh, Jesus and all twelve.

Sloan finished putting antibiotic cream on her stinging eye, one she could barely see out of, with a critical assessment and the purse of his lips. He was so gentle, his hands warming her chilled skin with the tenderness of them. You'd never know he liked women named Lollipop and Candy Bar who had fake boobs and made the bulk of their income in single-dollar bills.

Not that that was a bad thing, she reminded herself—but everyone made it sound so sleazy that she had to chastise herself for even considering throwing stones. Especially coming from where she came from. "The bigger problem being me."

"You're granting random wishes, Jeannie. Do you know how many people in a day must use the phrase, *I wish*? In jest alone there must be millions," Sloan said, brushing her bangs from her forehead and smiling at her. The crinkle on either side of his eyes was kind, making Jeannie lean back and away from her perch on the toilet seat.

When Sloan was this close, it made her dizzy and left her stomach feeling like a bottomless pit of butterflies. The sensation was unfamiliar and that meant, in her narrow world anyway, it shouldn't be explored.

Nina washed her hands in the sink and wiped them on a towel. "Not to mention, that was the fourth fucking wish you granted. What if we've used all that shit up? Where does that leave Marty?"

Sloan's sweater stretched across his pecs when he spread his arms wide. "Well, maybe, it isn't how you phrase the wish, then. The guy straight up wished everyone to hell, right?"

"Yeah, and you'd know that if you weren't passed out like some sissy-la-la in the backseat of Marty's fancy Sherman tank." Nina flashed her fangs at a smugly amused Sloan.

Jeannie put a hand on Nina's arm and squeezed. "Now, now, MWA. No arguing in front of the patient. She's fragile." Turning to Sloan, Jeannie nodded in answer to his question. "He did use very specific words, and poof, they were gone." She snapped her fingers while guilt ate her from the inside out. If only she'd had that kind of power twelve years ago, Victor would be where all pigs like him belonged.

Jeannie took a deep breath and let the notion sink deep into her bones. She'd literally sent people to hell.

Hell.

What if there'd been no Darnell and Casey? How many lives would she have ruined? How many families would she have torn apart? What if Nina hadn't been around to make everything better? Jeannie held in a shudder of horror.

"So she grants them telepathically, and frickin' randomly. So much awesome. Dude, she's a live cannon. Fuck only knows what she's capable of. I just know we need to fucking find Marty. I get hinky if she isn't up my ass about how I wear the wrong color hoodie for my whiter shade of pale complexion."

The three fell silent at yet another dead end. The only clue they'd had was that book. If the book they'd discovered online held answers, it was of no use to them if they couldn't locate it. Nina had even gone back to the library to try to read the mind of the librarian who'd checked the book out—but according to her, the librarian's mind was a complete blank.

Which meant something was rotten in Denmark. Was there someone else out there with the ability to erase your thoughts? Jeannie fought another shudder.

"There has to be a way to stop it," Jeannie insisted, wincing when she touched the area just above her eye. "If someone else disappears or is possibly hurt because of me, I just won't be able to live with that."

Nina bent at the waist and scooped up a wriggling, attention-needy Benito, letting him lick her face. She chucked him under the chin with an affectionate finger. "Tell Mommy she won't live much longer anyway, once Marty's man gets ahold of her ass." She chuckled, sticking Benito under her arm, leaving Jeannie and Sloan alone.

The already mediocre-sized bathroom became much smaller then, making her suck in a nervous breath of air. She rose from the toilet seat and skirted around Sloan, only to catch a glance of her reflection in the mirror. The bruise surrounding her swollen eye was mottled purple and red with shades of yellow to complement the enormous size of it.

Wow. Victor had really slugged her. And she'd missed her opportunity to slug him back. That was neither here nor there now. He'd found her. What was she going to do if he found her again? He knew about her karate lessons. Surely he knew where she lived, too.

How long had he known? How long had he waited to slither from his snake's nest to come after her and taunt her? Worse, what would she do if she'd put everyone else in danger because Victor had located her?

She had to contact Fullbright.

Sloan came up behind her, letting his hands cup her shoulders for a brief moment before removing them just as quickly, probably due to the memory of yesterday's freak-out.

Both regret and relief stung her gut in a simultaneous reaction.

His stunning face was full of concern as his blue eyes searched hers. "Christ, Jeannie. I'm sorry you got hurt because I wasn't paying attention. I've heard the girls talk about all kinds of crazy when they help an accident victim, but I guess I just didn't pay close enough attention. I'll be a better wingman next time. Promise." He winked at her, his lush lashes falling to his sharp cheekbones in a fell swoop.

"Maybe we should just never leave the house again? Seeing as I'm granting wishes like a crooked politician grants clemency—who knows what could happen out there?"

Sloan gave her a look that admonished her statement. "It's not your fault, Jeannie."

Jeannie's shoulders sagged and hot tears threatened. "We can only use that excuse for so long, Sloan. I get the impression not everyone's going to feel like it's not my fault forever. And I suppose the genie defense will get old fast."

Sloan's eyes met hers in the mirror, intense and blue. "You can't do anything about something you can't control."

Jeannie shook her head, noting the side of her hair was matted with blood. "You know, I swear I know that. But if I didn't feel enormous guilt for not only creating such havoc, but for not having any idea how to get control of it, what kind of person would I be?"

"We'll just have to keep you close so you can't telepathically or otherwise grant wishes."

Jeannie fought a shiver, running her hands along the arms of her old, navy blue sweater. *Close.* Being so close to Sloan made her heart race. They couldn't stay this way much longer. She wasn't emotionally ready to be in such close proximity to a man who was so unbelievably good-looking.

After twelve years, Jeannie? You're not ready after twelve years? Then just give up right now, Jeannie Carlyle. Give in to the notion that it's just going to be you and the twins forever. Better yet, why not just lie down and die? It's easier than doing the work, taking a chance. Her therapist's voice rang inside her head.

She gave him a shaky laugh, putting the heel of her hand to her head. "I don't know if close matters. I can do it telepathically, too, Sloan. Who knows the scope of my wish granting?"

"We'll figure this out, Jeannie. I promise." Sloan kept saying that, but she wondered if he wasn't saying it more to reassure himself than anyone else.

"Will I always be like this?"

Sloan gave a resigned sigh, his expression filled with hesitant concern. "Honestly?"

Jeannie closed her eyes and gulped, clutching the edge of her newly installed sink. "The straight skinny."

"I don't know for sure, but I'm guessing you'll always be a genie. From what the girls have told me, no one's gone back to their old way of life. There's no reversing it."

"So I'm your indentured slave for life?" she squeaked.

His lips thinned in distaste. "I really wish you'd quit looking at it like that. You're not my slave. I didn't ask for this, either, Jeannie. It was all an accident."

She gave him a look of apology, before letting her eyes flit to the floor. "You're right. You saved me, and because of it, you got stuck with me. But I promise you, whatever it takes, I'll be out of your hair as soon as I can be."

"Jeannie—lay off the whiny."

She took a shaky breath. "Too much conviction?"

"Too much poor me. I wasn't doing anything special. I was manning the phones for the girls. It was an accident. Period."

"But you have a life and a broad to bag somewhere. Surely you have a job? I'm keeping you from those things." Now that she'd let slip her interest in what Sloan Flaherty did with his time, she took solace in the fact that it wouldn't appear as though she were prying at all.

She was simply making sure his harem wouldn't suffer. How could she live with herself if he missed a good pole greasing by a woman named Almond Joy or Sweet Tart? At least she hoped that was how she came off—nothing more than mild curiosity with a dash of concern for his best interests due to the fact that they'd been thrown together, and it was polite to be concerned for your fellow victim of the paranormal.

"I have a job that can wait," Sloan said, interrupting her internal concern. "As to my life, while much less complicated sans you, it was a little staid and a lot boring as of late."

A snort slipped from her lips before she was able to stop it. "Oh, c'mon, Sloan. I just can't see you as boring."

His nod was curt. "Then maybe you don't see me. Either way, it doesn't matter. I'm here. I'm here for the long haul, and we'll figure this out—*together*."

"Can you do that without a flat screen?" A teasing smile lifted the corner of her chapped lips.

His eyebrow rose in haughty disdain. "I'm not really sure. I can only give my solemn vow I'll try to make do with what you've got, as archaic and thrift store as that may be."

Jeannie giggled, tucking her arms under her breasts. "I usually don't have a lot of time to watch TV anymore, with the catering business and all. It sort of boomed this last year."

Sloan fingered one of her hand towels, running his thumb over its shell pink surface. "What made you choose catering?"

She poked at her belly and grinned. She loved to cook. Her mother was responsible for that. It was the one bond they'd had—the one thing they'd agreed on in the millions of things they hadn't. Their love of a kitchen and a shiny utensil. "My love of a good canapé.

Food fills the soul, comforts it, sometimes even heals it. It's the one thing guaranteed to bring people together because everyone needs it to live. We associate it with all sorts of things. Good memories, sometimes bad, but it's something everyone can relate to."

Cooking was how she'd kept the memory of her old life alive. No matter how many things she'd had to change about herself in the name of survival, it was the one thing no one could take from her. There was nothing about gooey macaroni and cheese with a bacon and crumbled potato chip topping that screamed Jeannie Carlyle the way her old hair color or the fact that she was really green-eyed did.

Sloan leaned over her shoulder and captured her gaze in the mirror. "Food, huh? What's your favorite memory associated with food?"

Her smile held a shadow of regret—one that was a mixture of bitter remorse and the scent of lilacs, her mother's favorite perfume. "Chicken Kiev and mashed potatoes. It was the last thing my mother and I ever cooked together."

"She's gone?"

Jeannie fought the familiar rush of tears whenever she thought about her mother. Her gulp was hard, forcing the muscles in her neck to expand. "She is."

Sloan's sleek dark head dipped low in understanding. "Mine, too."

Jeannie turned away from the mirror. If she had to look at her lying face for one more second, she'd vomit right on Sloan's dirt-streaked black cowboy boots. She leaned back against her sink and looked up at him to avoid the subject of losing a parent. That had hurt far more than losing her old life. "What do you do for a living, Mr. Werewolf? Do werewolves have jobs?"

"We do. We have jobs and families and friends and all the same things humans do, believe it or not. And I work for Pack Cosmetics."

Pack Cosmetics? "Like the plant where they manufacture it?"

Sloan clucked his tongue at her. "It's because I'm pretty, right?"

Her look was confused. "What?"

"You think I work at the plant rather than, say, a desk job involving a suit and tie because I'm pretty, which completely means I can't be smart."

Guilt washed over her in a wave of judgmental remorse. "I suck. I guess, if I'm honest, that is what I thought."

"You do—suck, that is," he teased with an easy smile. "Actually, I have a degree in marketing. I work in corporate, where they pay me a lot of money to market their product."

"Ah. So you're the spin doctor, huh? No wonder you're so good with the ladies."

"I was good with the ladies long before I was good with the makeup and perfume."

"How long have you worked there?"

"All of my adult life, but it's only just recently that I took my career more seriously and became president of marketing. When Keegan decided to relocate headquarters from Buffalo to Manhattan, I decided I wanted a change—so I relocated."

Jeannie planted a hand on her hip and gave him a mock saucy look. "Are you going to stand there and try and convince me that you left Buffalo for Manhattan because of work? Or had you just tapped all that Buffalo had to offer in terms of women, and you needed a new hunting ground?"

"Okay, so there was that, too." He grinned unapologetically.

Which made her grin. "So what made you choose a cosmetics company?"

"I didn't. It chose me. My pack owns it."

Jeannie clapped a hand to her forehead. "Duh. Pack Cosmetics. What a clever way to hide out in the open. So do you hire only werewolves? Or are there trolls and ogres in your employ, too?"

Sloan's laughter filled her bathroom, the acoustics of it warm and deep. "No trolls that I know of. But I think we have an ogre in accounting."

Jeannie frowned.

"Joking. Most of us are werewolves, but we employ humans, too."

"Wait. Does the whole world but me know you guys exist?"

His smile was crooked and adorable and it made her heart skip beats. "Nope. Our human employees don't know about us. We've been blending with humans for centuries."

"That's a huge secret to keep." Secrets wore you down. Kept you up at night. Made you hate yourself.

"I disagree. I think the alternative is far worse. It would involve a witch hunt chock-full of silver bullets and a lot of entrails."

"A silver bullet really ki—" She bit back the word *kill*. "Silver really works?"

He held up his hands and gave her a sheepish glance. "Really-really."

"Are you guys immortal like Nina and Wanda?"

"We are. And we self-heal, which is why that crack on my head by that sonofabitch is now gone." He leaned down and let her glimpse his forehead where just an hour ago blood had spilled from his perfect flesh.

Awe made her reach out to brush his hair aside and touch it. Her fingers hovered, afraid.

Sloan took her wrist between his fingertips, wrapping them around it with a gentle touch. "It's okay, Jeannie," he whispered low, placing her fingers to his skin.

Jeannie held her breath, and for the first time in twelve years, didn't even consider snatching her hand back. There was no threat to Sloan's grip. There was no demand she do as he bid.

She relaxed then, letting her fingers connect with his warm flesh. When his thick, black hair brushed her fingertips, Jeannie fought a loud intake of breath. The soft ends bristled and shifted, making her stomach twist in excitement.

But then her throat closed up. The smell of him. The kid gloves he used with her without even realizing how important, how crucial it was to do so, overwhelmed her—touched her. Jeannie let her hand drop to her side and gulped. "The eternal-life thing—that has to be hard, huh?"

His eyes went dark and his expression sobered. "I haven't been around as long as some, but long enough to lose people who were important to me because of age. People who watched me stay the same while they changed as most humans do."

How dreadful and wonderful at the same time. Jeannie shook her head in yet more awe. "So you don't age?"

"We do. Just not quite the way humans do. It takes us much longer."

"How old are you?"

Sloan cracked another grin. "Old enough to know you aren't ready for this conversation yet."

Jeannie made a face at him. "Oh, and I was ready for 'you're a genie, suck it up—and while you're at it, have some ugly harem pants and chain mail thinly disguised as a push-up bra'?"

He laughed low and delicious, sending a wave of rippled delight along her spine. "Small doses. That's what the girls of OOPS recommend, and I'm not going to piss them off, because I'll have to go on living with them even when you don't."

Since Sloan had mentioned eternal life, it dredged up another question she was afraid to hear the answer to. She asked anyway—because she was a masochist like that. "Am I immortal, too?"

"Most genies are, according to the myths I read online, but again, another mystery to solve."

She took another deep breath, albeit shaky. "I'm not sure I'm up to living forever. Seems to me, it only prolongs the length of time I have to spend trying to keep my ass from hitting the back of my knees. The idea of taking Zumba class for an eternity is exhausting."

Maybe it was her tone of voice. Maybe it was the defeated way her shoulders slumped, but it was obvious Sloan picked up on her mood shift. He tilted her chin upward, running his thumb over her skin with his callused fingertip. "There are good things, too. Like the skin you have right now, which is pretty good, and I know skin. No one in the marketing department—who knows Marty—doesn't. Means you avoid plastic surgery for a long, long time."

If he only knew . . . "Best day ever," she said on a smile, noting how thready her voice sounded.

Sloan tilted his head. "It's going to be okay," he insisted again.

"Hey!" Nina snarled, reentering the bathroom and pushing her way between them. She poked Sloan in the chest. "Sloan, get the fuck off her. I swear to Christ, you make a move on a client, and when Marty gets back from Whereverthefuck, Egypt, she'll kick your ass. She ain't on the menu, buddy. No genies on my watch. Now get your ass in gear. Casey and Darnell are here, and they think they might have something that'll help us." She pointed to the door.

Sloan didn't say a word, but as he stepped around Nina, he pinched her cheek and grinned. "Have I told you I love you today, vampire? You're so helpful and warm, supportive—and soooo pre-ettty," he cooed, then laughed a deep chuckle.

"Fuck you."

Sloan's laughter lingered long after he'd gone to stand in the hallway to wait for Jeannie.

Jeannie closed the bathroom door and put a hand on Nina's arm. "He wasn't coming on to me. Swear it, MWA."

Nina shot her a bored look. "If a chick's hot enough, Sloan would come on to her even if she was on a morgue slab. He's a hole chaser. Period."

Hot? Phew. Problem solved. Hot would never apply to her again. Ever. "Well, I'm not exactly hot, so no fears there. And I just wanted you to know nothing untoward was going on. Absolutely no hole chasing. He was just showing me his forehead had healed. You know, the magic of werewolves?"

"Untoward? That's a big, fancy word for such a little chick. And you know what?"

"You don't give a shit."

Nina drove a light knuckle into her shoulder. "Fuck. Can you read minds now, too?"

Jeannie flashed her a coy grin. "No, you silly. I just get the impression you're doing what comes naturally to you."

Nina's eyebrow flew upward. "And that is?"

"Protecting the weak and helpless. Know that I appreciate you keeping man-whore Sloan the Werewolf from sinking his nasty teeth into my unsullied flesh."

Nina took a step back and crossed her arms over her chest with an arrogant gaze directed at her. "Is that your way of telling me you're a big girl, and you can handle this shit on your own?"

Jeannie shook her head until her swollen eye ached from the motion. "Oh, hell to the no. Not on your eternal life, Keeper of the Virgins. No way are you getting out of your bodyguard duties. No. Way. I got you, babe, and that means you got me, too."

"Then get the fuck out in the living room before I kick your midget ass, and when I look out for you—let me look out for your scrawny butt without any lip. Got that shit?"

Jeannie saluted Nina and retorted, "Got that shit, captain." She flung the door open and rushed out before Nina had the chance to utter another threat.

As Sloan followed her to the living room, Nina's rush to protect her virtue accomplished two things. First, it made her feel safer than she had in a long time. Safe and cared for. But it also led her to toy with a notion that was, at best, ludicrous. One that was probably as crazy as everything else going on right now.

But what was life without a little crazy?

* * *

INTRODUCTIONS had been made, and Casey had relayed what she'd learned from her college friend. Now, as Jeannie assessed these new paranormal people rather than address Casey's doom and gloom words, her eyes were instantly drawn to the enormous demon in high-tops and more bling than Marty.

As he crossed the room toward her, she instantly looked down at the floor to mask her curious stare and instead listened to the clank of his gold medallions slapping into one another.

He plopped down on her couch, consuming most of the exposed space, and smiled—so warm and teddy bearish, it made Jeannie's heart throb. But he was a demon . . . "You don't gotta worry, Miss Jeannie. I get why you starin', but s'okay. I'm a big dude. E'rybody stares one time o' 'notha. I'm used to it. And I know you thinkin', how can somebody who looks like a big ol' teddy bear be a demon, right? I ain't got no horns and pitchforks or nuthin'."

Darnell's warmth filled her, spreading through her chilled limbs and giving them a warm glow. She tucked her hands into her sweater self-consciously, her eyes downcast. "I'm sorry. It was very rude."

His chuckle was thick and hearty. "It ain't no thang. You ain't got nuthin' to fear from ol' Darnell. My good intentions is as big as I am. As to your eyeball, sho do make this demon wanna find the brotha and rough him up. Never you fear, though. If he comes round up in here, Darnell gonna make him wish he'd stayed in that hole he done crawled outta. I'll make him sorry he evah laid hands on yo little person. I got yer back, s'all I'm sayin'. Ain't no man hittin' no woman on my watch. Count on it." He followed his words with a solemn nod.

And Jeannie believed him. Darnell exuded all things good and kind. He also defied everything she'd ever been taught in vacation Bible school.

"So how's you, Miss Jeannie?" He planted a paw on her shoulder, and it didn't even make her flinch. "You a'ight, considerin'?"

"I think I am."

"You'll adjust. We'll help," was his simple answer.

This group of people confounded her. Clearly, they'd all been brought together by circumstance. Yet, they'd not just bonded in their supernatural states, they'd created a family dynamic that was unique to their situations.

The way Marty, Nina, and Wanda worked so fluidly together, even with their bickering, had amazed her, but that there were more people who so willingly gave of themselves to complete strangers had her rethinking her jaded view on humanity—or undead-manity. "I hear you're sort of the go-to guy when it comes to paranormal events. Do you always help Nina and Wanda like this?"

He nodded his big head like it was no sacrifice. "You bet. Least I sho try. Sometimes it's outta my wheelhouse, but I can usually find somebody that knows somethin'."

Jeannie shivered at his generosity—still incomprehensible with her cynical view of the world. "I feel guilty for taking you from your lives—your families."

Darnell sat forward, resting his elbows on his wide knees. When his chocolate brown eyes connected with hers, they were filled with fondness. "My family's all them crazy women and their men, their kids and pets, too. Family helps family. Thass just how it rolls, Miss Jeannie."

Jeannie's fingers twisted together in a knot. "But to give up so much of your time to someone you don't even know, and you don't get a dime to do it . . ."

Darnell looked her square in the face, a grin teasing his lips. "Now who says I don't know you? You Jeannie Carlyle, the wish-anator with the fancy pants and the brokeback magic carpet. I know you as good as I need to."

Her eyes searched for her brokeback magic carpet, finding him sleeping soundly by the entry to her kitchen.

A tear burned her swollen eyes and the fight to keep them in check made her head ache. This new transition in her life was very different from the last. The last had been rapid and institutionally cold.

She didn't know what to do with all this warmth. It left her feeling awkward and embarrassed. She'd somehow forgotten how to react to simple kindness. "That's a very kind thing to say. Thank you." Her words were stiff and noticeably uncomfortable, but she genuinely meant them.

"Nevah you mind, Miss Jeannie. I been around a long time. Know some stuff 'cus of the years I got under my XXL belt. Seen some things, too. Juss sharin' it is all. If it helps somebody, I'm glad to oblige. Got nuthin' better to do any ol' ways—you know, eternity and all. Might as well make the world easier to live in and help out where I can."

Tucking her chin into the collar of her sweater, she asked, "So is what Casey's college friend said really true? Someone has to replace me in the bottle in order for me to be released from this curse?" How could she possibly do something so heinous and still live with herself? Even if she put someone in the bottle who totally deserved it, like a mass murderer, what if they escaped the way Burt had? Then they'd be a mass murderer with out-of-control genie powers, too? She pinched the bridge of her nose and shook her head.

"Thass the best we got so far, Miss Jeannie. Same as what Mat told ya. Still don't know why you two stuck together, though."

Jeannie snorted in a go-figure way. "So either I hunt for a victim or I get used to the idea of bonding with that filthy college dorm of a bottle." She paused for a moment, then asked, "You think I could squeeze some throw pillows and a lava lamp into that tiny opening?

You know, just to freshen things up in there. Make it more Jeannie, less Burt the Twelve-year-old?"

He wrapped an arm around her shoulder and pulled her in close to his bulk with a rumbling chuckle. "A'ight now, Miss Jeanie. You got the right attitude. You all jokin' 'bout your lot in life. Thass a sure sign you gonna be okay." He held a thumb up at her.

Who wouldn't be okay with servitude and a new pad to decorate? It was like she'd hit the dream store and found the best dream ever on sale for half off. You just didn't take gifts like that for granted. "I *will* be okay. No matter what," she muttered with determination. Because she was a be-okay kind of girl.

Darnell leaned back and gave her a quizzical look, but she was thankful for Casey's appearance, which kept him from questioning the obvious vehemence in her statement. Casey, petite and slender in her conservative slacks, loafers, and brown turtleneck, eyed Jeannie with a critical gaze. "You okay?"

Jeannie nodded. "I'm fine, really, and I appreciate you finding out what you did, and saving those people from my wishes gone wild."

Casey perched herself on the edge of the couch where they sat and smiled down at Jeannie, placing a hand on her shoulder. "No worries. It's all part of the job," she said as though trips to hell were on par with a career as a filing clerk. "But our spells won't last long, Jeannie. You're the permanent fix to this—so we have to find some way for you to fix them in order for the spells to have a lasting effect. If only I had more info, but my friend's going to keep looking. We'll find something to help us . . . a clue . . . that damn book from the library, whatever. We always do. Or it finds us."

Casey's words and her smile were reassuring, but there'd also been a brief flash of the unknown in her eyes. Unfortunately, that was what stuck with Jeannie, and it made her already uptight stomach turn.

Casey gave her a nudge. "In the meantime, it could be worse, right? Sloan's not half bad to look at, don't you agree?"

Jeannie fought a dreamy sigh of agreement and kept her gaze steady with Casey's. "I guess I could have been tethered to a Jonas brother or, OMG, even Justin Bieber. There really are fates worse than death."

Casey slapped her hand on her thigh and let her head fall back on her shoulders with a laugh. "There you go. Go you, being all positive. And look at it this way—Nina could have been the one to open that bottle. You could be tethered to the beast. Now that would be total shit."

Nina was across the room in a blur of dark hair and hoodie. She loomed over Casey, defensive and rarin' to have a go at her. "Fuck you, fire starter."

Jeannie rose with a gulp, positioning herself between the two women. She reached upward and gave Nina's jaw an affectionate pat. Whether Nina liked it or not—and *not* was probably the case—she had a fan in Jeannie. "Now, MWA, no fighting. Remember me? Fragile and battered. I can only take so much chaos before I snap. Who knows what could happen with my wish granting if my emotional state's in utter turmoil."

The whole world could explode, for all she knew. Having the fate of the whole world on your shoulders was a lot. If stress activated a wish, she was an accident waiting to happen.

Casey stuck her head over Jeannie's shoulder, leering at Nina. "You're upsetting the client, Nina. So unlike your gooey, marshmallowy self."

Darnell shot up from the couch and wrapped a big paw around Casey's waist, hauling her to him while simultaneously patting Nina on the shoulder. "Ah, ladies, we got better things ta do than fight. We gotta find Marty and help Miss Jeannie. You don't wanna leave Miss Jeannie high and dry 'cus you two cain't play nice, do ya?"

Jeannie nodded and shot Darnell a grateful smile. "What he said. So let's focus on what to do now. All the evidence points to my ability to grant endless wishes——"

The crash of her front door opening startled Jeannie, making her mouth clamp shut and her eyes open wide. An older, but almost as handsome, version of Sloan stomped through her small living room. His face was a mask of a scowl, his eyes cold bits of blue.

He stalked toward Sloan, who'd been quietly searching the Internet with Wanda, and yanked him up by his collar, making Jeannie's stomach instantly heave. "Where the hell is my wife, Sloan? We never go more than a few hours without touching base, and it's been more than a few hours. So where the hell is Marty?"

Keegan's roaring voice made Jeannie's chest vibrate. She clenched her hands together and immediately went to step between the two men to run interference. None of this was Sloan's fault.

But Sloan was too quick. He gave Keegan a hard shove; the slap of his hands against the leather of his brother's jacket cracked sharply. "Back the hell off, Keegan," he said from clenched teeth.

His head swung around as he took in everyone in the room with a gaze so intense and hotly angry, Jeannie had to ward off a shudder. "Goddamn it all and you women with this quest to save the world!"

Wanda, always the peacemaker, took on a completely different role as she shook her finger at Keegan. Suddenly, she was a fierce mother, protecting her young.

Pushing Darnell out of the way, she stuck her waggling, elegantly polished nail right under the incited Keegan's nose. "Don't you dare swear at me, Keegan Flaherty! Marty loves OOPS. It's as much hers as it is any of ours. What happened was an accident. Period. Our safety is always at risk, and she knew that. But she does it anyway. Why? Because that's just who Marty is. Her theory has always been, as has been all of ours—well, except Mighty Mouth's—if we'd had this happen and there'd been no one to help us through it, what would have become of us? We had each other. People like Jeannie aren't so lucky. Now I'll tell you this once, Cro-Magnon man, back off! And you'd better watch your tone with me, werewolf! I know you don't want me to tell Marty you had the nerve to behave as though she isn't entitled to do with her life as she pleases. Because I think I know where that fight will leave you . . ."

Keegan's big body relaxed a bit, but only a little, before he was looming over Jeannie, his eyes filled with hot anger. "So *you're* the one who's got the 'problem'?" He swiped his fingers in the air. If fingers could portray sarcasm, his oozed it.

Jeannie gulped, shrinking beneath his hard gaze. God, he was big and scary. How had two such different men come from the same womb? Keegan was as intense as Sloan was devil-may-care. But she was the person responsible for sending Marty off wherever. She'd own it. "I . . . um . . . am. I'm so sorry. I would do anything to—"

Sloan's hand clamped on his brother's shoulder cut her off, the blue of his veins popping beneath his ruddy skin. He jammed his face in Keegan's. Eye to eye, Sloan's narrowed in warning. "I'll only tell you this one more time, and then we're gonna go, brother. Back the hell off the lady. It was an accident. *Got that?*"

Nina plucked Jeannie up by the waist of her jeans and moved her aside, then she stuck her face between the two men. She wrapped an arm around each of their necks and crowed, "Ass sniffers? I know you don't want another round like our last touch football game, do you? Remember that, motherfuckers? I slaughtered your asses. I'll damn well do it again. Take it down a notch and help us, you big, dummy werewolf. Don't make shit worse."

Keegan cracked his jaw and took a step back, moving from Nina's headlock with a grunt. "You know what, Nina? I wish Marty'd just keep her designer-clad backside where she belongs—with me. Because whenever she leaves the confines of my eagle eye, there's always hell to pay!"

Everyone in the room stood stock-still—not even an eyelash fluttered.

Damn that infernal word.

Jeannie's breath caught even as her body trembled and the heat in her cheeks flamed. This time, she felt something was going to happen and she knew she was powerless to stop it.

Oh, fire and brimstone.

The lights dimmed, winking on and off, and the floor shifted beneath their feet in a raucous rumble.

This time, the disturbance was followed by a high-pitched screech, an ear-shattering whine that made the windows of her brownstone quake then blow outward with the clink of flying glass. The frozen air from beyond her floor-to-ceiling windows whooshed into her living room in an icy wave.

Her eyes scanned the room for poor Mat and the twins. They'd be scared witless, but the twins were nowhere in sight, and Mat hadn't stirred from his spot by the kitchen.

Jeannie forgot everything when Sloan lunged for her just as all-out chaos erupted, covering her body with his and sheltering her already damaged face with his hands. She curled inward, forgetting that contact with a male was one of her biggest fears—forgetting that it was especially so with this male.

Bodies flew in all directions and Darnell gruffly shouted something Jeannie didn't quite catch with Sloan's hands pressed to her head.

In that moment, despite the shattering of glass and the roar of the floor ripping up in jagged tears, Jeannie allowed herself to experience the first moment of security she'd felt in over twelve years. A sigh escaped her lips, lips that were crushed against Sloan's rippling chest.

And then everything was still.

Well, until a voice shrilled, "Are you effin' kidding me, Drakaar?

Do you have any idea how much this haircut cost? A little warning the next time warp speed is on the menu, eh? I'll remember to pack my flatiron."

Ruh-roh. Was this wish number five?

One wish, two wish, red wish, blue wish.

CHAPTER 8

"It is *Nekaar*, madam," a regal, cultured voice corrected. There was a hint of indignation in the newest addition to Paranormal-Palooza's tone.

Jeannie's swollen eye twitched at the image in front of them; her eyes raced from the tips of this new person's ringed, bare toes to the top of his shiny tanned head.

Thank God, Mr. Clean was here. Everything just had to be okay now.

Marty, her legs wrapped around the waist of a man in MC Hammer pants similar to Burt's and a deep burgundy jeweled vest that revealed a hard, tanned wall of a chest, gave his sinewy shoulders a flick with her fingers. "I don't care what it is. You said you'd get me home safely. How was *that* safe? You almost ripped my face off. Where did you learn to drive that thing? The Big Truck rally?"

Keegan was on his feet and at Marty's side before Jeannie could process what had just happened. He leered at the man, lifting his wife from the stranger's well-muscled frame and throwing her over his shoulder fireman-style. "Who the hell are *you*?"

Yeah. What the big, intimidating werewolf said. Jeannie shuffled her cold feet, moving closer to Sloan while she eyed this new stranger.

Obviously, he was djinn, and despite his imposing appearance, he'd likely have some answers to their dilemma. From the way he wore his harem pants, if nothing else, maybe he could give her a tip or two on how to own them with the kind of no apologies that he wore his.

"I am Nekaar, the djinn," he stated, as though they should have all known that. He said it as if trumpets blaring should follow the words like an announcement. Then he lifted himself off the ground and hovered, crossing his legs and placing each ankle over his tree-trunk-sized thighs, scanning each of their faces with a look of haughty disdain.

From the floor, Jeannie ran her hand over her hair to push it from her eyes and fought to ignore his David Blaine trick so she could focus. His name. *Nekaar.* Where had she heard that? Mat. Mat was the one who'd said Nekaar had cursed Burt to the bottle, hadn't he?

He was the reason she was in this mess, but before she could accuse him of such, Marty sighed with a loud rasp of exasperation.

She blew her fringy bangs out of her face with a puff, making a face while she swung from her husband's shoulder. "Keegan, honey? Not today—especially not today. Now put away your ego, and put me down. I'm fine."

Keegan's grip grew visibly tighter around the backs of Marty's knees as he stared down the interloper.

She gave him a hard pinch on the ass. "Put me down, werewolf, or there'll be no more Me Tarzan, You Jane Tuesday nights," she warned, making Keegan go from insanely uptight to sheepishly chided.

His face relaxed as he let her slide over his shoulder and down the front of his chest, leaving the tip of her nose touching his. Clearly he'd been worried sick about Marty, if his anger with Sloan over her disappearance was any indication, but more evident was the love his gaze reflected.

A love he wasn't afraid to share with anyone who looked on. He dropped a kiss on her nose before setting her on her feet, which were encased in slippers much like the one's Jeannie had worn.

Marty's eyes twinkled when she cupped his jaw. "You're the best Neanderthal husband ever, honey. Now give me a kiss and let me get back to what I was doing." She stood on tiptoe, planted a peck on Keegan's lips, and then waved a hand at him to go.

But Keegan grabbed her arm, making the tassels on her sky blue, short-sleeved vest shake. "No more of this, Marty. You're coming home with me before you end up hurt, and you're doing it now. I'm not going to spend another damn second worried about you and this crazy OOPS deal."

Jeannie noted the concern and apprehension in Keegan's eyes for his wife, and she again wondered what it would be like to have someone that devoted to her.

"Oh, you've done it now, ass sniffer," Nina crowed as she rose to her feet, holding out a hand to Wanda to help her up.

Marty's blonde head cocked so sharply to the left, she resembled a bobblehead. She cast a disdainful glance at Keegan's hand before she pried his fingers from her flesh and slapped it away. "This *is* my *job*, lover."

"A job that could get you killed, *honey*. Especially dressed like that and hanging around nuts like him," Keegan remarked, pointing up at Nekaar, though his tone was much less demanding and far more appeasing now.

"This"—Marty waved a hand up and down her body and wriggled her filmy-covered hips—"was a gift from Nekaar. Don't you think it's cute? All those stupid crunches finally paid off. And excuse me, being a werewolf could get me killed. You sure fixed that, didn't you?" Marty jabbed a finger into his chest for emphasis.

As Sloan helped Jeannie to her feet, she prepared to apologize again even as she hesitantly eyed the silent man with the darting eyes Marty had ridden in on. "Keegan, I'm Jeannie Carlyle, and this is all my fault. I——"

Marty pressed her fingers together and summarily stuck them under Jeannie's nose to quiet her. "Do. Not," she blazed before turning to her husband. "I will not have you apologize for something so completely out of your control, Jeannie. I will, however, tell you, Mr. Flaherty, I can do as I please. And if it pleases me to be shipped off to whereverthehell I just was because I'm trying to help a client, then that's just how it'll be. I'm more than just your love bunny, sunshine. I have a career. One that makes me happy because I can help innocent people get on with their lives. I'm not just pretty, Keegan Flaherty, and not everything in my life revolves around you, head werewolf. Don't you forget it."

"And it's on," Nina bellowed with an abrasive chuckle, placing a hand on Darnell's shoulder and squeezing it, her face gleeful with anticipation.

Darnell grunted at her and rolled his big, brown eyes. "Don't you go makin' trouble now, vampire. You just hush."

Jeannie winced, worried Keegan would react badly to Marty's reprimand, but instead, he smiled and barked an indulgent laugh. "You'll be the death of me, cupcake."

"In a thousand lifetimes, no truer words have been spoken," Nekaar commented, sucking in his lean cheeks.

Sloan leaned into her, avoiding the hole in the floor to whisper a sensuous reminder, "I told you wherever Marty landed, she was making someone want to yank their hair out. Now, watch and see how she wraps Keegan around those perfectly manicured fingers of hers with just one pout. Did I tell you he was a Nazi when it came to Marty?"

He had. And Keegan was. And it was adorable.

But Marty didn't let Keegan say anything else. She placed a hand over his mouth and narrowed her eyes in definitive warning. "Not another word. Now, I love you. Be gone so I can work. Take Casey with you. She has that winter formal to help Naomi prepare for. Kiss Hollis and Muffin, tell them Mommy will see them soon." She blew him a kiss and waved him off.

Keegan's jaw hardened, but Marty hopped over several chunks of Jeannie's flooring and popped open her now crooked front door with a saccharine sweet smile. "Casey? Be an angel and set him on fire if he acts up, will you? Oh! Don't forget to ask Helga to water the plants in the kitchen when you get home, please. I might be gone for several days, but I'll call you like an obsessed teenage boy calls his stalking victim. Promise."

Casey nodded her head in the direction of the door and mouthed a "stay strong" to Jeannie. Keegan grunted, but clearly defeated, he slapped his brother on the back before trailing a finger down the side of his wife's face with an affectionate gaze. Then he was gone, following Casey out the door.

No sooner was Keegan gone than Marty was already turning to the stranger, who appeared to be assessing the mess of her brownstone with an eagle eye. Her gaze up at him was one of admonishment. "Make nice, would you?" She clucked her tongue when her eyes scanned the floor. "I don't know where you learned your reentry skills, but you need to go back and take that test over, because it blew chunks. So make your magic, Yul Brynner. We have much to discuss with Jeannie."

He scowled in all his hard hotness, first at Marty, then at the dismal condition of the room. "It is Nekaar, madam. *Nek-aar*," he said with slow precision, lifting his square chin in arrogant posture as he corrected her.

Marty shrugged her shoulders and hooked her feet at the ankles. "I don't care if it's Ruler of the Universe. Fix, Ali Baba. Please."

Craning his thick neck, Nekaar crossed his long arms over his vested chest, holding up a finger to his lips to silence everyone. He waited with a dramatic pause while the group quieted, then blinked his eyes twice. A loud rumble accompanied a shivering groan beneath their feet.

Order was restored in mere seconds in a cloudburst of blue smoke. In fact, her brownstone was cleaner than it had been in years. Though, no one batted an eye, so Jeannie kept her surprise on the inside in order to fit in. It was clearly all part and parcel of one's supernatural lifestyle. Still, she stayed close to Sloan as a just in case.

From the corner of the room, Mat woke with a start, exhaling a hacking cough before rising upward to almost his full length, launching into the air, his ends spread open wide. There was a wheezing whistle as he swerved to the left, appeared to locate Jeannie, zeroed in on her, and promptly hurled himself at her, knocking Sloan out of the way.

She fell hard to the ground in puffs of dirt with Mat wrapped around her like he'd done when they'd first met. Jeannie groaned and tapped his threads. "Mat! *What are you doing?*" she sputtered, blowing the dust particles from her eyes while everyone gathered around them, including Nekaar.

"Shhhh, doll. I'm protecting you from the bad genie. Stranger danger. We're invisible. No one can see us."

Jeannie scanned the room and all the surprised glances. "Mat?"

"Dollface?"

"Not invisible."

His fringe bristled with indignation. "The Internet said I'm supposed ta be able to make myself invisible."

"Oh, that crazy Internet," Jeannie responded.

"It says I can fly, too. It also said I'm your guardian forever or something. I didn't read it all on account a I fell asleep. There was a lotta words."

"What kind of guardian sleeps through an entire room splitting apart?" Sloan asked, his voice full of disbelief and aggravation.

Nekaar still hovering, peered over Sloan's shoulder and made a sour face full of displeasure. "Oh dear," he drawled from above, his gaze haughty.

"The room broke?" Mat asked, then coughed.

"Big," Jeannie assured, stroking him with an encouraging smile. "But it's okay now. I'm okay now, too."

Sloan peeled Mat off Jeannie, giving him a shake, and sending more dust into the air. He held out a hand to Jeannie to help her up, then eyed the carpet. "Mat?"

"Eye candy?"

"Not helping," Sloan retorted before spreading Mat out in the corner. "Stay put," he ordered.

Nina moved with swift feet, keeping her eyes on Nekaar while she pushed her way to Marty's side, giving the length of her friend's hair a tug. "Jesus, blondie. You okay?"

Marty smirked and threw her arms around Nina's neck, pressing a noisy kiss to it. "Did you miss me, Elvira?" she teased, her blue eyes twinkling.

Nina rolled her eyes in disgust, but Jeannie noted, she didn't deny it. For a moment, her gaze was chocolatey soft, but then it went hard when she sought out the newest addition to their paranormal sideshow.

She untangled herself from Marty, and as she approached Nekaar, her stance was wide and defensive, her fists tight. Nina hitched her jaw up at him. "You the freak who had Marty all this time?"

He held up a wide, long-fingered hand before squeezing his temples, his expression pained. "Indeed."

Nina leaned into him and grinned, evil mischief in her eyes. "She why your hair's gone?"

One deep brown eyebrow lifted, as did the corner of his lip, when he lowered himself to the ground. "Had I any to begin with, I assure you, madam, I would be without now."

Marty snorted and patted him on the back with a hard slap that jolted him forward. "Oh, c'mon. It wasn't that bad. I just made some suggestions to lighten up your bottle's living space. It's so drab and gloomy. All those deep purples and burgundies need some levity."

"So where have you been, Marty?" Wanda asked, giving her a tight hug and letting go a sigh that was obviously relief filled. "We've been worried sick."

"I was with Nekaar in his bottle. Don't ask how that's where I landed. What I want to know is, how the hell did I get there and who made that wish?" She paused, rolling her tongue along the inside of her cheek. "No. Wait. I know. It was Mighty Mouth, wasn't it?" She slapped her hand to her forehead. "Of course it was."

"Oh, for fuck's sake, I didn't say it out loud," Nina groused. "And I didn't wish for you to be in a bottle. I wished shit that was much fucking worse, but swear on Hollis, I just thought it in my head. Who the fuck knew the midget could grant wishes like she was handing out free samples at Costco?"

Marty's expression went from mildly annoyed to confused. She pressed her hands to her hips. "Oh, Cheebus. You just thought it? So Jeannie's granting wishes telepathically?"

Nekaar was suddenly all motion and sound. His ringed toes spread when he flew across her floor and stopped short in front of her. "Is what the flaxen-haired woman with the endless stream of nonsensical words says true, madam? You can grant wishes without hearing the spoken words?"

Jeannie hesitated only for a moment. Clearly, Marty didn't think he was a threat, which meant he'd gotten the paranormal green light. "That's how you ended up with Marty. Nina didn't actually speak her wish out loud. She just thought it, but she didn't wish Marty into a bottle. She wished something much worse. Which clearly means I need genie lessons . . ." Jeannie licked her lips nervously. None of this made any sense. Nina had wished Marty would fall off the face of the planet.

Pretty straightforward. In fact, most of the wishes she'd granted had all been granted exactly as they'd been requested. So what had gone wrong with Nina's?

Nekaar stared at her long and hard as though he were scanning the depths of her soul, making Sloan's arm around her tighten.

Jeannie fought a flinch, and rushed to apologize for her inadequacies again. "Okay, so just say it. I'm the crappiest genie ever. I guess a big fancy genie like you wouldn't understand what it is to suck like I do, but give me a little time and the djinn handbook, which I swear I'll study like I'm taking my driver's license test, and I'll be golden. I'm a super quick study—even with my bad memory. I also hear this gig is forever, so any help with getting control of this is more than a little appreciated."

Marty swept across the floor and poked Nekaar in his big, bronzed, Mr. Clean–like arm. "Talk, Yul. Tell her what you told me."

Nekaar crossed his arms over his chest and looked to Jeannie. "Is it as the woman with the crimson lips that always move says? Burt spoke before imprisoning you in his wretched bottle?"

Jeannie nodded hard. "Yes! I think. I don't know. He spoke in a foreign language . . . I think . . . and to be honest, it all happened so fast, and I was so shocked when he popped out . . ."

The djinn's eyes flashed hot and angry. "Then we must find Burt, for he has spit upon the djinn and brought great dishonor to our kind!" he thundered, the overdeveloped muscles in his shoulders flexing and tensing.

Jeannie held a tentative hand up, inching a little closer to Sloan. "Before you go curse-crazy here and let your temper get the better of you, you are the genie who cursed Burt to the bottle, right?"

He gave her a condescending look with sharp eyes. "I am. You knew this, how?"

"It's a long story, but my magic carpet, Mat, heard you do it. That's for later. So why did you curse him to the bottle?"

Regret flashed in Nekaar's eyes—regret and something else Jeannie didn't understand. "Burt is a blight on the djinn community. Unlike what you have obviously read on your computers and watched on your televisions with the screens so thin one would wish to feed it a cracker, we are an honorable people. We wish only to live out our centuries in peaceful coexistence. Thus, we primarily live beyond this realm and stay behind the veil."

"Veil . . ." Jeannie muttered. Yet more genie lingo. "Is that like an entire genie world separate from our human world? Because if being a genie means I have to live somewhere else, I want out." No more relocation, thank you very much.

"Indeed, madam. We do have a universe apart from yours. As you are not djinn by birth but rather by circumstance, I know not what this means for your future."

Oh, for sure it was so not bright she wouldn't need shades. Jeannie fought to keep her panic to herself. *One fact at a time, Jeannie.*

"So, back to Burt. Why did you curse him to the bottle?" Sloan asked, reading her mind, his eyes now intent on Nekaar.

"Alas, much like your human world, we have our share of upstarts—troubled souls who wish only to create mischief and discord with their gift of trickery. Burt was one of them. He could no longer be allowed to roam between the veils freely. He flaunted his magic. He abused it, using it on those whom were helpless to defend themselves."

"So he cracked on humans?" Nina asked.

Nekaar frowned, the solid stone of his features lining. "Cracked?"

"Took advantage of humans," Jeannie added helpfully.

Nekaar sighed long and put upon, his thick wall of a chest rising and falling under his vest. He dipped his shiny head low. "It is so. Thus, I imprisoned him to the bottle for eternity."

Jeannie spread her arms wide. "Well, glitch in the cursing thing, yes? Because here I am—stuck with a bottle and a man I can't get more than a few hundred feet from. So what happened? How did Burt manage to break your curse? Who would steal the bottle? And what's with this attached-at-the-hip thing?"

His look was dry, his words drier still. "The curse was broken because *you*, madam, let him out of the bottle."

Jeannie's anger spiked. "Well, hold the hell on now. I don't want to go all *Girl, Interrupted* on you, but why, if Burt is such a bad genie, would you ever leave his bottle just lying around so just anybody could open it? I mean, *hello*. It was at a party I was catering, for gravy's sake. Why wasn't it in a genie holding cell or something? And why would you imprison him, in of all things, a gin bottle? It's like putting him in a can of Coke! Maybe, if you'd locked him in, say, a can of spotted dick, or even Spam, your chances would have been less likely someone would have opened it, and he would have escaped. Who eats spotted dick? Never mind. I'm sure there are lots of people who do. But I think there are far more who drink booze. I mean, c'mon. *A bottle of gin?* If you ask me, that was just careless curse planning, genie. Weak, weak, weak!"

Nekaar rumbled his discontent, making the room shake and sway. "I will not have you defame my djinn capabilities, you disgraceful mortal!"

Sloan set Jeannie behind him in what she gathered was an effort to defend her, but she was tired. And cranky. And damn well fed up to her swollen eyeball with this whole genie bag.

She gave Sloan a shove and stepped in front of him, her nostrils flared in anger. On tippy toe, she rose, rolling her neck at him. "You listen here, you crazy, chick-trouser-wearing, crappy-cursing, elit-ist djinn *snob*. You back the hell off and quit calling names! I'm a disgrace, my eye! If it weren't for you, this wouldn't be happening! Now, if you have absolutely nothing useful to offer in the way of fixing the mess *you* created, get the hell out of my house!"

"Niiiice, homeslice. Way to slap an asshole down." Nina thumped her on the back, then stood behind her in protective mode, placing her hands on Jeannie's shoulder.

There, Nina approval. So, hah!

Nekaar lifted his chin in arrogance. "You, pale of skin"—he sneered at Nina—"have a vile mouth."

"And *you*, bald of head"—she sneered back—"have sissy pants." She pointed at the filmy cloth covering his tree-sized legs.

"Hold up!" Wanda ordered, parting the group and giving Nina a hand signal of warning. "Stop right there. You may not like it, Nina, but Nekaar's our only solid lead to the djinn world. So don't razz the caged tiger, huh? Jeannie? While it's super-duper awesome to see you stand up for yourself and find your voice, there's a time and a place, agreed?"

Jeannie let her head fall to her chest. "Sorry," she mumbled. In truth, she was really just taking her frustration out on Nekaar. He'd done the right thing by capturing Burt. His intentions, if nothing else, were good. Wanda was right. They needed this nutball to help them.

"Okay, so, put away your easily affronted genie sensibilities and help us. Tell them what you told me about Burt," Marty encouraged with a smile.

Nekaar stood silent and regal.

Marty sighed, running a hand over her neck to massage it. "Now, don't be petty, Yul; do it or I'll hunt down your bottle again. And this time, I'm bringing swatches and as many fluffy, pink pillows as I can wrap my werewolf hands around."

Nekaar's stiff posture slumped slightly. "Burt's bottle was stolen from me. I do not know who took it, nor do I know how it ended up on this plane. I am responsible for your plight. There. We have cleansed in a group setting. I consider that absolution. Now, may I go, madam?" he asked Marty in a peevish tone.

Marty planted her hands on her slender hips and shook her head. "No. No, you may not go. You're more than a little responsible for losing track of Burt's bottle. If you're the upstanding djinn you say you are, you'll not only help, but you'll tell me why your face was flashing all sorts of signals when we told you Jeannie had granted more than three wishes. Which, if I remember as we chatted over a pot of jasmine tea, you said was all you were obligated to grant the person who sets you free. In turn, the genie is set free from enslavement. End contract. As you can see, that's not the case with Jeannie. We're on wish number five, if we're counting Keegan's wish, pal. Ante up, genie." She snapped her fingers under his nose.

Nekaar rolled his genie eyes at a very bossy Marty. He shook his fingers at her, glistening with rings. "You are maddening."

"And you're going to sleep amongst a bunch of throw pillows in three, two, one . . ." Marty threatened, the tassels on her vest quivering when she shook her finger at Nekaar.

The genie cleared his throat, the thick cords moving up and down his deeply bronzed neck. "This is the dilemma as I see it. Upon release from his eternal prison, Burt cursed Jeannie to the bottle. If he were an honorable genie, of which I have informed you, he is not, he would have granted you your three wishes and been freed from the curse I placed upon his dark soul. As is quite obvious, Burt defies honor and sought only to gain his freedom. It is also my assumption that when he blathered his curse upon Jeannie, he somehow confused his words and tethered you to your master for eternity. Burt was never very adept academically. He was always mucking something up. Often, he would create havoc during lessons. That he doomed you to another poor soul makes enormous sense to this djinn. Burt and I practiced often together. I still bear the scars of our class on creating thunderstorms for botanical purposes."

Sloan, who'd remained silent while he absorbed the information bandied about, finally spoke. His deep, gravel-hard voice sent chills up Jeannie's spine. "So Burt, the guy *you* lost track of, cursed us to be together for eternity? Eternity?"

"It is so," Nekaar said in his hushed, yet somehow booming voice.

"Jesus Christ," Sloan murmured.

Jeannie heard the disbelief in Sloan's voice, and she was sure she heard disappointment, too. Deep disappointment, the kind that should be expected when one found out they had a forever albatross around their neck. Even though she was experiencing the same disappointment, she found it still hurt a little. So she wasn't blonde. She was still funny—and a little interesting.

Taking a deep breath, Jeannie plowed onward. Good or bad, she had to know what could be around the corner. "So how do we fix it? Can't I just wish my way out of this?" She'd given that notion some thought. If she was just granting any old wish, why not her own?

Thunderclouds flashed across Nekaar's angular face. "No, madam. You must never, ever, *ev-er* make a wish for personal gain. Djinn code strictly prohibits it. Burt often abused his magic, and you see what happened to him."

Silly, Jeannie. You didn't think it would be that easy, did you? Her snort dripped sarcasm. "Yeah. Because as a result of what happened to him, *this* happened to me." Jeannie circled the space between her and Nekaar.

"A thousand apologies, madam," the genie offered with a bow. Yet, she wasn't convinced he really had any sincerity going on to match his contrite look.

"Spilled milk and all," Jeannie retorted. "So, if I have to be a genie forever, fine. I'll figure out the death-by-push-up-bra thing, but I can't have Sloan stuck to me forever. This isn't his fault. He was just helping me, and because he was just being a decent person, he has to be stuck with me forever? That's crazy—and unjust—and crazy. So what do we do?" She closed her eyes then, waiting for the inevitable.

Nekaar's sigh was full of remorse. "I am afraid only Burt can reverse a curse of this magnitude. To do otherwise would be to meddle in another djinn's magic. Magic, in our world, is quite personal in nature. It is the signature mark of each djinn's work, much in the way you identify a popular singer's voice or a particular author's writing style. It is unique and carefully cultivated over thousands of years. I have seen but one attempt to break a bond by a djinn who meddled in another's magic, and then only once in all my thousands of years . . ."

Jeannie's eyes popped open. "And?" Wait for it because for certain the answer would be exactly what she didn't want to hear.

Nekaar's Adam's apple bobbed up and down in a gulp. "And one of the two parties no longer roam your plane. Or any plane."

Bingo. "So this person is dead?" she squeaked, the tremor in her voice pounding in her ears.

His eyes, for all their snooty arrogance, flashed a moment of sincere sympathy at her. "It is so, madam."

Forever. It was really true. She was stuck to Sloan forever. How did you ask the person who saved you from death by beer stank to also consider finding a way to break a curse that could leave him dead?

She'd been telling herself over and over it could be worse, but even the best relationships in the world couldn't withstand that kind of twenty-four-seven pressure. How in the world could she and Sloan survive something like continual proximity when they hardly knew each other? Choosing to be with someone forever had a whole new meaning with this new information.

"Well, then, there's some good news," Sloan offered, letting his fingers stray to her in reassurance. "I'm a werewolf. I have eternal life. Problem solved. Can't kill me if we break the curse. The only person we have to worry about is Jeannie."

Nekaar sighed again. "I am aware of your paranormal origins due to the incessant ramble of the one with the crimson lips and sunshine-dappled hair. However, I am afraid your nature can be trumped by djinn magic. Nothing, and, sir, I do mean nothing, can trump the magic of the djinn."

Jeannie warred with her knees, silently directing them to stay locked in place.

Nina put her hands under Jeannie's elbows to keep her from swaying. "Fine. So we need to find the greasy asshole who cursed her to the bottle. That's on you as far as I'm concerned, Aladdin. You fucked up when you lost that damn bottle. So when, note I'm using the word *when*, you get your hands on this Burt, just give him to me. I'll fucking make sure he reverses this curse. Count on it. In the meantime, explain the wishes gone wild, dude. Why the hell aren't her wishes all dried up by now? Last count was five."

Confusion skittered across Nekaar's elegant face, and then he replaced it with his haughty mask. "I have not the answer to this, angry one. Yet, I find Jeannie's dilemma most troublesome. There are no djinn I know of with this magnitude of power. We grant three wishes and we are, as you of this realm say, out. And wishes bestowed upon another are only allowed upon release from captivity as rather a courtesy for our freedom. That you have been granted this gift is quite puzzling. I shall chalk your unlimited power up to Burt and his irresponsible desecration of a curse with the proper intent."

"So this all leads back to Burt. Which means you'd better get to doin' whatever it is you genies do when you got a shitty djinn on the lamb, and fucking fix this," Nina demanded. "So find Burt. Find him fast, frilly pants, or I'm gonna take your ass out."

Jeannie found her voice again and asked, "What if we can't find

Burt? Is it really true that, in order for me to get out of the bottle for good, I have to curse someone else to it?"

"Without Burt, yes, madam, that would be the answer."

Nina shook her head. "But what does that do to the rest of this shit? Like her wishes gone wild? Sloan stuck to the midget like she's one of those beds in a sleazy hotel with the coin operated massage machines is one thing. Her sending people to hell just because someone wished it out of the GD blue from five hundred feet away is a whole other ball of wax."

"You are truly made up of all parts distasteful." Nekaar turned his nose up at Nina.

"And you're truly going to be the limbs I gnaw on from my plate at genie lunchtime if you don't shut the hell up. Quit dickin' us around and help find Burt," Nina growled.

"As you wish, madam," Nekaar replied with unusual obedience. He snapped his fingers, and out of a thin air, a cell phone appeared. His fingers flew over the face of the phone, his smooth brow wrinkled.

Nina patted Jeannie on her trembling back then stepped from behind her and tugged on a strand of her hair. "So, it's gonna be okay, right, shawty? Dude will find Burt, and we'll get you unhitched, and then you can go on your genie way. Yeah, you might still be a genie, but you can work with that shit. If I can be a vampire, you can be a genie. Good news all round, right, kiddo?"

"Do you think finding Burt is going to help with the wish thing?" Jeannie's eyes pierced Nina's. If she could count on anyone to tell her the God's honest truth, it was Nina, simply because she didn't really care if it upset you.

Noting her shiver, Nina buttoned her sweater like she was a child needing tending, tucking the lapels under Jeannie's chin. "Yep. It's gonna be fucking awesome. And if Burt gives us a hard time—I'll show him the way of the vampire." She flashed her fangs.

And then another thought occurred to her. How did one go about living their life as a genie? If you couldn't grant wishes for the greater good unless you were freed from a bottle, what did genies do all day?

"Don't let that imagination get the better of you, Jeannie," Sloan warned, cupping her chin so their eyes met.

"My imagination has officially been bested by real life. I keep asking myself, what next?"

"Look. I'm here to tell you that, even if we never find Burt, it'll be okay. We'll just figure something out."

Her glance was filled with skeptical disbelief. "Do you think your leggy blonde dates are going to feel that way? You know, when I'm unwillingly pressed up against the door that just beyond holds your Lair of Love?"

"Don't be ridiculous. It's not called the Lair of Love. It's called the Haven of Heat. Lairs are for sissies," he teased, squeezing her jaw. "I know I keep saying this, but it bears repeating. It's going to be okay."

"Dreadful news," Nekaar muttered, his head low when he held up the phone for Jeannie to see.

Her eyes scanned what appeared to be a Facebook page. She squinted at the avatar in the upper-left-hand corner—a picture of the Robin Williams–voiced character of Genie from *Aladdin*. Live out loud, right? The banner flying across Genie's jovial face read BOTTLE BABES.

Jeannie shook her head in disbelief. "The djinn have a Facebook page?"

Nekaar's chuckle was oddly watery. "Hide in plain sight, yes, madam? Nary a soul believes it is real. We allow the outside realm the belief that we are all, um . . . 'cracked-out wannabes' is what I believe the most crude of social networking have labeled us."

Nina cackled her understanding. "We get that shit all the time."

Jeannie's gasp interrupted Nina. Sloan came instantly to her side, placing an arm around her shoulder to lean in and read Nekaar's phone from over her shoulder. Instead of fearing Sloan's comfort, Jeannie leaned into it this time without a second thought. "Well, shit," he spat.

"Fuck, now what?" Nina demanded. "Did they run out of little genie pants in your size, Aladdin?"

Oh, look. Omar made harem pants now. Buy one get one free. Jeannie shook her head. "No. They have plenty of harem pants," she responded, now even more familiar with defeat. "Pants aren't the problem. This is." She cleared her throat and read the post dated yesterday—the very day she'd been cursed to Burt's bottle. "It is with sadness that we bid fellow djinn Burt safe passage to the Realm of New Beginnings." Then she lowered her voice out of respect. "And four hundred and eighty-two people like this." It appeared Burt didn't have a whole lot of love, the genie community.

Nina plucked the phone from Jeannie's trembling hands. "I guess the Realm of New Beginnings isn't like genie rehab, huh, Gunga Din?"

Nina scrolled some of the comments, making Jeannie bite the inside of her cheek. Oh, genies were mean. How cruel to wish the tread marks of a rabid camel upon Burt's black soul.

Jeannie gazed at Nekaar's crumpling face with sympathy, pushing her own worst fears aside. "This Realm of New Beginnings is bad, isn't it?"

Pressing his fingers to his eyes, Nekaar shook his head up and down hard. He shook it so hard, Jeannie feared it would fall off his neck, and then he collapsed on her couch in a dramatic, gulping sob. His wide shoulders quivered when he buried his face in one of her throw pillows.

The group passed bewildered looks. Jeannie knelt in front of him, putting a tentative hand on his arm. "Nekaar? I don't understand. What's wrong?"

"Buuuurrrrt," he cried. "Burt's dead!"

Yeah. Things just kept getting shinier. Poor Burt. Poor her. Poor Sloan. "And this makes you sad because?"

He took in a huge gulp of air before letting it out into the pillow with a muffled shudder. He lifted his head "This saddens me because Burt, for all his dastardly ways, is my—my—was my . . . Burt was my brother!"

CHAPTER 9

Sloan cracked his neck and stuffed his hands in the pockets of his jeans, uncomfortable with the tears of a man, especially one as big and imposing as Nekaar. This was very obviously bad news. They'd needed Burt to break this curse. If he was dead, that meant he and Jeannie were like the Rick Astley song—together forever. Talk about being Rick-rolled.

Though, as he watched Jeannie comfort Nekaar by cradling his head against her shoulder and patting his broad back, when it was Jeannie who really needed the comfort after having her world turned upside down, Sloan found he wasn't nearly as pissed as he should be that he and Jeannie had an imposed future together.

It also made him pause. Pause big. He should be all kinds of pissed off that not only had he been dragged into this mess by Marty and the girls, but that he was going to be stuck with a woman he never would have considered was in his wheelhouse.

It wasn't that Jeannie wasn't cute as hell. It wasn't that she wasn't appealing to his eye on every level. It wasn't that she didn't have full lips and rounded hips. It wasn't that she wasn't adorable—period.

So what was it?

What was keeping him from beating this Nekaar to within an inch of his life so he'd produce an answer that left him free of Jeannie?

Jeannie was troubled. He felt it—smelled it. What troubled her was a mystery, but it was there. It was there in the way she stiffened when he moved closer to her. It was there when she tripped over herself to keep him and Nina from arguing. Jeannie had no filter when it came to their harsh words. She clearly didn't understand that while he and Nina gave each other regular hell, it meant nothing. They both just got a kick out of poking each other. No harm, no foul. They'd always done it. But to Jeannie, it was discord. It rattled her need for harmony.

And that need for harmony was bigger than she was. She had more CDs with monks chanting than she had room for in her bedroom closet. There were dream catcher wind chimes hanging outside her bedroom window on the small fire escape, and all sorts of books on relaxation techniques on her nightstand. Muscle relaxers and anxiety reducers littered the lining of her medicine cabinet in her bathroom, and she had about as many soothing candle scents that invoked said harmony as Bath and Body Works did.

Jeannie was easy to figure out. What had created the Jeannie of today was going to take a lesson in patience and more sleuthing.

And there he went again, wondering how he could get inside Jeannie's head without damaging her tenuous trust. Unheard of from Sloan Flaherty. He didn't want to get into heads. He wanted to get under miniskirts and, equally so, a set of Egyptian cotton sheets.

Or he'd wanted to as far back as last year. Until everything had changed for him and someone he'd been fond of had died in an accident. Her funeral had been attended by the men she'd slid around on a pole for instead of family and the young women she should have been having lunch with at the mall while they giggled over men their own age.

That moment, that funeral, with its cheap casket and cheaper send-off, had been what everyone called a defining moment. It was when he'd realized that no one should die with a stream of mourners who carried that many dollar bills in their wallets—at least, not someone as young as Sable had been. The girls who'd surrounded her had known the score. They were older—they got the big stripper picture.

But Sable . . .

She'd been too young to die. Too naïve to realize the path she'd taken wasn't going to lead to some Hollywood agent, but instead a life of catcalls and whistles that slid from between cracked, dry lips in a darkened room where "Pour Some Sugar on Me" thumped in the speakers. She'd made him think of his niece, Hollis, and Casey's daughter, Naomi. A career like the one she'd chosen to make ends meet after losing her parents was unthinkable for the children in Sloan's life.

Watching the slew of men pay their respects to Sable had done something to him. Did he want to be one of those men someday? Would he attend the funerals of strippers and bartenders because they were the only people he'd allowed in his life other than his family?

It was also when he'd realized if he didn't start at least living cleaner and respecting himself, if he eventually did kick the bucket, there were going to be maybe four people at his funeral, and they'd only be there because they were obligated to attend—one of them would surely be Nina, who'd remind him in his cold, dead ear that he was a hole-chasing pig.

Just because a werewolf could live for an eternity didn't mean he would. Did he want to spend the rest of forever sleeping with whoever caught his very short attention span? Or did he want to smile the way Keegan did when he saw Marty and Hollis?

Did he always want to be the dick who showed up at their

paranormal picnics with a woman he'd never share any memories with but the vague, booze-riddled scent of their one night together? Or did he want to make some memories of his own? Did he want to have someone to share his meals with, his troubles? Or did he just want to keep pretending he didn't? Did he want to pretend that the lure of an endless stream of women, whose first names eluded him completely, wasn't wearing his ass out?

The definitive answer had been no.

He'd left that nondenominational church with its ragtag bunch of mourners and he'd never looked back

He'd straightened up. He'd paid better attention to his duties at Pack. And he hadn't dated anyone—if that's what you'd call what he'd been doing—in over a year.

Ah. Now that might be it. He'd fought the ghost of his horn-dog on more than one occasion since he'd laid off the women and lightened up on the booze. He was just needy.

And that perfectly summed up his attraction to Jeannie.

She was everything he wasn't interested in—and he was just hankering the bed sport.

Except what is that shit that goes on in your stomach every time you look at her swollen eye and want to kill the fucker who hurt her? Why does your heart pound harder when you get a whiff of her after she's bathed in chamomile and cucumber?

His gut said his fascination with Jeannie couldn't be dismissed as long overdue lust. There'd been plenty of temptation in the way of women in his path since he'd decided on celibacy. They just hadn't been Jeannie.

"Sloan?"

Wanda's voice drew him from his thoughts of Jeannie. "How's Nekaar?" Sloan had felt the tug of his feet when Jeannie had taken Nekaar to her kitchen to help him freshen up. Every couple of minutes, he could still hear a small whimper from just beyond the doorway.

Her smile was a little forlorn, her eyes full of warmth. "How anyone would be when they realize their brother is dead. Good or bad, he was still Nekaar's brother, I guess. Sadder still? The awful reality that he was the one who had to curse his brother to a bottle to keep him out of trouble. If only we could do that with Nina."

"Don't tempt me," he said on a laugh.

Wanda squeezed his arm with her hand. "Nekaar and this newest information aside, I'm concerned about you. How are you? I think we all tend to forget that, while Jeannie is the victim here, she has casualties of war."

Suddenly, Sloan felt like she'd seen right through him. Like Wanda sensed he was having impure thoughts about Jeannie. Straightening, he visualized a hike in his man-panties. "I'm fine, Wanda. No worse for the wear."

"But eternity, Sloan? I know you well enough to know that, while deep down you're a good man, and you'll do the right thing, you do like your playtime . . ."

Yeah. He deserved that. "Are you checking to be sure I won't do something crazy like find some stray djinn to attempt to break the curse so I can have my blonde supermodel time? Are you making sure I won't risk Jeannie's life for a six-pack and some strippers?"

Wanda gave him a sheepish glance before looking down at the sleeves of her silky green shirt to avoid his direct question. "I kinda am . . . I'm sorry, Sloan," she was quick to back her harsh words up. "It's just that . . ." She sighed. "Okay, so I'll just be honest. We all know how much you like women. You always have a new one, and she never lasts for more than half the time of a family event before you're bored and eyeing the next kill. Do you remember the Not So Barbequed/Champagne Blood party Casey hosted over two summers ago?"

Shit. He remembered. "Yep."

"Do you also remember that you came to the party with one woman and left with another?"

"Well, to be fair, my date did desert me for Clayton's vampire friend. Remember? She was all about him when she found out he'd once been a Viking. Personally, I think they're way overrated, but there you have it. She thought the guy was a god. Who am I to say he wasn't?" After a couple of beers, she'd been a red-hot she-wolf, but over potato salad the next day, she'd ended up just being like most of the women he surrounded himself with. Ready for the next kill.

"Point. But what I'm saying is, you didn't exactly have a mourning period over it, either."

He cracked his jaw. That was because she hadn't been important enough to mourn. But he was who he was—or had been. "Fair enough."

"I'm not trying to beat you down, Sloan. Swear it. Your life is your life and you can live it as you see fit. No judgment here. I mean, I am BFFs with Nina. Who am I to judge? But Jeannie's got something else going on, which, while I can smell it, I can't pinpoint it. I think for all her jokes and bravado, something else is happening aside from the genie thing. I just don't know what, but it entails a fragility she reeks of. I want to see that you're helped, too. You're just stronger than she is. Period. So I haven't paid as much attention to you, but I wanted you to know that I get you're stuck in this unwillingly, too."

Sloan lifted his chin. "And?"

"And I just don't want Jeannie to end up hurt until we can find some help. I don't want you to . . ."

"In the process, you just don't want me to help myself to Jeannie, right?" He deserved that, too. He'd been a contributor to the Shitty Club for Men. He'd own that.

Wanda sighed, but her eyes were sharp, and he knew she meant it. "Desperate times and all."

He knew exactly what his sister-in-law and the rest of the women were thinking. He'd sleep with Jeannie simply because she was there. Also a label he deserved. "I'm not desperate, Wanda, and I can assure you, Jeannie's safe with me—from me."

Nina came up behind Wanda and made a face at Sloan. "Are we giving him the speech about keeping his desperate dick inside his 501s?"

"Mind your own beeswax, Mighty Mouth," Wanda snapped, as though reminding Sloan he was a cad made her feel badly.

Nina stuck a finger out at him over Wanda's shoulder and shook it. "You hurt shawty, and you got me right up your ass, gnawing my way to your spleen."

"What's the attachment to Jeannie, Nina? Do you liiike her?" He knew what it was. He knew Nina had a weak spot for the helpless, but he also knew she hated it pointed out to her. And he liked to point it out.

She flipped him the bird. "Oh, fuck you, ass sniffer. She's just a kid with nobody to look out for her. You're the Big Bad Wolf with sharp teeth. I don't want more bullshit drama than we already have. So hands to yourself, freakazoid. Feel me?"

"Felt, Defender of All Things Great and Small." Instead of making him angry, Nina's strange and rather sudden attachment to Jeannie comforted him.

He knew, no matter what happened to him, Nina would look out for Jeannie, because Nina was champion of all things needing a champion. For all her mouthy ways, she was badass if she was on your side.

"Good," she grunted, leaning into them. "So lemme just say this between us three, some shit ain't right about that dude who clobbered her today. Some shit ain't right about Jeannie. I know you've all been feelin' it, too. Smellin' it, whatever."

Sloan's antennae went instantly into alert mode. Jesus, his wolfie senses were really off. "What do you mean something isn't right about the guy who hit her? Of course something's not right about him. He hit a damn woman for money." His fists tightened at his sides.

Wanda's head moved back and forth. "No, she knew his name, Sloan. According to Nina, she said this supposed mugger's name in the process of the mugging. She claims he told her his name when she tried to reason him out of robbing her. You know, know your enemy, personalize yourself to your attacker sort of thing, so they'll sympathize with you—connect with you?"

"Bullshit is what I call," Nina spat, jamming her hands into her hoodie's pockets. "That dude had a hold on her like he was lookin' for more than money. I can't explain it, but it was fucking personal. Maybe even intimate, and I didn't get it, but it was there. He knows her—or knows something about her. I dunno. But I say we sniff the freak out. I still have his scent in my nostrils. Booze and more booze. Whiskey, to be precise. How many bars can there be in the city?"

Sloan put his hands up. "So the bastard might know her? Ex-boyfriend? Husband? What do we really know about her besides the fact that she owns a catering business?"

"Only what she's told us," Wanda said.

"I so wanna dig around in her head. But I can't do that because of vampire code. If things get worse, or that fuckerly fuck shows back up, heads up, I'll do it. For now, we focus on the worst. That being she grants wishes like Dr. Beverly Hills 90210 hands out boob jobs. That's a problem, and somebody needs to be with her twenty-four-seven to try and keep track of it. As to her knowing the sleazy shit who clocked her, I'll keep watching her to see if she gives me any more suspicious signs. But I can tell you this—she looked me right in the eye and told me she had no idea who he was. If she's lyin', she's fucking aces at it. I was this close to convinced."

"Ladies!" Darnell called from the living room. "You might wanna come watch this here five o'clock newscast. We got mo' trouble."

They piled into Jeannie's small living room and turned their attention to her TV. The reporter, slender, with her hair sharply pulled back from her face and eyes like hazel razor blades, was standing in front of Forever Bridal. When the camera panned to the store behind her, Sloan swore softly. He didn't need to hear what had happened. The visual was enough to show him.

A man . . . There was a man that was . . . Jesus. He couldn't digest this. Not today.

As the short clip ran and as the reporter's voice droned on, Sloan rubbed his temple.

Hoo, boy.

The reporter jammed the mic into a distraught twenty-something woman's tear-streaked face and asked, "We're here with eyewitness, Kris Burns. Kris, can you tell us exactly what happened here today?" The reporter's tone, a reporter Sloan recognized, usually so even and unbiased, trembled ever so slightly to his sensitive ear. As though what happened to this group of women could happen to her, too, if she didn't watch her step.

The interviewee's eyes, dazed and already the size of half-dollars, widened. Her voice began as a hushed whisper of fearful awe, wobbling as she told her tale. "We were all part of the scavenger hunt. You know, to win the free wedding and an all-expense-paid trip to the Cayman Islands . . ." The woman's voice drifted off into a moan. She bit her lip and shook her head, clearly refocusing. "We had to find the dress with the golden ticket on it. Ohhhh," she groaned, and shot a confused look into the camera.

The reporter nodded, placing a hand on the young woman's shoulder, portraying a look of deep sympathy while the camera scanned her porcelain features.

Kris appeared to regain her composure after several more shallow, rhythmic breaths. "Anyway, two women found the golden ticket at the same time. There was a lot of screaming and arguing over who put hands on the dress first and neither of them would let go. I swear, we all thought they were going to rip it in half. So some of the store employees intervened, and it just got worse from there. One of the women . . . Her name was . . ." She grabbed the reporter's arm and squeezed, scrunching up her face as though she were in agonizing pain.

The reporter looked into the camera and said, "The alleged perpetrator of the crime, Monica Gilson?"

"Yes! Monica was yelling at the other lady. She said she deserved the dress more than her. But the other lady said, in her condition, she'd kind of skipped the need for a wedding and a fancy honeymoon. Then she asked Monica if whales wore wedding dresses. It was pretty mean, and I'm ashamed to admit, we all laughed. So then——" The eyewitness paused and took a huge gulp of air before bravely soldiering on. "Then that Monica lady, who didn't really need a wedding dress, just went ballistic and screamed, 'Who the hell do you think you are, you bunch of judgmental sluts? How dare you laugh at me! I wish . . .'"

Sloan winced and tuned out the woman's next words. He didn't need to hear what this Monica had wished for. He had the visual. Jesus Christ. What a visual.

The camera panned away from the terrified woman while the reporter gave a solemn nod amidst the shrill pre-labor screams. "You heard that right, Five-Alive viewers——"

Nina flipped the TV off; her look of genuine disbelief shocked Sloan. "Oh, Jesus Christ and a cradle, I thought we'd seen it fucking all. You don't think this was Jeannie, do you? How . . . ? Can you even believe this shit?"

Marty scoffed at her friend. "Did you really just ask that? Really, vampire?"

Nina gave her head a shake, her eyes as stunned as the woman's on TV. "But it was a dude, Marty. A fucking dude. Jeannie got a whole store full of women knocked up and a *dude*. And she did it without even being in their vicinity. Hell, she didn't even *hear* the wish that chick made. She couldn't have. Last time I checked, she wasn't anywhere near a bridal store. Which means, anyone, *anywhere* in the world could use those two fucking dreaded words and shit could go down, yo."

Wanda's sigh was ragged when she let her head fall back on her shoulders. "Every time we put out a fire, she sets another one." She raised her fist to the ceiling and muttered, "What? What do you want?"

Sloan had to fight a laugh. It was a helluva lot funnier when it was someone else's wish granted. "So what do we do about this?" he asked, forcing a snort deep down in his throat. Because in truth, it wasn't funny. Shame on him for thinking it was funny.

Wanda turned to Darnell, her eyes weary. "Say we can fix this, Darnell. We need to fix this, demon. If that reporter was right about her facts, there were over two hundred women in that store—now all expecting little bundles of joy—including, as Nina so succinctly put it, a dude."

"C'mon," Darnell said, putting his hand under Wanda's elbow and leading her to the door. "We gonna go see where Casey is and fix what needs fixin'. But if me an Casey do the demon hoodoo and make it all go away like we did them people landin' in hell, it won't last but a coupla days because it ain't our spell. Jeannie's the only one who can break the spell and make it right."

Mass pregnancy. Jeannie'd created a mass pregnancy.

Sloan had to hide another chuckle. So twelve. So inappropriate.

JEANNIE leaned over Nekaar and patted a cold compress to his face, pressing a second one to her own. She didn't think she had anything left in her in the way of surprise, but knocking up a whole store full of women, including a man, after someone threw a random wish out she'd never even heard with her own ears? It was a little too much like Moses parting the Red Sea from, say, Albuquerque for her. It had to stop or she'd never have any genie friends. Not to mention, she could be creating havoc all over the world and have no prior knowledge it was her in charge of the havoc just because someone had used the words *I wish*.

Turning her attention to Nekaar, she asked, "Better?"

"It is so, madam," he mumbled, clearly ashamed of his outburst. He hadn't met her eyes since she'd sat him down in the kitchen.

She slid into the chair beside him at her table for one and reached out a hand, cupping his forearm. "I'm sorry about Burt. I'm sure he had good qualities. Those people on Facebook are just meanie butts is all." Maybe he was kind to small animals, seniors, and little children?

"No," he whispered, his voice heavy with sadness. "No. They are right, madam. Burt was a blight on the djinn community. He did more bad than good, and he lived as though djinn law did not apply to him. No one liked Burt. Not a soul. He was scum. He was also a fashion disaster. It is so."

She made a face of sympathy, but Burt's imprisonment had her very curious. What did you have to do to end up locked in genie jail—forever? "May I ask a very personal question?"

His nod was that of agreement, his square chin remaining close to his chest.

She hesitated for a moment and then decided it was better to just get it over with so she had a frame of reference for things not to do when you're a genie. "What did Burt do that made you curse him into the bottle?" What was so horrible that your own brother would curse you away forever?

Nekaar's lower lip trembled when he lifted his shiny head. "His trickery and deceit sent my beloved away. In return, I sent Burt away."

"Djinn have girlfriends?" This was refreshing to know. Because someday, when she got back on that dating horse, she'd have a whole new realm to ride it in. Or veil . . . or whatever.

"They do indeed, madam."

"May I pry further? I don't want to dredge up painful memories at such a sensitive time."

He rolled his hand in a *proceed* motion, then folded them together into a large fist.

"What did he do to your beloved that would make you take such harsh measures?"

Nekaar's sigh was bereft, his somber expression distorted with pain. "As I've said, Burt was full of trickery. A real King of Snark, as you'd say here in your land. He often put himself in a bottle to lie in wait for an unsuspecting victim. He thought it was humorous to dupe the innocent. When the poor soul opened the bottle, Burt would, as all djinn must, offer him his three obligatory wishes."

She remembered what Sloan had said about headaches, losing your head, and something about wording your wishes distinctly. "I'm guessing a lot of people got *exactly* what they wished for?"

His wide shoulders, shoulders that filled her small chair and over-powered the back of it, shuddered. "Oh, madam, if only you knew the depths of my brother's deceit and the lengths at which I have gone to correct them. When your heart is pure, the wishes you grant are as such. Contrary to your pop culture beliefs, the majority of recipients use their wishes to bring joy. Do those recipients ask for riches? Indeed. Though, I find in most cases, they ask due to a life-time of great financial struggle. Do they ask for love? Again, indeed, and it is almost always with good intent. Also, contrary to what you may have read or heard, an imprisoned genie is quite rare. Obliga-tory wishes are not as common as you'd think."

"Well, that's a relief. Who knows what could happen if I ever get stuck in another bottle again. I think Genie World might explode the way I hand them out like they're Halloween candy. So we've established Burt played games when it came to granting wishes."

He sniffed his disapproval. "Sadly, when your heart is black and cold, you do not grant joyful wishes. Burt had done this one too many times, and had been given several warnings after we had to tidy up yet another of his messes. There was always a fire to put out where my brother was concerned. I grew weary, madam, as I would hope you can surely understand. I had detached myself from Burt and his hijinks—banished him from my life with the strict order that if he were to tarnish our name again, there would be consequences. His reputation was that of a hooligan, and I wanted no part of it. I warned him!" he shouted with vehemence, then shrank back in his chair again. "During this time of peace and reflection in my life, I met my one true love, Leila. We had a lovely romance . . ." His words were thwarted by a sniffle.

Jeannie winced. This wasn't going to be an HEA. She just knew it. "But?"

"But Burt, as with everything else, tore her from me," he yelled, reanimated again as he dropped his large fist to the table. Squaring his wide shoulders, he sucked in a breath. "Burt was jealous of Leila, pathetically so. So jealous he used his gift of trickery, and one night, taking on my visage . . . He convinced Leila that he . . ."

Jeannie blanched, putting her hand to Nekaar's mouth to quiet him. She didn't want to hurt him. No one knew how painful it was to dredge up your past than she did. "Shhh. Enough said. I think I know where this is going."

He shook his head, the pain of losing his girlfriend evident. "Alas, Leila was infuriated. As was I, you understand. So infuriated, I summoned the most horrific of all curses in my ire. It was better this way. Better that Burt could no longer hurt not just mere mortals, but my beloved. Yet, now see what I have done. You are doomed to an eternity with a man you did not wish for. Though, I see the pretty man's eyes as he watches you, and there are emotions you shall soon address. I see emotions in you, too, madam. Powerful. Painful. Emotions *you* must address . . ." He spoke the last words low, as though he was a soothsayer sharing a secret.

Tears stung Jeannie's eyes at Nekaar's uncanny insight. "I have lots of things to address. What I don't have is a clue about how to be a genie."

His finger whipped into the air in an excited gesture, the pain in his eyes now replaced with a glitter of excitement. "*This* I can fix! You have no control over your magic, nor do you have any idea the ways of the djinn, as it was thrust upon you rather than given as a gift. But I promise you, in return for my egregious error, I shall be your guide. I will teach you all there is to know about the genie lifestyle. Until then, I beg your forgiveness with a thousand deep regrets."

"Any ideas on who would want to steal the bottle, and how it ended up at the party I was catering? Someone who was maybe in cahoots with Burt?"

His bald head moved in definitive motion. "I know not, madam. I know only that Burt's bottle turned up missing a week ago when I did my weekly bottle cleaning. But fear not, I shall search the veils high and low to find the scoundrel who brought this disaster upon you!"

"Why didn't whoever stole the bottle just open it themselves and let Burt out?"

"Because, madam, I must remind you of djinn law. When one leaves the bottle, another unfortunate soul must replace him."

Right. Djinn law. "So that more than likely means that the person who got me to open the bottle was in this thing with Burt?" Damn, if only she could remember who that person was. Yay, short-term memory.

Nekaar's nod was solemn, as if the very idea there could be someone as dirty as Burt out there pained him. "It is quite possibly so."

"Why would this person who helped Burt, be at the party I was catering? Do genies live here"—she looked around her kitchen with suspicion—"on this plane?"

"They do, indeed, madam. If they are inclined to mischief, a party with the rich and indulgent is certainly appealing for one such heathen. We are simple in our lifestyle, madam. Not all of us require the toys you humans so treasure. And as I have stated, we are not allowed to wish for personal gain. Some djinn find this intolerable after a taste of life on this plane. Thus, they must earn their play-things much in the way you do. Or like Burt, they, as you say, sponge off the kindness of others."

"So whipping up a flat screen is like totally off the table?" she joked, squeezing his arm.

Nekaar finally let slip a chuckle, and Jeannie found it was pleas-ant to her ears. "Without question, madam."

Hopelessness welled in the pit of her stomach again. "Isn't there anyone we can appeal to about this curse? You know, like the High Priestess of Magic Makers or the Grand Poo-Bah of Djinn? Surely there's someone who can overrule a huge mistake like this? Maybe pardon me? Parole? Community service? Something?"

Nekaar paused in thought. "There is, of course, a ruler of our realm, and would that we appeal to him."

She slapped her hand on the table and smiled at him. "That's good news, Nekaar! How do we find him? Does he Facebook, too? Tweet, maybe?"

Nekaar's face fell. "No, madam. Yet, even if he did, it would bring you naught."

Naught. Nay. Nada. *Nyet*. Nine. If she only had a hundred bucks for every time she'd heard the word *no* in the past two days. "Why is everything *no* with you people? I mean it's always, no, Jeannie, you can't break your mystical bond with Sloan or someone gets dead. No, Jeannie. You're right; you don't look so hot in your genie uniform. No, Jeannie. You can't grant endless wishes because the djinn say that's impossible. No, no, no. Don't you think whoever the big guy is in your world would want to do something about me? I'm out—of—control here. I just got a whole store full of women pregnant. I got a *man* pregnant. I'm like the special ops, ninja genie. I'm clearly a burden to your society—so why is the answer no?"

Nekaar put a finger on his phone and dragged it toward them. He clicked the screen on and pointed to its face. "This is why, madam."

Jeannie read yet another Facebook post, pausing before nodding in defeat. Of course.

She let her head fall to her arms on the table.

Oh, woe was the life of this djinn.

She tucked her chin into her palms, her next words muffled when she addressed the Facebook post. "Kidnapped?"

"It is so, madam. Our Grand Poo-Bah, our great leader of the Realm has been absconded with."

So much shiny.

AFTER her chat with Nekaar, his promise to teach her how to fix the damage she'd done at the bridal store and the burger joint, and Darnell, Wanda, and Casey's Surprise, You're Expecting reconnaissance mission, they'd all gone to bed heavy of heart and with no answers.

As she lay in bed, Mat in the living room with Benito and Boris, and Sloan on her bedroom floor, and after the devastating revelation from Nekaar, she made an impulsive choice. One she didn't allow herself to think about for long before she said, "Sloan?" Jeannie leaned over the side of her bed, placing her cheek on the edge and straining to see his sharp features in the dark. Then she closed her eyes.

"Jeannie?"

"Will you have sex with me?"

His silence made her want to spork her eyes out in humiliation. She'd summoned up the courage to just blurt it out, and he was staring at her as if she'd just asked him to do the closest thing to death.

Her world had narrowed even more today. It was time to take control of something, namely, how attracted she was to Sloan. Hesitant, but still attracted.

"I don't think you're ready for this jelly," he quipped, smiling at her from the floor.

She ignored his Beyoncé joke. "So will you?"

"Are you going to hurl dollar bills at me next?"

"Forget it." She flopped back on the mattress, her cheeks hot.

Sloan's head shot up. He peered at her over the edge of her bed, his blue eyes twinkling. "Hold on there, pardner. Where is this coming from?"

It was coming from her long-ignored hormones. "I'm not sure."

His eyes narrowed in twinkling suspicion. "Oh, you're sure, Jeannie. Don't bullshit the bullshitter."

"Okay. I know where it's coming from. Does my knowing where it's coming from really make a difference?"

He flicked her fingers playfully. "Yep. It does."

She pulled the covers over her head. "Why?"

"Because it does. So talk or I walk." Sloan poked his head beneath the comforter and pointed to the door by way of threat.

Jeannie uncovered her head, though her eyes still couldn't meet his. "This is a very uncomfortable conversation for me to have. You don't need to know my motives to have sex with me, do you?" Were motives all the rage in one-night stands? She'd always thought there was only one. Sex.

"This is an uncomfortable conversation for *you*?" Sloan scratched his head. "Huh. You just propositioned me and *you're* uncomfortable?"

Her face was getting redder by the second. "I figured you wouldn't be offended. You do it all the time, and I'm sure there are plenty of bold blondes out there who've propositioned you. Turnabout and all."

He paused for a moment, giving her a thoughtful look. "This is about my being pretty, right?" Sloan let out a mocking dramatic sigh. "I know, I know. I'm irresistible, charming, fun, fun, fun, but I'm not just pretty, you know," he teased, tracing the tip of her nose with his finger, making her shiver.

"I know that." She did. He had a job as something or other of marketing at Pack, yada, yada, yada. He was smart *and* pretty. Point taken.

"So then, answer the question. Where is this coming from?" he drilled.

Jeannie shook her head. "Why does this have to be so deep? Why don't you just answer my question and stay out of my psyche?"

"Because I'm not that kind of guy."

Jeannie rolled her eyes at him and flicked his knuckles. "Oh, you are, too. You're exactly that guy. That's why I asked you. Or did you forget Tootsie Pop?"

He chuckled and leaned closer to her, their lips but inches apart, his warm breath fanning her face. "It's *Lollipop*, and I didn't have sex with her. Not once." He said it with such conviction it was as if he'd placed his hand on a Bible.

"Oh, but there have been plenty of others by your own admission. Did you ask them where their motivations lay?"

He grinned all white and pretty. "Nope."

How unfair. "So why are mine so important?"

"Do you want me to list the reasons?"

Jeannie's eyes widened. Did she? "Yeah. Yeah, I do."

"Let me count them." He held up three fingers and ticked them off. "Nina, Marty, Wanda. That's just for starters. Add in Casey, Darnell, Heath, Clayton, Greg, and Keegan and we have a red carpet of reasons."

She let out an exasperated sigh. "They don't have to know. We'll be quiet. Er, won't we? I mean, is sex with you a loud affair? Never mind. We can keep it on the down low. Do you tell them about every encounter you have? Because if you do, that's just creepy and we can call this a no-go."

Sloan's expression went from light and playful to ultraserious. "No. No, I don't. Which is why they think I still have them."

Jeannie's eyes purposely widened again, this time in mock shame. "You don't have sex with random women anymore? The stripper community weeps."

"I don't have sex period."

She snorted so hard, it hurt her throat. "That was a joke, right?"

"No. It wasn't a joke at all. I've been celibate for almost a year."

How convenient. "Because?"

He smiled again, all Cheshire cat–like. "I'll show you mine if you show me yours."

Jeannie's shoulders sagged back into the pillow in defeat. She wanted to stomp her feet in two-year-old protest. Instead she slapped her comforter. "You've just ruined everything."

"How do you figure?" He ran his finger down the length of her nose, making her limbs warm and so buttery Jeannie had to remember she was angry with him for suddenly being celibate.

"Because you're the only man I've been in close proximity to in several years that I'm semi-comfortable with—you have all your teeth—and you bang your gong at regular intervals without looking back. All that no-regrets thing. You remember, right? The thing I so admired about you? *Still* admire about you, but everyone else seems to hate?"

"Aha! So what you're saying is I'm an easy mark because I played the field."

"Yes!" She jabbed a finger into the air to punctuate her point. "And let's not be coy. They named the field after you. And now you've ruined everything. How dare you be celibate, Sloan Flaherty." She shook her finger at him. "I feel like you did this just to spite me." Or maybe he was just lying to keep from hurting her feelings . . . God, that would suck. If she couldn't get the man who'd sleep with Satan to sleep with her, she might as well just forget foraging the veils for her hunky genie soul mate.

But Sloan interrupted her thoughts with a very serious statement. "I did it because my life needed to change."

"Why?" Why did it need to change when she needed it not to change?

"I'm not answering why until you answer why. You brought the dirty up first. You tell me why you suddenly want to have sex when, if I get even a little too close to you, you all but run away from me. Talk or forget it."

She was just going to be honest. He didn't need to know the whys and wherefores, just that they were. "Sometimes when I'm caught off guard, I panic a little. More importantly, intimacy is difficult for me, really difficult for me. But I've worked long and hard to get it together and—and . . ."

He folded his arms under his chin and shot her a playful smile. "I guess you haven't worked hard enough."

"What?"

"A one-night stand does not intimacy make, Jeannie. It's meaningless, and I don't have meaningless sex anymore."

"That's so unfair."

"I didn't make that choice just to piss you off. I made it for a reason, and I made it long before I met you."

"I'm still considering it was just to spite me. I just thought . . ."

He gave her a knowing smile, the muscles of his biceps flexing when he shook his finger at her. "I know what you thought. You thought, because I was a real chick hustler, I'd require very little of you when I was done banging my gong. No fuss, no muss. Then you could run right back to the cave you hide in that keeps you from having a relationship."

B-I-N-G-O. "Yes!" Yes, yes, *yessss.*

"Well, guess what, Jeannie Carlyle? Not gonna happen. It's obvious you have issues with intimacy. You have clear issues with men in general, judging by the way you cringe if I so much as brush against you when you don't see it coming. And FYI, I hate it. I want to annihilate whoever made you feel like this. It's keeping you from a lot of pretty great things. But guess what else? No can do. If you don't want to share with me what made you so afraid, if you think I'm somehow unworthy of your trust, you're not gettin' a piece of this." He slapped his ass, sharp and jarring. His delicious, hard, tight, encased-in-boxer-briefs ass.

"Is it because I'm not blonde?"

"It's because I want making love to you to count."

Jeannie's breath caught in her throat and her stomach tingled. "So you've thought about it?" His honesty made her feel less like she was a desperate Sloan groupie and more like she was on equal footing with him.

Sloan nodded his dark head, reaching for her fingers. "Oh, you bet your sweet genie ass. I've thought about it every night since I met you."

"Which is all of two nights."

"That's a lot in One-night Stand-ville," he teased, his breath fanning her face.

Her throat began to constrict. Fear. Effin' fear controlled everything she did, said, thought. But she just couldn't. Not yet . . . "I can't talk about it, Sloan. I just can't."

"And I can't be your one-night stand," he drawled with finality.

She stuck her tongue out at him. "You so suck right now."

Sloan caught the tip of it and chuckled, the gesture somehow intimate. "Back atcha."

"I can't believe you went and got morals. Did you shop online for them?"

"I can't believe you went and forgot yours."

"Maybe I never had them."

"Maybe you're a liar."

"I chose you because I thought it would be uncomplicated, and I could trust you to be gentle with me."

His eyes narrowed and his jaw clenched. "Oh, you *can* trust me to be gentle with you. I'd never hurt you, Jeannie. *Never*. I'm going to assume the animal that did this to you really did some number on you, but I'm not an animal, despite my origins. I'm also unavailable for one night."

"Would you consider two if I like it?" Her grin was mischievous even if her bravado was shaky.

"Two's still closer to one than I'd like. And make no mistake, Jeannie. You'll like it."

She shivered in response to his confident words, tucking her chin to the bed to keep its trembling hidden. "I can't know that unless you let me try it out for myself," she taunted, letting herself run her fingers over his forearm.

He caught them and brought them to his lips, whispering a kiss over her fingertips. A hot, promising kiss. "Or unless you tell me what happened to you, and we work through it—together."

She just didn't understand. "You hardly know me. Why is what you think happened to me so important to you?"

"I don't know." His eyes pierced hers for a moment, and she was suddenly grateful it was dark in the room. "I just know that's how it has to be with you, or it can't be at all."

"How definitive."

Sloan smiled, obviously pleased with himself. "Yeah."

"So are you proud of yourself for turning temptation down?"

"I'll probably be in the shower later regretting that I turned temptation down, but for now, I'm feeling pretty good about it."

"I feel like an idiot."

"How long did it take you to work up the courage to ask?"

"Does the time frame matter?"

"Not really."

"It was a little impulsive on my part. In fact, it was a lot impulsive. I don't typically make decisions without thinking them through a hundred times over. So thanks for crushing my first attempt at impulsivity," she teased.

But Sloan's expression was serious. "I'm not asking you that to humiliate you, Jeannie. I'm asking because I want to know how long it took for you to be comfortable enough to do it."

She didn't know if she'd ever be totally comfortable in an intimate setting or requesting intimacy, but semi-comfortable wouldn't upset her. Yet, even though she'd been turned down, she wanted to pat herself on the back and call her therapist to tell her she'd finally taken a chance. "Comfortable? Nothing about this rejection is comfortable."

He shook his head again, his luscious lips pursed. "I'm not rejecting you. I'm *requiring* you to give me something more of yourself. If and when we make love, Jeannie, I want you to enjoy every nasty, dirty, sweaty, hot moment of it, and I want you to do it because you want something more than just some relief from a long stretch of lonesome. I'm not a guinea pig. I'm a man who's interested in making love to a woman. A woman who wants more than just a dip of her frightened toes back in the intimacy pool only to yank them out if the water gets too rough. I want a woman who wants to explore something deeper. You're that woman. If you decide you want to join me in a venture like that—I won't be far away."

Her heart raced at his words. Words she was inclined to

believe and she couldn't quite figure why they were so believable, coming from a player like Sloan. "I don't want anything serious, Sloan. I *can't* get involved. I just wanted to attempt to reenter a world I haven't dabbled in for a long time with someone I've come to like. Someone who isn't or wasn't afraid to be honest about who he is . . . Uh, was."

He cupped her jaw, making her want to curl her cheek into his warm palm. "Can't or won't, Jeannie?"

"Maybe a little of both."

He brushed her hair from her eyes with a tender finger. "This is killing me, you know."

"Saying no to sex?"

Sloan laughed, but it wasn't the warm chuckle it had been ten minutes ago. "No. What's killing me is that you've equated an intimate relationship with the loss of your independence—like you lose you or something. Don't ask me how I know that's what freaks you out. I just do. You seem to think that somehow, if you become involved with anyone, they'll take everything away from you and make it theirs. That it'll be something you can't ever get back. That's not how deep, equal relationships are. At least from what I'm told—or what I've seen with Marty and Keegan. You saw it, too. They had a little power struggle over OOPS, but Marty asserted herself and told my bossy brother he couldn't have what was hers. He realized he'd gone too far and overstepped into a place Marty's damn protective of and backed off. His temper flared and he spoke irrationally. She checked it. They worked it out. End of. That's what I've observed as healthy."

Her next admission was brutally honest, and the first time she'd shared her feelings with anyone other than when she was in therapy. "I'm not as afraid of you as I am of me."

"Care to explain? Or is that asking too much again?"

Her lips trembled and her heart crashed in her chest, but she was determined to just spit it out. "I'm afraid that thing most women have, the thing that keeps them from losing themselves entirely to someone, is something I don't have. The thing Marty has. She told Keegan no without an ounce of fear. And to me that said she's secure about her place in his life, but even more, she's secure with herself. I don't have that alarm bell that says, 'No. You can't take this from me. It's mine. Live with it.' In light of that, I'd almost rather be a one-night stand than become involved." She swallowed hard when he leaned back and glanced at her with obvious confusion.

"Then we both have our lines in the sand, don't we?"

She shot Sloan a tentative smile. "Couldn't we blur them a little?"

"Not this time. Go big or go home."

"You're a stupidhead."

"You're a beautiful woman with a dilemma."

"I could have just lied to you to get you into bed, had wild, uninhibited sex with you, and given you the I'll-call-you-in-the-morning routine. You know that game, right?"

He winked. "Oh, I know that game. I owned that game, which is why I'd have never fallen for it. You can't pull that with me because I'm the master—you're nothing but a noob to this rodeo. Know why I know that?"

Her chest rose up and down with laughter. "Werewolves can read souls, too?"

"No, ex-shitheads like me can read when someone's lying like you. You'd have failed miserably. Not to mention, there'd be no getting away from me even if you did have regrets. Or have you forgotten we're a magical genie couple."

There was that. It was why she'd asked in the first place. Because being near him all the damn time had awakened sparks of desire she hoped to fan into a flame. "I haven't forgotten."

Sloan dropped a light kiss on her cheek. "Then clearly you didn't think this through to the end. Oh, and do me a favor? The next time you want to sleep with me—look me in the eye and ask me. When you can look me in the eye and tell me you want me as much as I want you is when I might reconsider." He dropped back to the floor and sighed. The rustle of the covers below her was a signal he was preparing to sleep, and suddenly, their conversation was over.

And to think she'd opened up a brand-new package of flannel pajamas for this nonevent. Her last-minute plans to woo Sloan to her bed of iniquity had made her do it.

Still, she smiled.

She'd done it. She'd propositioned a man all by herself and he'd said no.

Yay, healing.

CHAPTER 10

"So where are we?" Sloan asked from beneath a clear, cold November night sky. He eyed the glass front of the door with discreet silver etching.

"We're at the Jeannie-needs-therapy store. A place where she can forget that the king genie, and probably the only man on the planet who can help us, has been nabbed." Oh, and that Sloan wouldn't sleep with her. He'd probably sleep with a zombie—just not if that zombie was her.

The next morning and afternoon had been filled with Nekaar's unsuccessful attempts to help her control her magic and teach Mat how to fly and become invisible. He'd brought the *Djinn Book of Magic* or something like that, complete with laws and bylaws and more laws. A book that also contained spells she'd have to learn, curses she should avoid, and even a section devoted to choosing the right harem pants for your frame. It was harder than studying for the SATs.

They'd begun with small things like wishing her dead plants back to life. According to Nekaar, she should be able to harness her magic and keep it in control.

Jeannie had told him to tell that to the jungle she'd created in her bedroom, complete with a palm tree. Her fingers didn't allow her to keep anything in the air for more than a couple of seconds before it broke or grew flapping wings. And when she'd attempted to curse her—as Nekaar called it—fashion-apocalypse wardrobe and change it to something cute and flirty, it caught fire.

Mat hadn't fared any better with flying. He could only top three miles an hour, according to the speedometer attached to him, and getting him started was on par with attaching jumper cables to a dead battery.

He chugged and sputtered, hacked phlegm-filled coughs, left trails of dust, and could only stay in the air for less than a minute. And forget invisibility. He was as invisible as an elephant in the room.

There was lots of lavender smoke, a whole lot of swearing, and the end result? She sucked at being a genie and her sidekick magic carpet really was brokeback. Nekaar had assured her it was just practice, and after more lessons, both she and Mat would excel at their new skill set, but Jeannie had her doubts. If she didn't get control of this madness soon, for sure she was going to minimally create the apocalypse.

The long day had finally taken its toll on her and she needed to walk, not just to take care of business, but to let off some steam and fight her damn caged-tiger demons. Risking someone might make an errant wish while she was in public troubled her, but Nekaar assured her he would hover from his realm and protect any innocent bystanders by creating a spell that shielded her from granting a single wish.

But that spell would only last for a couple of hours, he informed her; making haste was advised. Yet, Jeannie had no choice but to do what she planned to do next.

Jeannie yanked the door to the store open with determination, trudging in with Sloan in tow. Soft music played, adding to the atmosphere of the seductively dim lighting.

His eyebrow rose when his eyes instantly went to the worst possible display. "Dildos?"

She grabbed aimlessly at a package that read, THE CRIPPLER II. "You have an aversion to sparklies? Or is it the color pink?"

Sloan looked confused. "No. I just . . ."

"You just what? Thought that ugly girls don't like to wear pretty lingerie or masturbate?" Oh! Oh, yes. She'd said it. Anything to keep her cover.

He leaned into her, his whisper silky and hot, his body big and radiating the sort of warmth that almost made her purr. "No. I just thought purple was more in your color wheel." He looked at the display and grabbed The Crippler II in purple.

Okay. He won this round of lewd and lascivious.

Putting his hands on her shoulders and pulling her flush to him, Sloan eyed the racks of lacy underwear, row upon row of lingerie in pastels, and bras with fuzzy marabou on them. "I like," he said, with a smile in his voice.

She waved a dismissive hand up at him and ran her fingers over an ivory camisole like she cared what kind of fabric it was made of. "And to think I so worried you'd rather be at the army-navy store."

His smile was deliciously amused when she turned and pulled from his embrace. "So you're into this kind of stuff?"

Jeannie gave him an uncomfortable shrug. "Sort of." Total lie. She couldn't remember the last time she'd bought anything but Hanes underwear. The ones that didn't give you a wedgie were some of her personal favorites. This stuff was all too revealing and much more suited to someone who had far more confidence than she ever would.

But she'd needed to get Sloan away from her house, and somewhere she could call Fullbright at a location where Sloan's big wolfie ears couldn't hear her do it—yet still manage to be in their accepted range of coupledom.

How she'd explain Fullbright when he showed up with guns blazing was a whole other problem she couldn't dwell on. But he had to be kept informed. If Victor was on the hunt again, the hell he'd hurt more people while she was still alive to prevent it. If he was looking for her, he was looking for all of them.

She grabbed a bunch of whatever lacey item was in front of her and turned to Sloan, who was watching her intently. Her face was red. She just knew it. After last night's conversation, looking at lingerie made it appear as though she were baiting him.

But she knew the dressing rooms here, and they'd afford her just the privacy she'd need to make her call. So let Sloan think what he wanted. "I'll be right back. I'm going to go try these on. I think I can get into the dressing room and still manage to be within our range. You chick watch, okay? Or better still, imagine this"—she held up a teeny tiny scrap of silk—"on a hot blonde. Dream away, lover. I'll be right back."

He slid his big body into a chair in front of a set of mirrors and smiled again. Clearly, a store of this nature was like homecoming to him. "You bet."

Thankfully, the dressing rooms were quiet. She knew about them because she'd been here before on a lunchtime shopping trip with Betzi, filled with humiliating demonstrations involving dildos that bent like a Gumby doll. One even sang to you . . . Trudging to a dressing room door, Jeannie let the saleswoman unlock it for her, ignoring her reflection in the door's mirror. Old jeans with holes at the knees and an ugly, lumpy black down jacket looked painfully out of place in a store with all these beautiful things.

She closed the door behind her and sat down on the bench provided, dropping the pile of multicolored fluff on the floor to dig around in her jacket pocket while she sent up a mental order for Nekaar, wherever he was in his realm, to keep his genie mouth shut about the phone call she was going to place. She had a disposable cell and Fullbright's number memorized, but it was the first time in five years she'd had to make a call to him. Maybe he'd quit.

That would be okay by her. He was cranky and curt. She imagined it was in the effort to not become too attached to any one assignee. Sometimes they ended up dead. After a while, that could wear on you.

But Fullbright didn't have even an ounce of happy in him. He was all business, all the time.

"Fullbright," he barked in her ear.

"It's . . . Jeannie," she whispered, cupping the phone.

"What's wrong?"

She gulped, catching a glimpse of herself in the long mirror. Nekaar had worked his magic on her face and her swollen eye in order for her to see properly, but her hair needed brushing, and she noted her clothing choice again. Instead of wearing something that flattered her figure, everything she wore swallowed her curves up. As she'd watched Wanda and Marty, so pretty and put-together, she was reminded of a time when she'd cared about her appearance.

But for twelve years it had been about flying under the radar and keeping her low profile. Doing that meant not standing out.

"Jeannie?" Fullbright snapped with impatience.

She refocused. "He found me."

"Victor's resurfaced?"

She heard the surprise in his voice. "In a big way. He clobbered me." She didn't need to mince words with him. He liked everyone much better if they kept to minimal chatter.

"When?"

Panic warred with reason. She'd kept telling herself that due to the fact that Sloan had to be with her all the time, Victor couldn't possibly hurt her again. Sloan was a werewolf—a big, badass one who had the gift of eternal life, at that. But Victor was nothing if not resourceful. He'd caught Sloan off guard once. Why couldn't he do it again? She wouldn't jeopardize the man who'd selflessly saved her from bottle doomage. "Yesterday afternoon. He's going to kill me."

"We'll move you. I'll have a team there in twenty minutes. Where are you?"

"No!" she yelled, then coughed to hide the rise of her voice. "Please don't. Please. I have a life now. A business . . ." *Oh, and I'm a genie now, too, BTW . . . I can make magics and stuffs. Bad magics, but magics nonetheless.*

His sigh was grating. Fullbright didn't cotton to babies. "You won't have anything if he gets his hands on you again. How the hell did you get away from that maniac?"

She dragged a hand through her hair. "He'd been drinking—he was unsteady. I take karate." Lies and more lies. But she was between a rock and a hard place. If she didn't tell Fullbright Victor had found her, more innocent people could end up dead. Victor had a long hit list. She might be at the top of it, but there were others . . . Others she couldn't bear to feel responsible for if something happened to them.

Yet, telling Fullbright was exposing the very people who had, from the start, set out to protect her, minimal questions asked. What would happen to them if Fullbright found out who and *what* they were? Or for that matter, what she was now, too. Fullbright would investigate—interrogate every one of them in an effort to find Victor. She wouldn't allow it, and she wouldn't compromise their paranormal lifestyle.

Jesus, this was all such a mess. She was taught at all costs to never expose herself, but by doing that, she was risking giving Sloan and the others up.

"I've got you on my radar. Meet me outside in five."

"No! Wait. I need you to listen to me. I have . . . a . . . boyfriend now!" Yeah. That's what she had. Referring to Sloan in that manner made her cheeks blush and her knees weak. "He's shopping with me, and I haven't told him anything because, you know, that breaks every rule you ever taught me. So we have to be discreet." And not stray too far from my ball and chain, but still keep him out of hearing distance.

She rubbed a weary hand over her eyes. Jesus. Being a genie on the lam was stressful.

His laugh was gruff and cutting. She could just imagine him letting his squarely cropped head fall back on his shoulders with a derisive laugh. "A boyfriend, huh? 'Bout time."

Right. Because snaring a man was what this life was all about. "Look, I have an idea. You knock on the store window and I'll come outside. I'll tell him you're a client."

"Can't take a chance the *boyfriend'll* see me." He said the word *boyfriend* like it was dirty.

Her lips thinned. "Then wear a hat or something. Just do it. You don't want me to blow my cover, do you?"

"Five minutes," he warned and ended their conversation.

"Jeannie?" Sloan called. "How's it goin' in there?" His question sounded skeptical to her ears.

The hairs on the back of her neck rose. Reaching down, she clanged the hangers together. "Pretty good. I think I found a couple of things I like." Gathering some of the items, she jammed the cell into her jacket in order to yank the memory card and flush it down the toilet later, then let herself out of the dressing room.

She looked past Sloan and over his shoulder to see Fullbright was already there. Shit. *Think, Jeannie. You know how to rock the improv.*

Holding up a couple of the nighties, she unceremoniously dropped them in Sloan's lap and then pointed to the store's window. "Oh, look! It's one of my clients! Be a peach, and hang on to those, would you? A couple of those flimsy things are one-of-a-kind items, and I don't want them snatched out from under my nose by some blonde with better hair. Guard them with your life, fine warrior, while I go say hello, okay? But wait here. It's a little awkward being in the"— she lowered her voice—"store of dirty with a man. You know? He's a repeat client—gotta schmooze."

No sooner was Sloan turning around to see what she was talking about than she was opening the door and running right into Fullbright.

He thumbed over his wide, grimly clad shoulder. "That him?"

"Yes. My boy . . . friend. Boyfriend." The word was so stilted and awkward she had to hope Fullbright didn't notice with his trained ear.

"Shake my hand," she ordered, peering over her shoulder at a very curious Sloan. She smiled up at Fullbright and muttered, fighting to keep it together, "Victor knows everything about me. He knows I've been taking karate. He said he knows where I live."

Fullbright took her hand in his cold, dry one and squeezed it limply for show. "We've gotta move you, Jeannie. You know the rules. To stay in the program, you gotta act fast. Besides, if we don't, Victor will kill—"

His words were drowned out by the sound of shattering glass, screaming women, and Sloan—with a pair of emerald green panties still clinging to the collar of his leather jacket—all up in Fullbright's space as they sprawled to the ground in a pile of struggling limbs.

Beautiful.

"I said I was sorry, okay? I heard the word *kill* and reacted like all good bonded-to-a-woman men do. I was trying not to eavesdrop, but werewolf ears and all. How was I supposed to know he wasn't the guy who mugged you the other day?" Sloan had hauled a limp, dangling Fullbright over his shoulder and taken him to the end of the street, where they now hid in the shadows.

"Because I said he was a client. That's how." Jeannie rolled her eyes and brushed shattered glass from an unconscious Fullbright's face. He was covered in scratches. This had turned into a disaster. He'd make her relocate now, and if she wouldn't, he'd threaten her with those stupid papers she'd signed.

Sloan knelt down beside her. "He's no client, Jeannie," he said low and deep. She didn't love his tone. It screamed liar. While that was true—it wasn't something she enjoyed or did out of malice.

She did it to survive.

Sloan's face hovered close to hers, the dark evening playing shadows over his face. A face that was now hard with condemnation. "I heard him say Victor. *Victor* was our mugger, wasn't he, Jeannie?"

The insinuation in Sloan's voice cut her to the quick. No matter how deserved. "I don't know what you're talking about." Surely Nina had told the others of her suspicions. The clock was ticking on her ruse.

"Yeah, you do, midget." Nina's voice rasped from the sidewalk, making Jeannie jump. She took two long steps toward them—long, angry steps. "That ain't the dude I saw with you yesterday," she confirmed, her lips thin in irritation. "So who the fuck is he?"

"He's a *client*," she insisted, though it was weak and pathetic. All this subterfuge had become too much *Mission Impossible* for her.

Nina slapped her hand against the side of the brick building, the sound resonating in Jeannie's ears. "Oh, the fuck you say. Listen, you two go hash this shit out, and I'll wait for princess here to wake up so nobody loots him. Then I'll erase his memory. But I'm tellin' you now, kiddo—we can only put out so many fires before you fucking set one too big for us to catch. Some shit's goin' on, and it has nothing to do with being a genie. I can smell it, and I wanna know what it is. If you don't give it up by the time I get back to your place, I'm gonna squeeze it outta your short ass, yo. Now bounce," she ordered, pointing to the street.

Nina upset with her was, for some unexplained reason, like a dagger in her genie heart. She reached out a hand to touch Nina's arm. "Nina. Please don't be angry—"

"I said go the fuck home!" She shook Jeannie off with a grunt.

Oh, this was so *Old Yeller*.

She let her head hang low as though Nina had slapped her. From hooded eyes, Jeannie glanced at Sloan, who was still just as cute seriously pissed off as he was when he was just a smiling womanizer.

He clapped Nina on the back. "Appreciate it. See you back at Jeannie's." He began to walk toward the street, Jeannie stumbling behind him.

"Could you walk slower?" she gasped, her feet tangling.

"Could you lie less?"

"I'm not—" She cut herself off. She was tired of defending herself. What truly sucked about this whole thing was even though she lied to protect, she was always going to play the part of the bad guy unless she let the cat out of the bag.

She clamped her mouth shut and began a light jog in order to keep up with Sloan. When they rounded the corner to her house, he stopped short, making her ram into his back.

She huffed, trying to fill her lungs with air. Bending at the waist, Jeannie took deep breaths. "You're just gonna have to wait for the weaker sex or risk breaking our bond. I need to catch my breath."

Sloan bent at the waist, too, and cupped her chin, his breathing even but for the flare of his nostrils. "Wanna tell me what's going on before that pack of women gets ahold of you? You stand a better chance if I have your back than you do on your own."

Closing her eyes, Jeannie battled tears. "Nothing's going on. I'm tired and I'm a genie who's taken wish granting to a new low. That's all it is. So, leave me the eff alone already."

Instead of reacting with the kind of anger she deserved, Sloan pulled her up by her hand, pushing the stray strands of hair from her face with tender fingers that made her shiver. His eyes held concern. Concern she just couldn't bear. Concern she definitely didn't deserve. It was all she could do not to lean into him and soak up the comfort he offered. "We have to learn to trust each other, Jeannie. Who knows how long this could go on."

Her eyes avoided his. "I trust you."

"Ah. But I don't trust you," he replied, pushing her against the back of the railing leading to her brownstone's steps.

"I understand. Trust takes time."

"Apparently not for you."

"I don't have a lot of choice. I have to choose to trust someone in all this. Tag, you're it by default."

"I don't have a choice, either," he answered stiffly, lifting her jaw so she either had to close her eyes or look at him directly.

She gave him a cocky, knowing smile. "Are you sad because today is TGIF? Is that what this is about? Would a blonde make it better? I know. We could always go barhopping. I can wait at a discreet distance if you wanna hit the Grease Your Pole and hang out with Lollipop or maybe even Twizzler. I'll close my eyes. I'll drink while you watch them grease. I love Fuzzy Navels."

Leaning even farther in, he eyeballed her, the lines on either side of his mouth deeply grooved with discontent. "Jesus Christ, would you lay off the funny? I don't want a blonde, Jeannie," he ground out, wrapping an arm around her waist and hauling her so close her spine arched.

"Then what *do* you want?" she yelped in frustration, stomping her feet childishly as she pressed her hands to the bands of steel that were his forearms. Frustration created by his nearness. Frustration created by the comfort his nearness brought—and the damn consistent tremor of her heart.

She'd experienced it whenever he was near, but it had been nothing compared to this. He smelled so good. He looked so good. He felt so good. Their lengths molded together like this made her dizzy. She wanted to cling to him, burrow against him and just let go.

Sloan's heart pounded, too, crashing against her chest. She heard it invade her ears, soar through her nerve endings, and make her blood pulse hot. Felt it throb in harsh beats.

His lips descended on hers before she had the chance to even consider her deeply rooted fears about such close contact with a man.

And it was delicious. Demanding. Probing. Hard and soft. Jeannie sighed into his mouth before she could stop it.

His stance widened as he enveloped her smaller frame with his strong arms, her thighs pressed to his before they were cradled between his legs, hard and flexing, rippling against hers until she thought she'd pass out from the bliss of it.

Jeannie's lips moved beneath his, relishing the fresh scent of his breath and the slick slide of his tongue delving between her lips. A moan slipped from her mouth when he hissed his appreciation. Their tongues dueled with one another's, gliding, tentatively touching before sweeping into scorching oblivion.

Hot, wet heat swept over her, making her nipples hard, hard enough to scrape against the fabric of her thick coat. She squirmed against Sloan, inhaling every inch of him.

Sloan's hands slid under the ends of her jacket, pulling her closer, devouring her lips as he pressed into her, ground his hips against hers in an agonizing rhythm. And Jeannie responded completely unafraid, wanton and wickedly needy.

It had been a long time. A long, long time since she'd enjoyed a man's touch, and every nerve in her body responded to the sweet heat Sloan evoked in her. Her arms went around his neck.

She luxuriated in the stretch of her muscles when she closed the final distance between them, pulling Sloan tightly to her. She drove her hands into his hair, clutching the silky strands, gasping when his hand touched the flesh just under her sweater.

Oh, this kiss. Oh, this man kissing her. She wanted to take this moment and freeze it. Freeze it so she'd always remember what it was like to want someone this much without fear.

Sloan hiked her leg around his waist, pulling her, drawing her deeper into the vortex of his kiss. Naked images flashed before her eyes. Hot, sweaty, dirty images of Sloan. In her bed.

In her.

A dog's sharp bark piercing the night had them pulling apart and readjusting Jeannie's jacket with hasty hands. "Yoda! Hush," a woman ordered, then chuckled as she strolled past them with a small, snarling dog. "Young love. Grand. So grand," she chirped her appreciation and waved at them.

Love. Jeannie looked down at her feet and gulped.

Sloan tipped her chin up, his blue eyes flashing all sorts of emotions Jeannie didn't know how to read. His jaw pulsed and his teeth were clenched.

"Jeannie Carlyle!" Nina hollered from out of the dark, making them pull apart in guilt. When she came into view, her nostrils were flaring. "Get the fuck upstairs now before I drag you up by your flippin' hair!" she roared, flashing her fangs at Jeannie.

"Hey! What the hell, vampire?" Sloan yelled back at her, pushing Jeannie behind him, the protective gesture making her smile. But only briefly.

Because Nina was angry. Like, wow, looked downright murderous angry, and she wasn't calling her *shawty* or *midget* or *kiddo*. She'd used her given name. Jeannie's stomach sank.

"You, shut the fuck up, ass sniffer. You're gonna wanna hear what I have to say." Nina stomped up the steps, the sound of her work boots sharp in Jeannie's ears. *"Now, Jeannie!"* she bellowed.

She didn't even think twice. Nina ordering you to do something was like getting a personal visit from God. You didn't ask why he'd stopped in. You just dropped everything because he had. She ran up the steps, ignoring the confusion on Sloan's face.

When she flew into her living room, everyone was staring at her, and it wasn't because she was having a fabulous hair day. The stares were a mixture of condemnation and confusion. The looks on their faces, faces she'd in such a short time grown to want approval from, broke her, stabbed at her very soul.

Nina was the first to speak or yell, depending on how good your hearing was. "Who in the ever lovin' fuck are you, Jeannie Carlyle?"

Her chest tightened, constricting her breathing, and her legs went all butter soft.

"And don't you give me that wide-eyed asshat bullshit. Because if you say, 'I don't know what you mean, MWA,' I'll beat your genie ass until you bleed!"

Wanda stepped in front of Nina while Marty put a hand on her friend's shoulder from behind. "Stop it. Stop it now, Nina!" When she looked Jeannie in the eye, Jeannie shrank. In those eyes was betrayal. Anger. Hot anger. Her tone was cool and no longer held the nurturing warmth of just hours ago. "I suggest you spill, Jeannie—or we'll leave you to your own devices if we have to take you out to save Sloan. Got that?"

"What the hell is wrong with you three women?" Sloan snapped at them, putting an arm around Jeannie's waist to shield her. "What's going on?"

Nina opened her mouth again, but Darnell clamped a hand over it and shook his head, his eyes, too, full of bitter disappointment.

Marty spoke now, her voice raw and full of crystal-clear displeasure. "Nina went through Jeannie's alleged client's phone before she erased his memory. To cover all the bases, you know? He texted someone about Jeannie and the text had nothing to do with catering."

Sloan's head cocked in her direction, but then Jeannie looked away. On top of everyone else, she couldn't bear to have Sloan's eyes look on her with disappointment, too. "What *did* it have to do with, Marty?"

Marty's eyebrow rose in disdain. "The man called her his informant—said she was in trouble and they might have to pull her out."

Nina ripped Darnell's beefy hand from her lips and came at Jeannie with fists balled. "You're a fucking snitch? *Who the hell are you?*" With each word Nina screamed at her, she drew closer to Jeannie, menacing, threatening, until Jeannie couldn't breathe from one more second filled with lies.

"Wait! Please. Please, just wait!" she cried, putting her hands up to protect her face. "It's true. I'm not really Jeannie Carlyle! I mean, I am, but I'm not. It was a name that was given to me."

Nina instantly retreated, but her presence was no less intimidating. "Given to you? You mean like a fucking code name?"

Immediately, Jeannie's hands clasped together, knotting into a fist of worry and tension. Her thick jacket stuck to her, perspiration gluing it to her neck. "I didn't want to lie. I swear it, Nina—all of you. But I've been doing it for so long. I mean, I've been Jeannie for so long, I don't know any other way."

Wanda's cold expression shifted only a little. "What are you lying about besides your name? You have five minutes and then we end this."

Sloan intervened with a hand up, his next words tight with tension. "Ease off, Wanda. Let's at least hear what she has to say."

"I'm sorry, but the program teaches you to . . ." Jeannie bowed her head, the tears she'd tried to keep from falling, slipping down her face in humiliation. "Stay hidden at all costs. Don't draw attention to yourself. Blend, blend, blend." She'd blended so well, everything about her old self was almost nonexistent. Drab and gray like her wardrobe.

Darnell, bless his sweet soul, took pity on her. "Why did you have to blend, Miss Jeannie?"

The jig was up, and even if it wasn't, she was tired. Tired of hiding. Tired of lying. Bone-deep tired. If Victor was going to kill her, then bring it on. She'd lost enough because of his sick, twisted mind.

She might go down, but it wouldn't be without a fight, and it wouldn't be without telling the truth to these people who'd welcomed her like she was one of their own with open arms.

Head bent, she whispered, "I have to blend because I'm part of the Witness Protection Program."

CHAPTER
II

"I yelled at you," Nina stated, her face so full of anger ten minutes ago, now held the Nina brand of remorse. Still defiant but with a dash of apologetic.

"It was loud," Jeannie agreed before blowing her nose.

Nina poked her arm, but it was done with a gentle finger. "You made me fucking yell. You should have just told us from the beginning."

"Guilty, MWA." The sounds of Wanda and Marty making tea for her in her kitchen soothed her. Mat, snoring softly by her feet, brought comfort, too. The bubble of fear in her chest had dissipated some and eased in size. Now all that remained was the explanation.

Nina sat on the couch beside her, nudging her knee. "I'm sorry."

Jeannie's mouth fell open. "Shut up?" she retorted in disbelief.

Nina grabbed her hand from her lap and massaged her stiff fingers. "Don't gift horse this bullshit. Just accept and live to fight another day."

Jeannie squeezed Nina's fingers back in gratitude. "Done."

Wanda breezed in, teapot and cups on one of her serving trays. Her old smile was back again—warm and kind, a relief for sure.

Jeannie had the feeling that it wasn't Nina you had to worry about when the shit went down. She let you know she was angry. Her anger oozed like an open sore. It was Wanda who was the force to be reckoned with. Nina's anger was a living entity—all out in the open and loud. But Wanda's kind of anger simmered quietly—condemned without saying a word, and it probably stung the most in the end.

When she was finally able to look at Wanda, Jeannie said, "I'm sorry I lied."

Wanda shook a finger at her before reaching for the teapot and pouring it into a mug. "No, no. No apologies. Please. My behavior was abominable. We're very protective of our kind, and when we think someone might not be on the up-and-up with us, we get hinky. Me especially so. We're suspicious by nature. We have to be. So, I'm the one who's sorry, Jeannie. Now that I understand, you'll never know how sorry I am."

Marty nodded, flopping down in the armchair and pulling a blanket over her lap. "Me, too, Jeannie. It's like Wanda said, we're a little defensive. We had a recent experience that left us cautious about just how easily we can be exposed."

"And I picked the scab off the wound. I'm sorry."

Darnell crossed the room, his big lumbering body oddly lighter than air. He stood before her and opened his arms without saying a word.

Jeannie rose and let him envelop her, pressing her cheek to his bulky chest, ignoring the big gold medallion that dug into her chapped cheek. Darnell was like milk and cookies. Meat loaf and macaroni and cheese. Comfort food. "I'm sorry, Miss Jeannie. I knew somethin' wasn't right 'bout you being bad." He gave her a final squeeze and set her back between Sloan and Nina on the couch.

"I checked your story," Nina commented, her words tinted with sadness.

Jeannie's hackles rose again. If anyone found out she'd given up her cover, they'd set her free and there'd be no protection from Victor. Eventually, everyone would have to go home, and that left just her and Victor. "How?" she asked on a gulp.

Nina's face was grim. "My brother-in-law. Name's Sam, mated to my sister, Phoebe, and he's the reason we're so cagey about being exposed. Sam's ex-FBI, but we didn't know it until it was almost too late. Long story, but shit with him is good now. So, you don't have to worry about anyone knowing he was poking around. He has more connections than the A train. All on the QT. He said you're telling the truth."

Yet Jeannie found little comfort in that. She gripped Nina's hand. "You're sure? If the bureau finds out I had a run-in with Victor, and I didn't report it, they'll cut me off and leave me with no protection at all." She clenched a fist as panic began to resurge in a harsh wave of her reality.

Nina gripped her hand tighter, her eyes hard and determined. "Swear it. No fucking way will anyone know." Then her eyes grew soft and encouraging. "So you wanna talk about this shit? I hear it makes you feel better. Or have you had enough in your government-facilitated therapy sessions?"

One of her worst fears was that she'd be exposed for the coward she was. But to expose herself in front of a ninja warrior like Nina was like getting naked in front of a perfect-ten body.

And yet, they'd stuck close to her these last few days. They'd protected her—defended her—coddled her. The truth was the least they deserved from her. "My real name is Charlotte Gorman or Charlie was what I preferred . . ."

"Before you go on, Jeannie, we know what happened from Sam. Some very basic details anyway. If this is too painful, we don't want you to feel like you have to rehash it, okay? We only inquired in order to be aware and keep everyone involved safe," Wanda said, handing her a steaming mug of tea and then running a gentle hand over Jeannie's mussed hair in a soothing gesture.

Shame washed over her. Shame and remorse so thick she could cut it with a knife. "So you know about Victor?"

Sloan leaned into her and reached for her hand, caressing it with pressure-free fingers. "You're tired. Why don't you sleep on it? It's been a long day, and she's wrung out, ladies. Is this really necessary?" he pressed, glaring at Nina.

Jeannie squeezed his hand in return, but shook her head. "Because I've slept on it for twelve years and never said a single word to anyone. I've spent twelve years in therapy and in my head going over and over what I could have done differently. I just can't hide anymore. I don't want to hide anymore . . ."

Marty sat up and reached across the coffee table to grasp Jeannie's knee, her hand warm and strong. "You have us. You don't have to hide anymore, Jeannie. Or would you rather we call you Charlie?"

The sob that escaped her throat was raw and held years' and years' worth of pent-up fear. "I just want to be called free."

Sloan's arm tightened around her. His calming strength helped her to find the courage to finally just say it.

"I was young when I got involved with Victor. Twenty-three. But that's not really a good enough excuse. Stupid is the only answer I have to offer, and in light of what happened, youth as an explanation is weak at best."

"But who isn't stupid at twenty-three?" Nina asked in her defense. "Like two fucking people in the world, and they're practicing Tibetan monks, I bet."

Jeannie wanted to laugh at Nina's attempt to ease her fears, but her throat was too tight. Yes. She'd been twenty-three, and Victor had been the answer to all her girlish dreams. "Victor Alejandro Lopez was charming and gorgeous, dark and sultry. And he had an accent, so incredibly compelling to someone like me. I was small town and kind of sheltered as a kid—had no huge ambitions of my own when I graduated high school. But in our house, you earned your keep if you chose not to attend college. So I decided to work at a bank until a career inspiration struck. Victor played me from the second he met me. I was the teller who opened his account for him. An account that was, of course, a total front for the . . . things he did . . ."

"He was handsome, I bet," Wanda said, holding Jeannie's hand, warming it with her own.

Jeannie shuddered. "He was very handsome—and older. Unlike any of the boys I'd ever dated. He was sexy and worldly and he wore crisp suits. He was nothing like this South Dakota girl had ever seen, unless you counted TV and movies."

Marty's blonde head nodded in understanding. "And he wooed you with all the things only a mysterious stranger can woo you with. It wasn't like dating some awkward boy from the country, right?"

Her smile was bitter at the recollection. "Right. He took me to nice restaurants and we even went on trips to Mexico. Flew first class. Lots of luxuries. I didn't know what the trips were really for. I swear, I didn't know. It wasn't even that I didn't want to know. I just didn't. I didn't have even a clue about the world outside South Dakota. I certainly had no idea Victor was on the FBI's most-wanted list. I just knew he made me feel good. He told me I was beautiful all the time. That I considered what he said was true should show you just how besotted I was with him." She'd really thought she was something back then—until she wasn't.

"No, Jeannie. You're the only one who thinks that's untrue," Wanda whispered, her eyes shimmering with tears. "You let him teach you to believe he was the only one who saw your beauty, but that's just not the way the rest of the world views you."

It didn't matter now. Now everything about her had changed, even her appearance. "But he could be cruel, too. He wasn't physically abusive until the end . . . But looking back, there were moments of verbal abuse I chalked up to stress because he had me convinced he was some investment banker who was responsible for truckloads of other people's money. My friends, after the awe of his fancy car picking me up from work wore off, told me that, too. They pointed out how controlling and possessive he really was. I just didn't listen. I dubbed them jealous and small town, because I was living the princess dream we'd all stayed up late at night giggling about when we were teenagers."

"So he isolated you, didn't the motherfucker?" Nina seethed, tightening the strings of her hoodie around her face and wrapping them around her index finger. "He enforced the fact that your friends were just jealous bitches because you had something they'd always wanted, and then he convinced you they were fucking trying to come between you. He picked them off one by one so you eventually had no one but him. You and him against the shitty-bad world, right?" she spat, the tension in her body palpable.

Jeannie nodded; the memory of those conversations sprang to life again with a painful knot forming in her stomach to go along with them. "He convinced me that he was the only person I could truly count on. I *let* him convince me. I did whatever Victor said whenever he said it."

And she had. Because if she hadn't exactly known where she was going on a path to a career back then, there was one thing she did know—she wanted what Victor offered. A big house. A big minivan filled with their children. A big bunch of bullshit.

"I married him," she confessed, more tears pushing beneath her eyelids, hot and salty with regret. God, it was all so sick. "My mother hated the idea. She hated Victor, hated that he was almost fifteen years older than me, but she never had any solid reasons why she hated him. She'd just say there was something about him . . . I thought she was angry that I was moving away. My dad had died four years before, and she was lonely." Jeannie paused and gulped at the memory of her mother's face when she'd told her she'd never support her daughter marrying filth.

"She didn't come to the wedding." Damn. That still hurt even though her mother had been right. "We moved to Mexico. I left everything and everyone behind and skipped off to my beautiful, rich life where I was going to raise Victor's babies and drive a big, fully loaded SUV."

Jesus Christ forgive her, but those were the things she had thought about. Not trust and devotion. Not compatibility. Not anything but the passion Victor stirred in her and the life he could give her with his riches.

"How long were you married before you found out what he was really doing?" Sloan asked, his lips thin. "What *was* he really doing, Jeannie?"

Jeannie paused, gathering her words so they'd come out coherently instead of in gulping sobs. "I was married to him for six months before I found out Victor was a drug dealer. A big drug dealer—lord—whatever they call them, with a cartel and all the trimmings. Then I found out he was on the FBI's most-wanted list. They were just never able to nail him down until me. I told them everything because everyone else was too afraid. Even when they caught him red-handed, no one would talk." All of Mexico was afraid of Victor. She should have been smart enough to be afraid of Victor.

The hiss of silence singed her heavy conscience. "I swear I didn't know. I believed him when he said he was an investor, and his brothers, who were always skulking somewhere, were his employees. His bank account sure said he did something big. But then, after he . . . After the mess with the FBI, I found out he had all sorts of fake businesses and letterheads, and bank account numbers. He was always on the phone making some deal in Spanish. Now that I look back, he mostly spoke Spanish on the phone. I took French in high school . . ." *Lame defense. So weak, Jeannie.*

"You don't have to explain why you didn't know, honey," Wanda soothed. "We believe you when you say you had no clue. What ended up getting him caught?"

Pain invaded her limbs, acute, gnawing pain while more hot tears fell from her cheeks to land in guilty puddles on her lap. *Go big or go home, Jeannie,* a voice taunted. "I walked in on him and Jorge . . . Jorge was nine . . . He was one of Victor's drug mules." Nine and so innocent—so willing—to do whatever he could to help his family.

The visual of little Jorge, his trusting face looking up to the man he thought was going to save him from poverty, made her stomach heave. "I was supposed to be out shopping, but I didn't feel well, so I went home early, and that's how I found them together . . ."

Wanda's arms went around her waist, her face contorted in pain. "Dear God—he didn't . . . Please say he didn't. I can't bear it."

Jeannie's head shook in Victor's defense. Probably because it was the only heinous thing he hadn't done. "No. He didn't do what you're thinking. But he did violate them. Victor had a doctor implant the children with his drugs. I guess because they were the least likely suspects, and hiding them, however they got them over the border, was easier. He used women, too. Breast implants filled with heroin. Some girls, teenagers really, would have three or four pair inserted then taken out in as little as a year's time, and all to get across the border to what they thought was the freedom Victor promised them."

They all sat in astonished silence until Jeannie summoned the will to finish her tale. "When I caught him with Jorge, at first I thought what you thought, Wanda. So I hid and listened. They were speaking Spanish, so it was fuzzy. Though, by then I'd picked up a little of the language, and it was enough to know Victor was doing something illegal. I finally got the big picture when I saw him show Jorge the packets of drugs next to the piles and piles of money I'm assuming he'd promised little Jorge. I admit I was naïve, but I knew drugs when I saw them. But Victor sold dreams. Jorge's family, like most of the people he drew into his web, bought into the dream."

"Jesus, that motherfucker! I should have killed him when I had the chance," Nina muttered.

Sloan tensed next to her, and Jeannie guessed it was because he never had the chance to have at Victor. "If he ever comes near you again, I'll kill the bastard," he growled.

"There's more?" Wanda prompted softly.

There was more. The worst of it was yet to come. The problem was just getting her tight throat to let the words loose.

Jeannie closed her eyes and recounted the horror she relived almost every night. "So, I didn't tell Victor I was home, and I waited until Jorge was on his way out the door. I told him to run as far away as he could and go to the nearest police station, explain what Victor had done to him. And that's where it began. The plan was to get away from him as fast as I could and tell the authorities, but . . . He caught me calling home," she said, her voice hoarse, her nerves raw.

Wanda reached out and squeezed her hand. "So you confronted him, threatened to tell the police?"

Jeannie's fingers tightened on the ends of her sweater, twisting them. "I did and it's something I've regretted every day of my life since. If I had just shut my big mouth and made him think I was going to go along with it . . ." One stupid choice. Just one, and it had ruined so many lives.

She took a deep, shuddering breath. "When I finally understood exactly what was going on and the true horror of it was staring me in the face, yes. I reacted. Now, looking back, it was just foolish. Ridiculously foolish. I didn't think. I didn't even consider, in all my youthful arrogance, that Victor would be able to stop me. I knew nothing about drug cartels and blackmail and everything else he was involved in. I'm from a small town in South Dakota where the most exciting thing that happens is when someone discovers roadkill." Her laughter was acidic and bitter. "I don't even remember being afraid when I told him I was going to the police. I just remember thinking he had to be stopped. How's that for moron?"

"You were so young, Jeannie . . ." Wanda sympathized.

"It's no excuse!" She shouted her stupidity into the room so everyone would know what a fool she was. There was no excuse for thinking she could just threaten Victor with tattling on him like she was simply telling the teacher he'd pulled her hair.

The rage of that insane notion, that one misguided choice that had left seven people dead, still had the ability to consume every cell in her body. It made her quiver, ache, and fight to quell the urge to crawl out of her skin.

Charlie Gormon from Nowhereville, South Dakota, who'd once thought her life was boring and staid, had been a foolish, impressionable, immature idiot.

When Victor was done with her, her life had been anything but boring.

"By the time I was done being 'so young' and making foolish choices," she spat sourly, "seven people were dead."

WANDA didn't say anything. Instead, she put a hand on Jeannie's shoulder and squeezed it in comfort.

Sloan was so filled with rage—so hot to bash this Victor's head in—he almost couldn't think. What had happened to Jeannie explained so much. That it had happened at all made him want to take her somewhere where she'd never be frightened again. He wanted to shelter her—protect her—and the emotion scared the shit out of him.

As Jeannie continued, he had to war with himself to stay seated and not yank Nina's cell from her hands, call Sam, and demand he tell him where this bastard Victor was.

"Anyway, after he caught me, it's a bit of a blur. Victor had one of his emotionally stunted goons of a brother tie me up and handcuff me to a bed in the basement of his house. After all this time, I still don't know why he kept me alive. I guess it was so he could terrorize me—toy with me. He said he was beating me because he loved me, and that I'd made him do it. He said it was because I belonged to him, and when he was done, I'd never forget it.

"The FBI tells me it was just asserting more control over me. Victor had far more control over me than I ever realized. He told me how to dress. He told me what to do, what to eat, what to wear. He had people watching me all the time. They went everywhere with me. He convinced me it was because he was so rich and powerful and with those riches and power came enemies, and I didn't even realize it was all bullshit until it was too late. The FBI says it's kind of a conditioning, because in his sick, twisted mind, I was his possession, and he couldn't stand to lose me."

"But you got out?" Marty encouraged, pulling the throw blanket up under her chin with a shiver.

Jeannie's face distorted. "I got out. But not before a lot of people were hurt and a little boy was brutally murdered. Because of me, he's dead. He was just trying to help me like he thought I'd helped him . . . God. The sight of that poor baby . . . will never, ever have less impact. It never goes away."

Sloan had to physically hang on to the couch to keep from rearing up and howling his fury—tearing something into small, angry pieces.

"Sweet Jesus," Darnell whispered.

"Jorge came back for you, didn't he?" Nina asked, her tone quiet.

Jeannie nodded, letting her head drop to her chest. "Yes. Yes, he came back. The FBI told me later that he told his parents what was going on, but they didn't believe him . . . What I didn't know was the FBI had been watching us for months, and when Jorge snuck in unnoticed, thinking he could untie me and help me escape, was the exact moment the FBI raided Victor's house. But Victor wasn't going down without a fight. He caught Jorge in the basement with me . . ." She sobbed, closing her eyes tight, as though that would block the horror. "I heard the chaos, the footsteps. Doors breaking. Windows smashing. I wanted to scream for help, but Victor told me not to scream. He said if I screamed for help, someone would die."

And Sloan was guessing he hadn't lied.

Jeannie dragged her knuckles over her wet eyes, making his gut ache. "Victor always kept his word," she whispered, her eyes wide with a terror Sloan couldn't bear. "He dragged us out of the basement at gunpoint. I could hardly see because my eyes were almost swollen shut. I didn't see the signal from the FBI agent, or I swear I would have protected Jorge," she rasped. "All I saw was a gun—a big gun—and I screamed to Jorge to run . . . I forgot. Jesus forgive me, I was so panicked—it was so hard to see anything, I forgot that Victor ordered me not to scream." There was no controlling her sobs. They ripped through her, wracking her chest visibly.

Sloan wanted to make it stop. He wanted to put his fingers to her mouth, to hush the painful memories, but he couldn't without letting on that he was interested in Jeannie and, thus, risk the wrath of the women. Jeannie needed another hassle like she needed a hole in her head. So he fought to stay still.

But Nina was there then, putting her arms around Jeannie and rocking her while tears streamed from Marty and Wanda's eyes, and Darnell gripped Sloan's shoulder.

She'd had so much bad, so many years of it haunting her. But saying it out loud didn't appear as though it had cleansed her one bit.

Rather, her pain was so physical, so palpable, it looked more like it was tearing her in two reliving it.

"Jorge, as well as our housekeeper Rosalita, an FBI agent, two of Victor's brothers, and two of the groundskeepers were killed in the shoot-out with Victor," she said into Nina's shoulder, inhaling a deep breath. "It was a massacre. I'll never forget the sound of that first bullet exploding from the barrel of a gun or the roar of helicopter blades circling overhead. The stench of gunpowder and death. And the screams. The terrifying screams."

"So Victor got away, and they put you in the Witness Protection Program to keep you safe," Sloan finished with tight words, his nostrils flaring.

She lifted her head and accepted a tissue from Sloan, who dabbed at her eyes with his thumb. "I was unconscious for a few days—or at least that's what the FBI told me. When I woke up, they offered me the program as part of my stoolie package. Truthfully, I wasn't much help. I really didn't know a lot about anything other than what I witnessed. But I knew Victor considered me a betrayal. He was always very big on honor and *familia*, as he called it." She snorted in irony. "I knew he'd kill me, if he could get his hands on me. He told me he would when he tied me up in that basement."

He couldn't take any more. As Jeannie finished out her story, he had to clench the arm of the couch to keep from ripping it the hell apart. This Victor would pay. He'd find him and make the fucker pay.

THE basement. That ugly, moldy room with peeling paint and nothing but a filthy bed.

It was where she'd derived her fear of the dark and of dirty sheets. She could still summon up the vile odor of her own sweat on those sheets, and it never failed to make her gag. "I don't remember a lot of what he did to me while I was in the basement. I was in and out of consciousness. My therapist calls that a blessing. I only know when I woke up, I wasn't Charlotte Gorman anymore. Not literally or physically."

Nina held up her phone, her face grim. "The text from Sam says you had three reconstructive surgeries. I shoulda killed the fuckwad that day. I should have chewed off his filthy limbs and buried him in my fucking backyard."

Jeannie's nod of acknowledgment was defeated. Three. Three had been the magic number. Victor had beaten her so badly that it had taken a team of government doctors to patch her up. He'd punctured her spleen, broken her arm and two of her toes, deflated one of her lungs, and changed her face forever, but worse, she'd lost the child she was carrying. She hadn't even told Victor yet; the pregnancy had been so new. "I look very different than the old Charlie. She was, in my estimation, much prettier. She always got lots of attention from the boys. Jeannie's nose is crooked and her left eye droops just a smidge more than her right. But she can still see out of it—which was a little touch and go for a time. That's something, right?"

"Oh, Jeannie," Wanda whispered, wiping her eyes. "I wish you could see what we see."

It was uncomfortable for her to talk about what she'd looked like before Victor. She'd wooed him with those good looks. In fact, she hadn't been that much different than Sloan. Okay, maybe she hadn't been as active as he was or had near the amount of partners he probably had, but she'd smiled and winked on more than one occasion to get what she'd wanted.

At times, since she'd met Sloan, she'd wondered if he would have been attracted to Charlie. Charlie had been right up his alley minus the height deficit.

"I lost a child, too," she whispered in hushed tones. "I was only ten weeks pregnant, but that was why I was so nauseous that day

I went home and found Victor with Jorge." She'd told herself it was for the best. What would hiding have done to a child? Yet, it still ached.

Wanda sucked in a long breath, her face hard. "I will kill him, you know. Without hesitation. I will pulverize the bastard."

Jeannie gulped. "It doesn't matter anymore. I am who I am *now*. Or that's what my therapist says. So they put me in the program, taught me all kinds of things, conditioned me for beginning again all alone. Made me come to terms with never seeing my family and friends again, not that I had any left anyway. Then they gave me a job here in New York at a restaurant. I worked as a waitress for a while. Then I managed a restaurant, and finally I decided to take the money I'd saved and start my own business. The rest you already know. There isn't much that's interesting about Jeannie Carlyle's life after that, and I like it that way."

"So where do you suppose we can find this Victor?" Sloan asked, his jaw clenched, the veins in his hands pulsing as he made a fist.

"Yeah," Nina crowed her agreement. "You didn't have us back when Victor was beating the shit out of you and killin' little kids. No fucking way he can get near you now that we're around. Especially with Sloan tied to your ass. He knows to look out for the motherfucker. We'll all just be at DEFCON Five."

Jeannie shook her head. "And what happens if Victor doesn't show back up or we can't find him, we finally find an answer to this crazy genie thing, and you all go home? I have to tell someone Victor's on the loose, or I lose my protection as part of the program. I have a business I worked hard to build. It's *all* I have. And there's more than just me to consider. I'm not the only person he wants dead. According to the FBI, he had a mole in his organization who disappeared after the big showdown. I don't know who it was, but he was the person who gave the FBI the final information on where I was located."

"Maybe I can find out from Sam who the stoolie was?" Nina offered.

Jeannie tightened her sweater around her. "The stoolie helped save my life. Does he deserve to die because I withheld new information? If I contact Fullbright again, that's whose memory Nina erased, I would put all of you in jeopardy because they'll want to investigate everyone who's been in contact with me. And Fullbright said they'd relocate me the second I said Victor's name. If I don't contact him, Victor's out there freestyling with a grudge list a mile long.

"I don't even know who's on the list. I just know there were more. Maybe some of his mules turned on him? God knows those poor women he mutilated should have lined up to hand over evidence on him. How fair is it that I get the chance to survive because you can erase memories, and I have vampires and werewolves to protect me, but no one else does? I can't take any more deaths on my conscience. I just can't."

"Here's something to ponder," Marty said, slipping to the end of the armchair. "Can genies die? Do they have a kryptonite like werewolves and vampires? Victor's chances just slimmed big-time if not."

Jeannie scrubbed her eyes with her knuckles. Confessions were exhausting and so was that book of djinn law. "I don't know, but when Nekaar gets back from wherever he's gone off to, to find out who kidnapped the Grand Poo-Bah of Genie-ville, I'll be sure to ask. In the meantime, my life span is insignificant at this point. I don't care what happens to me. It's those other people Victor wants dead who're mortals that worry me." She gnawed one of her nails. Everything just kept getting bigger and bigger. Badder and badder.

Wanda rose from her chair, her phone in hand. She gave Jeannie a quick hug before saying, "We won't let that happen, Jeannie. I promise you, Victor won't hurt anyone anymore. Not if I have to take him out myself. Just give me a little time."

Time.

She had plenty of that if the djinn law book was right.

But could she really afford to just carelessly throw around the time other people might not be granted if Victor found them?

Tick-tock.

CHAPTER
12

"Hey," Sloan called softly from her bathroom door, still sexy-damp from his shower. "You did it."

A floating candle almost crashed to the ground when she heard Sloan's voice. Jeannie nodded and smiled distractedly. She had, in fact, done two things, un-impregnated all those women and that poor man from the bridal shop, and made sure all those customers from the burger joint were out of hell for good. Yay, Nekaar and his skills. She'd also done this—made inanimate objects float. Not for long, but long enough to know it was possible. She could make things levitate all on her own. It wouldn't save the world, but she was becoming more genie by the second.

Lou Rawls crooned in soft tones in the background, caressing her ears. Her mother had loved Lou Rawls. Jeannie played his CDs often, and when she did, it was like her mother was right here with her, singing in the kitchen as she made dinner.

The big book of genies was on the bed, open to the page where, among other menial genie abilities, levitating items was detailed. It was a small feat, but it made her proud to have simply read the directions and performed the task.

Sloan crossed the room and stuck his finger in the air with a smile, his eyes taking in the rather romantic setting she'd created. "Pretty great."

Jeannie nodded, hoping that losing her focus wouldn't make the rest of the twenty or so candles she'd levitated fall. "Well, I'm sure it's not as amazeballs as shifting into a werewolf or scoring a super-blonde, but it's a start."

The room's soft glow, glittering with star shapes illuminated from the floating decorative tin holders, twirled through the air with kaleidoscope grace. Practicing what Nekaar had taught her brought her a small measure of peace. It gave her mind something to do while Wanda and the others looked into how to find Victor, and she waited to find out what happened next. She'd told them everything Victor had threatened her with. Confessed every detail she could remember about their conversation.

Now there was nothing to do but wait.

The shapes swirled above their heads, the flames flickering and dimming. "It's pretty, right? Not terribly useful for anything more than atmosphere, but a start. I just followed the directions and relaxed like Nekaar said to."

Sloan came to stand in front of her, a towel around his lean waist. She looked past him and right over his shoulder. The sight of his naked pecs and rippled abdomen made her mouth water and her legs quiver, but she would lose her concentration if she didn't ignore him.

Plus, she wasn't up for the torture of wondering what was going on under his towel. Since her admission the other night and tonight's confession, her confidence had shifted without warning.

Something in her had broken loose—she felt freer than she had in almost as long as she'd been part of the program. In the moment, talking about what Victor had done, what she'd been too blind to see had hurt as though it had happened just yesterday. But now, a few hours later, she'd found she was sick with relief to have no more secrets. Good or bad, it was all out there.

"Jeannie?" his low voice grumbled.

"Sloan?"

"Wanna have sex with me?"

Two of the candles she was floating with sheer will alone, waffled and tilted. Bouncing her finger, she righted them, still looking past Sloan. "It's the flannel pj's, right? Super-duper hot. Knew you couldn't resist. Who can resist pink with fluffy sheep?"

"It's your everything," he growled low, moving in closer to her, invading her space, sucking up her life force, making her want to throw herself at him and beg him to take her.

"Huh. Funny that. The other night my *everything* couldn't make you budge."

"Things change."

"Horny changes everything." She forgot about the candles and planted her hands on her hips. "Aren't you celibate? I wouldn't want you to break any vows you made with yourself because of me."

"I was just waiting for the right woman to come along to break it with."

"You do see with your special werewolf eyes, I'm neither blonde nor leggy, yes?"

"I see just fine with my special werewolf eyes, and I like what I see."

Sloan stepped closer and snaked an arm out to wrap around her waist, hauling her up tight to him. The rigid line of his shaft pressed to the space between her thighs, making her fight a gasp. "I asked a question."

Her arms dangled at her sides noncommittally despite her pounding heart and her racing pulse. She was afraid this was some kind of weird test she'd fail. "What changed your mind? Was it my pathetic tale of woe? Or did all the subterfuge and 007 stuff make you wild with desire? Men love spy stuff."

Sloan put his hand to the back of her head and drove his fingers into her hair, tilting her head back. "No more jokes," he ordered, gruffly.

Her eyebrow rose. "Totally not joking here. This was sudden and unexpected and, I think, after the not-so-subtle interrogation I got the other night from you, I deserve an answer."

Sloan's eyes penetrated hers, forcing her to connect gazes with him. "Because I know that tonight changed everything for you. You don't have to hide anymore. Hiding from Victor, keeping all those secrets kept you from investing in a relationship. You were afraid it would be taken away. It's easier not to take a chance. But no one's taking me anywhere. I know that. You know that, too. I also know you're ready. I can smell it. Now I want to taste it."

Her pulse pounded. She wanted him so much it hurt.

He lowered his mouth to hers until their lips were only inches apart. "Are you in or not?"

Jeannie's breath rasped. Was she in? Was all that new confidence she'd been thinking about just moments ago real or imagined?

The press of Sloan's hard chest, huffing in and out, mirroring her breaths, was maddening and delicious and frightening all at once. She wanted. God, she wanted.

It was all there for the taking if she just reached out.

In that brief moment, when indecision warred with need, her need won. Good, bad, or indifferent, she was ready to recognize that she was a healthy woman with healthy desires and Sloan was willing to look beyond her scars, and his love of blondes, and fulfill them.

And that was right and good. Wanting to make love with an attractive man was healthy.

"I'm in," she whispered, husky and breathy.

"Where's Mat?" he demanded, running his hands along the curve of her hips.

"In the living room with the twins."

And those were the last words either of them spoke before he was pulling her tighter to him, dragging his hands over her length, teasing her with his touch.

His mouth descended on hers, gentle at first until she wound her arms around his neck and demanded more. Flashes of white light flitted behind her eyelids when his tongue rasped over hers, tasting, touching, driving into her mouth.

Sloan's muscled limbs flexed and tensed when he scooped her up and carried her to the bed.

She kept her eyes closed tight when her back pressed into the mattress, afraid if she opened them and saw Sloan assessing her, she'd see distaste in his eyes and this magical moment would be ruined forever.

But Sloan's voice, thick and grumbling, demanded she open them. "Look at me, Jeannie. I want to know you know who I am."

A deep breath later, and she popped her eyes open. Sloan sat above her, gloriously hard and bronzed, a veritable Rodin sculpture of near perfection. His skin was still damp from his shower, small beads of water still clinging to the hair beneath his belly button. His chest was smooth and hard, his pecs developed but not overly so.

When he rose and let the towel slip from his waist, Jeannie shivered, and it wasn't due to anything other than lust. His cock was thick, jutting forward in clear desire, and it made her almost gasp a sharp intake of breath.

Her hands clenched at her sides, tightening until she was clinging to the sheets. Her eyes followed him when he sat at the edge of the bed, his breathing rapid and harsh.

When his lean fingers reached for the buttons on her pajama top, she stopped him, catching the look of hesitation that flashed in his blue eyes. "I'll do it," she whispered.

She needed to be the one to reveal the scars on her chest. They weren't pretty, though they had healed well. Her fingers trembled as she freed button after button, then let her pajama top fall open. She pointed to the cluster of tiny lines, white and rigid. "These are from the glass that exploded and sprayed us."

Sloan's hiss made her heart stop, but he hadn't hissed due to distaste. Instead, he leaned forward and traced, with light fingers, the lines that kept her from wearing a neckline lower than her collarbone. He explored them, smoothed them away.

"The doctors said I could have another plastic surgery to minimize them even more, but I was just so tired by then. Maybe someday—"

He pressed his fingers to her lips, his eyes searching hers, demanding she see him. "*I don't care, Jeannie.* I don't care about them. I only care that they caused pain."

A tear slipped from her eye, falling into the pillow beneath her head, and then Sloan was replacing his fingers with his lips, nipping at her mouth, tasting it.

The hot flesh of his skin pressed to her bare torso made her arch upward, seeking closer contact, melding to him until they were one endless loop of entwined limbs.

When his lips traveled from hers and moved along the column of her neck, grazing her scars, her heart stood still. They were scorching hot, gliding over her skin, leaving her needy. As his tongue tasted her nipple for the first time, she lifted off the bed, her hips rising. Her hands tugged at him, encouraging him to cover her body with his delicious weight—to press her so far into the mattress there'd be no beginning or end to their union.

When his cock brushed along the fabric of her pajama bottoms, Jeannie tensed, but Sloan licked her nipple with a long swipe, savoring the bud with a hum of appreciation, making her forget everything else.

Her hands went to his hair, burying them in the silky strands as he drew her nipple in and out of his hot, wet mouth. Her heart clamored as Sloan's fingers skimmed the top of her pajama bottoms, slipping over her flesh, teasing it until she moaned with need.

Jeannie's hands roamed at will, too, slipping over his broad back, tracing each set of muscles, relishing the feel of a man's skin beneath her fingertips. She found it was natural to wrap her thigh around his waist, encouraging him to grind against her.

His moan of pleasure slipped into the room, echoing in her ears, leaving her squirming beneath him. Sloan's lips slipped away from her breast. Moving over her ribs in slow increments, he consumed her flesh with wet kisses, trailing a path to the top of her pajama bottoms.

Jeannie's muscles tightened, tensing when Sloan's hot breath caressed her lower abdomen. She fought not to cry out as he moved the fabric lower, hooking his thumbs under the waistband and dragging the material down along her hips with an agonizingly slow rasp. He pushed the bottoms to her ankles and shoved them over her feet.

White-hot heat flushed her veins and her pulse raced when Sloan leaned forward and spread the lips of her sex. The moment stood still for her. Sloan gazing upon the most intimate part of her body made her shiver with delight. It was carnal and decadent, naughty and exciting, all rolled into one big package. The anticipation made her chest heave and her fingers clench her sheets into balls of fabric.

Jeannie's eyes flitted open for a brief moment to find Sloan held himself suspended over her, his nostrils flaring.

His eyes, deeply blue and darkened with something feral, connected with hers for mere seconds as though he were asking her a question.

And then Jeannie understood. She let her own eyes break contact and slide closed as she lifted her hips.

Sloan's growl was husky and thick in her ears. His hair brushed her thighs just before he dipped his head low and took a long swipe of her clit, lashing out at it with his tongue and circling the tight bud.

Jeannie fought a scream, the pleasure was so intense; she reached a hand out to clutch locks of his hair, tugging at them as he explored her needy flesh. She ached with want. Every nerve ending in her body screamed for more.

When he slid his finger into her, easing into her tight passage, she jolted. A hoarse cry stuck in her throat. She clenched her eyes tight as he stroked her with his finger, driving it into her as he licked the swollen bud of flesh. Lights flashed behind her eyelids, streaking colors of brilliance, making her head thrash against the pillow with the need for release.

As waves of sweet heat rose and fell, Jeannie fell further into the abyss, allowing herself to do nothing more than feel the stroke of Sloan's slick tongue and the drive of his finger within her.

Her release was so swift it took her by surprise. There was no warning, no subtle shift in pressure. Instead, it slammed into her, assaulting her with its intensity. She bolted upward to an almost half-sitting position and grasped Sloan's hair, biting her lip to keep from crying out. Her orgasm tore through her, clawing its way to her very depths, leaving a trail of white-hot residue in its wake.

Falling back on the bed, she heard the harsh intake of her breaths, short and choppy. Sloan slid up over her length, letting his hands roam across her skin, wiping away the beads of sweat that had gathered between her breasts with his kisses.

Jeannie clung to him, pressing her face into his neck when he spread her thighs and positioned himself between them. His cock, rigid and warm, brushed her clit enticingly, creating just enough friction to make her hot with need all over again.

He bracketed her face. "Look at me, Jeannie," he demanded as his chest drove against her with harsh intakes of breath.

Her eyes popped open to find him staring down at her. She searched his blue gaze, waiting.

Poised at her entry, Sloan didn't say another word. Instead, he hiked her thigh up over his hip and slipped into her, stretching her, filling her with his width until her breath left her lungs. He moved with ease, inching into her, using the slick wetness of her passage to guide him.

"Christ, Jeannie. So damn good," he murmured.

Jeannie's eyelids slipped closed again as her neck arched and she adjusted to Sloan's cock moving deep within her. It was delicious; the grind of his hips, the slap of their skin connecting with each thrust Sloan took, the pound of his heart in rhythmic time with hers.

And so it began again, that hot climb upward, that needy, desperate ache for fulfillment from deep within her belly.

Sloan's breath was hot on the shell of her ear, hot and uneven. He reached under her, cupping her ass, kneading the globe of flesh, pressing them closer together until the crisp hairs above the head of his cock scraped her clit. The friction was decadent, ratcheting her desire up yet another notch.

Sloan tensed above her, each muscle in his body hardening as he, too, fell deeper. His lips sought hers, hard and demanding. His tongue drove into her mouth and she savored the combination of his cock deep within her coupled with the skill of his kiss.

Again, there was no warning to the call of release. It drove into her hard and fast, making her hips lift in desperation when Sloan took a final thrust.

He gripped her flesh, driving upward into her with a low groan, the cords of his neck stretching and tensing, the grind of his hips swift.

Jeannie clung to his neck, driving her body against his, matching him thrust for thrust until she was almost dizzy.

Sloan slumped against her, his weight laden with his release. Their chests crashed together, their harsh breathing mingled.

Jeannie didn't move. She never wanted to move. What had just happened between them had been earth shattering for her in more ways than just their physical union.

She had made love to a man, and it had been good—so good. She didn't regret the choice to do it, and she almost didn't care if she turned out to be just another notch on Sloan's belt. Sure, it would hurt if his spiel about celibacy were all a lie.

But that was insignificant in comparison to the huge leap she'd just made.

A leap of control in her life.

A leap of faith that, if nothing else, she wouldn't lose anything by making love with Sloan. Rather, she'd gain yet another freedom—the freedom to choose to make love and take it for exactly what it had been.

A new level of physical connection she'd denied herself all these years because of fear.

Nothing more. Nothing less.

Sloan's finger trailed across her cheek. "Question?"

"Is it going to be the kind that has you shining a light in my eyes and telling me you have ways of making me talk?" she teased, snuggling under him, remorseful when he pulled out of her.

He chuckled and rolled to his side, pulling her with him. "Nope. But it's personal."

"Is there anything more personal than naked?"

"How long has it been since you've made love?"

She giggled. "I was rusty, right? I'm easily confused by slot A and tab B. I'll try harder."

His hand framed her cheek and his smile was warm. "It has nothing to do with rust or tabs."

Her eyes avoided his for a moment, and then she decided, no more hiding. Not even her sexual inexperience. "Back in the day, I wasn't much different than you. Well, I was more the kiddie version of you."

"Meaning?"

"Meaning, we're more alike than you think, and it's why I don't judge your vast and varied field of blondes. Before Victor, I wasn't above a little cleavage flashing or a coy smile to get what I wanted. I had a few not so serious boyfriends until I met him, all acquired with my beguiling charm."

"And since Victor?"

"A couple of years. And my last three attempts failed on almost all levels." There'd been a man or two who'd been willing to look past the boring clothes she wore and the colorless lifestyle she led.

"You know why they failed?"

"I can't wait to hear, Doc Sloan."

"You weren't free."

Her breathing hitched. *Yes.* Sloan got it, leading her to believe his celibacy had a reason behind it. It had been a long time since she'd been able to share what had happened to her in anything but a clinical setting where someone who was supposed to observe her and be impartial held court. It just wasn't the same as telling Marty, Nina, and Wanda—women who, to a degree, still lived out loud despite the fact that they, too, hid.

To keep the secrets she'd had to keep took more energy than she'd ever imagined. In fact, twelve years ago, had she known what it was like to have to stay hidden, to always have your guard up and monitor every little word that slipped from your lips, she might have just walked away from the program and let fate have its way. She'd been that desperate a time or two over the years.

But confession cleansed the soul.

"Yes. I feel freer than I have in a long time. I'm not running-arms-open-wide, *Sound of Music*–style just yet, because I have to always temper my freedom with caution, but that's part of the reason my attempts at romance or even close friends have failed. I viewed any physical contact as possession instead of simply seeing it for what it was or could be, if I let it. Two people enjoying each other."

His lips tightened. "Might I remind you, that wasn't only what this was about with us."

"Oh, you just say that now because you don't have a choice. You're stuck to me like gum on a shoe. Wait until you're free, and you have the opportunity to hit Club Greasy. Then we'll talk."

He shook his head with a teasing grin. "No. That's not why I say that, and I don't go to Grease Your Pole anymore. I say that because I want you to give this attraction between us the chance to maybe grow. I gave up celibacy for you tonight. That was big. You owe me more than just a phone call in the morning."

"So, a question for you?"

"Shoot."

"You clearly understand this defining-moment thing I had tonight. Why? And why the celibacy?"

His eyes held a faraway gleam. "Because of a stripper named Sable. She worked at the Pole with Lollipop. She was just a kid, and she was killed in a car accident. She started out here with big dreams, got roped into stripping to make ends meet. The girls at the Pole all told her not to do it, because she *was* just a kid. Most of the women at the Pole know how it goes when you tell everyone you'll only be stripping for a little while, until you can get on your feet. They've all been there. They're still there. They looked out for Sable, loved her, cared for her when her family wouldn't. Long story short, as I sat at her funeral, mostly attended by the men who'd watched her take her clothes off—including me—and the strippers from the club, something just clicked with me. I know you'll find the comparison strange, and werewolves have eternal life for the most part, but if something happened to me, I didn't want to end up with no one at my funeral but my drinking buddies who only care where the next six-pack of beer and a bucket of chicken wings is coming from, and a string of one-night stands who couldn't identify me in a lineup."

She tweaked his chest playfully. "Oh, surely Nina would come, if only just to call you *ass sniffer* one last time."

He barked a laugh, his hard chest rising and falling beneath her cheek. "My brother would come, too, and Marty. My pack members would come, but they wouldn't have come out of respect for me. They would have come out of respect for *Keegan*. There's a difference."

"So you were sort of looking for a purpose?"

"Yep. I had nothing deeper in my life than a bottle of Budweiser and a shallow blonde. I was restless and bored. It was time to change, make like a grown-up. So I eased off the booze, quit the blondes altogether, and focused on Pack. It was sort of a test to find out what I really wanted in life without my judgment so clouded by alcohol and partying."

"And you found what, Sloan Flaherty?"

He pressed a kiss to her lips before saying, "I found, Jeannie Carlyle, that for the first time since I became an adult, which was a long, long time ago, that I wanted someone to come home to every night. I wanted to know where I was going to bed each evening, and where and with whom I'd wake up. I started participating more with my family, though if you listened to Nina, you'd never know it. And I got serious about my career. One that was handed to me, I might add. I didn't have to scrape like Sable did to make ends meet. I got a paycheck whether I showed up or not. And that just wasn't okay. I lived on Easy Street, but Sable fought for everything she wanted, and she died working her ass off to get it. She was killed when she fell asleep at the wheel after a double at the Pole. That's what I found."

Her heart clenched and shuddered, her throat thick. "Wow, when you find, you really find."

"I'm nothing if not tenacious," he said on a chuckle.

Jeannie caught his hand in hers, her eyes moist with tears. "You helped me find something I never thought I'd find again, Sloan. But I want you to know, there are no strings attached here." Even if some small part of her would now always be Sloan's, it would be meta- phorical, and she was finding out, she had begun to recognize the difference.

"I like your strings, and I don't mind them being attached to mine at all. You'll learn to like them, too."

A strange shift occurred in her chest, one Jeannie imagined was more of her baggage yanking itself free from baggage claim. Sloan's possessive tone turned her on rather than frightened her like it might have even just as little as a month ago. "So then, we'll see, right?" The promise of anything else right now was too much to hope for. People said all kinds of things in dire situations. Men said all sorts of things in sexual situations . . .

"Oh, you'll see," he teased, planting a sensuous kiss on her lips. "And don't think I don't know what you're thinking. Because I do. You think I'm spinning some bullshit because we're in deep crap, and when two people are in deep crap together, they'll say anything."

"Oh, how do you do it, great and powerful Sloan?"

His laughter was deep and resonant, bouncing in her eardrum pressed to the wide span of his chest. "It's my hair gel. It has mind-reading properties."

Jeannie giggled, luxuriating in being safe and warm.

"Hey, look—the candles are still floating," Sloan remarked on a smile, tucking her closer and letting his chin rest on the top of her head. "I think that's a sign, Jeannie Carlyle."

"I'm sure it's a sign I'll be a huge hit at the next Bath and Body Works sale."

"More with the funny."

She shrugged, reluctant to look at him. "That's just who I am."

Sloan tipped her chin up, running his thumb over her chin. "Is it? Or is it who you became because of what happened to you?"

She shrugged, unsure how the wisecracking Jeannie had come to be. She just had. "It's the me that developed over time. When you have to leave everything behind forever, and you can't ever contact the people in your old life again, not even just to let them know you're okay, you either laugh or cry. I did cry. I cried a lot. So much. Everything happened so fast. There was no time for good-byes or anything. One day you exist—the next, you don't. But you can only cry for so long before you have to do something to survive. So I chose to stop crying—well, mostly—and find a way to come to terms with it. I started a new life here in New York, and I have Charlene, Betzi, and the twins, and it's mostly good."

Tracing the scars on her chest, Jeannie watched his jaw harden. "You do know I'll kill him, don't you? If he comes anywhere near you ever again, I'll kill the bastard."

Jeannie shivered, closing her eyes and praying Victor would be found before she had to reveal she knew she'd seen him. "He's been watching me. He knew so much about my life, Sloan."

"Well, now I'm watching you. And I'm watching for him, too. He'll never take anything from you again, Jeannie. *Never.*"

Never was a long time. She'd once been condemned to never.

But tonight, it didn't seem so bad.

CHAPTER
13

Jeannie woke to the sound of voices outside her door and Sloan gone from her bed. She ran a hand over the imprint he'd left on the pillow and smiled foolishly at the warmth that spread through her limbs before throwing her legs over the side of the bed, taking the sheet with her.

The voices grew louder, angrier, making her rush to press her ear to the door, the warmth in her limbs turning cold.

"You did the grown-up with her, didn't you, ass sniffer? Jesus, Sloan, is everything fucking fair game to you? Is there a single fucking thing you can leave untouched by your dick? Why are you always spoogein' all over anything that moves?" Nina yelled.

Jeannie didn't have to open the door to know Sloan's jaw had gone hard. "That's none of your business," was his cold reply.

Jeannie popped the door open to witness Wanda jam her finger in Nina's ear. "It's none of your business, Nina."

Nina gave her the finger with one hand and held Boris in the other. "The hell it's not, Wanda. I told you this shit was gonna happen. Every case we work on, somebody's always sexin'. It's a GD cliché, for fuck's sake. And we're supposed to be protecting our fucking stupid clients, not feeding them to the werewolf."

Sloan rocked back on his heels, glaring at Nina. "It isn't what you think, Nina."

She rolled her beautiful eyes. "Oh, it is, too, what the fuck I think, dicknuckle. And you made it my business by crankin' so loud it was like an amusement park ride. All screams and your hands up in the air, catching the wind of the humpty-hump." Nina poked Sloan in the chest. "I have vampire ears, Sloan. Kinda hard to avoid hearin' your oversexed ass, yo."

Wanda shook her head in staunch disapproval. "You promised me, Sloan Flaherty! *Promised me.* I thought even if you were a dirty bird, your word was good."

They'd made him give them their word that he wouldn't have sex with her? Okay, she'd give that she probably came off a little helpless, and, too, she probably oozed fragility, but Jeannie Carlyle was a big girl and she could make big-girl decisions.

Jeannie popped the bedroom door open entirely. Her eyes blazing, sheet trailing, she flew across the room, startling Benito from his dog bed. "Hey! Guess what? Adult here. Sloan didn't force me to do the 'grown-up' with him. *I* propped *him* to do the grown-up with me. So whaddya think about that?"

Wanda and Nina were stunned into silence, their eyes glued to Jeannie and the sheet she held tight to her chest.

Rolling her neck, she seethed, "That's right. I said it. I did something for me. Something healthy. Something I wanted to do, and I did it without fear, and I sure did it without looking back. Is that okay with you two—or should I get written permission for the next time? Because there will be a next time! So lay off the werewolf!" Jeannie's eyes widened. She'd just told anyone who would listen she'd had sex. Good sex.

Outrageously awesometastic sex.

And she'd clearly stated she wanted to do it again. Right in front of Sloan.

Okay. Maybe this empowerment thing made you a little mouthy and presumptuous. It was, after all, the morning after. Maybe Sloan had changed his mind.

Sloan dropped a light kiss on the top of her head and gave the girls a smug look. "What she said."

Nina's stunned expression turned into a grin. "Look at you, all ownin' yer lady parts again. Knuck it up with me, Slice." She held her fist forward for Jeannie to bump. "Proud to know ya, midget. Now, here's the paranormal crisis speech." She cracked her knuckles in preparation, then looked at Jeannie.

"So, you've known Sloan like three days. Intense time spent together in a major life crisis means huge adrenaline rush of out-of-control bullshit emotions. That means, you ain't readin' your personal shiz with a clear head. In a nutshell, let me repeat, emotions are running high. Common sense is at an all-time low. If he fucks you up, it's on you, 'cus we warned yer ass. In fact, I think we should have, like, an OOPS disclaimer for this kind of shit. Anyway, just don't think you're gonna fulfill your white-knight wishes and fucking happily-ever-after dreams with this numbnuts. But for now, ain't nuthin' wrong with takin' care a some girlie business. End speech."

"Nina should know," Marty crowed with a dry snort, twirling the end of a royal blue scarf tied fashionably around her neck. "Before Greg, she had more business than a pretzel stand in Central Park. Oh, and good on you, honey!" She gave Jeannie a hug, enveloping her in the scent of lilacs. "Way to own." She leaned in closer to Jeannie and whispered, "But what Nina said about Sloan . . ."

"Fuck you, blondie. Swear to Christ, you always got some shit to say, don't you, Virgin Marty?" Nina yelled at her friend, jabbing her finger under Marty's pert nose.

"Ladies!" Sloan yelled with a scowl, putting his body between Nina and Marty. "This is between me and Jeannie, and it isn't what you women think. I'd be happy to explain it to you—"

A loud whizzing noise stopped their arguing cold. Just as Jeannie's head swerved around to see where it was coming from, she was flattened to the floor by Mat. "Invisible!" he spat in an intense whisper as if just saying it made it so.

Jeannie groaned at his suction cup–like grip on her. "God, Mat. Could I get a little warning next time? These sneak attacks are going to leave me with a broken skull."

"Sorry, doll. I heard all the yellin', figured there was more trouble. I'm doin' my guardian bit."

She tucked a hand around him and gave him an affectionate stroke. "Sooo, still practicing?"

Mat coughed, his fringe blowing in Jeannie's face. "Whatever it takes to protect ya."

"Mat?" Sloan said, kneeling down on the floor near Jeannie.

"Eyeball candy?" he groused.

"Not invisible."

Mat moaned, his cigarette-smoky voice rippling through the room. "Jesus. Whaddo I gotta do? I read your damn genie book until my eyeballs rolled around in my head while you two were in there swappin' uglies. And still, I ain't gettin' it right. I don't think I was cut out for this guardian thing, dollface. I can hardly keep my eyes open long enough to read the damn directions anyway."

Jeannie patted him on his matted threads in sympathy. "It's okay. Guardians are crazy overrated any ol' way."

Sloan chuckled, peeling Mat off Jeannie and helping her up. He pulled her tight to his side, making her cheeks flush and her heart pound with the possessiveness of his embrace.

Jeannie looked at the three women and avoided Wanda's critical eye. "So, any news on Victor?" She was more hopeful this morning than she'd been last night. If anyone could find Victor, it was these three women.

Wanda's lips thinned and she sighed. "No. But I've been on the phone all morning with Sam, and I promise you, it won't be long until we find him. We've got a tentative list of the people the FBI suspects he'd go after, and we have plenty of backup watching from a safe distance from the werewolf-vampire community. We're not going anywhere until we catch the pig."

Nina crossed her arms over a T-shirt that read, Off Is the General Direction in Which You Would Fuck, and nodded. "You know thass right, midget."

Jeannie warmed from her toes to the top of her head. It felt so good to have someone on her side. Four someones, to be precise. Yet she couldn't help but experience some small sense of defeat—they really weren't any closer to finding solutions than they had been when this began. "So we're still on square one."

"Yep," Marty said on a smile, fluffing Jeannie's couch pillows, her multitude of bracelets jangling. "You're still stuck to Sloan. Your magic is still all kinds of haywire, and we still have to find that sleazy mothereffin', woman-beating, child killer, Victor. On the bright side, it's a beautiful crisp, sunny day. So while we wait for news on Victor, we've decided to let Nina get her vampire sleep, because she's long past due. Wanda and I are going to catch a sale at Macy's and grab some lunch. You should be safe with Sloan. And Darnell's always on call if you need backup. In the meantime, let's hope Nekaar shows up with some news on what's happened to the president of Djinn-ville."

Before she'd gone to bed last night, Jeannie had checked the Bottle Babes Facebook page again. There was now what amounted to the human Amber Alert out for the leader of the genie pack, and her hopes of figuring this out any time soon were dashed.

She'd offered to help Nekaar, but with Sloan tethered to her, Nekaar claimed she couldn't cross into the veil due to the fact that he wasn't djinn. Which was probably one of the weirdest things she'd ever heard.

Well, almost. To know there was another world somewhere but where she was standing awed and frightened her. It was just too much to take in right now. She could live with being tethered to Sloan. She couldn't live with the idea Victor was on the loose with a vengeance for blood.

Marty and Wanda gathered their coats and scarves while Nina scooped up the twins and told her friends to watch their backs before stomping off to the guest bedroom. For a moment, Jeannie envied their friendship. It was so easy and fluid, if at times noisy.

Marty brushed Jeannie's hair from her face with a gloved hand. "Go relax for a little while. And hey," she said on a smile, thumbing a finger at Sloan, "when we can get rid of your excess baggage, you really should shop with us. I can think of a million colors other than gray and black that are suited to your pretty complexion."

Wanda nodded her agreement, scooping up her purse and letting it slide to her elbow. "That'll be our reward when this is all over with. We'll shop, because I know deep down inside, our little Jeannie's a shopper," she teased.

Yeah, Jeannie, er, Charlie, had been a shopper. Once. "Deal," she chirped, touched by their offer.

Marty and Wanda swept out her door in a wave of perfume and laughter, leaving just her and Sloan.

He eyed her from across the room—dark and sultry.

"I Dream Of?" Nina howled from the guest bedroom.

"MWA?"

"I've been up all damn night, trying to find that fucker Victor. Swear to fucking God, if you two make a bunch of horny racket in there while I'm tryin' to sleep, I'll come and take you both out at once—and it'll be bloody. Big and bloody."

Jeannie put her hand over her mouth to keep from laughing out loud. "Aye-aye, captain."

Nina slammed the door, making the walls shake.

Sloan held out his hand to her. "Coffee?" he asked in a whisper, wiggling his eyebrows.

"I'm sure we should waste this precious alone time drinking coffee," she teased, suddenly uninhibited and wanton.

Sloan dragged her to him, kissing the tip of her nose while he molded her body to his. "Is there something else you had in mind, Ms. Carlyle?"

Her cheeks flushed at the rigid press of his cock to her thigh. Yet, today she felt flirty and sexy, emotions she'd forgotten existed in her. "There was."

"Like?"

"The toilet could use a good scrubbing. Oh, and I need to do laundry. How are you with delicates?"

Parting the sheet, he drove his hand between her legs and spread the delicate flesh of her sex, teasing her clit. "Oh, I'm magical when it comes to delicates."

Her head fell back on her shoulders, and Sloan took the opportunity to run his tongue along the column of her neck. "So, delicates, is it?" she gasped the question.

Sloan lifted her, wrapping her legs around his waist, his breath coming in harsh puffs as he walked back to her bedroom and kicked the door shut.

Her need for Sloan was instant, so intense she had to mentally war with her fingers to keep from tearing his clothes off. He'd paid such attention to detail with her last night, it was time she returned the favor.

With her eyes closed, she dropped the sheet.

Sloan's low moan of pleasure was all she needed to encourage her. She ran her hands over his shoulders before tugging at his sweater, lifting it over his head and throwing it to the floor. With trembling fingers, she yanked at his belt, unbuckling it and finding the button to his jeans. She flipped it open, then reached for his zipper. The sound of metal against fabric was harsh to her ears, making what she planned to do next very real.

Her hands pushed at his jeans before she lost her nerve, shoving them to his hips and over the thick muscles of his thighs down to his feet. Sloan kicked his shoes off, shoving them away along with his jeans before grasping her by her shoulders and lifting her to meet his eyes.

She gazed back into his. Sure. Unafraid.

The groan he let go was thick and husky, turning her limbs to butter. She wrapped her arms around his neck and pulled him in close for a long kiss. The delicious slide of his mouth meeting hers made her shiver as she allowed her body to mold to his.

The connection of flesh meeting flesh, hot and sweet, now had her groaning, too. His cock brushed the cleft of her sex, spearing her clit, swollen and aching.

She dragged her mouth from his, allowing him one last lick of her lips before sliding down his body to settle between his legs.

Sloan's hand reached for the top of her head. The hiss of sound he made when her breath grazed his cock spurred her on.

Her eyes admired the strength of his thighs, the dark sprinkle of hair covering them. She curved her arms around each one and leaned forward against his strong frame.

Sloan moaned in response, and when her tongue flicked out to taste the head of his cock, he bucked forward. Resting her head against his lower abdomen, Jeannie took one long pass over his entire length, savoring the silken flesh against her tongue, reveling in the veins, which pulsed hot with life.

Jeannie massaged his thighs, running her hands over the rigid planes of muscle as her tongue flitted over his shaft. She let her fingers explore his crisp pubic hair, running her nails through it, teasing him.

Sloan's legs trembled against her hands when she enveloped his cock fully, drawing him deep into her mouth. She wrapped her hands around his shaft then, twisting her way along the length, chasing her hands with her lips. That white-hot heat in her belly began to grow, spiraling upward and leaving her almost dizzy.

Sloan drove his hips against her face. He pulled her flush to him, rocking forward until he choked out, "No more!" and tore himself from her mouth.

Sloan yanked her upward, letting their flesh meet and scrape one another's. His skin was hot and slick with sweat. His eyes met hers once more, sultry and dark with passion. "I need you now, Jeannie, but I don't want to frighten you."

Her heart crashed against her ribs. His words were so urgent and thick with desire. But she wasn't afraid—only hot with need. In response, Jeannie kissed him hard, driving her tongue into his mouth, luxuriating in the ability to turn a man this beautiful on.

His harsh intake of breath was followed by a blur of his large hands turning her around and pushing her forward to the bed.

Her cheek met the comforter, cool and crisp. Her pulse raced with what was to come.

Leaning over her, Sloan kneaded her spine, ran his hands along the curves of her hips, dipped between her legs to slide between the fold of her flesh. His breath was hot on her skin. His lips were silken as they trailed a path along her lower back, making her shiver with anticipation.

When his tongue slid into her, teasing her clit, bolts of heat sliced through her, making her cling to the comforter, twisting the fabric in her hands. She fought not to cry out. The sweet sharp feel of his tongue was so delicious. His hair brushed against her inner thighs, soft and silky, making her nipples bead into tight buds.

He retreated quickly, replacing his tongue with his fingers, stroking her to madness as he rose and positioned himself between her legs.

The thrust of his cock was swift and hard, almost forceful in its intensity. She was slick with need. Wickedly, she raised her hips to meet his first drive into her, humming her pleasure.

Sloan placed his hands on her hips, gripping them, pulling back, then pushing forward, withdrawing, retreating until her hips rolled with his rhythm. He reached around her body, cupping her breasts. He toyed with the nipples until small explosions began to erupt in her.

The slap of their flesh, moving in unison, drove her desperate need for fulfillment to a new height. It was sticky and dirty and all the things Sloan had described and more.

Sloan's breathing grew quick, mingling with hers until she thought her lungs would explode. Desperate for release, Jeannie hiked her ass up, taunted him—dared him to make her come.

Sloan took the challenge, rolling his hips against hers, driving upward into her until she had to jam her knuckles into her mouth to keep from screaming.

Her orgasm was a hard jolt to her gut, wending its way from the tips of her toes to the top of her head in a wave of sweet heat. She came hard, choking out a cry of gratitude.

Sloan responded in kind, taking one last driven thrust into her before tensing, gripping her flesh with hard hands, hissing her name, and then collapsing on top of her.

They fell together on the bed, a tangle of limbs and heavy breathing.

Sloan was the first to stir. He rolled her boneless body over and pressed a kiss to her lips as he enveloped her in his arms. She inhaled a shuddering breath against the smooth skin of his chest.

"So, good morning," he teased, rumbling and husky.

"You really are magical with delicates," she responded, her cheeks flushing hot with color.

"Wait until you see the magic that is my whites."

Jeannie giggled, burrowing next to him and letting her eyes slide shut.

The shrill ringtone of her phone had them both groaning. Jeannie reached for it. It was the first time it had rung in three days, and she'd been so caught up in her genie-ness, she'd forgotten to even touch base with Charlene and Betzi. Guilt stabbed at her when she saw it was Betzi's number.

"Betzi! Oh, God, I'm sorry, but you know these past few days have been nuts."

Betzi's breathing rang in her ear for only a moment before she said, "It's okay, Jeannie. No worries. Charlene and I have it handled. But we're having a problem with a vendor down here at his warehouse. You remember Mr. Mitzenkowski, right? Can you come give us a hand? Swear I wouldn't have called you, but this guy's a real shizwad. He said he'll only deal with you." She ran off an unfamiliar address to Jeannie, who grabbed a pen and wrote it down while Sloan kissed his way up her spine, making her nipples tight with need.

She cocked her head, shooing Sloan away and muffling a giggle. "Maybe I could just talk to him? Is it for the Warsham wedding? I thought all systems were a go?"

Betzi cleared her throat. She sounded like she was coming down with a cold, her voice was so hoarse and raspy when she replied. "Yeah. It's about the Warsham wedding. So come, please?"

In the past three days, she'd realized, she'd never once taken any time off since she'd been thrown into the Witness Protection Program. Although these three days had been anything but a vacation, they'd definitely shown her that some personal time was in order.

Still, the guilt she felt for neglecting Charlene and Betzi, leaving them alone to virtually handle everything, ate at her. "I'm on it. Be right there."

Betzi didn't say good-bye. Instead, she hung up abruptly.

Jeannie stared at the phone for a minute, her head cocked. They had every right to be angry with her for not touching base.

"Work trouble?" Sloan asked, cupping her breasts.

She fought a moan at his delicious fingers tugging her nipple. "Sounds like it. So I have to go make nice. Which means you have to come with. Put on some pants, werewolf," she teased, letting him take one last sip of her lips before heading to the bathroom to give her hair a quick comb-through and her teeth a good brushing.

Catching the first glimpse of herself in the mirror since her miraculous return to the world of the naughty, Jeannie giggled like a schoolgirl. Her cheeks were flushed and her eyes sparkled. She ran her fingers through her chin-length hair. She brushed her bangs over her forehead instead of pushing them back with some hair gel into the severe style she'd grown accustomed to.

All of these new revelations made her yearn for the old Charlie. She wanted to touch base with this new version of herself—the happier-than-she'd-been-in-almost-half-her-life self. She wanted to discover how she could breathe new life into a Charlie that was intentionally without color. She wanted to match her exterior with her more hopeful interior.

But that would have to wait. For now it was enough that she *felt* the inner changes.

"Jeannie?"

She slipped on her jeans. She noted the sag in them and promised herself she'd buy a pair that fit her once they had this all straightened out. Poking her head out of the bathroom, she smiled at Sloan, dressed in a deep navy blue sweater that highlighted his hair, and tight jeans. He pulled a black knit cap over his head. "Ready?"

"Let's do it," she chimed, taking his hand in hers, filling her with hot-gooeyness all over again.

JEANNIE peered out of the window of her passenger seat at her unfamiliar surroundings. She'd let Sloan drive her car so she could get her head together about where they stood for the Warsham wedding. She took one last glance at her phone and shook her head. She'd sewn this all up two weeks ago. What could possibly be the problem?

"Pretty deserted," Sloan commented, popping open the door and rounding the car to her side to let her out. He smiled at her, his raven hair shining under the sunlight in streaks of chocolate.

God. Every time she looked at him, her heart stopped. She slid from her passenger seat and nodded, taking his hand when he offered it. "Yeah. Funny thing, I don't remember a vendor named Mitzenkowski that I use having a warehouse in this area or even having a vendor with the name Mitzenkowski. But vendors move for bigger spaces all the time." She squinted in the sunlight. "It's very *Footloose*, huh?"

"Kick off your Sunday shoes," he replied on a wide grin.

"Look," she pointed. "That's Betzi's car."

Betzi's cute, red VW Beetle was parked in one of the many empty parking spaces.

Sloan looked up at the large stack of gray and green buildings, his nostrils flaring. "They're here. I can smell them, among a thousand other scents. Most of which are unpleasant."

Jeannie frowned and cocked her head. "You can smell them?"

"Werewolf here. I don't just smell scents. I remember scents, and I remember Betzi's and Charlene's." He began to walk toward where his nose apparently led him.

As they entered a dark cavernous opening, Jeannie asked, "You mean like you recognize the scent of their perfume?"

He shook his head, his dark hair brushing the collar of his leather jacket. "No. I mean each human has a scent, and once you've smelled it, you almost always remember it. I smell another one I recognize, I just can't get a grasp on where I recognize it from."

"Okay, Sloan Flaherty. I can't even wrap my brain around identifying humans by their smells. I think I need more time to absorb. In the meantime, where the heck is Betzi?" She wondered this out loud as, hand in hand, they made their way past stacks of wood pallets and aluminum barrels.

"Jeannie?" Betzi called her name. It sounded like it was coming from far away, deep into the darkness of the building.

Sloan's head cocked. "Hold on," he said, grabbing Jeannie's arm and pushing her behind him.

A whistling noise from over her left shoulder made them both turn.

Out of the darkness came the sick thud of a bat crashing against Sloan's head. He dropped to the ground at her feet so suddenly she barely had time to fall to her knees, her hands reaching for him before she got the big picture.

That's when it hit her—probably as hard as the baseball bat that had knocked Sloan out cold.

She didn't have a vendor named Mitzenkowski. Her memory sucked, but she remembered every name of every single vendor she dealt with.

Mitzenkowski had been Betzi's code word for, "Hey, dummy. We got trouble." But she'd been so busy relocating her libido, she'd missed the signal.

Oh.

And surely, when she turned around to find out whose hand was attached to that bat, things were gonna go all kaplooey.

CHAPTER
14

An apt description of kaplooey could surely be described as facing the barrel of a gun, no?

Jeannie stared at the black hole of Victor's pistol, remembering vaguely what Marty had said about finding her kryptonite. Unwilling to find out if her personal kryptonite was bullets, she instead fought the swarm of bubbling fear in her gut and remained still.

Victor jammed a needle, most likely filled with a sedative, into Sloan's neck with a grunt while he held her at gunpoint.

He wasn't the man he had once been, and it wasn't just age that had changed him. No longer lean and well muscled, now he was simply gaunt and lacked definition. His movements were jerky and stuttered. His once beautiful raven hair now hung in greasy strands around his face and straggled down to his shoulders.

Strangely, her temper flared.

Here we are again, Jeannie. You helpless. Him with a big, big gun.

Fuck, fuck, and bigger fuck.

"Move," he snarled, jamming the gun in the direction of the dark void she'd just peered into before ramming it into her back. The barrel drove between her shoulder blades and right through her thick winter coat. As they walked, she noted her surroundings. The stench of booze. Fast-food wrappers littering the path they took. A picture of her pasted to the cement wall. A picture of the old Charlie before plastic surgery and the unwilling abortion of her baby.

He'd been living here. Waiting.

Before she had the chance to let that sink in, her ear cocked to the tune of whimpers and a low growl.

Betzi. It was Betzi, and she was pissed.

That was the growl she used when a client had complained her corn bread biscuits were too dry. It was the sound she'd used when Jeannie had told her she'd have to learn to love making hot dogs for children's events because foie gras in a foot-long bun glazed with a garlic butter wash wasn't just messy, but wasn't going to cut it with the kiddies. It was the growl she used when Jeannie had told her she couldn't have the day off so she could scope couples yoga for men who wanted a little some-some on the side.

It had never occurred to her that Betzi would be in any danger. Jesus, why hadn't that occurred to her? Of all the people she thought Victor would go after, they were all people who'd been in his organization—or the family members of the victims who were shot. They might not have talked back then, but he was going to ensure they never even considered it.

But taking out those people wouldn't hurt her the way it would if she lost the only people who were even a little involved in her new life.

And he wanted her to hurt. She'd taken down his whole operation in one fell swoop and sent him into hiding for twelve years. That he was this dedicated to finding her said something about the kind of sick rage Victor harbored.

Victor dragged Sloan's big body behind him, limp and heavy, his leather jacket scraping against the hard cement floor.

She stole a breath, forcing air into her lungs. Sloan wasn't dead. He wasn't. She knew that. He'd said it would take a silver bullet. So whatever Victor had jammed into his veins, it wouldn't kill him. Because he had eternal life.

And if Victor were to turn that gun on her, she also had eternal life. So all she had to do was get him away from Betzi. Nekaar had said so.

Right?

Oh, God, her memory was so bad. Please, please be right.

When they arrived at their destination, a huge room that had probably once been used as storage, with only the sway of a lightbulb dangling from the ceiling, Jeannie had to bite the inside of her cheek to keep from screaming her horror.

He didn't just have Betzi. He had Charlene, too.

Go big or go home, motherfucker.

Charlene sat back-to-back with Betzi in a huddle in the corner. They were tied together in a mass of duct tape and rope, bound at the ankles and wrists. Their mouths were taped shut, too. The silver gag on Betzi's mouth flapped at the edges, and an angry patch of red had formed just above her upper lip where Victor had probably yanked it off in order to force Betzi to call Jeannie's name.

Charlene's mouth puffed outward with the need for air. Her brown tweed skirt was torn, her shirt dark with blood. Her sleek blonde hair, usually smooth and capping her head, was mussed and sticking up at odd angles. Her fashionable, yet practical, glasses hung off her nose crookedly. But her eyes . . . Oh, her eyes were filled with defiance. She was angry, and that was good. Jeannie was going to need to harness some of that if they were going to survive.

Betzi, as dark as Charlene was light, arms bound behind her, clenched her fists so tightly the veins in her hands bulged. Her fair skin held a faint red tint to it at the cheeks, almost matching her sweatshirt. A thin line of blood dripped from the corner of her eye where Victor had clearly hit her.

Probably with his big, bad gun. Victor was nothing without his gun, and he loved a good pistol-whipping. A flash of light, followed by a startlingly clear vision ricocheted in her mind's eye, one of Victor bringing the butt of the gun down on her face over and over.

It was as clear as if it was happening to her right now. So stunningly real she had to close her eyes and shake her head.

The sound of Victor dumping Sloan in the corner, letting his head fall unprotected against the wall, drove her from her recollection with a jolt. Her instant reaction was to run to him, cradle his head in her hands. But she knew if she showed even a little sympathy for Sloan, if Victor were to see her feelings in her eyes, he'd do something drastic.

Victor rounded her, coming up behind her and pressing his length to her back. "Look, *mi amiga*," he whispered in a husky chuckle. "Here we are again. You and me. As you can see, I invited your friends. I'm still not sure that was a good idea. The one with the dark hair has a big mouth. One I want to shove my gun into and pull the trigger."

Jeannie fought a shiver and reached deep inside for calm. This time would be different. *Please, God, let this time be different.* "So what do you want, Victor?" she asked evenly, her breathing slow and sure.

Charlene and Betzi shot confused eyes in her direction. They clearly hadn't known she knew their attacker. But they did now.

"I want you, daffodil. There was no other way to get near you. Seems you always have friends around you. Friends and him," he spat in her ear, the greasy smell of his breath wafting into her nose. "Is he your lover?"

Jeannie remained silent, silent but for the crash of her heart. To deny who Sloan was would only evoke more suspicion in Victor, and that would incite him. Because everyone had a dirty secret as far as Victor was concerned. But to tell the truth would enrage him just as much.

"Is he your lover?" he repeated, tightening his hold on her neck until she almost couldn't breathe.

She twisted her head. "He's just a friend."

With a hard jab of his knee to her back, he asked, "Since when do your male *friends* sleep over?"

Jeannie coughed, her lower back almost crumbling. "Since I became a lesbian."

Charlene and Betzi's heads popped up, but her eyes directed them to stay silent with a flash of urgent warning. Victor's grip loosened at her confession, but only for a second.

She put a hand on his forearm, the one with the snake tattoo, and lifted her chin, easing the pull of the skin on her neck. "So, yeah. Gay. I'm gay. Sloan is, too. We have gay sleepovers. You know, in celebration of us coming out of the closet? Nothing to get excited over. In fact, why don't we just leave everyone here and go somewhere we can talk? Because you don't really want them, Victor. You want me. Once Sloan wakes up, he can untie everyone, and they'll all go home and forget this ever happened."

Wrapping his arm around her waist, he pulled her hips to his, grinding against her. Victor jammed the barrel of the gun to her temple, driving it against her skin. "You lie, *bitch*. You lie."

She tried to shake her head. "Nope. No lie. Look at how pretty Sloan is. Are men that pretty ever straight? No. I know. It cuts women deep far and wide, his gayness. It's like the Village People all over again or Ricky Martin. I, too, felt your brand of disbelief, when I found out Ricky wasn't straight. I can't tell you how many times I lived *la vida loca* in my bedroom mirror while I danced around and dreamed he'd come whisk me off and marry me. God, that news was such a disappointing time in my life. But there it is. So I decided

Ricky must see something I was missing. That's when I decided no more men."

He reached upward, rested his elbow on her collarbone, then snatched her hair, yanking her head back so far her neck strained until it felt like it would break. Victor jammed his face into hers. "You were always with the funny, petunia. Shut the fuck up. *Now!*" he screamed, making Charlene and Betzi cringe.

But Jeannie didn't cringe. She fought it with every fiber of her being. Fought to hold on to the anger she felt instead of allowing her fear to preside.

As Victor gazed down at her, his eyes wild and glassy hot, Jeannie realized he was no longer the dealer. He was the addict. Through the FBI, she'd found out that almost all dealers, including Victor, didn't touch the stuff they sold. They collected the money and left the sad journey of addiction to everyone else.

But that was no longer the case with Victor. He was using. She'd watched *Intervention* a time or two. She'd seen all the signs of an addict. His face, once so beautiful and exotic, had been lean, but chiseled to hard perfection. Now, it was hungry lean, sagging at his once sharp jaw. And his eyes, so dark they were like hot fudge, were now just dark holes in his head surrounded by darker shadows beneath them.

Jeannie's hands reached upward, gripping the fistful of hair he had as her feet began to slide out from under her. She fought to get her footing, refusing to utter even a gasp for air.

No. This time, Victor wasn't going to use his intimidation tactics. Even if he forced her to do whatever it was he planned to do with her, she would not scream or beg.

Her eyes locked with his and she waited, silently accusing him with her cold stare. Waited for what was next while she looked for a way out.

His eyes, so dark and clouded by whatever he was on, went wide for a moment. As if, in that very second, he realized she was no longer the girl he'd known twelve years ago. As if he sensed the change in her.

He threw her to the ground, driving her face into the floor with his hand at the back of her head before kicking her so hard she had only a second to tuck inward and roll toward Charlene and Betzi.

And then her tormentor was staring down at her past the barrel of a gun. *"You fucking bitch!"* he screeched, saliva spraying across the room. "You took everything from me, and now I'm going to take everything from you! So choose, *whore*. Choose who dies first."

Jeannie bit the inside of her cheek to keep from screaming her pain. His blow to her side left a searing trail of an agonizing throb in her ribs and her nose bled profusely. Huge drops of crimson fell from it, dripping down her face and splattering on the floor.

Yet, she would not fear him.

And if she had to have another rhinoplasty to fix her nose, she was going to rip off his face, because that shit hurt and took forever to heal.

She scrambled to sit up, using Charlene and Betzi's bodies as leverage. The room tilted and swayed before righting itself. The nerves of her face were on fire with a ravaging sting.

Betzi's fingers connected with hers, touching them briefly before flitting away. Her harsh huffs of breath made contact with Jeannie's ear. The short pants, choppy and wheezing, were raspy.

Damn you, Victor Alejandro Lopez. Damn. You.

Show no fear. No. Fear.

Jeannie didn't budge. Instead, she glued her narrowed eyes to his face and refused to look away. Even though it hurt like a mother-fucker, she lifted her chin in defiance.

Victor, clearly unnerved by the silence, moved in closer and circled her neck with his big hand, slamming her back against the two women and holding her in place. "Choose, whore! Who will it be? Maybe it should be the gay boy, huh, *mi amiga?*"

Sloan, still prone against the wall, helpless and crumpled in a heap, hadn't stirred. It incited her. Made her pulse race and her fury rise to a new height.

And still, she didn't look away when she said with cold calculation, "Victor. I swear to you, on everything I have, I'll kill you if you hurt them."

Victor laughed, letting his head slide back on his shoulders, cackling with a deep gurgle of lunacy as he jammed the gun under her nose. "How will you do that, tulip? With your Mr. Miyagi brand of karate? I have a gun, whore!" He held on to her neck and reached around her, jamming it into Charlene's temple, making her whimper while tears streamed down her face.

Okay. Point. Could she wish for a gun of her own? Was that considered wishing for something in the personal-gain category? She decided to bargain, forcing her words to find a calm execution from her trembling lips. "Aw, c'mon. It's not them you really want, Victor. You know that and I know that. You really want me. Remember what you told me while you bashed my face in? You said it was for my own good. So take me, Victor, and let them go."

He leaned back, his eyes filled with hatred, but there was a slight tremor in his hand—one she hoped to take advantage of. "No one's going anywhere, you slut. Choose. Choose now or I'll choose for you." He gave her a hard shake before shoving her back against Charlene and Betzi again.

"So who's it going to be, rose petal? The bitchy brunette with the big mouth or the whiny blonde? On the count of three . . . One." He smacked his lips, then grinned in the way only the truly insane did. "Twoooo . . ."

Do it now, Jeannie. Do it like you fucking mean it. Do it before someone eats the barrel of that gun again. She closed her eyes, clamping her lips shut, visualizing Victor's exact position and seeing in her mind's eye exactly how she'd strike.

"Three, whore!" he bellowed with twisted glee.

A surge of howling anger thrust her upward as she steamrolled him, barreling into his gut and knocking him to the floor. The gun clattered to the cement, falling out of Victor's hand and sliding sideways toward Charlene.

Jeannie threw herself on top of him, straddling his large body. She grabbed his shirt with one hand and put every last bit of power she had into balling her fist up and landing a clean blow to his nose.

Victor's head jolted backward, blood spraying from it and spattering her in the face. The moment his head snapped back up was the second she struck again, screaming, "I'll kill you!"

Her breaths came in sharp gasps when Victor fell limp against the floor. She leaned forward and bracketed his head, almost unaware his eyes were closed. "I hate you! I hate you!" she sobbed, hoarse and raw. Tears splashed on Victor's torn flannel shirt, tears of shame, tears of finality.

Jeannie planted her hands on his chest and pushed herself back upward, gagging on his booze-riddled scent.

She forced air into her lungs while she stared down at the man who'd ruined her life. The eerie silence of the room met her ears, stifling her urge to smash Victor's face in. To kick him, tear at him, scar him the way he'd scarred her.

Wiping the back of her hand across her mouth, she lifted her leg to move off him and locate the gun. She was going to tie Victor up like a trussed turkey and duct tape him so securely he wouldn't be able to move an inch. Then she was going to set everyone free, send them home, and call Fullbright. And her nightmare would be over.

Forever.

Jeannie fell backward on the floor as a wave of dizziness accosted her, ignoring the humming noises Charlene and Betzi were making. She held up a hand, still trying to catch her breath. "Hold on. I'll untie you. Lemme just catch my breath."

But instead of her words quieting them, their muted noises grew louder, more urgent.

Jeannie's eyes popped open.

Okay, so using the word *forever* in terms of ridding herself of Victor just moments ago had been maybe a little rash.

And, Jesus, she was really crappy at picking up signals lately. Warehouses that belonged to vendors who didn't exist, muffled screams of warning—all missed signs. Missed in a big way. A relearning of the girlfriend code was in serious order when this was all over.

Victor's howl resonated in her ears, high and enraged as he slammed into her again, hurling her to her back just as she'd fought to sit upright.

Seconds before he took his first blow, before the huge ball of his flesh slammed into her face, she caught sight of the gun out of the corner of her eye and memorized its position.

She let his fist connect with her face. Heard the bones crunch in her cheek. Welcomed the ire it drew from deep within her soul. Jeannie fell limp for a moment, allowing Victor to think she'd passed out just as he'd played her.

Her hands flattened on the floor on either side of her to give her leverage, and she counted in her head, waiting for Victor to relax. Letting him think she was once more, his prey.

Three, two, one!

Rearing upward, Jeannie lifted her hips, crashing upward against Victor's groin and catching him off guard. He lifted off her just enough for her to roll out from under him and tuck her legs to her chest, giving her the kind of force she needed to ram the soles of her feet into his gut.

She drove upward hard, sending him flying backward. Jeannie didn't waste time in scrambling to her haunches, reassessing where she was in the room, and making a dive for the gun.

With an infuriated Victor hot on her ass.

SLOAN woke to the sound of muffled cries and Jeannie, flat on the floor, a man sprawled on her back, yanking at the back of her head, wrapping his fist into her hair and preparing to slam her face to the hard ground beneath him.

There was no time to think. There was no time to plan an attack. His shift, in all its raging fury, took care of that for him.

Sloan keened a howl, low and feral from his throat, when his clothes split and tore at the seams. Buttons from his shirt flew in every direction, fabric arced in the air in swirling colors, his change was so fierce.

As his bones twisted and morphed, Jeannie clawed her way across the floor to something he couldn't see for the red haze of his change. So intent was her focus, she didn't even turn her head at his howling screech. Determination, palpable and agonizingly raw, filled his nose. He felt it. Tasted it. Cheered it.

The man on her back, greasy, bloodied, his stench of disease and despair, clawed with her, racing her to get to something . . . Sloan's blood coursed through his veins, hot and pulsing, while thick patches of hair sprouted from his body. He fell forward, moving from his human position of erect to that of his animal half on all fours. Sloan sniffed again and finally pinpointed the scent.

Victor. Ah. At last. That was who he had smelled when they'd first entered the warehouse. His scent had been all over Jeannie after the first attack. Anticipation, greedy and hungry, swelled in his chest.

For all he'd done to Jeannie, for all he'd stolen from her, Sloan would see to his death. And it would hurt. It would so bloody hurt.

A gun. Oh, Jesus Christ, there was a gun. Sloan spotted it moments before the last vestiges of the shift roared through his body.

"Shawty!" someone bellowed, as something dark and musty flew overhead.

Nina. He recognized the voice as Nina's. Fuck. If she rushed into the middle of this and let her anger take control without realizing Victor had a gun, humans could die.

Sloan's shift completed just as Victor reached for the gun while Jeannie tore at his fingers, trying to keep his hands from latching on to it, her nails leaving thick lines of blood in his ravaged skin.

Sloan lunged for the gun, launching himself in the air in a smooth leap, intent on keeping Jeannie within his sights.

As Victor's fingers peeled Jeannie's from his, he reached forward with his other hand and made contact with the gun. He reared upward and aimed at Charlene and Betzi, who slammed their eyes shut and cowered in the corner.

Helpless. They were helpless to even move to defend themselves, and it sent raw fury through his veins.

Jeannie's scream, mingled with a hovering noise, was the last thing Sloan saw before he collided with something fuzzy and smelling of mildew.

Mat—it was Mat, aimed right for Victor's head until he'd intercepted him.

Sloan crashed into the wall, breaking the cement blocks like they were made of cardboard. Chunks flew about the room, pelting the two women in the corner. He howled his outrage when he righted himself on all fours and saw that Victor had managed to get away from Jeannie, and he still held the gun.

Victor waved it wildly, his breath coming in harsh wheezes from his chest as he aimed it directly at Jeannie. "You fucking whore!" he raged, his teeth clenched and his legs wobbling as he stumbled backward.

And then Jeannie was using her hands to pull her bloody body across the floor, screaming, daring Victor in a white-hot rage that filled Sloan's nostrils. Taunting him, daring him, while spreading her arms wide to block Victor's view of Betzi and Charlene. "Do it, you fucking pig! Do it! Take me, you animal! Kill me! I dare you!" she ranted, driving forward, crawling, inching toward him as though her body were made of cement. She rose up on her knees, pitching to and fro, unsteady, enraged. "Do you hear me, you fucking spineless coward? *Do iiit!*" she bellowed, spit spraying from her mouth as she pounded her chest with her fists.

That very gesture on Jeannie's part, the beating of her hands to her heaving chest, created a maelstrom of activity. Empty cardboard boxes rose up from the floor as if on two legs and leapt to the air, dancing in frenzied circles. Lavender smoke swirled in small tornadoes while wood pallets clacked together as though they were head butting. Paper soared like birds in a blue-hued sky, diving and twisting, attacking Victor's head and making it difficult for him to see.

Nina took advantage of the storm Jeannie created and raced across the room toward Sloan, rearing up short when she caught his eyes. He felt the slight nudge of his brain where she rooted around to read his intent and then she screamed, "Midget! Duck!"

Sloan ran, directing his simmering hatred in one snarling leap at Victor, aiming for the gun.

Victor's finger poised at the trigger, twitched erratically. Sloan heard the click of the first barrel loading with an eerie slow motion of sound and movement.

Victor hesitated as his wild eyes took in the scene before him, and his hesitation, the crazed uncertainty in his eyes, was exactly what Sloan needed.

"Invisible!" Mat screamed in a rumbling rage.

Sloan watched below him as Mat crashed into Jeannie, knocking her to the ground and covering her with his entire surface just as he arced over them and drove into Victor, pounding him into the ground.

He landed on Victor with a heavy grunt, driving him so firmly into the cement flooring Victor's eyes rolled to the back of his head.

And now, he would die.

CHAPTER 15

"Invisible!" Mat honked again, coughing and wheezing.

Jeannie, battered and bloody, rolled her eyes to the left and let out a shaky sigh that hurt almost every part of her body. "Mat?" she croaked.

"Dollface?"

"Not invisible!" she and Nina yelped in unison.

Nina sat on her knees, clapping Mat's threads. "But aces on that fucking takedown, dude. You rolled shawty like she was a Weeble. Knuck that shit up, brother." She held out her fist to his fringe.

Mat's fringe lifted, but just barely. He groaned. "Jesus, doll. I tried. My aim's still shittier 'n a drunk palooka shootin' fish in a barrel."

Jeannie reached a hand upward, stroking his matted threads. The effort to move set off a string of deep aches. "But you saved me, Mat. If not for you and Nina, Victor would have shot me. What more can a girl ask for in a guardian?"

He purred, then shot out a cough that released more dust.

Her eyes turned to Nina. *"How?"*

"Brokeback carpet," she answered with a grin. "He sensed something was wrong just like he did the last time this fuck got his hands on you. So he used his crazy fucking Jeannie GPS and got a line on where you were. He even flew a little. Yeah, we coulda gotten here faster if we'd crawled, but he had your back."

Jeannie's eyes filled with tears of gratitude. "Oh, Mat. Thank you . . ."

"Ain't nuthin', dollface. Anything for you," he crooned.

Sloan's snarl, ragged and feral, made Jeannie give Mat an urgent pluck of her fingers to his fabric. "Sloan!" she yelled. During the chaos, she'd caught a brief glimpse of Sloan when he'd sailed across the room and slammed into the warehouse wall.

But it hadn't registered. Hearing his puffing breath and low growl made it real. Really real. He was a werewolf. And she was a genie.

Oh, Jesus Christ.

Mat rolled away from her, and Nina helped her up, the tug she gave her so hard Jeannie had to fight back a sharp gasp of pain.

Nina eyeballed her while she helped her hobble to Sloan. "I say we let Sloan eat the motherfucker—but that's just me. This is more about you. Either way, shawty, he's gotta go. He's seen. Heard. And he's a wife-beating, kid-killing fuck. I'll let you decide how it happens, if you want the choice on your shoulders. But go his ass will."

Victor's life in her hands.

How ironic.

Letting Nina help her, she caught her first real glimpse of Sloan in werewolf form, and it was many things. Awesome. Wondrous. Hairy. He was enormous and fierce.

She gripped Nina's arm. "Ohhh . . ."

"Scary shit, right?" Nina quipped, tightening her grip around Jeannie's waist. "No worries. He can understand everything you say. I love when he's in were-form. Means he can't fucking talk back."

More humming noises rang in the air, echoing in the cavernous space.

Jeannie's head whipped around. Charlene and Betzi were still tied up, and by now, probably so petrified after Sloan's shift and her shit storm of debris they were going to need to borrow her therapist. "Nina, get Charlene and Betzi. I can do this."

"A'ight, Slice, but you remember what I said." Her warning was clear. Victor would be disposed of. Somehow. Some way.

Jeannie nodded, wincing at the pain she experienced in her ribs when she knelt beside Sloan.

He loomed over Victor, all four of his paws planted firmly on each side of him. His dark fur glistened under the one lightbulb, almost blue black. His teeth dripped saliva, letting it fall to Victor's petrified face. He dropped his jaw wide open when she put a hand on his enormous head and thrust her fingers into his fur. "Sloan. Let him go. Please."

Victor gulped, his eyes pleading with Jeannie. "What . . . What the fuck *is* it?" he squeaked as his chest rose up and down and sweat rolled off his forehead.

Sloan bared his teeth, starkly white and pointy, opening his mouth wide.

Jeannie tugged on his ear. "Sloan! Stop. Please, *please stop*." She couldn't stand any more blood, any more violence. "Please," she whispered in his ear, stroking the velvet of it.

"Get it off me!" Victor screamed, thrashing his head from side to side, barely able to move. "Get it off!"

Like lightning striking, Jeannie knew exactly what to do with Victor. "Sloan," she urged. "Let him go. *Please*. I know what to do."

Easing back some, Sloan plunked back on his haunches, still pinning Victor's torso to the floor. He cocked his head in question.

Charlene and Betzi ran to her side, stopping short at the sight of Sloan. Charlene sobbed, pressing a fist to her mouth while Betzi grabbed Jeannie's hand and squeezed it. "You got some splainin' to do. But until then—wow. Like wow-wow. You are one badass, boss."

Jeannie's smile was wan, but she turned to them and rose. She threw her arms around both their necks, cringing at the stabbing pain in her ribs. "I'm sorry. Oh, my God, I'm *so sorry*." And then her fingers were wiping at the residual glue at the corners of their mouths from the duct tape and rubbing their hands to promote circulation. Touching them reassured her they were still alive, and she hadn't caused two more senseless deaths. "Are you two okay?"

Betzi waved a hand in the air with careless abandon. "Like this was all that much different than a night out at The Dawg House for me? *Please*. Well, okay. There're usually no guns and whatever he is"—she pointed to Sloan—"at The Dawg House, but still. Now our girl Charlene? Miss Unicorns and Twizzle Sticks? Probably not so much."

Charlene nudged Betzi with her toe. "Oh, hush, mate," she said, her spine straightening until she caught a glimpse of Sloan. Her voice trembled, but as was the Charlene way, she sought to reassure. "I'm fine. So fine. Fine, fine, *fine*!" she shouted, then winced at the echo of her voice. "Sorry," she repeated more quietly. "I'm okay. I just want out of here."

Jeannie grabbed Charlene's hand and brought it to her face. Tears wet her cheeks again. "I'll explain. I swear. Everything from start to finish. Go back to my place. Wait for me. I'll be right behind you."

Betzi shook her dark head in a firm no. "The hell. We're not leaving you here alone with a dog, whatever the heck that thing was that flew through the air like some kind of shag rug UFO, and a guy who's just this shy of the cray-cray and clearly wants you to die for reasons unknown. Um, no. You come with us."

Nina tapped Jeannie on the shoulder. "Your friend with the wiseass mouth's right. You go back to your place with them. Take Mat. I got this fuck covered."

Jeannie emphatically shook her head, which made her nose throb. "No. No more violence. I'm not leaving him alone with you, MWA. Besides, I have an idea." She leaned into Nina, tugging her down to her level so she could whisper her thoughts.

Nina grinned with so much malice, Jeannie hesitated, until she said, "You go with your little girlies here. You need bandages and shit. Promise I won't hurt the fuck—*much*."

Jeannie ran her hand over Sloan's head once more, reveling in his soft fur and valiant chivalry on her behalf. "Please, Sloan. Let it go, okay?" she begged.

He nudged her with his muzzle, his enormous body still firmly planted on Victor's. She took it as acknowledgment of her plea that he would respect her wishes.

"Take her. *Now*," Nina demanded, hitching her jaw in the women's direction.

Charlene and Betzi said no more, huddling Jeannie into their sheltering embraces and walking her out of the warehouse.

Victor's screams pierced the warehouse walls, so pitiful and heart wrenching that she almost turned around. "Tulip! Don't leave me here! Don't leave meeee!"

But Betzi and Charlene tightened their grip. "No!" Charlene reprimanded, stopping the trio cold. Her eyes, always so soft and friendly, were full of fire when her gaze fell upon Jeannie. "You will not look back. I don't know what just happened back there, mate. But I know whatever that man did to you was horrible. You will come with us and you will never, *ever*, look back."

Victor's last petrified scream was drowned out by Charlene's hands over Jeannie's ears.

Betzi dragged her out of the dark warehouse and into the blinding sunlight. Stopping, she looked down at Jeannie, and without saying a word, flung her arms around her. Sobs wracked her body— loud, gulping sobs in a release of pent-up terror.

Betzi was the tougher of the two. The least sympathetic. The quickest to anger. To see her sob so openly made Jeannie's heart ache with sympathy.

Charlene, the tallest of the three, enveloped them both, resting her head atop Betzi's and letting out a shuddering breath.

The sunlight shone down on them.

The cold air bit at their quaking huddle of bodies.

Explanations and apologies could be made later.

For now, there was this.

As Charlene and Betzi had patched her up, putting salve on her wounds, icing her nose, and checking her ribs to be sure they weren't broken, Jeannie heard how Victor had lured them to the warehouse. He'd simply called Cee-Gee Catering and booked an appointment, claiming the abandoned warehouse was his place of business where he planned to hold a party for his employees. Betzi and Charlene, being the employees they were, had gone to scout the location. He'd made Betzi call her at gunpoint, for which Jeannie would never forgive herself.

Jeannie, in turn, told them everything about the last few days. It was a lot to absorb. Not just her past and her relationship with Victor, and the lie after lie she'd told them concerning her former life, but what Sloan and Nina were, and how her crazy genie powers had continued to evolve since she'd first discovered them.

They'd nodded with wide eyes, but as Jeannie sent them home, she wondered if she wouldn't lose them as employees for all she'd put them through. For all she'd hidden. While their words had been sympathetic and kind, their eyes still held residual fear.

Jeannie had to wonder if that was what the paranormal lifestyle was always going to be about. Lots and lots of fear followed by lots and lots of alone time while people avoided you and distanced themselves from your life.

Now, Jeannie and Nina sat together, side by side on her bed, looking down at Jeannie's bottle.

"You know, the next time someone has the unmitigated gall to tell me they had a bad day, I'm going to slug them in the head."

Nina snorted, her eyes distant. "You sure know how to bring the crazy."

"What's on your mind, MWA?" Jeannie patted Nina's hand.

She popped her lips. "You and Sloan."

"Look, it's like I said. He had nothing to do with our . . . you know. I mean, he had something to do with it, but I was the one who forced him to have something to do with it. It's all on me. Promise. And despite all the saving I've needed lately, I'm a big girl."

"It's not that." She paused, rolling her tongue along the inside of her cheek as if she were deciding if she should make a confession of some sort. "Today, in the warehouse . . . I'm gonna tell you a little something about Sloan—and if you fucking share it with anyone, especially him, I'll chew my way through your esophagus. Got it?"

"Esophagus." She nodded. "Check."

"It wasn't so much that I didn't or don't like Sloan. He's nice enough. He's good to his nieces and nephews, he loves that little shit Hollis like nobody else—even me. He's also pretty good to his pack. He's loyal and all that bullshit. What I didn't like were the chicks he dated and I was forced to hang out with at every fucking party we've ever had with Marty and Keegan. Every last one of them has so much air between their dumb-ass ears, they were like a vortex of asshat. Yeah, he's banged a lot of broads, and I haven't been shy about telling him he's a dick for it. I understood for a while because I wasn't exactly above a one-night stand from time to time before Greg. But I fucking grew up. Sloan's been around a lot longer than me, and he's still living like he's twenty. But after today's crazy, I see him a whole lot different."

Jeannie's hairs bristled on the back of her neck. She wanted to share Sloan's revelation with Nina, but it wasn't her story to share. "How so?"

"Because of you. There's something about *you* that makes Sloan want to be fucking better. I felt it today in the warehouse. He didn't just want to protect you and slaughter that son of a whore, Victor. He was *proud* of that crazy crap you whipped up with all that shit flying around. Pride in someone else when you're as fucking selfish as Sloan is don't happen often. That usually only happens when you find someone you really dig."

"Am I hearing experience talking?"

She turned to Jeannie. "You know what? Yeah. Yeah, you are. I'm not ashamed to admit I wasn't exactly all cuddles and shit before I met Greg."

"And this post Greg is what you'd define as teddy-bear-ish?"

Nina chuckled, nudging Jeannie's shoulder. "It's fucking closer than I was before. When I met Greg, after we got past all the crazy bullshit of the vampire thing, I wanted to be a better person."

Jeannie fought a visible shudder. "So you were even worse before your mate?"

"I know. You're having trouble believing that shit."

Jeannie laughed, holding her sides with a wince. "It's a big pill to swallow."

"Here's my point. I actually like Sloan with you, dude."

Old fears, and the habits they wrought, were hard to break. Suddenly, she was overwhelmed with the feelings Sloan was evoking in her. The utter agony she'd experienced when she was unsure at the warehouse what exactly would end Sloan's life. Their intimacy, an intimacy she hadn't ever experienced in her entire life as an adult.

Jeannie's breath was ragged. "I'm afraid to like him, too much. I'm so afraid to like him and then get lost in him, like I did with Victor." Last night and earlier today had begun to sink in, and her brave performance in front of Nina and Wanda when she'd declared her sexual independence was beginning to lose its luster.

Nina's snort was sharp. "First, midget, who the fuck wants to like a guy like Sloan? Seriously. He's a total player. Second, he's a shit, but he'd never let you get as far as Victor let you go. Sloan's an ass, but he's not a controlling one. Anyway, he's different with you. Really different, I'm not sayin' me-and-him-are-gonna-hit-the-blood-bank-together-like-BFFs different, but I am saying I know when he tells you he gives a shit about you, he means it."

Jeannie pointed to her forehead with a finger while her stomach did somersaults. "The mind-reading thing?"

"Yeah. He deserved a good probe. I'm a cranky bitch, and I know it seems like I hate everything—"

"Your admission. See my shock and dismay."

Nina slapped a hand over her mouth with a gentle squeeze. "Here's the thing, you had one shitty past where men are concerned. I'm not so much of a bitch I won't look out for another chick if she needs looking out for, and the fuck I'll ever let a man beat on a woman. But I def wouldn't let you trust someone I thought was a total dick through and through if I knew different. I know you've probably heard all this shit from a therapist. Who wouldn't need some time on a GD couch after what happened to you? That you're still standing is some shit to be admired, shawty. You're one badass broad. So own it. Just like you told Sloan to."

Jeannie pulled Nina's hand from her mouth. "You heard that conversation?" She blushed. That had been in the confines of her bedroom . . .

Nina tugged at her ears. "Vampire hearing. I blocked the two of you Chatty Cathys out after that, but that's not the point. This is the point. Own that you've got some shit—some bad, bad, fuckerly fuck shit that's happened in your life. But don't let it keep you from at least trying to reach the hell out. Fight like hell not to let that happen. I saw the way you were looking at Sloan. You want to—you just don't know how. So say that to him. That's all. Just say it."

Jeannie gulped, but Nina's observations didn't make her feel defensive. It was the first time she was able to hear the words without wanting to crawl back into her dark cave. She didn't want to live her life by rule of her past. But this last step toward Sloan frightened her like no other.

"Look, you deserve a nice guy. I definitely never would have thought Sloan was it—but he digs you. And that's all I'll say because of the vampire-code crap I have to stick to. We're not supposed to probe anyone's mind unless it's necessary. I'm not sure finding out if Sloan's righteous is a good enough reason for the clan, but I say fuck 'em. No one ever beat the living shit out of them the way that fuck did to you. So bad you had to hide from the motherfucker for all these years. Just know I'm telling you that you don't have to be afraid Sloan's just amusing himself with you. Because you deserve something nice, Jeannie, for everything you had to sacrifice. Something really nice."

A tear stung her eye. Nice would be . . . well, nice.

So nice.

"You helped save my life today, Nina. I won't ever forget that."

Nina reached out her hand and put it on Jeannie's. "Nah. I didn't do that. You did that with your nutty genie shit. Which, you should note, you totally fucking nailed. *You* saved you. You and Sloan and your brokeback magic carpet. I just helped a little. But don't think there wasn't somethin' in it for me, too, kiddo. I got my pissed-off on in a big way when you left. Victor was what I like to call a saucy motherfucker. I figured he'd put up a fight because I'm a girl. He likes beatin' on chicks. He had to be checked. I did the checking. There's nothin' like a little throw down to relieve some stress."

Another wave of relief washed over her. "I don't care why you did it. I'm just glad you did."

"Yeah? So am I, midget. End girlie sharing time."

Jeannie held up her gin bottle. The bottle that had begun this madness. The bottle, that now, thanks to her big book of genies' directions and a little thing called a curse, contained Victor.

Forever.

She couldn't have lived with his blood on her hands, but this? This she could live with. Victor's imprisonment brought up a million questions, but she was too tired and too battered to address them tonight. For tonight, she just wanted peace.

She shook the bottle at Nina. "And we'll always have this, huh?"

Nina took the bottle from her hands and gave it a hard shake, her hands blurring with the motion. Then she cackled. "You bet, midget."

Jeannie laughed, but it was through silent tears that slid down her cheeks and plopped with wet splats on her dark jeans.

Nina put an arm around her shoulder and let Jeannie rest her head on hers. Jeannie allowed Nina's clean, soapy scent to soothe her while the slight sway of her rocking motion eased her tension.

And they sat for some time like that.

The savior and the saved.

The once broken now healed and the desperately wanting to heal, on the mend.

Just sitting.

CHAPTER 16

The next morning she awoke to the clatter of dishes and something scraping across her floor just outside her door. She'd fallen asleep while sitting with Nina, whom, she vaguely remembered, had tucked her in. But it hadn't given her the chance to see Sloan.

Her heart began to throb and ache as she slid off the bed, avoiding Mat and the twins, and headed to her bathroom to brush her teeth. She and Sloan had to talk now that the imminent danger of Victor had passed.

Her first glimpse of herself in the mirror didn't even make her gasp. She'd been down this bruised, discolored, distorted road before. It just took time to heal. Running a brush through her hair, she threw on her robe and wrinkled her nose. It was too big. Everything she owned was too big or too colorless and as nondescript as she could get. She hoped to change that soon.

Because she could. Because it was time.

A renewed sense of hope welled in her. One she planned to foster.

As she made her way out of the bathroom and toward her door, her head cocked. Where was her other half? Her eyes flew to the bed; the half Sloan had slept on the two prior nights was still neatly made-up.

She raced to the door, flinging it open to see suitcases and coats littering her floor.

Nina gave her a tired smile as Wanda rushed up to hug her. "You're free!"

"Free?" Jeannie repeated, bewildered.

"Yes!" Wanda crowed, a smile wreathing her face. "I can't believe not one of us geniuses even noticed that when you came back from the warehouse yesterday, Sloan wasn't trailing behind you like some stray dog."

"Yeah, yeah," Nina moaned. "Big fucking high-fives all round. Now let's get yer shit together so I can get the fuck home to my man where I plan to sleep for the next GD year."

Leave? They were leaving?

Marty, in a swirl of perfume and sunshine, enveloped Jeannie in a gentle hug so as not to hurt her wrapped ribs. "Good news, right?"

"News?" Jeannie murmured, wincing at the sunlight blaring in from her living room window.

Nina lifted her sunglasses and looked at Jeannie. "Yeah, midget. You're free of the ass sniffer."

Her head spun. How could she be free? She tightened her robe's belt around her waist. "I don't get it."

Wanda stopped buttoning her coat and gave Jeannie a soft pat on the cheek. "You're no longer tethered to him, honey. When you put Victor in the bottle, you must have freed yourself from Sloan, according to Nekaar. I'm not going to pretend to understand it, but I'm certainly not going to question it, either."

Oh. Right. And that was good.

Wasn't it?

"So while you're still a genie, you're in no more immediate danger," Wanda continued. "Which means we can go home, and we can let Nekaar handle it from here. You don't need the head djinn, or whatever they call him, to untether you. Yes, he's still missing, if the update on the Bottle Babes Facebook page is right, but Nekaar seems to have a good grip on keeping you from granting random wishes with his genie force field or whatever. And Nina tells us your warehouse adventure was quite something—one to be applauded, FYI. That means you're getting your magic under control, too.

"We tweeted Nekaar to see if he'd come and take care of you until you're totally back on your feet, and he'll be here later for more genie lessons. We just wanted to let you sleep in. It's been a rough week, so we asked him to wait until tonight. Betzi and Charlene, now that they're over their shock, are going to pop over tonight, too, to make sure you've eaten and rested. They'll take the twins out, as well. Other than that, our paranormal part in this is done, sweetie."

Yep. All the bases were covered. That was it? It was just over?

Nina wrapped an arm around her neck and brought it in close to her chest. "But don't worry, midget. We're not far if you need us. I texted you all our shit like our Twitter and Facebook info, and we'll do follow-ups to see how you're adjusting. And we'll hang soon. 'Kay?"

Follow-ups? Like she'd just been to the dentist and had a root canal. Well, okay. *Chin up, Jeannie.* "Okay . . ."

Wanda held her arms out and gave Jeannie a hug. "Don't look so glum, kiddo. We'll see each other soon. For now, I really need to get back home and see my husband."

"Ditto," Marty chimed in, pressing a quick kiss to Jeannie's cheek before turning and grabbing one of her many suitcases. "And, God, it'll be good to sleep somewhere Nina isn't."

Nina slung a large brown bag over her shoulder, poking Marty in the shoulder. "Fuck you, Marty. And what the fuck is in this bag? Jesus Christ, even you don't need this much makeup." She grinned at Jeannie, pinching her cheek. "Laterz, shawty. Remember what I said last night." And with that, she was gone.

They were all gone. Off to their already established lives.

And here she was with a brand-new one she didn't have a clue how to live.

And where was Sloan? She'd had too much pride to ask. But he certainly hadn't wasted any time, now had he?

Once he'd realized he wasn't tethered to her anymore, he'd probably skipped off to somewhere flocks of blondes gathered and dove right in.

The loss of the OOPS women's suitcases and shoes stacked in her corner left her feeling lonelier than she ever had before. The only thing that remained was the mixed scent of their perfumes and the lingering sound of their laughter.

She made her way to her bedroom, peeking at Mat and the twins to see they still slept soundly. Her eyes were drawn to the side of the bed Sloan had slept on. As if looking at it would make him reappear.

Sitting at the edge of the bed, she fought the visual that Sloan was immersed in a pool of leggy women, laughing at her because he'd managed to talk her into bed with his snazzy reverse psychology.

But Nina had said . . .

Yeah. Nina had read his mind and he was all gushy stupid about her.

Of course, you couldn't tell that from his lack of presence, now could you?

Wow. This sucked.

SLOAN texted Jeannie once more in order to let her know he was grabbing some things at the store so they could have a decent meal together tonight, but only after he checked on some things long needing checking at the Pack offices.

The freedom their broken bond allowed him didn't feel quite as good as he'd thought it would. He missed the warmth of her presence next to him and knowing when he looked down, she'd be right next to him. He'd been as surprised as anyone when they'd all realized he and Jeannie were no longer stuck. But it also afforded him the opportunity to get some things together for them, and free up some of his time so he could woo her properly.

He glanced at his phone. Nothing.

Damn, he should have woken her before he'd left so abruptly, but she'd been sleeping so soundly, and if anyone deserved some rest after yesterday, it was Jeannie.

His chest tightened with pride. She'd clawed at that fuck Victor like a cage fighter, refusing to allow him to win again.

Of course, there was no way in hell he would have with him and Nina in the picture, but Jeannie had rallied without even realizing they could take Victor out in one shot. He'd smelled her determination. Sensed that she would try to protect Charlene and Betzi at all costs—even if it meant her life was up for the taking.

The sight of her screaming at Victor to shoot her had broken him, torn at him until he wanted Nina to let him finish Victor off. But Nina had made a promise to Jeannie, and if Nina was nothing else, she was a woman of her word.

Sloan made his way to the elevator at the Pack offices and pressed the button, nodding at fellow Pack employees. Lost in the fastest route to get back to Jeannie, he checked his phone once more.

Nothing. She was probably still sleeping.

He'd hit his office, check his messages about the big meeting they had next week, then he'd grab some food and be back with her within the next couple of hours.

"Sloan!" his brother Keegan greeted him as he stepped off the elevator. His rough features and hard good looks were filled with concern.

"Bro." He gave him a quick shoulder bump.

Keegan flung his arm around Sloan's shoulder, walking with him toward his office. Shutting the door behind them, he gave his brother a concerned glance. "You okay? My wife tells me yesterday was a shit storm."

"Like you wouldn't friggin' believe," Sloan answered, scanning the pink slips of paper filled with messages on his desk.

Keegan plopped down in one of the leather chairs. "Jeannie okay?"

He smiled. Yeah. She was okay. "Yep."

"Holy shit!" Keegan yelped, slapping a hand to his knee and shaking his head.

"What?"

"You're in, brother." Keegan chuckled sinisterly, mimicking Vincent Price.

"In?"

"Hot for Jeannie. I've never seen you look like that when I mentioned a woman's name before. Does she know?"

Sloan gave him a grin. "She has an idea."

"And she likes you, too?"

"I think she does."

Keegan barked a laugh. "Hah! You're the luckiest sonofabitch I know, brother. With your past, I can't believe she didn't run the hell screaming from you the minute she knew you two didn't have to be in the same space."

"She doesn't exactly know yet. She's still sleeping. But hope burns alive she'll still feel the same when she finds out."

Keegan steepled his hands under his chin. "You tell my incredibly hot, but seriously nosy wife and her two busybody friends what you been up to lately? Or do they still think you're shit on their shoes?"

He rolled his tongue in his cheek. It was better the girls didn't know just yet. He wasn't up to the shit they'd surely lob at him. For now, he just wanted to be with Jeannie. "I'm stickin' with shit on their shoes. There's no pressure to perform that way."

"You know they're not known for their subtlety. They've probably trashed the idea of your horn-dog past and hiding it with Jeannie."

Sloan shot off a snort of derision. "Oh. Trust me, brother. They've had their say. But it's cool. They didn't say anything that wasn't true."

Keegan let a low whistle escape his lips before smiling. "You got it bad."

His stomach tightened into that knot of anticipation that meant his mind was on Jeannie. "I think I do."

"She's got a pretty shitty past to overcome," he warned in only the way an overprotective brother could.

"That she does."

Keegan rose, reaching over the desk to slap his brother on the shoulder. "Don't fuck with her, okay?"

"Not a chance," he responded, holding Keegan's warning gaze with one of his own.

"So, I guess you get it now, huh?"

Oh, he got it. He totally, unequivocally got it. His smile was stupidly high school, but he didn't give a damn. "You bet your ass I get it."

Keegan broke into a grin and clapped him once more on his back. "I'm goin' home to see my wife. Keep me in the loop. Oh, and good luck. Go get your woman."

If it were the last thing he did, he'd make sure he worked it out.

AFTER a long bath, iPod in her ears, Jeannie was feeling better and more optimistic. While she'd bathed, she remembered she'd forgotten to check her phone to see if Sloan had left her a message.

Now, she tore her nightstand apart looking for it while Mat and the twins looked on.

"What's all the racket about, dollface?" Mat sputtered.

She frowned. God save her, but one fine day, she was actually going to organize her life. It would include listing the places she put things after she'd bought them or carelessly flung them somewhere without remembering where somewhere's location was. "I can't find my cell phone."

It occurred to her that she was being rather dramatic over Sloan's disappearance. Last night, before she and Nina had cursed Victor to the bottle, she'd turned her cell on vibrate and completely forgotten about it. Maybe she'd condemned Sloan before he deserved to be.

Mat grumbled and hunkered down on her bed. "You look. I'll take a nap. I wanna be wide awake when that joker shows up for our genie lessons. I'm damn tired a bein' labeled brokeback, thank ya very much."

Her answer was distracted. "You're not brokeback, Mat. You just need some fine-tuning. You stay with the twins while I go look in the kitchen, okay?"

"Won't hear me complain," he groused, and almost as quickly, he was snoring.

As she made her way from the bedroom to the kitchen, she noted how much she missed Sloan's presence next to her. Missed looking up and seeing his tall frame and handsome face smiling down at her. Cell—she had to find it.

Jeannie flipped on the light in the kitchen, eyeing her phone on the counter, but a voice nearly had her jumping out of her skin when she heard the words, "Boo, tulip!"

As her eyes adjusted, they widened.

Victor, in sparkling genie garb, floated in her kitchen with Nekaar, who hung by his neck from Victor's grasp.

With a shiny jeweled knife to his neck.

Whoomp, there it is.

SLOAN glanced at his watch and cursed. He'd forgotten that he'd left his spare set of keys to his apartment at the OOPS office just before this whole thing had begun. He frowned as he unlocked the door and pushed his way in. The door stuck, reminding him he needed to come over and oil it for the girls.

Flipping on the lights, he scanned the desktop and located his keys when the phone rang.

Sloan cocked his head. Shit. He'd forgotten to have the calls rerouted to the girls' cell phones as he'd promised he'd do just before he left Jeannie's this morning. He'd told them he was whipping up a surprise for Jeannie, made them promise that they wouldn't tell her where he was, and offered to drop by the OOPS office because he had to pick up his keys anyway.

But he'd forgotten that he'd promised to drop by OOPS first—before he went to Pack and got involved in the thirty or so small fires he'd ended up putting out before leaving.

The shrill continual ring pierced his ears.

Damn. If he didn't pick up, he was a total shit.

If he did, who the hell knew what was in store on the other end of the line. Next he'd be shackled to a mermaid . . .

It was probably just a crank call. *Right, Flaherty. Wasn't that how this all began with Jeannie?* Okay, so he hoped it was a crank.

Sloan glanced at the phone. "Okay. This is me raising my hands like white flags in defeat," he said to the room. He snatched up the phone. "Thank you for calling OOPS. We're here to serve all your paranormal crisis needs. This is Sloan Flaherty—werewolf at large. How can I help you?"

"Sloan?" Jeannie's voice hissed through the phone, panicked and hushed.

But he figured it was just because she hadn't been able to touch base with him all day. "Jeannie? Jesus, woman! Where have you been all day? I've texted you at least twenty times in the last six hours. Is this what our relationship is going to be like, Ms. Carlyle? Will I always be waiting for you to call me back?" he teased, that ridiculous lump in his chest throbbing at the sound of her voice.

"If you don't shut up and listen to me, I'm never going to call you back again. Unless it's from the afterlife." She choked on the words.

Sloan's nose flared, and his chest tightened. "What the hell's going on?"

"Nothing. I was joking. You know me, always with the funny? Anyway, I just got your texts. Wow. You really meant it when you said you were into me, huh?"

His chuckle was warm, fluid, but his ear was finely tuned to something that wasn't sitting right with him. "And you're just as into me. You know it. So do I."

Her sigh was breathy for a moment and then she was all business. "Right. So this is me, the chick who's super into you, calling you to tell you, the guy who's just as super into me, that I need a little space tonight. The plans you texted are awesome. Like otherworldly. In fact, I bet you cooking in the kitchen is so hot, it's like watching molten lava with an apron on. But I need some girl time. Okay? So let's do this dinner date tomorrow night. You know, when my face feels less like it was put in a grinder and my ribs don't feel like a vise grip is squeezing the life out of them. That work?"

Sloan frowned, tapping the desk with his forefinger. "But I was going to put more ointment on your face, maybe rub your back . . ."

"And all while you cooked me a meal. God, the nerve of some people calling you a jerk. If they only knew the Sloan Flaherty I've come to know. Anyway, gotta go. A hot bath awaits me and bubbles. Lots and lots of bubbles. Call me tomorrow, m'kay? Byeeee."

She clicked the phone off before Sloan had the chance to protest.

His nostrils flared again.

Something wasn't right. Not the tone of Jeannie's voice, or her ridiculous request for girl time. She wasn't just blowing him off—she was warning him off.

Shit. What now?

He dug his cell out of his pocket and texted Nina, Wanda, Marty, and Darnell while his jaw clenched tight and the animal inside him itched to make an appearance.

Making sure he covered all the bases, he tweeted them, too. *2Furry4U @OOPS 911 @Jeannie's!*

JEANNIE, chained by her feet to what had once been her bedroom wall and now was some monstrosity of brick and stone, moaned. Shit and shit! Pleading for her brain to calm, she turned to her right. "Did that phone call to Sloan sound convincing enough? Or too much?"

Nekaar, chained alongside her, raised one regal eyebrow in her direction. "If I laughed at you, madam, would thou be offended?"

She shook her head, tucking the cell phone back behind her. "Thou would not. Okay, fine. Nobody ever said I was winning any awards for my acting, but I had to keep Sloan away somehow, right?"

"Oh, indeed, madam. I'm certain your thespian performance, delivered with a great flair for overexaggeration, I might add, was on point. I expect you shall never see him again."

Perfect. No way was she risking Sloan's life. According to master djinn Nekaar, werewolf and vampire were trumped by genie magic. Which meant their lives weren't so eternal while she was holding court. Her heart ached to see Sloan one last time. After she'd read his texts about a surprise, not only had guilt eaten her up, but also the idea that she might never see him again. Or any of the people she'd come to care about and trust these last few days, for that matter.

No. This time, she was handling this on her own.

She turned to the stranger who was tied up beside she and Nekaar. "Can you chill for just a few minutes while I straighten some things out and then we'll talk?"

There was an affirmative nod from the latest addition to this newest hell she found herself stuck in, and it was all Jeannie needed to move forward.

So first up, their imprisonment. She held up her ankle in Nekaar's direction, wincing when her ribs screamed in protest. "What is this and why does it take our genie powers away again?"

"It is cursed silver, madam. Cursed with the power to strip us of our magic. No one can remove the curse and release us but another djinn."

"Have any djinn friends available?" Jeannie asked with hope, knowing the answer before Nekaar had the chance to say anything.

"Only the genie who placed the curse on these cuffs—"

"Can break it," she mimicked. *Beautiful.* Jeannie rolled her eyes. Well, Marty would be happy to know she'd found their kryptonite. Cursed silver—a common, yet mostly unused curse.

Yay.

But that wasn't the worst of it, according to Nekaar. There was also some ancient curse only one djinn in all of Genie-ville knew about.

Burt.

She was all on the edge of her seat just waiting to hear what this curse entailed.

"So hang on," Jeannie hissed in his ear as Burt and Victor rooted around in her kitchen for whatever they needed to perform this ritual she was still unclear of. "You mean to tell me that Burt, the genie who, according to you, can't remember one curse from another—the genie who bonded me to Sloan but didn't really mean to—was the one who managed to whip up the macdaddy curse of them all from the afterlife? You said he was dead!"

Nekaar nodded his head. "It is so. Burt clearly put his sentence in that bottle to good use, for this curse is so ancient, not even I knew of its existence."

Jeannie's head hung low as she tried to free even just one ankle from the super-duper, magical, mystical ankle cuffs. She grimaced when her ribs began to ache from leaning forward. "And you don't have a rad curse to sling back at him? Oh, Nekaar . . . tsk-tsk."

His regal face hardened. "I hear your disappointment and return it with a renewed sense of frustration, madam."

She was stunned with disbelief. "How could you, the better student of the two of you, not know about a curse like this?"

He sucked in his lean cheeks in righteous indignation. "Because I, madam, do not seek such devices as an outlet for my magic. I am the good cop. Burt is the bad. Like on the *SVU* TV show."

Jeannie clucked her tongue. She'd heard that before. "Right, right. Genies are mostly peace loving, hang ten, love thy neighbor, yada, yada, yada. All I know is, since I met you crazy bunch of djinn, I've been trapped in a bottle, forced to call a man master, tethered to said man, sent a dozen or so people to hell, and managed to get a store full of women pregnant. Oh, plus a man. So I hope you won't be offended if I don't buy this genies-love-lollipops-and-sunshine rhetoric."

Nekaar cleared his throat, and putting his hands in his lap, he remained silently admonished.

She gave him a poke in his bulging bicep. "And another thing, you know, before we get to this curse, Mr. Clean, why, why, why would you let Victor out of the bottle?"

He lifted his strong jaw in clear discomfort. "I was not made aware he was in the bottle, madam. Clearly, I was left out of the loop, as your people say. I was seeking *you*, madam. As you recall, we had lessons this evening. Upon my arrival, I could not find you. Thusly, I checked your bottle, which is your home away from home, is it not? I mean, there was talk of throw pillows and the hanging of pictures. I believed you had grown comfortable with the idea and had chosen it as your me-time destination."

Apparently, she'd been in the bathtub with her iPod blaring "Footloose" when Nekaar had arrived. "All I wanted to do was get out of the stupid thing, why would I choose to get back in it?" she asked, dumbfounded by his reasoning.

"I do not know, madam. It seemed as likely a place as any. I knew you could not go far. The pale woman informed me you had injuries via Twitter. Injuries I planned to teach you how to heal in our first exercise tonight."

Jeannie made a face at him. "Well, surprise."

He nodded sagely. "Indeed. Surprise, madam."

"We put Victor in the bottle because he's a maniac. Now he's a maniac with genie powers. I fear we won't fare well in this battle, my fine djinn friend."

"Had I only known, madam." He shrugged his wide shoulders with nonchalance, making his vest gape at his chest. "But alas"—he paused, clenching his perfect white teeth together and jamming his face into hers—"*no one informed me* of this Victor," he hissed back.

She let her head fall back on the wall. "Fine. Guilty. But it all happened so fast, you know. The idea to put him in the bottle struck me, and blamo, I looked up how to do it in the big book of genies, and there you have it."

"Oh, we'll have it, madam. We shall have it and then some."

Yet, she was still confused. "How did Victor become a genie again?"

"I'm unclear, but I believe your magic is so powerful and out of control it, in a sense, rubbed off on Victor via your bottle."

Check. "Okay, so how did Burt find me?"

Nekaar's chin hung to his broad chest. "Burt followed me here, madam."

"And why is that again, Nekaar?"

"Because he now knows you are the successor, the great ruler of all djinn."

Jeannie popped her lips. Yeah. That. "What does that mean. And we know that how?" God. All these rules and curses were a maddening maze of total chaos.

"Via my investigation through the veils, madam. It was one of the many things I'd planned to share with you upon my return this eve. It's all very exciting, do you not agree?"

Cue majestic music full of excitement.

She didn't even have time to react to her newest title before she asked, "And Burt found out I'm head genie how, loose lips?"

Nekaar's head sunk to his chest in obvious shame. "Via, as you dubbed it, my sinking-ships lips. I was not aware, when I sought information on your dilemma throughout the veils, that Burt was still alive, madam. Surely you saw my grief when news of his passing came. When Burt realized that he had, in his utterly moronic shameful luck, indeed not only cursed you to the bottle and enslaved you to Sloan, but in the process gave you a far bigger gift, he sought to find a way to retrieve it."

"So this, all of this crazy, me being head djinn, was a total accident on Burt's part?"

Nekaar dipped his head once more. "I did mention he was dreadful academically speaking, did I not? Only Burt, the worst djinn in centuries could make such a blunder as to give you this sort of power when he meant to bestow it upon himself."

Jeannie sighed, the air escaping her lungs stinging on its way out.

She got it now. "So he posted his death on Facebook under a false account to keep suspicion at bay and buy himself some time to find me?"

"Yes, in the effort to distract the attention from himself and his nefarious plan. He is quite aware of his reputation in and amongst the veils. Knowing he'd be the likely suspect when word was out our ruler had been kidnapped, he furthered his ruse."

"Riiiight. So now, for the moment anyway, I'm the great and powerful Oz."

Nekaar gulped, his bronzed throat moving up and down with the effort. "He wishes to dethrone you."

"By dethrone, you don't suppose he's just going to ask nicely for the title, perchance?"

Nekaar sighed. "Nay, madam. I fear there shall be bloodshed."

She clapped him on his broad, tree-trunk-sized thigh. "Thanks for keepin' it real."

"I am so dreadfully sorry, madam. I had no idea. I knew your powers were askew. I did not know it was, as is with Mat, a mere matter of fine-tuning them to prepare you for your maiden voyage as our ruler. I also did not know the curse Burt bestowed upon you was only just past half in its completion. Though, with Burt, I should have known," he said in disgust. "I confess I am mostly blind to the inner workings of our world and its government. I was not aware our ruler could even be dethroned—by anything or anyone, and certainly not Burt. He is, as the pale one says, a moron."

"Know your government, Nekaar," she chided.

"Ah," he groused. "But Burt knew—or found out. I do not know why I find myself astonished that he faked his own death in order to prepare for the kidnapping of our ruler. Nor do I know how he could have possibly found you. I spoke quietly with my interveil connections when I queried this most unusual turn of events. Which means there is a mole among the veils, a despicable informant for Burt, and should we live, which I highly doubt, I shall turn every stone until I find this traitorous genie!"

Leave it to her to become not just any old genie but top genie. "So the only way to usurp yon current ruler is if, say, someone like me, you know, special genie, is by some freak set of circumstances, gifted with rare and unlimited powers that are more rare and more unlimited than our current ruler?"

"Indeed. You have now, according to the universe's great plan for you, become our ruler, for you are more powerful than any other djinn as a result of Burt's treachery. Our current ruler has returned to his normal djinn status. Consider yourself a prophet. Did you not impregnate a mass count of women? Your magic is clearly more powerful than our current ruler's—stronger. How Burt managed this, again I say I do not know. There must have been a glitch . . . The universe is a strange and delightful place, yes?"

"Dee-lightful," Jeannie agreed with sarcasm tempered with a smile. Because it wasn't Nekaar's fault. Well, not really. How was he to know if Burt were freed from his bottle he'd turn into some power-hungry madman? How was he to know Burt would actually spend his imprisonment researching when he'd sucked at all things academic?

They each paused in reflective silence.

Then she cocked her head at him. "I just don't get it . . ."

Nekaar's sigh was dramatic and drawn out. "I do not, either, madam. However, I blame everything on Burt. He is the—"

"Feces of a thousand camels. I know, I know." She waved a weak hand at him. "His black soul is neither here nor there. So how did Victor get mixed up with Burt?"

"It is as I stated. When Victor was released from the bottle, my surprise was great. Little did I know, his visit to your bottle left him with the gift of the djinn. Burt followed me to your home and popped in at the very moment Victor was holding me captive. The rest is, as you say, history."

Right. Bad dude meets another bad dude and they make beautiful bad music together. Now she really shook her head. "So Victor's djinn because of one screwed-up curse. And all these rules, they just keep changing. Could we please just have one set of rules?"

"Again, madam, it is my duty to remind you that your powers are far greater than even you realize. There are no rules in your case, as yet. Clearly, in this Victor's case anyway, they remain askew. It is as I said before; your bottle contains djinn magic. The point is rather moot, wouldn't you agree? Victor is now djinn. Thusly, when Burt followed here, demanding I tell him of your whereabouts, he and Victor found a common bond."

"*Me*, and their hatred thereof."

"It is so, madam."

Jeannie snorted, then winced when her nose began to throb. "So I'm sure there was a lot of smack talk about me. Stuff like 'I'll get that bitch if it's the last thing I do.' And 'Damn her for getting all the power. Let's join interveil forces. Make a dirty deal, and get the bitch,' right?"

Nekaar's face fell, despair lining it. "Oh, the things they said about your person, madam. All lies, I say!" he whisper-yelled. "Alas, yes. That is what occurred. In return for Victor's help with stripping you of your ruling powers in ritual fashion, Burt cut a deal, as Victor called it."

"Which was?"

"Victor would help Burt strip you of your powers, powers that are, as I said, currently stronger than any other djinn. Yet, it is my understanding, through their despicable conversations, when Burt cast this spell upon you, due to lack of thorough research, he spoke a portion of the words incorrectly."

Jeannie rolled her eyes. "Well, duh. What does Burt do correctly?"

Nekaar grimaced. "The spell, while strong, was not completed.

Burt however, has come upon the actual book with the correct spell in its entirety. Thus, he plans to steal your powers and merge them with the powers from the spell in the book. Should he complete this, it will make him virtually omnipotent. This is totally unacceptable, madam. With such magic available to him, Burt's reign will be that of terror and treachery!"

Oh, Jesus. "So I'm betting my fez, somehow, we have to keep Burt from getting my power and the other power." Or some power.

Nekaar winced. "Yes. We must find a way to give the rest of this magic to you. You would be the kinder, fairer ruler."

"And what does Victor get out of this again?"

"Burt will allow Victor to remain djinn."

Jeannie shook her head. "If you think Burt was trouble in Genie Land, my friend, you have no idea the kind of feces of a thousand camels Victor is. And as an FYI, in my former life, he was a drug lord. A big one—like on the FBI's most-wanted list. He killed people, Nekaar. He killed a small child. *A child.* He's not afraid to take someone out, and he definitely wouldn't be afraid to join forces with a dolt like Burt—one he can run roughshod over. He knows how to run an operation." *Oh, God.* "So this is bad."

Nekaar's head bounced up and down, catching the light on his glistening head. "So bad."

She wasn't giving up yet. Not yet. She grabbed Nekaar's hand and squeezed it, even though they were raw and scabbing over from yesterday. "We need to think, Nekaar. Really think. Like dig deep into your genie brain and think of something to get us out of this. We need to find a way to restore my power, your power, *someone's* power."

"I shall ponder, madam. Might I ask for a peaceful setting in which to do so?"

Jeannie nodded, then turned to her left and finally addressed the stranger's presence. "Jeannie Carlyle. You are?"

"Najim, ex-head genie."

Aha. "Right, the current reigning great and powerful Oz. Good to finally meet you. I hear you've had quite an ordeal."

His smile was crooked, his youthful face the color of light teak. "In a nutshell."

"So Burt's had you all this time?"

He winced and she wasn't sure if it was in shame or he was in pain. He looked pretty roughed up. "Scum of the Veils Burt. Yep. He's who kidnapped me."

Concern flooded her. He might be older in years than her, but he mostly looked like a fifteen-year-old. A tired, fed-up fifteen-year-old. When she'd pictured the Big Kahuna of genies in her mind, he'd been wearing long flowing robes to match his long, flowing beard. Oh, and he'd had a wizard's hat on. Wrong fairy tale.

"I don't mind saying, I'm completely confused. What good did kidnapping you do?"

Najim sighed. "Burt thought I knew how to find out where he could locate my replacement with my *special powers*."

Jeannie nodded, blowing a wisp of her hair from her mouth. "So Burt knew he'd created a new ruler, but when I let him out of the bottle, he meant for that new ruler to be him, except he screwed up the curse and gave it all to me." Saying it out loud helped define it for her.

"Irony, yes?" Najim looked defeated.

"She reached out her hand to Najim. "Are you okay? Did he hurt you?"

"You mean aside from the headache from all of that whack Burt's screaming because he didn't know how to find you, or the right hook to the head when I mistakenly giggled—my critical bad, BTW, after he found out that he was essentially the one who sort of handed it to you? I'm golden. Nay, I'm platinum."

Jeannie's glance was sheepish. "I'm sorry. I didn't know. If we get out of this, I'll grant you, like, deluxe vacay. Somewhere warm. Soothing. Spa trip, maybe?"

"You're awesomely kind," was Najim's reply as he stretched a long, lean leg covered in a whole new level of cool genie garb out in front of him.

"Soooo, thoughts on where we're at?" She lifted the cuff surrounding his ankle and massaged the place where they had begun to dig into his beautiful skin.

"Not a one. I apologize. It's been a rough week. Add to that, my magic is waning due to your life-force suck."

She snuck a glance upward at him—so calm, so resigned. "Yeah. Who knew, right?" According to Nekaar, since she'd unwittingly become mondo genie, she'd also been draining Najim's power. "So, are you kind of pissed that I took your title? I don't want there to be hard feelings. If there's a way to give it back, and you know, on the off chance we live, I'm on it."

"The djinn with the most power wins. End of."

"But are you all gonna grudge on me because of it? You know, in secret, while you plot my overthrow on Facebook?"

Najim snorted. "Oh, hells to the no. It means I can catch up on my Netflix."

His reply, full of disinterest and boredom, sent an APB to her brain. "You do know your people are doomed if Victor and Burt become the controlling parties, don't you?"

He shook his shortly cropped, dark hair, his blacker than black eyes bright and determined. "They're not my people anymore, lady. They're yours, and I have to tell you, it's a relief. I'm exhausted. You have no idea what thousands and thousands of years of ruling can do to a soul. The djinn dress code alone is hard enough. Add in the fact that I have no life, I hardly ever date, and it's purgatory."

She nodded. "Yeah. Not a fan of the harem pants, either. Maybe, if we live to see this through, something can be done about them and those push-up bras."

Najim sighed. "Also, if you live, you might want to look into the traffic problem in veil four. I get more complaints about this one intersection there than any other veil."

"Huh," she muttered, pondering the idea that she'd actually have to deal with traffic violations. "So here we are. Two great and powerful Ozs and one average djinn. What to do, what to do, boys?"

Mat coughed from the bed, hacking and phlegm filled, startling them.

She'd forgotten about Mat and apparently, so had Burt and Victor. Score!

It was slim, but it was hope redefined in a sort of brokeback way.

The three of them looked at each other, but it was Nekaar's eyes that narrowed with sinister glee. "I believe I have a plan, madam."

Jeannie's eyes narrowed, too.

She prayed it was a good plan.

As of right now, they were livin' on a prayer.

And in the words of the great Bon Jovi—Oo-wa-oowa-oowa-oo.

CHAPTER 17

Sloan paced the length of OOPS, glaring at Nina, Wanda, and Marty. "Something's just not right. I know it. She sounded strange."

Nina scoffed, twirling around in her office chair. "Like you'd fucking know what sounds like *normal* from her, Sloan? Jesus. You hardly know her at all. And hell to the low, you don't even know what the shit normal is period. Maybe she just needed a second to breathe, dude. I know you find that shiz hard to believe, but there are some chicks left in the world who don't want to be up your ass twenty-four-seven."

He slammed his fist down on the desk, making the phone leap in the air and scattering the colorful sticky pads. "Something's not right, Nina, and it has nothing to do with my charm or lack thereof. If you don't wanna back me the hell up, I'll go myself!" he roared, grabbing his keys and wallet.

Wanda popped out of her chair in a huff of silk and heels. "Sloan!" She pointed to the chair. "Sit—this instant!" Squaring her shoulders, she inhaled, then turned to him. "Look, Jeannie was in personal crisis while whatever intimacy went down between the two of you, and we've told you what the typical reactions to those crises are. Emotions run high—very high. Add in the fact that yesterday was brutal from what Nina shared with us. I mean, she did finally beat her inner demons, didn't she? Maybe she just needs time to absorb all of this. Just give her time, Sloan. Just because you say it should happen, doesn't mean it will."

Marty rose and put her hands on his shoulders, massaging the tight muscles of his neck. "That's what having a real relationship with a woman who has a brain is like, werewolf. I think you have some adjusting to do, too."

He clenched his jaw and his fists in unison. No. That's not what this was. He was attuned to Jeannie. He understood the inflection in her voice; he knew the rise and fall of it like he knew his own name. And something wasn't right.

If they didn't want to find out what the hell it was, he'd do it alone.

BURT lit the last candle while Victor tightened the chains around their ankles. He lingered at Jeannie's, twisting them so taut she had to bite the inside of her lip to keep from screaming. Blood ran down her ankle and dripped onto her floor where they cut into her bone.

And her anger grew. Goddamn him. Every time she was anywhere near him, she was the one who ended up needing a surgeon.

Nekaar growled low, baring his teeth at Victor, who laughed in mockery. "Shut the fuck up, fairy," he threatened in harsh tones, pressing a gun to Nekaar's temple—which, now that his powers had been stripped, essentially left him killable.

Reaching behind her, Jeannie grabbed Nekaar's finger and squeezed it. To rile Victor was to wake the sleeping beast. Let him think he'd won. Her stomach roiled, filled with a sour, acidic burn at what they were about to try to pull off. And then she closed her eyes and prayed that Nekaar's crazy plan would work.

As Victor gave Nekaar a final shove and went back to his tasks in the kitchen, Jeannie vaguely wondered what he planned to do with a spatula, some baking soda, and a meat tenderizer. She leaned into Nekaar and whispered, "Is this like the MacGyver of power stripping? Or is he just baking cookies for the Burt Reigns Supreme after party?"

"Oh, madam, betwixt the two, they nary share a fully functioning brain. Did you expect less?"

Leaning to her left, she eyeballed Najim. "Thoughts? Hints? Any visible clues as to what this curse is about, oh wise one?"

"You know," Najim whispered back, his breath smelling faintly of jasmine, "I wanna say chocolate cake, but I don't get where the meat tenderizer comes in. I'm as stumped as you."

A shuffling noise from Burt's scuffed, torn sandals made them all sit up while Jeannie kept half an eye on Mat, who hadn't stirred.

Burt leaned down and chucked her under the chin. The T-shirt he wore *did* smell like the stench of a thousand desert mongers, torn and streaked with dirt. His sandaled feet were grimy, his toenails embedded with grunge, and his breath reeked of beer and cigarettes. She fought not to gag. Instead, she lifted her chin and gazed right back at his sunken eye sockets.

He pinched her skin, twisting it between his yellow-stained fingertips. "Look at this shit, would ya? I gave you all the power. Just gave it to you with one stupid spell. Can you even believe how awesome I am?"

As Nekaar squeezed her finger, the signal that Mat had slithered successfully from the bed, she enacted phase one of the plan. Mock Burt. Mock hard.

"Your IQ must be at least in the double digits to have given me all this power instead of giving it to *yourself*." She smiled up at him, squeezing Nekaar's fingers again to quiet him when he snorted at her snark. "And from what I hear, you still didn't get it right, because these powers that I have, you know the powers you want to complete your spell? Fucked up, buddy. You might wanna reconsider taking my magic from me and finishing up this half-assed spell you conjured up. The Great Djinn only knows what you'll screw up next."

But Burt didn't seem to get the joke. He flicked at her lips with his fingers. "This will all be over in seconds. You won't know what hit you."

Jeannie didn't flinch. She kept her eyes fixed on him. "Did you hear me? Are you sure you got it right this time, Burt?" she taunted, stalling him and praying it was enough time for Mat to get back to the bedroom while Victor was in the kitchen and Burt was taking her verbal beating. "I mean, you did give me this power when you could have given it to yourself. That would have been the easier plan. I hear you get things kinda backward sometimes. It happens. I don't want to judge, but word around town is you suck as a genie."

He leaned back on his haunches; the thin braid trailing from the back of his head fell over his shoulder. His blank eyes now held confusion. "Did you just make fun of me?"

"A total and utter mockery," she said, with a somber gaze.

Now his confusion doubled, making his dull eyes almost bright. "A *what*?"

Nekaar, clearly fed up with his brother's asshattery, snapped. "Oh, you insufferable fool! Yes. She is making fun at your idiotic expense. Oh, Burt. How could you?" Nekaar spat. "How could you betray your own kind this way?"

Burt's face fell, but he was in and engaged, and that's all they needed. "Shut up, Nekaar! I screw things up sometimes. So I gave her all the power? Big deal. Now I'll just get it back."

Her eyes flashed a warning at Nekaar. He needed to tap some of that emotionless stuff he was so good at. "So here's the thing, Burt. If you didn't know you were doing it the first time, how do you know you're doing it right this time?"

He shrugged his thin shoulders. "I guess we'll find out," he said on a grin. What Nekaar said about his brother was true. He was reckless. Oh, and smelly.

Burt stood to leave, claiming he had to help Victor, but Nekaar squeezed her finger again, signaling they needed just a bit more time. "But wait! How did you find this curse? I mean, I've gotten a bunch of brides to be pregnant—all at once. I sent people to hell, buddy. *Hell*. I'm a perfect example of genie magic gone kaplooey. What if you blow up Genie-dom? There'll be nothing to rule but ashes. And all the bottle dwellers in Bottle-ville will haz a sad."

Burt paused for a moment as though he, too, wondered what he'd do, but then he shrugged again. "I won't. I have the directions on how to do it."

Plant that seed of doubt, Jeannie, and water the shit out of it. "But where did the directions come from? Maybe they're bad directions like the first set of directions you found. You know, like sometimes on a hot day when your satellite on your GPS gets overheated. It messes up. I had a GPS system that would talk to me in French when it was overheated. *Oui, oui!* How do you know the directions aren't in French? Where did you get them?"

Now Burt looked like he was unsure. He jammed his hands into his MC Hammer pants and waffled, jumping from foot to foot. "I got them from a book in the library."

Ah. So the book she and Sloan had gone looking for was *the* book Nekaar had spoken of when he'd overheard Victor and Burt in the kitchen. Burt had taken it from the library. "A book? You got this power-meld curse from a *book*?" she asked in whispered disbelief.

Burt's face fell again. He twisted the braid at his shoulder with a grimy finger. "Well, some was from the Internet."

"And the Internet never lies, right, Burt?" Jeannie shook her head in open disapproval and clucked her tongue for good measure. "Oh, Burt . . . Whatever shall we do with you?"

Seconds before Victor's return, Jeannie caught Mat's return to his place on the bed. He lay motionless as though he'd never left. She fought a sigh of relief and a scream of triumph.

Victor suddenly loomed in front of them. Standing behind Burt, he reached over his shoulder and went straight for Jeannie's neck. "Violence?" she squeaked. "So predictable, Victor."

"*Shut up, you bitch!*" he screamed, making Burt jump back and fall to the floor. Victor shoved her back to the wall with a hard crack to her head, his face full of hot rage.

She fought the whimper of pain in her skull and sucked in a shuddering breath of air as Victor went for Burt. "Get up, you dumb ass! Didn't I tell you not to talk to her? Now get out there and help me!" he bellowed, pointing a shaky finger toward the kitchen.

Burt skittered backward in a crablike walk before rolling over and jumping to his feet to do Victor's bidding.

Nekaar squeezed her fingers again, his tone worried. "Madam, do you fare well?"

Najim reached out a hand to her head to examine the back of it to find blood. "He's an animal!" he spat. "Are you all right?"

Jeannie gulped and swallowed hard, seeing stars behind her eyelids. "I'm fine. I survived several plastic surgeries among other things after Victor had his way with me the first time. A bump like this is like a trip to Disneyland." Yet, her little trip to Disneyland felt like she'd just ridden the teacup ride—over and over. Nausea assaulted her stomach and her ribs throbbed with screaming fire.

"Madam!" Nekaar shook her as she felt herself begin to fade, his whisper-yell urgent. "You must stay with us just a bit longer. They will come for you soon!"

"Mat!" she whispered, inching as close to the bed as her dizzy spell and newest aches and pains would allow. "Mat! Did you get the spell?"

* * *

"DUDE, wait the hell up!"

Sloan, head down, turned the corner to Jeannie's just as he heard Nina's voice from behind him. He stopped short and turned to glare at her, the air from his lungs huffing from his mouth with condensation. "Vampire? Aren't you supposed to be back with the Jeannie Doesn't Want You Up Her Ass Twenty-four-seven club?" he mimicked in a female voice.

Nina tightened her hoodie around her face before punching him in the arm. "Oh, shut the fuck up, ass sniffer. I just got a bad feeling, and decided to come see for myself. I figure if she doesn't want to see your cad ass, she'll at least see mine. 'Cus I'm a girl, and all."

"So you believe me when I say something's not right?"

She rolled her eyes. "Fine. I just know Jeannie digs you, and I'm pretty fucking sure what you told us didn't sound like her. She'd have been down with this surprise you planned for her. So let's go see, dude. Because if somebody's got my midget, shit's gonna fly."

He assessed her for a moment, dark and beautiful, and admired her loyalty to Jeannie. Whatever the bond was between the two of them, he didn't get it. He was just glad for it. "You do know if this has something to do with the djinn, as paranormals we're not immune to spells and curses, right?"

"Like I'd let that shit stop me?" She shot him a look of disbelief. "Do you even know me at all, dude? I don't give a shit if we go down, but I'm gonna fight like hell when I do. We can't just leave her helpless and defenseless. Not happenin'."

Sloan held out his hand to her. "I appreciate this."

Nina grasped it but for a moment, then shook it off. "You didn't think I was gonna let you pull a kamikaze on your own, did you? Just because I think you're a pig, doesn't mean I don't have your sweat-hog back. Now quit with the girlie talk and let's roll." She pointed to the stairs of the brownstone.

He took them two at a time, his nose flaring at the scent of danger and his heart crashing at the thought of losing Jeannie.

CALM, don't fail me now. Jeannie repeated the words in her head as Nekaar mouthed the word "*Phoenix.*"

Right. Plan Phoenix. Which was in Arizona, but had nothing to do with the plan. But it did, if she recalled, have something to do with Jack Bauer.

Oh, yes. She was going to be the Jack Bauer of genies and take the hit.

A big, fat, save—Genie Land hit.

She sent up one last prayer of thanks that Victor had somehow become distracted from his evil, power-stealing plan when Burt entered the kitchen and they began to joke about all the booty they'd chase as powerful djinn. Burt busied himself teaching Victor how to summon up the chick of his wet dreams, and the notion kept Victor's rapt attention.

It had given Mat time to relay the spell word for word to Nekaar and Najim. It had also allowed them not only to understand how the transfer of power would occur, but what Jeannie's part in this plan would be.

As an aside, her part sucked. Her fear Mat might have read the spell wrong, something he was infamous for, was matched only by what she had to do next.

So now, here she was, doing her part in this crazy plan. That entailed baiting Victor. Baiting Victor entailed a shiny knife.

Victor held that very shiny knife at her neck while Burt hopped from foot to foot, nervous and jittery. He made it hard for her to focus on nothing but her core. Nekaar's instructions had been to find the center of her calm and just float.

No matter how Victor taunted or even if he physically tortured her, she had to focus on the one goal.

"Any last words, tulip?" Victor asked, sultry and smooth, his lips on the shell of her ear.

Her eyes popped open and she stared him down just like she had at the warehouse. "Nope. Slice away. But do me this—you know, thinking ahead to a possible open-casket funeral—keep it neat, 'kay?"

If he was taken aback, it was only for seconds before he was giving her that hard glare again. "I can't believe you have no last words. You always have words."

She sighed, slumping back against the wall. "It's not like you understand most of them anyway. They're too big. So I don't see the point."

He leered at her, ramming his face into hers while his hot breath lanced her nostrils. "You were always so high and mighty, weren't you, *Charlie*? With your big words and your high school diploma? Too smart for a drug dealer, right?"

She laughed in his face. If she was going, it was all the way. "Oh, c'mon, don't sell yourself short. The FBI called you a drug *lord*. Muuch bigger than small-time dealer. You were on the most-wanted list. Still are, as far as I know. Pat yourself on the back. You've done your mother proud."

His hand snaked back around her neck—so cliché. "Fuck the FBI! They killed my brothers! And as to mothers"—he lowered his voice, adding that deep hum of a threat—"I plan to pay her a little visit—very soon."

The mention of her mother made her blood boil. If he touched her mother . . . Nekaar's eyes flashed a warning in her peripheral vision, and she fought the urge to strike back in anger. Clenching her hands tight to stave off the instinct to spit in his face, she said, "Make sure she offers to whip you up a batch of her white chocolate macadamia nut cookies. Badass. All the drug *lords* like 'em."

Victor's head cocked for a moment in wonder at her, making Jeannie's intestines knot up. She had to play this right. If he questioned her intentions, they were ruined. In comedy, timing was everything. That held weight in genie death, too. Yet it was much different when you knew what the outcome would be. Or thought you knew . . . She gave him a bland look. "So are we doing this? C'mon, drug lord, you know you got it in you."

Leaning into her face, he sneered at her, his eyes full of the hatred he'd nurtured for so long. "I've waited twelve years for this, you traitorous whore," he seethed. Sweat dotted his upper lip as he leered at her.

Yet, he lingered, tracing the knife in a shaky pattern over her neck. Jesus Christ and a crack whore.

Phase two of this plan clearly needed to be set in motion. Praying her voice wouldn't give out on her, Jeannie reared up against him, feeling the tip of the knife prick her flesh. "Do it, coward! Do it, you spineless piece of uneducated shit!" she screamed, making her eyes bulge, spraying his face with spit. "Do it just like you did to Jorge. C'mon, you know how to kill innocent babies! I should be a piece o' cake! Kill me and get it over with, you motherfuckerrrr!" she bellowed so loud it made his greasy hair sway from her exhale of breath.

And it hurt her throat. But it was for the cause—so, whatever.

Victor dragged her forward by the hair, digging his fingers deep into her scalp, tilting her neck back so her throat was revealed. He yanked her upward with a furious hand, dragging her as far away as the ankle cuffs would allow. Jesus. If he didn't do this soon, she was going to have a dislocated hip, too.

Briefly, she caught sight of Najim and Nekaar, their faces appropriately fearful. Yet, the flicker in Nekaar's eyes was real. This plan they'd hatched was risky, and she felt Nekaar's cool facade slip, but she warned him with her eyes, begging him to just let this play out. He twitched his thumb in an upward motion, pretending he was wiping the corner of his mouth.

All systems go.

Burt was still behind Victor, his sunken eyes wide with fear, his body visibly trembling. He continued to hop from foot to foot in nervous anticipation—like some methed-out cheerleader. "C'mon, Victor!" he whined. "Do it before one of her stupid dogs starts to bark—they're tearing shit up in the bathroom."

Victor shook her violently, arching her spine at an awkward position, breathing heavily as he raised the knife, gleaming and sharp. She saw it then. The anticipation in his eyes. The gleam of excitement he drew from literally being handed the opportunity to finally get his revenge made keeping her mouth shut and not screaming a neener, neener in his face really hard.

Victor held that pose for a long, drawn-out moment. He looked macabre in his new genie garb. Dark and glistening with sweat, his teeth white in his swarthy face, he shook with maniacal joy as he prepared to end her life.

Sweat dripped from his brow. His wild eyes looked down at her when he opened his mouth wide to screech, "This is for *mi familia*, you backstabbing snitch!"

"*Fuck—you*, Victor!" she screamed just as the knife sliced through her flesh, cutting her so deep, she heard the gurgle of blood spew from her neck.

Oh, and she also heard Sloan burst through the door with Nina right behind him roaring, "Jeannnniieee!"

What was it about hell and a road?

Oh, right. The road to hell is paved with good intentions.

* * *

SLOAN lunged for Victor seconds too late, snarling his agony in a howl so earsplitting that even from where Jeannie sat, for all intents and purposes dead to the casual observer's eye and still propped up against the wall Victor had slammed her into after he'd slit her throat, made her want to put her hands over her ears. As she watched, helplessly immobile, her rage rose to a new level of hatred.

"I'll kill you, you bastard!" Sloan bellowed, Nina charging in behind him.

Jeannie realized, from this strange in-between place, she was almost glad Sloan and Nina had shown up. It meant Nekaar and Najim would suffer far less abuse at the hands of Burt and Victor while she did this crazy thing called transition. Her thoughts warmed when she realized, both genies had gone into this crazy plan knowing they'd be rendered helpless until she transformed.

As Sloan went for Victor's throat, Nina, her eyes full of momentary anguish at the sight of Jeannie, hesitated for only a moment before she was prying the cuffs from Nekaar's ankles like they were made of butter.

For all the good it would do him, Jeannie mused. Hadn't Nekaar said no one could remove the curse on the ankle bracelets but the genie who'd cursed it in the first place? Wasn't that why she'd taken this ugly, gaping-wound hit? Didn't Nekaar say there was no other way but for her to die? Oh, if this crazy idea worked, she was going to banish him to the realm of eternal stupidhead!

But to Jeannie's surprise, Nekaar was up and springing into action, removing Najim's cuffs as the ex-ruler scrambled toward Jeannie to perform the ritual as they'd planned. His eyes held terror when his gaze fixed on Jeannie.

Yet, Najim's words for the spell were strong if not hushed and quick and when he rose to join Nekaar in the fight, his last glance at Jeannie was that of reassurance.

Nekaar became a force, leaping into the air to raise an angry fist in Victor's direction. He screamed something in a language Jeannie didn't understand, his face a mask of tight fury.

A thunderbolt of a multicolored beam shot from his large fingers, knocking Victor against the wall and smashing her dresser. Wood pieces exploded into the air, jutting into the walls in sharp splinters, making a whizzing sound as they flew by. The wall separating her bedroom and living room blew apart with an explosion of sheetrock and nails.

The beam of light, menacingly blue, sought Victor as though it were a missile in search of its target. It headed straight for him, grazing his head so it slammed against the wall and bounced back off, giving Sloan just the opportunity he needed.

Sloan dodged the hissing beam and went for Victor, clearly mindless to the fact that Nekaar was now in control of the situation.

Nekaar screamed above the shrill howl of wind Burt had created, "No, Sloan!"

But Sloan was single-minded as he raced across the room at the speed of light, heading straight for Victor's throat.

But Victor had semi-recovered, rising up and levitating to hover over the room. His hand morphed into a sledgehammer, oversized and square. He brought it down with the sound of thunder on Sloan's head.

Sloan dropped to the ground, crashing against the floor and leaving an imprint of his twisted form in the remains of the wood.

Jeannie's surprise at how swiftly Victor had taken to djinn magic was quickly replaced with sorrow for Sloan. Fear for his safety washed over her. A fear she couldn't express while this transition kept her imprisoned as nothing more than a corporeal observer.

This stupid spell better friggin' work or she was going to hunt Nekaar down from her genie afterlife. Sprawled up against the wall and helpless was nothing short of maddening. And, in a moment of lunacy, she thought, this position she was propped up in was probably going to leave her with a crick in her neck due to its odd angle. On top of everything else, if she survived this, someone owed her a massage.

Victor set his malicious eyes on Nekaar. Throwing his hands up like a conductor at a symphony, he lifted Nekaar in the air, and for a moment, suspended the regal genie before balling him up and throwing him across the room like a human baseball.

Nekaar crashed into her living room wall, falling to the ground in a pile of limbs and harem pants.

Nina flashed her fangs in anger, setting her sights on Victor just as Najim twirled his finger in the air, creating a tornadolike effect of rain and wind. As rain slashed against her face, Nina launched herself at Victor. Grabbing him by the neck and raising her hand high, she slammed him into what was left of the springs of the bed, piercing his skin with the sharp coils of the mattress.

Then Burt was in the mix, too, finally grasping what was really going on around him—he sprang into action. Using both arms, he raised them high and spread his fingers, flinging his hands as though there were excess water on them he was attempting to shake off.

Bolts of fire came from out of nowhere, hitting Nina in the head with a sizzling crack. She screamed her rage, straightening with her arms open wide, her fists clenched. She narrowed her eyes, pinpointing Burt as her new target. As she leapt through the room, hurling pieces of debris from her path, she lifted the chair and flung it at Burt, just catching him in the side of his head and knocking him sideways.

She screamed a rebel yell so untamed and fierce, Jeannie, from her strange, ethereal view, shuddered. Yet, even as Nina immobilized

Burt, Victor was back on top again, soaring through the air and directly toward Nina.

Then Marty and Wanda were at her door, eyeing the situation with a critical glance before rushing in and shifting to their were-forms. Snarling and screeching, they lunged into the melee. Howls rose up in the air, flesh tore, hair flew, and still, they waged.

All in an effort to avenge her supposed death.

Jeannie wanted to scream into the falling debris and howling wind, to warn them they weren't immune to a genie's magic. There was no eternal life when up against a djinn, but she was trapped until this transformation occurred. Her fear ratcheted up a notch, as the people she'd come to care for fought for their lives.

Sloan shifted then—his clothes splitting and ripping apart in chunks of material. He fell to the floor with a crash. He growled, his mouth opening wide, revealing his teeth; his howl was feral when he reared back on all fours and located Victor.

Victor had Nina clamped to the wall, imprisoned by some invisible force while she struggled to free herself, the veins in her arms pulsing visibly.

And Team Paranormal was suckin' wind.

Najim eyed the spot in the room they'd chosen for her to wait and gave a slight nod of acknowledgment to her before he began to spin like a top. The centrifugal force of it created a windstorm even Victor's newly acquired magic couldn't contain.

Nina was suddenly thrown free of the wall, dropping to her feet with catlike grace. "I'll kill you, motherfucker!" Her eyes met Najim's, and Jeannie wanted to scream to her that he wasn't the enemy.

But she had no choice in the matter. *Completion is important, madam. These things take time*, Nekaar had said.

Yet, while she waited for completion, devastation was occurring all around her.

Nekaar noted Nina's lunge for Najim and roared, "He is not the enemy, angry one! Get Victor!"

Glass flew in every direction, loud clashes of thunder and screeching metal clanged around the room in resounding echoes.

And still Jeannie waited as Nina rose up again and again, doing whatever was in her power to thwart Burt and Victor.

Jeannie's eyes followed Sloan as he lunged for Victor over and over, snarling, bellowing his rage until she wanted to scream for them to stop.

As suddenly as that thought came was how suddenly she felt the return of her soul to her body. In the blink of an eye, she felt her arm move, her toes twitch, and her head throb from the brutal blow she'd taken to the back of her head.

Like a phoenix rising from the ashes, literally, Jeannie plowed upward, taking the debris of Sheetrock and glass that had fallen on her prone body with her as she went.

So, yeah, in the immortal words of Nina Blackman-Statleon—it was time to roll some bitchez.

CHAPTER
18

Power surged through her limbs, rocketing her skyward. The room quaked, crashing and shaking with such vengeance her teeth chattered together.

Victor, his eyes wide in disbelief, backed away, staggering to press himself against a wall.

Nekaar had managed to untwist himself and locate her old bottle. He held it up like he'd just won the mirror ball on *Dancing with the Stars*, shaking it wildly and jumping up and down. His face was weary. Blood dripped from the top of his shiny head as his strong, bronzed arm began to tremble in an effort to hold up the bottle.

Burt now hovered in a corner, cowering and quaking. His face was covered in Sheetrock dust, marked only by the tracks of his frightened tears. He curled into a ball, whimpering and begging.

Jeannie flew at Burt's face while debris swirled around her, and yelled the words Nekaar had taught her. "I, master of all djinn . . ." she stumbled.

Hoo, shit. She'd forgotten. Damn her short-term memory. Wait.

Was it, *I, master of all djinn, do so solemnly curse you to this bottle for eternity*? Or was it *forever*? Wait. Didn't the curse rhyme?

Crap, crap, crap! If she got one word wrong, it could all go to hell.

Nekaar ran toward her like a football player headed for the goal post. He jumped up on what remained of her bedpost, wobbling momentarily before perching himself there and repeated the words in a flurry of frantic gestures. "Madam, listen! I, master of all djinn *near and far*, curse you to live in this bottle wherever you are!"

Well, hell. There was no *eternity* at all in there, now was there?

Her voice flew from her throat in a boom when she repeated the words, "I, master of all djinn near and far, curse you to live in this bottle wherever you are!"

"Not agaiiiinnn!" Burt wailed, making a break for what was left of her doorway only to become a stream of green smoke with the faint smell of garbage to it. Nekaar held the bottle up, waving his hand and directing the stream of wispy tendrils into it like an air traffic controller.

One down, one to go.

And there was no choice in the matter. As vile as Victor was, as much as Jeannie found the only solution to this problem as reprehensible as what Victor had done, Nekaar had reminded her, she had more than just herself to think about now.

"Act quickly, madam!" Nekaar directed frantically, as Najim continued to try to pry Victor's hands from an object she couldn't quite see, and Sloan, attached to Victor's back, began tearing at his flesh with his razorlike teeth.

As fast as Sloan's teeth tore gouges of skin from Victor's back was as fast as they healed. Marty and Wanda ripped pieces of his flesh from his legs to no avail.

But Mat was there like a shot out of the dark, soaring through the air like an Air Force fighter plane. He aimed right for Sloan,

Marty, and Wanda, spreading his fibers until he encompassed them all, knocking them off Victor. "Invisiiiibbbblllee!" he yelled, clear as day, nary a phlegm-riddled cough in sight.

OMG. He'd done it! Jeannie roared her approval, fighting back a tear of pride. "Totally invisible!"

Najim, through clenched teeth, yelled to her, "Jeannie—*do this*! I can't hold him off"—he clamped his jaw tight—"much longer!"

Victor lunged for Nina and dug his fingers into her neck, ramming her against the wall. Her eyes had gone glassy and her long legs dangled.

The scent of garlic and burning flesh rose to Jeannie's nose, and it was then that she realized, Victor must have materialized a cross out of thin air, a cross decorated with a rope of garlic. He drove the cross against her chest, singeing her flesh and immobilizing her.

She didn't think she could hate Victor any more than she already did for the life he'd stolen from so many, but his hands around Nina's neck, burning her flesh, made Jeannie's anger spike to a new height.

Her eyes zeroed in on Victor, her voice flew from her lips like a sonic boom. "You will die, Victor Lopez! For all the wrong you've done, for the lives you've stolen, you will die!" she spat, shooting hot flames from her mouth so they nipped at his limbs.

Throwing her hands into the air, she fisted them, releasing what Nekaar had called the Walk of Shame curse—or spell—or whatever.

Their eyes connected, and with the help of her newly bestowed power, Jeannie created a startling visual—the visual she'd lived with in her head for the last twelve years.

An ugly picture of agonizing suffering—the movie reel of the deaths that had dirtied his hands. Jorge, broken on the ground, their housekeeper, bloodied and riddled with bullets, Victor's brothers in twisted piles of limbs. Him as he brought the butt of that gun down on her relentlessly, screaming she was his forever.

It was all there for him to see in living color.

Victor dropped Nina, whimpering in fear. He looked up at this entity she'd become, his mouth open wide in a silent scream of horror.

Jeannie wasted no time, striking hard and fast. Whirling around, Jeannie put her hands together, one on top of the other, then opened them, keeping the heels of them pressed tight and curling her fingers inward. She repeated the words in her head, words she must never speak aloud, just as Nekaar had taught her but moments ago.

I banish thee, oh foulest of foul, I banish thee with this dragon's howl!

To her shaking amazement, her hands twisted, reshaping themselves into the mouth of a scaled, mottled blue dragon. Its head bobbled, rearing back, then up in a fierce howl. Opening her hands wide, she breathed fire on him, hot and searing. A long tongue, pink and ringed with ridges, snapped at Victor once before snatching him from the air and rolling his body up like a weenie in a blanket.

He wailed in agony, twisting and tearing at the tongue just before it swallowed him whole.

Silence, in all its eerie bliss, settled on the room.

Jeannie dropped to the floor, falling to the ground in a puff of Sheetrock and wood. Nekaar was above her in an instant. "Oh, madam." He clapped his hands together with a rapid motion. "You were stunning!"

She looked up at him, her eyes crossing. "You know this genie thing?" She held up her red palms for inspection. "It burns. The next time you tell me to dragon-up, a little warning, m'kay?"

Nekaar swept her up in his arms and twirled her around, laughing and lifting her off her feet to bounce her up and down. "You did it. Never have I seen such vivid execution!"

She winced at the pain in her ribs and tried to squirm out of his grasp. Nina, immobile on the floor, caught her eye. She waved a hand, a hand that made Nekaar release her without saying a word.

Wow. Goooo, genies.

Dropping to Nina's side, she threw herself on the vampire's chest and sobbed, "MWA! Don't you do this to me. Don't you dare die. Not today. Do you hear me? If you die, there'll be no one to call me midget!" Tears stung her eyes.

Nina groaned, making Jeannie's head pop up. Nina's eyes flew open. "Shut up, shawty. I'm not dead, but I want explanations—like right fucking now." She rubbed at the spot, where a faint imprint of the cross Victor held to her chest remained.

"Jeannie!"

Her eyes lifted to the tune of Sloan's voice. Sloan, who'd come to get her despite the fact she'd asked him to stay away.

A buck-naked Sloan who was fighting his way out from under Mat.

She snapped her fingers like she'd been doing it all her life, restoring Sloan's clothing to the precise shape they'd been in before he came charging in to save his damsel in distress. Jeannie stared at her fingers, confused. After all that frickin' struggle to keep some candles floating in the air, she was suddenly genie extraordinaire? The magic had just happened without effort or even much thought.

Jeannie hopped over a grumbling Nina and hurled herself into his arms, forgetting the screaming ache of her ribs and the continual throb of her head. "Sloan! Oh, God. Why did you come here? I told you to stay home!"

He pulled her tight to him, his cologne drifting to her nose as she buried her face in his neck. "You didn't really think I believed you, did you? That was some of the worst acting I've ever witnessed. It's good you cook," he teased.

She planted a warm kiss to his lips, running her hands over his jaw. "You could have been killed." Her heart clenched at the thought.

"Um, excuse me, Ms. Carlyle. You *were* killed," he reminded her, his eyes taking on a haunted look. "I saw it with my own two eyes."

She nodded, squeezing his neck. "That was the plan, silly."

Nina was leering at her over Sloan's shoulder, her head bald in spots where the fire had singed it, her clothes torn and blackened. She waved her hand. "Explanation. Now. 'Cus I'm feelin' a little pissy about the state of my hoodie." She held up the burned edge of it and narrowed her eyes.

Jeannie slid from Sloan's body, planting her feet on the floor. "Okay, so here's the deal. I'm now officially the master of the djinn."

"Well, la-dee-da." Nina crowed sarcastic approval.

Jeannie curtsied in response and smiled.

"So, queen djinn, how the fuck did the whack Victor get out of the bottle?" Nina demanded.

Nekaar was instantly at Jeannie's side. "It was I, pale one. I am responsible for Victor's release. Should ire be your choice of emotion, please direct such at me," he stated with an arrogant lift to his chin as he crossed his arms over his chest and widened his stance.

Nina's lips thinned. She jammed her face into Nekaar's. "You know, cue ball, that motherfucking wife beater almost killed me and the paranormal posse. How is it that whenever your Aladdin ass is in the vicinity, bad shit's happenin'?"

Jeannie stepped between Nina and Nekaar. "Nekaar mistakenly let Victor out of the bottle. Long story—I'll share the details later. Anyway, Burt was the one who kidnapped Najim, er, the former ruler of the djinn."

Sloan's eyes held confusion. "Na-who?"

Najim crossed the room, his elegant silver jacket, cropped at the waist, still smoking. His raven hair was almost white from the sheetrock dust, and his harem pants, garnished with red rubies, were flapping behind him. Placing his palms together, he bowed before Nina and Sloan. "I'm Najim. It's an honor."

Nina scoffed and made a face, wiping a hand over her soot-streaked face. "You're the head genie? Did you win that title on your Xbox 360, dude?"

Instead of taking offense, he leaned into Jeannie and gave her a brilliant smile. "No. But it's just one more thing I can add to my list of stuff to catch up on now that Jeannie's taking over."

Jeannie couldn't help but giggle. "Najim was the ruler of Genie Land. When Burt cursed me after he escaped from the bottle, he didn't just turn me into a genie or simply screw up and tether Sloan and I together—he somehow released this crazy power that sort of landed on me. So the reason I was granting random wishes was because not only was my magic untrained, it was all screwed up. It had to be tweaked, so to speak."

Nina scruffed her soot-covered hair up and grinned. "Badass, midget. So explain the shiz that just went down. You were dead, kiddo. Scared the living shit out of me."

Jeannie saw the flash of concern in Nina's eyes before she slapped her tough exterior back on, and it made her heart shift in her chest. "I was dead, that's true. Very dead. And you'd have never seen any of it if you'd just stayed away," she admonished, rolling her eyes in Sloan's direction. "Genie magic trumps *all* magic. So your paranormal superpowers, as you saw, did little good." She went on to explain how Burt had found her and what he and Victor had planned to do to Jeannie in their quest to steal her power.

Nina's eyes went directly to Nekaar with accusation flashing in them. "So, if Burt was the dummy in this relationship, how the fuck is it that you didn't know he could do something like this?"

Nekaar's sigh was of exaggerated exasperation. "Because, madam, I do not seek such atrocities. I was not aware anyone could take our ruler's place. I was also unaware that a book existed with instructions on how to do so. I am not malevolent in nature!"

Sloan patted Nekaar on the back. "Burt was who checked out the book from the library? The book had real information? Information that worked?" Sloan asked.

Jeannie squeezed Nekaar's arm. "Yep, and the curse Burt originally hurled at me was totally a screwup on his part. He didn't complete the curse. When he found out what he'd done, he looked for ways to get the magic back."

Nina planted her hands on her hips. "Get to the death part, midget."

Jeannie smiled in Nekaar and Najim's direction. "My death was all part of the plan. I distracted Burt while Victor was in the kitchen cooking up my destruction and Mat, the most awsometastic magic carpet ever, slithered off into the living room, found that damn book, read the spell they planned to perform on me, and slithered back in. Originally, Victor was going to kill me, transfer my power to Burt, making Burt the new ruler because as you know, genies can't use magic for personal gain. So I let Victor do what he's wanted to do all these years. Kill me."

"I fucking told you we shouldn't have put Victor in the bottle. You shoulda let me kill him," Nina said, balling her fists.

Sloan put an arm around Nina and said, "Hush, vampire." His warm eyes fell on Jeannie as she continued.

"Anyway, we didn't have much choice. We were all rendered powerless by those stupid ankle cuffs. So the only choice we had was to let Victor kill me, have Najim repeat the words to the spell, which, by the way, you don't even have to be a genie to perform, and pray Najim and Nekaar didn't suffer too long, chained to that damn wall, while I made the transition. Talk about a leap of faith, right? What they didn't count on was Najim performing the spell on me before they could get there first." Jeannie followed her words with a smug smile. "And speaking of spells . . ." She turned to Nekaar, her eyes flashing. "Didn't you tell me no one but the genie who cursed those cuffs could remove the curse? Nina's not a genie."

Nekaar's eyes were sheepish. "I spoke too soon, I fear. My most informed guess is, Burt cursed the cuffs, madam. And we all know how Burt's curses roll, as you say."

Jeannie's giggle bordered hysterical. "So I let Victor slit my throat for nothing?"

"Nay! Nothing you have done tonight was in vain, madam. Who could have guessed the pale, angry one would show up with your pretty male? You died for the cause, madam!" Nekaar said fiercely.

"Yeah, about that. You dying. *Explain*," Sloan insisted, his gaze intense as he brushed the hair from her eyes. "Because I'm still a little lost about why you had to die for this all to work. And it better never happen again. I don't think I'll live through it."

"According to the book, I had to die and experience a rebirth by way of the spell, the sort of final phase of me becoming ruler. I was only three quarters of the way there all this time because Burt screwed up originally, which explains why my magic was so haywire. I just needed the other quarter of it to complete me. Under normal circumstances, according to this book, this ritual would have been a happy occasion, and once I was reborn, there would have been celebrations and all sorts of jazz. But the magic I had can also be stolen upon my death—if you know how to do it, that is. So my half-assed magic, plus this spell no one seemed to know about but Burt, equals the most powerful genie ever."

Nina's eyes narrowed. "So that dicknuckle Burt only spewed half the spell when he got out of the bottle?"

Jeannie winced when she ran her hand over the back of her head. "That's basically what it boils down to, MWA. He found pieces of the spell on the Internet, but the entirety of it was in that book. A book I fully intend to burn as new ruler. Can you even believe just anyone can repeat it? You don't have to be djinn to cast it. That worked to our advantage, too, because Najim was powerless at that point."

Sloan shook his head. "So why didn't Najim take the spell and use it for himself, so he could continue to rule the djinn?"

Najim smiled at Sloan. "Because Najim is tired after a buttload of centuries as ruler. And remember, in order for someone to accumulate all of the power, your Jeannie would have had to die for me to steal it."

Sloan slapped him on the back with a smile. "You made the right choice, my friend. Because if you'd harmed a hair on her head, no genie magic would have saved you."

Jeannie smiled impishly up at him, her eyes warm.

Najim gave Sloan a sheepish glance. "I'm sorry I wasn't more help. My magic was a little neglected during my week of captivity, and as you grew stronger, I grew weaker."

Jeannie ran a hand over his arm and smiled. "You were still pretty awesome."

Nina shook her head, her dark hair now beginning to grow back before Jeannie's eyes. "So you actually let that fuck put a knife to your throat and slit it?"

Jeannie nodded, forcing the utter terror of that decision from her mind. "A knife dipped in some kind of genie magic. What they didn't count on was what a brilliant spy Mat turned out to be. He saved us."

"Jesus Christ and a pair of Hanes, you are one righteous broad, midget. Gimme the knuck," Nina encouraged, her fist facing forward.

Jeannie bumped fists with her and grinned, though she ached from head to toe.

Marty and Wanda began to squeak from beneath Mat, sending Nina off to help them.

Sloan's jaw clenched and a vein in his forehead pulsed. Always a sure sign he was bent out of shape.

She put her hands on his chest and glanced up at him with hangdog eyes. "So you're mad."

He held up a hand. "Pretty people have feelings, too."

She walked her fingers up his arm and batted her eyelashes—even though the batting hurt like hell. "Would it help if I said I'm über-sorry, and I was just trying to keep you out of harm's way like you all did for me?"

He shrugged his shoulder and sighed comically. "Maybe."

Throwing her arms around him, she clung to his middle. "I'm sooorrry. So, so desperately, dreadfully, incredibly sorry."

Sloan scooped her up and met her gaze, his filled with fire. "Don't ever, ever, so long as your little genie life lasts, ever do that again, young lady. I think I lost a good fifty years off my eternity."

Her heart clenched tight and her arms tightened around him. "Promise. I think. I hope."

"You're one brave warrior, Jeannie Carlyle."

As the reality of what she'd done began to sink in, she found herself beginning to wobble.

Sloan put his lips to hers, kissing her soundly before pulling away to ask, "So, about that dinner date . . . We might have to reschedule due to the remodel your kitchen's going to need. We can't play *Top Chef* like this." He waved his hand around at the total annihilation of her brownstone.

Jeannie giggled against his lips and sighed. "I get to be Padma," she teased. She didn't care that her brownstone was ruined. She didn't care that her body felt like it had been run over by a 747. The only thing that mattered was Sloan was here with her and safe.

"All right you two, leave the lip-lock for later, huh?" Nina razzed them as Wanda and Marty followed behind her, both wrapped in one sheet. Nina held up Mat and gave him a shake.

Tears stung Jeannie's eyes when she took him from Nina. She cradled him close to her chest. "You are the best guardian ever."

He coughed, blowing more Sheetrock dust up in a white cloud. "Invisible," he reminded her.

Jeannie laughed. "Like totally. I'm so proud of you."

"Aw," he grumbled. "It's the least I could do for ya, dollface."

She held him up, struggling to hold his heavy weight. "You know, there's something else I can do for you if what Nekaar says is true."

He shuddered, making his fibers ripple. "Dyson?"

Jeannie shook her head. "Way more awesome. I can lift your curse . . . You could be human again, Mat. I'd miss you as my guardian, but all you have to do is wish . . ."

Mat held perfectly still for a moment as though paused in thought. "Can I think on it, doll? I dunno if I can handle bein' human again. I'm so used to bein' just some throw rug."

She pulled him back to her chest and squeezed him hard. "You're not just some throw rug. You're my throw rug, and you take all the time you need." Dropping a kiss on his fringe that made him purr, she set him down on the floor. Mat slid off over the chunks of her brownstone and disappeared under the bathroom door where Boris and Benito barked wildly and scratched at the door.

Jeannie turned to Wanda and Marty, more tears stinging her eyes. "Thank you. I never could have done this without you—all of you."

Marty blew a strand of her mussed hair from her face and enveloped Jeannie in a hug. "Please. You were a force, kiddo. Way to take a sonofabitch out, honey," she cooed.

Wanda bobbed her head, tugging at a piece of wood stuck in her shoulder before examining Jeannie's head, which was still crusted with blood. She wrapped her arm around Jeannie's neck, squeezing it before clucking her tongue. "What a disaster. Nina, get the Dust-Buster. Wait. Scratch that. See if Darnell can hire a bulldozer. Marty? See if we can find some rubber gloves. You know how my hands chafe when they're submerged in water."

And they were off, unaware that Jeannie could simply snap her fingers and restore everything to its former disorganized mess.

She was about to reveal that when Sloan took her by the hand

and pulled her aside. "Before you do the hocus-pocus and make everything all better, give me a second."

"For?"

"For this," he murmured before swooping down and covering her lips with his.

And in the midst of Wanda barking orders, and Marty carrying on about how itchy Jeannie's sheets were, and Nina complaining that Marty was a diva-whiner, Jeannie sighed against Sloan's mouth.

This was what magic was made of.

JEANNIE and Nina sat side by side on her bed once more while Sloan was at the store picking up more antibiotic cream to tend to the wounds he promised he'd care for when they were alone if he could just get rid of all the yakking women who seemed to think he was incapable of nurturing her properly. She didn't bother to tell him that the next spell on her list to learn was that of self-healing. She needed a moment alone with Nina.

Sloan had insisted she wait here and rest under Nina's watchful eye.

Jeannie nudged Nina's shoulder. "Can I ask you something, MWA?"

Nina eyed her. "Is it gonna require a long, touchy-feely talk? Gotta tell ya, after tonight, I'm just not up to a bunch of therapeutic, girlie-talk bullshit. I'm all girl'd out."

Jeannie giggled, letting her legs dangle from the bed. "Nope."

"Then ask and make it quick. I need to go home and see my man the minute the ass sniffer gets back from the store."

She gave Nina a tentative look. "If I had been your genie—"

"If you'd been mine, I'd have stuffed your midget ass back in that bottle and sealed that shit tighter than a virgin's chastity belt and none of this would have gone down. End of."

Jeannie chuckled again, knowing full well Nina would have

rescued her like she had so many others. "Just listen to the question." She paused and waited for Nina to nod her head in consent. "If I'd been your genie, what would you have wished for? Would you have even wished at all?"

Nina made a face at her. "Is this some kind of fucking test? Like that Rorschach thing with all the pictures that are supposed to mean something? 'Cus I can tell you for sure, they don't look like cuddly puppies and rainbows to me. Just looks like carnage and innards."

Jeannie stifled a giggle. "Nope, I was just curious. You don't have to answer."

Nina's pause was long, myriad emotions flitted across her face, and then she shot Jeannie a faraway smile. "Yeah, I would have wished. But not for the shit most people wish for: money, cars, boobs, whatever."

"Ruler of the universe, right?"

"You're funny, squirt. Like I'd fucking wanna have to deal with that kind of responsibility. Nah. Nothing that big. Well, not big to some, but big to me because it's impossible."

"Aha!" Jeannie shook her finger at her. "The chance to eat chicken wings and Ring Dings again, right?"

"Don't think I wouldn't dig a bucket o' wings and a fucking Ho Hos."

"So that's what you'd wish for?"

"Nope."

"Then what? The suspense, she kills me."

"Kids."

Jeannie's breath caught in her throat. Nina was great with children and animals and anything helpless, but Jeannie'd never considered she'd wanted any of her own. At first encounter, Nina came off very selfish, but Jeannie knew that wasn't who this vampire really was on the inside. She was loyal, protective—and honest to her core.

She'd given up her eternity to the man she loved when push came to shove and she'd had the choice to become a vampire or let Greg perish.

That kind of devotion, that kind of sacrifice, came from a deeply selfless soul. It came from someone who loved hard and loved forever.

Jeannie slung an arm over Nina's shoulder. "No shit?"

"No shit. I dig kids. You know that. Never really wanted them until Greg—and even then, I didn't want 'em until we'd been married a little while. But when I hang with Hollis and my sister Penny, I get this fucked-up feeling in my stomach—like just a little something's missing. But I gave that shit up when I mated with Greg. He's enough for me, and I have Hollis and Penny and Katie's twins from time to time. It's a good life."

Jeannie believed that was true—to her core. "I wonder if you had children if they'd live for an eternity, too? I mean, vampire children."

She shrugged her shoulders. "I guess they would, but it's never happened to a vampire. So it ain't shit you need to worry your midget head over."

But there was this one festering question . . . "Would you want them to live for an eternity, too?"

"Probably fucking selfish of me, but, yeah. I don't know if I could deal with my kid kickin' it before me. Ever. That's more than I think even I got in me. I'm a badass—but I'm a marshmallow when it comes to the little shits."

"But what about the little one? How would you explain eternity?"

"I guess it would just grow up that way, right? Like Sloan and Keegan, Casey's kid, Naomi, too. It's just part of their world. It would meet other vampires or werewolves at paranormal playgroup or some shit. So, yeah. I would have wished for a kid." She shook her head, a scowl returning to her face. "Look, this is kind of a moot point. Now shut the fuck up and quit talkin' about crap that ain't gonna happen and go get with your man. I just heard him pull up with my super vampire hearing. So, shoo-shoo." She waved her hands at the door.

Jeannie smiled and, on impulse, threw her arms around Nina's neck and squeezed tight. "You're the best evah, MWA. *Evah.*"

Nina gave her an awkward pat on the back before saying, "Get the fuck off me. What is it with you and a PDA, dude?"

It was freedom.

The freedom to express your joy—your love for another person—without being afraid it would be taken away.

And now, she decided as she rose and made her way to the door, she was going to go express that freedom with Sloan.

Opening the door, a door that deep down inside Jeannie knew led to her future, she stepped out just in time to see Sloan with a bag from CVS.

He held it up and smiled, wiggling his eyebrows. His handsome face taking her breath away. "Wanna try something kinky with Neosporin?"

Jeannie giggled and wrapped her arms around his waist, burrowing her aching head against his chest. "Oh, yeah. I always wanna try something kinky with Neosporin."

He scooped her up gently, touching his lips to her forehead. "I've got bandages and peroxide, too. Just to keep things fresh and exciting."

Jeannie let her head fall back on her shoulders when she laughed loud and strong. "I don't know how I could ever be expected to resist bandages and peroxide. I'm giddy with desire."

"So you wanna go explore that? You know." He tilted his jaw toward the door and gave her a lewd smile. "In there?"

Jeannie's return smile was warm even as tears formed in the corner of her eyes. She cupped his jaw. "Only if I get to play the part of Christopher Columbus."

He rolled his eyes. "God, you're so demanding. Is this how it's always going to be? You making demands and me giving in?"

Always—the word made her heart throb with joy. "We'll never know until we try," she said, mentally stepping aside and leaving room for Sloan, giving him the opportunity to walk into that metaphorical door she'd just opened.

"Then let's try," he said, his eyes connecting with hers in unspoken understanding.

Jeannie didn't say another word. Instead, she sealed their silent commitment with a kiss.

A kiss full of promise.

A kiss full of always.

EPILOGUE

Nine Months and Four Days Later—Seven and Counting Freaky-deaky Paranormal Accidents, a New Head Honcho in Genie-ville, a Reformed, Sickly Besotted Playah Werewolf, a Hot Pairing Between Two of the Most Unlikely People in the World, a Brokeback Magic Carpet Turned Human, an Even Super-duper Freakier Paranormal Pregnancy, and a Vampini in a Pear Tree . . .

"Martyyyy! I swear to fucking Christ, if you don't get the fuck away from me with your goddamn squishy-feely Lamaze, I'm gonna beat the fake blonde out of you when this is done."

Marty beamed a smile and wiped Nina's brow with a cool cloth, clearly smothering her with motherly love. "Now, now, Mistress of the Dark, remember what I told you about babies in utero. They can hear everything. Do you want your precious angel's first word to be"—she leaned down close to Nina's ear and whispered—"*fucktard*?"

"No. I want them to be *Hello, Auntie Fucktard!*" she spat in Marty's face from between clenched teeth.

Jeannie cringed and winced, but she refused to believe Nina

would be anything but an outstanding parent once the baby was
within hearing distance.

Wanda watched the monitor, and if she marveled at the miracle
that there was a little heartbeat registering on it, she didn't show it.
"Deep breaths, now, honey. Another contraction's on its way. It's
time to push, Nina—puuuussshhhh!" Wanda chirped, squeezing
Nina's hand with encouragement while Casey stood by, cheering
with pretend pom-poms.

"What the fuck is this bullshit?" Nina roared, rearing upward in
her bed, her long, dark hair sticking up at odd places, saturated with
the sweat she wasn't supposed to be able to produce. "I can't breathe,
dummy! I'm a vampire, for fuck's sake—I'm not supposed to feel
any of this. I have no working frickin' uterus—how the hell can it
be contracting?" she yelped, then set her sights on Jeannie, who stood
at the doorway to Nina and Greg's bedroom. "Swear to God, midget,
if I live through this shit and my chuckie doesn't split in half, I comin'
to get your ass right after Marty's!"

Jeannie smiled wide. Ah, the strange, yet awe-inspiring magic
of a genie's wish granted.

When Jeannie'd been given permission from Najim to grant herself her one heart's desire, she'd chosen not to use it for herself.
Instead, for all that Nina had taught her, for all she'd given in the
name of her "midget," Jeannie had chosen to forgo her wish and use
it to give Nina and Greg a child.

She'd had no idea Nina'd actually carry that child—full term.

She'd also never in a million years anticipated Nina would experience what every human woman experiences when with child.

Who knew her wish, one she'd granted because Nina was one of
the kindest, most selfless people Jeannie had ever known, would
involve morning sickness, sciatica, mood swings—oh, Lord, the
mood swings—and a *uterus*?

But here they were—nine months later, finally at an end to Nina's continual bitching in sight.

Greg held Nina's other hand, his face that of a worried, expectant father. He'd arranged to have all the birthing equipment brought to their castle so they wouldn't have to go to a hospital and risk exposure.

Not to mention, on several occasions, Nina had openly considered her fears about what the rug rat would turn out to be, supernaturally speaking. Thus, no one wanted to take the chance in such a public place.

So Marty had read books about homebirths on her e-reader out loud to Wanda while Wanda knitted baby booties, blankets, and hats in neutral colors. Casey read tips on successful breast-feeding on the off chance Nina had also gained that particular human trait.

They'd thrown Nina a baby shower, too. A big one with as many pink and blue items as they could get their hands on. Nina had squawked her protests near and far, but nothing could stop them from making her wear the paper plate hat decorated with all the bows from the shower presents she'd received. She'd had no choice, Marty had joked. It wasn't like Nina could get her whalelike ass out of its own way to get away from them anyhow.

During Nina's pregnancy, she and Sloan had decided to try this relationship thing out sans forced entrapment. Since that decision, her world had grown so much bigger, stretching to new limits with new experiences. It was full of friends who invited her and Sloan to the strangest barbeques she'd ever been to, entailing champagne-glass, blood waterfalls and steaks that merely grazed the grill before they were yanked.

They'd spent long nights just sitting up talking while they watched football and baseball and any sport Sloan could get his hands on. In return, he watched *Top Chef* with her, daring her to try some of the recipes. He'd taught her the wonders of HDTV and flat screens.

He'd even bought her one for her birthday, but they both knew whom the present was really for.

They ate out often, saw movies together—celebrated Christmas at Marty and Keegan's, where Jeannie experienced a full-moon shift. Most of all, their intimate relationship had deepened. Jeannie was now a regular at Victoria's Secret, and she loved that she shared her purchases unabashedly while Sloan whistled his approval and cat-called as she strut past him.

So many changes.

Mat had decided he'd like to give a go at being human again. The result of his restoration was nothing short of fantastic. Thankfully, he was restored to his former age, and while his zoot suit left a lot to be desired, he was also incredibly handsome with sandy brown hair and deep brown eyes.

The girls were still working on breaking him of using the term *dollface*, but he'd proven his weight in gold in, of all places, the kitchen, where he and Betzi now shared space and worked side by side as Jeannie's catering business continued to grow.

Charlene and Betzi, now completely in on her status as Head Honcho of Djinn Land, had become closer to Jeannie in the ensuing months since Victor had held them hostage.

They had girls' night twice a month, wherein they'd taken Jeannie shopping for a new, more colorful wardrobe. The Live Out Loud wardrobe is what they'd titled it over Fuzzy Navels and enchiladas at Miguel's.

Most of all, they'd agreed to be her bridesmaids in the wedding she and Sloan had planned in just two months' time. Nina'd asked them to wait out of courtesy for the fucking beach ball she'd swallowed. If she was gonna have to wear an ugly color like persimmon, she wasn't doing it looking like an olive on a toothpick, she'd groused.

In between planning the catering of her own wedding, Jeannie had also spent long hours with Nekaar and Najim, learning the djinn law, practicing for the time when Najim would fully retire and she would take over completely.

It wouldn't be easy to travel beyond the veil and handle her life here on this plane, but with Nekaar as her right-hand djinn, and Najim still consulting, she had no fear she wouldn't be able to keep the balance of genie order. Nekaar had found their genie mole, and indeed, Burt had summoned the help of one of his old friends to find someone to release him from the bottle.

He'd been the genie who'd swapped the bottle of gin at the party she'd catered what seemed like a thousand years ago. That very djinn was now in what Jeannie liked to call her Genie Time-out program, wherein all djinn, after a first-time offense, enjoyed a bit of Nina boot camp as they atoned their sins.

As the time for Nina, who'd had a very human pregnancy the entire way, approached, they'd all waited for the call from Darnell to tell them it was a go.

And here they were, the fruits of Jeannie's literal labor almost ready to make its entry into the world.

Phoebe, Nina's vampire sister, poked her head outside the heavy oak door where Jeannie stood. "Loud enough for you?" she quipped, pushing her way out with her sister Penny in tow. "Penny opted out. She said Aunt Nina yells too much."

Penny nodded from her wheelchair, covering her ears and smiling impishly up at Jeannie.

Jeannie nodded, stooping down to give Penny a quick kiss and a smile. "I hear there're some freshly baked cookies downstairs, courtesy of Uncle Arch."

Penny put her hands to the wheels on either side of her chair. "Vroom-vroom, Phoebe."

Phoebe chuckled. "Yes, yes. Cookies. I'll get her settled and then I'll be right back up. Yell for me if Nina needs me. Wait. Never mind. I can't believe I said that. I'll hear her if she needs me. Commence with the big mouth," she said on a laugh, lifting Penny like she were nothing more than a new dress instead of a child in a wheelchair, and carried her down the wide staircase.

Another long scream erupted from Nina's room just as Sloan flew up the stairs and scooped her up in a hug. "Sorry, I got here as soon as I could. The office was a total hell today. So we there yet?" he asked, cocking his dark head at the door to the birthing room.

She smiled up at him, cupping his jaw and running her thumb over the delicious stubble that had formed after a long day. "Not yet, but we're close—I can feel it."

"So . . . I have a surprise for you. I was going to wait until tonight, but Team Nina was obviously needed."

Throwing her arms around his neck, she cocked her head in question. "A surprise?" she asked, nibbling at his lips.

"It's a good one, too, if I do say so myself. I'm in for lots of the bed sport for this one—like bed sport for life," was his confident reply.

"Oh, really?" she cooed, shooting him a flirty smile. "I still can't believe you're willing to cop to spending the rest of your eternity with a brunette."

He grinned down at her. "But I am."

"Then I have good news," she assured him, kissing his jaw.

"More? I don't know if I can contain myself." He nuzzled her cheek, making her sigh.

"I'm really blonde—blonde and green-eyed."

"Shut the front door." He leaned back from her, assessing her face with a grin.

"Swear it. I changed my hair color and wore contacts because of the witness-protection thing. And because we still weren't sure if any of Victor's enemies would show up, I kept doing it. It was second nature anyway. But lately, I've been thinking of changing it back."

"How could I not have seen you were wearing contacts?"

"Because you're always busy looking at other things?" she teased.

"But you're not really five-ten, are you?" Sloan made a mock sad face.

"No. I really am. If you put me in water, I grow."

"I like you, Jeannie Carlyle Charlotte Gorman."

"Really? Because I was just thinking I like you, too."

"Of course you do. I'm pretty and I have good hair. What's not to like?"

"Oh, right. All good reasons to begin a marriage."

"So, ready for your surprise?"

"You've asked Lollipop to move in and be our housekeeper?"

"Damn. You're always one-upping me."

Jeannie snickered. "I hope she likes piles. I'm a notorious pile maker."

"Jeannie?" He tweaked her side.

"Sloan?"

"Look behind you."

Jeannie turned around, pivoting on the new heels she'd just bought when she'd shopped with Nina for strollers.

He hadn't. She strained her eyes along the dark hallway that led to the stairs.

Her breathing came to a halt. *"Mom?"* she squeaked, peering closer, her legs wobbling.

Her mother closed the distance between them, hurling herself at Jeannie and wrapping her arms around her daughter. "I can't believe it's you, Charlie. After all these years, I just can't believe you're alive. Thank God, you're alive," she sobbed, squeezing Jeannie tight.

Tears streamed down Jeannie's face, falling to her mother's shoulders. She inhaled her mother's familiar scent of lilacs and smiled up at Sloan.

And she was home at last.

Pulling from her mother, she took her by the hand and led her to where Sloan stood, smiling. "Mom, this is my fiancé, Sloan Flaherty." She introduced him with so much pride, her heart throbbed. "Sloan, this is my mother, Nancy Gorman."

"I know all about this handsome devil," she chirped, clutching Jeannie's hand to her cheek. "We've been having lunch together all week long. I know everything, Charlie. *Everything.* Oh, God. I never thought I'd see you again. It's a miracle." She pulled Jeannie back into her embrace again, caressing her face. "It's all going to be fine now, honey. I've missed you so much."

Sloan handed Jeannie's mother a tissue just as Nina howled another squealing contraction.

"Is that the lady in there having the baby?" Nancy asked.

"And screaming like the end of the world is near? Yep," Sloan said. "That's Nina."

"Why don't I go see if I can help?"

"Wait, Mom. That might not be such a good idea." She cast Sloan an are-you-kidding look.

"It's okay, sugarplum. She knows everything—everything there is to know about us—and I gotta give it up to Moms, she's pretty tough. But she also has a nursing degree. So why don't we let her go do her thing?"

Nancy gave Jeannie one more quick hug before scooting into Nina's bedroom.

Jeannie's head fell to her chest, tears streaming down her new silk blouse. "You are the best man in manlandia. Ever."

Sloan didn't say anything, but he pulled her close, letting her burrow her face in his shirt.

When her wave of tears passed, she asked, "I thought the FBI said I had to wait to contact her? Until they were sure none of Victor's enemies might come looking for him."

He let his head rest on top of hers. "They lifted it just last week, and it's all clear—everyone's either dead or in prison. Sam contacted Fullbright on the sly. I knew it would be hard to find a way to just pick up the phone and call, or show up on her doorstep after so long. So I figured I'd break the ice for you."

She had no words to express the kind of gratitude she felt for this man—for this new life that had been given to her—for her new friends—for a future.

"So this is the part where I tell you I'm nuts about you, right? Because you're such a great guy and an even better fiancé?"

He tipped her chin up and smiled, running his finger over her lower lip. "Yep. And it better be good, all hearts and flowers. If I don't feel a tear spring to my eye? It's off, lady."

Lifting her lips to his, Jeannie whispered against his mouth with a chuckle, "I love you more than I love *Top Chef*. No, no. Don't say it. I'm amazingly gifted in word."

Nina's scream, and the shout of "You're almost there!" had Sloan and Jeannie rushing into the room just as Nina grunted her final push with a sharp yelp.

"It's a girl!" Wanda cried. "Oh look, honey—she's beautiful!" The loud wails of the newborn, music to everyone's ears, echoed through Nina and Greg's bedroom.

Jeannie smiled to herself. A girl. Of all the things for Nina to have, she'd gone and had a girl. Oh, the shit that would fly when Marty and Wanda tried to put bows in her hair.

The dark thatch of hair on top of the baby's head stood out against the white T-shirt Nina wore. Nina's hands instantly curled around the baby possessively before Jeannie's mother took her and wiped her clean, then wrapped her tightly in a blanket.

Nancy handed the baby back to Nina, patting the bed so an even-paler-than-usual Greg would sit next to his wife. "Would you just look at you?" Nina cooed while Greg let his head rest on top of his wife's and closed his eyes.

Though Nina was unable to shed tears, her eyes were glassy when they met Jeannie's. She mouthed a "thank you" to her, for which Jeannie threw her hand up to her forehead in an aye-aye-captain gesture.

Sloan pulled her back to his chest, curving his arms around her waist, and she settled back against him—content to watch Nina and the baby.

"So did you two ever come up with a name for the newest Statleon?" Wanda asked, reaching out for her husband Heath's hand and squeezing it. He brought it to his lips and kissed it.

Nina's nod was curt, but her words were oddly thick and heavy with emotion. So un-Nina-like. "Janine, after my mother. Janine *Charlotte* Statleon. Charlie for short," she said, gazing directly at Jeannie.

Jeannie's throat became tight. So Charlie would live on. She'd decided to keep her new name. It was easier for her catering business and the people she dealt with. But in her heart, she'd always be Charlotte Gorman from Nowhere, South Dakota, who'd made a horrible decision, but had fought her way back.

"Thank you," she mouthed back at Nina, and Nina in turn gave her the aye-aye-captain response with a watery grin.

Little Charlie yawned then, wide and with a long grunt. "Holy fangs," Marty muttered when they all got a good glimpse of the inside of Charlie's mouth. Two tiny incisors, or fangs as Nina had titled them, poked from Charlie's gums.

Keegan slapped Greg on the back with a hearty smile, wrapping his other arm around Marty. "So we've got a little vampire—booyah, buddy."

Darnell leaned down and chucked the baby under the chin. "Ol' Uncle Darnell sho gonna have his work cut out fo him, ain't he, half-pint?"

The men all took turns giving Greg a clap on the back before

Wanda was shooing them out. "Baby and Mommy need quiet time now and lots of rest. Take your man-child thumps on the back downstairs. Arch made a feast for you bunch of Neanderthals."

Heath dropped a kiss on his wife's lips before taking his leave, followed by Keegan, Darnell, Sam, Phoebe's mate, and Clay, Casey's mate.

Jeannie left Sloan's embrace to drop a kiss on Nina's forehead. She held out her fist to the woman who'd shown her what survival and strength were all about. "Nice job, MWA. Or is it Mom now?"

"My cootchie-la-la's gonna need an overhaul thanks to you, midget," Nina said, though it was playful and light. She nuzzled the dark head at her chest, and the baby snuggled deeper.

"I am the head wishmaster," Jeannie teased, running a tender hand over the baby's hair before standing upright. "We're going to go now and take advantage of all that free food, but make sure you call me if you need anything at all. 'Kay?"

Marty was back at Nina's head, wiping her with a cool cloth and, in general, fussing. "Jesus, Marty!" Nina flapped a hand at her. "Knock it off already. Stop flippin' treating me like an invalid. I had a kid—not a freakin' lobotomy."

Marty made a face at her. She rubbed a finger along Charlie's cheek before planting her hands on her hips and giving Nina *the look*. "You know, Mistress of the Dark, you're the most ungrateful person alive. All you've done is complain for nine solid months. Honestly, you could make a living doing it. So guess what, Elvira? I wish you'd knock it off with the complaining already! Whaddya think about that?"

The room trembled ever so slightly and a tiny tendril of pink smoke wafted above Charlie's head before disappearing altogether.

Oh.

Oh. No way.

Jeannie's eyes flew to Nina.

Nina, whose mouth was moving in typical payback-Marty-style, yet wasn't omitting any sound.

Oh, hell's bells.

Jeannie jammed a knuckle into her mouth to keep from laughing too loudly and frightening the baby. Clearly, her help was going to be in order. She rushed to the bed, scooping the baby from Nina's arms and cuddling her close while Nina reached a hand out and dove for Marty's hair, silently, mind you, but still with the intent of assault.

Jeannie pressed her lips to the baby's forehead, so soft and warm, and waited. She gasped when she felt the vibration, drawing Sloan's attention.

She'd learned much from Nekaar and Najim, and she knew the sign of the djinn. It was distant, and it was as yet fully developed, but if everyone thought Nina was a handful—wait till they got a load of Charlie.

Sloan leaned over her shoulder, stroking the baby's cheek with a knuckle. "Noooo," he drawled.

Jeannie nodded in wonder. "Yes." Oh, yes.

"So there's work to be done, sensei?"

Jeannie giggled, her heart so full. She snuggled closer to Charlie as Nina went for Marty's throat and Wanda jumped between them. "Ladies!" she called, snapping her fingers so that each woman was frozen in place.

The Insta-Freeze magic spell was high on her list of favorites. High. "We have some work ahead of us. Look, girls." She held up the baby with a warm grin. "We have our first ever vampini!"

She pulled the baby back to her chest, cradling her tight while Sloan pulled her to his side, right where she belonged.

Her sense of belonging, her newfound confidence, and her love for Sloan were all the magic she'd ever need.

Ever.